# SNOWGLOBE

2

스노볼2

## Books by Soyoung Park

### THE SNOWGLOBE DUOLOGY
Translated by Joungmin Lee Comfort

*Snowglobe*

*Snowglobe 2*

# SNOWGLOBE

스노볼 2

## SOYOUNG PARK

Translated by Joungmin Lee Comfort

DELACORTE PRESS

Delacorte Press
An imprint of Random House Children's Books
A division of Penguin Random House LLC
1745 Broadway, New York, NY 10019

penguinrandomhouse.com
GetUnderlined.com

Editor: Krista Marino
Cover Designer: Casey Moses
Interior Designer: Michelle Canoni
Production Editor: Colleen Fellingham
Managing Editor: Tamar Schwartz
Production Manager: Tracy Heydweiller

Library of Congress Cataloging-in-Publication Data is available upon request.
ISBN 978-0-593-80914-3 (trade)—ISBN 978-0-593-80915-0 (ebook)—
ISBN 978-0-593-80917-4 (trade pbk.)

Originally published in Korean by Changbi Publishers in 2021.
This book is published with the support of the Literature
Translation Institute of Korea (LTI Korea).

The text of this book is set in 11.5-point Bembo MT.

Manufactured in the United States of America
10 9 8 7 6 5 4 3 2 1

The authorized representative in the EU for product safety and compliance
is Penguin Random House Ireland, Morrison Chambers, 32 Nassau Street,
Dublin D02 YH68, Ireland, https://eu-contact.penguin.ie.

# CAST OF CHARACTERS

## ACTORS

Jeon Chobahm

Bae Serin

Myung Somyung

Shin Shinae

Jo Yeosu

Jo Miryu

Goh Maeryung

Goh Sanghui

Goh Rhim

Goh Shihwang

Goh Wooyo

Hwang Sannah

Jin Jinsuh

Fran

## PRODUCERS

Yibonn Media Group:

Yi Bonyung

Yi Bonshim

Yi Bonwhe

## PLANT WORKERS

Boss

Heart

Healer

Diver

Violet

Knife

Sky

Wisher

## DIRECTORS

Cha Seol

Cha Guibahng

Cha Hyang

## ENGINEERS

Shin Ichae

# PART 1

# SEVEN DEGREES TO DISASTER

At once, all the lights go out and the TV goes dead. On the dark screen, ghostly afterimages linger for another moment before they, too, dissipate, plunging us into darkness.

"For real?" Beside me, Somyung balls her fists at her sides and squeals with a nervous laugh.

My brother Ongi sighs softly with wonder.

"The news was on point . . ."

It was just minutes ago that *News at 9* announced an imminent power outage for District 1, our home district, located on the east side of Snowglobe—the domed, temperature-controlled city where we live, and the only warm refuge in our otherwise-frozen world. Inside the dome, a record-setting heat wave has been raging for five days straight, with tropical conditions continuing into the nights without remit, resulting in round-the-clock use of air-conditioning and fans everywhere by people seeking relief. Needless to say, this has put a major strain on our electrical grids. All week, experts have been warning us of shortages and blackouts, but we ignored them. What else could we do? Roast ourselves alive? And now here we are, dealing with the first outage of the season.

On the table, a small desk clock dutifully ticks on. Nineteen past nine, according to its luminescent dial. My eyes are still adjusting to the dark, when heat and humidity begin pressing from all sides. Overhead, the fan stops completely, finally losing the last of its momentum, and it doesn't matter if all it did was chop uselessly at the ovenlike air settling thick over us. Our discomfort is absolute.

"Damn, it's hot," Somyung mutters. Beneath her short hair, her face is identical to mine—as both she and I are identical to Haeri, the onetime megastar of Snowglobe's most popular reality show. It seems like only recently that I saw her for the first time in the break room of the Ja-B-6 plant in the open world; that the two of us, along with others, realized we were integral parts of the sinister Director Cha's plot to create the perfect TV heroine.

That the Haeri we grew up watching on our screens never existed . . . at least, not in the way we thought she did.

We might as well have kept the air on all afternoon instead of doing our part as responsible citizens and trying to conserve energy. That's probably what everyone else did, maximize consumption, believing that if they didn't do it, someone else would anyway.

Then the third of us, Shinae, quips, while fumbling in the dark for a handheld fan, "Ha! Running out of electricity because people are trying desperately to cool down? What a concept!"

This induces a chuckle from everyone—everyone but Hyang, that is, who glares at us, unimpressed, from where she is sitting. For the rest of us non-natives who are used to an annual temperature of negative fifty degrees, Snowglobe's sizzling summer is at once intimidating and kind of amazing. But for Hyang, who grew up in luxury as Director Cha's sister and a onetime director herself before being exiled to the retirees' village where I met her, this heat must be a familiar foe.

Hyang and Miryu, another former Snowglobe actor whose show—a brutal murder program starring Miryu herself as the merciless killer—also resulted in her ostracization and banishment before she and Hyang reunited recently, move deftly through the dark, lighting candles, drawing a huge pitcher of ice water, and even getting ice pops from the freezer. Meanwhile, all Shinae and I can do is lie plastered to the wooden floor while fanning ourselves. Ongi and Somyung head off to cool down with cold showers in the first- and second-floor bathrooms, respectively.

"Man, it's hot!" I cry out for the dozenth time, crunching ice cubes between my teeth, but the cool relief they offer stays with me for all of a few seconds before escaping through my sweating pores. I know from experience, it's the same with cold showers. Just moments after you step out and towel off, the warm, waterlogged air welcomes you back into its sticky embrace. Outside the wide-open windows of the living room, cars and trucks zip by, kicking up gusts of heat and exhaust into our already-boiling house.

"Ugh . . . Should we forget the candles? They've gotta be adding to the heat," Shinae suggests, squinting at the tiny flames. Like me, she was raised in the open world, completely unaware that the people she thought were her parents were in fact just foster parents—that she, also like me, was conceived as one of a number of Haeri clones. It still sickens me to think of it. How Director Cha introduced the world to Haeri as a baby, then created a host of stand-ins to swap out when her perfect star started acting less-than-perfect. I myself was brought in only after the previous "Haeri"—whose true name was Jo Yeosu—took her own life. And even then, I was only meant to reside in Snowglobe for a short time, as a replacement for the intended replacement, Serin, while Serin underwent surgery to remove childhood scars.

But Director Cha didn't realize her creations could fight back. She didn't think any of us, if given the chance, would turn down the opportunity to become Haeri—Snowglobe's most famous girl—even if it meant stepping over one another.

She was wrong.

Suddenly, Hyang springs to her feet and claps her hands in sudden excitement, bringing me back to the present.

"I have an idea," she says, and tapping Somyung, who's lying listlessly on the floor, snow-angel style, with her foot. "Get up! Let's go!"

Somyung looks up at her in annoyance, but then her eyes light up in the next moment, and she's suddenly on her feet, crying, "You're right! Why didn't we think of it before? We'll go to a district with electricity!"

She stares at Hyang with breathless expectation, which Hyang returns with an exaggerated look of pity. Being older than us, and the only adult along with Miryu, she's taken on the role of our de facto guardian since we've been in Snowglobe. Tut-tutting with her tongue, Hyang shuffles to the entryway closet and fishes out a large picnic basket.

"Electricity?" she huffs. "Let me show you how to cool off in style."

Then, as we watch her with curiosity, she goes around the house, stuffing the basket with a variety of items. When she casually suggests that someone should go upstairs and get Serin, Shinae and I just exchange a glance.

**It's been about a month since we moved out of the Yibonn** estate—home to the founding family and guardians of Snow-globe, as well as the heads of all its programming—and into this two-story house we share. Like us, Serin is a Haeri clone—the clone I was meant to act as a stand-in for, until unknown to me, Director Cha decided to make my role as Haeri permanent. But unlike the rest of us, Serin would have done anything to keep the Haeri illusion up. She resents us for revealing the truth behind Cha's plot, and though Serin's white-hot hatred and animosity toward us might have cooled a bit over the past weeks, she still keeps her distance. Apparently, even the outage isn't enough to drive her from her room in search of comfort in our company.

We continue to stall as Hyang urges, "Come on, girls. We're not going to let Serin roast in the dark house by herself."

Serin's resentment of us is profound. In her mind, we swooped in with our exposé to rob her of her life as Haeri, which she had earned tooth-and-claw. And how have we been dealing with her? Sad to admit, but none of us seems especially capable of loving thy enemy or of blessing those who curse you, not in the face of her daily venomous attitude.

"I'll go get her." Ongi, back from the showers, voluntarily steps in and heads for the stairs, always the peacemaker. I appreciate my brother's joviality even more now.

I have the impulse to go help Hyang gather this and that in the kitchen just so I have an excuse not to join them, but after seeing Somyung and Shinae join Hyang, I cave under pressure and drag myself up the stairs.

*You, Me, and Us,* the hottest new Snowglobe show in which we all star, breaks the age-old mold in many aspects, the most notable of which is that it's available to residents of Snowglobe, rather than just being filmed here and streamed to the outer world as all other Snowglobe programming is. Since all shows are reality-based and most actors live their roles, allowing the stars to watch their own programs could result in spoilers—something that directors avoid at all costs. As the only actors with access to their own show, we have watched a total of four episodes so far.

After each viewing, the three of us invariably find ourselves asking each other, "Is it just me, or do we come across as . . . kind of mean to Serin?"

We're not mean to Serin, of course not. At least not intentionally. It's Serin who chooses to ostracize herself in her self-sabotaging contempt for us; and Hyang, our director, doesn't engage in the kind of editorial cutting and manipulating that other directors use to twist that truth into a streamlined story. Funny thing is, though, the Serin in our show does seem lonelier and sadder than the Serin full-of-barbs we all know in real life.

For instance, in the show, Serin would be all alone in her darkened room, lying in her bed and staring vacantly at the ceiling as gales of merry laughter drift up from downstairs. And when she'd blink—slowly and dramatically—tears would release from her liquid eyes and roll down her temples, which the high-power lenses of Snowglobe cameras would capture with crystalline clarity even in the low light.

I admit that I never imagined a sad, lonely, or vulnerable Serin until I saw her in our own show. And though it's entirely possible that it's pure playacting for the camera, what if she's indeed sad, lonely, and struggling to reach out to us because of some stupid pride or fear of rejection? If so, I'm willing to extend the olive branch. I just need to know.

And yet I'm already feeling tense, nearing Serin's room in the hallway. Thank god for my brother's presence, which tends to soften the hostile air between her and me.

"Go where?" Serin's voice flows out of her room, meek and anxious.

Creeping up to her open doorway, I peek in to see her sitting crouched on her bed against the headboard with her knees drawn to her chest, her empty gaze fixed on a spot on the comforter. Ongi sits on the edge of the far end with one foot on the floor.

"I don't know. Hyang knows a place, apparently. She says it's real nice," Ongi answers cheerfully, his voice full of warmth.

But Serin sits frozen in her chronic sourness, refusing to even glance up at him. Ongi dips his head to one side and tries to catch her eye.

"Come on, Serin. Come with us," he pleads softly, and the most attentive, caring tone he uses with her somehow transports me to fourth grade when we used to bicker and fight like two badgers. Following such a bout, I'd shut him out completely, refusing to speak to him or even to acknowledge his presence in that tiny house of ours; but he'd always make the first gesture for peace, cajoling and clowning to draw me out in that same tone of voice as if we hadn't been at each other's throat mere hours before. And soon enough, I'd be laughing at his antics, forgetting that I was even angry with him. The message I internalized through all this was Ongi will always have my back, no matter what. But as we grew older, our fights got worse, and we drifted apart. It's been a long time since I've heard him speak like this.

"*Oppa . . . ,*" Serin mewls then, yanking me out of my reverie.

Did she just call him oppa, a term of familial respect and affection that is long extinct between Ongi and me?

She continues in the same wronged, pitiable tone, "If I do go, will you stay close to me? You already know, oppa. The girls hate me. And it's clear whose side Hyang and Miryu are on. I hope you understand how uncomfortable and awkward it is for me to even be around them."

What? Who hates who?

My bighearted intent to casually slip into their conversation flies out of me.

"You know that's not true," Ongi denies. "We care so much about you. All of us do."

"See? That's what I'm talking about, oppa. You, too, speak for them—from their side," Serin says, letting her voice fall. "No one's on my side."

The hurt in her eyes is almost real. I don't have a good view of Ongi's face from this angle, but his silence tells me he's hard-pressed for a counterpoint. This is where I need to insert myself. I'm debating between harsh rapping on the door and savage throat-clearing, but then Ongi speaks up.

"Point taken," he says, and raising his right hand in the way of a court witness, he goes on brightly. "From now on, I, Jeon Ongi, am on Serin's side."

My heart squeezes in my chest. What?

Serin gives Ongi a long look. Then she finally lets the makings of a smile emerge on her lips, and she says, "Really?"

Ongi lets out an expansive, oppa-like chuckle, and nods his head.

"Really. So let's go. Everyone's waiting for you," he says, pushing up to his feet and offering his hand to Serin. "Embrace the awkward. Lean into it. That's the fastest way to get close to anyone."

Meanwhile, the tiny camera perched on the bedside lamp faithfully rolls on, unaffected by the blackout. It's fed by the Central Power Plant's nuclear energy, as are the hundred million other Snowglobe cameras. Typical Snowglobe: content comes above everything else, even the comfort of its residents.

I swing around and flee toward the bathroom, already thinking about asking Hyang to edit out the scene where I'm listening in on these two. My heart's heavy, and for no good reason I can think of. Yes, I'm guilty of eavesdropping, but so what? It wasn't intentional, anyway. Not really. Then there is the hurt and embarrassment I'm feeling after being betrayed on camera by Ongi, my twin brother who has just pledged his allegiance to Serin?

Slipping into the bathroom and locking the door behind

me, I remind myself that Ongi is no longer blood. We never have been, in fact. Like with the other clones, my parents were only surrogates, meant to foster me until Director Cha had need of me in Snowglobe. I keep forgetting this cold fact, though I was the one who let the world know when the rest of the Haeris and I interrupted a live weathercast to expose Cha's plot.

**Soon we're all riding in Hyang's van to the mystery destination.** The vehicle is crowded, and Ongi won't stop chatting up Serin as if it's his duty to keep her engaged and entertained, which bugs me more than I want to admit.

It stinks—it does—to know that he has chosen Serin, of all people, over me. But I curb my impulse to throttle him because . . . I'm not jealous of or threatened by her in the least. I'm way cooler than that, aren't I? Plus, I can't let Somyung or Shinae—or, god forbid, Ongi—get wind of it, even if I were.

But just who does he think he is? A peacemaker? Patron saint of self-alienating antisocial girls? Why does he try so hard to pull her in?

"Gosh . . . Look, Serin! The Disaster Meter is already up by ten degrees," he's saying now.

I'm fighting the impulse to repeat what he said in a mocking voice, when the sight of said meter glowing menacingly in the distance sobers me up. Ninety-three, it reads.

The Disaster Meter is an instrument much like a thermometer but for measuring and indicating how close we are to the next Snowglobe disaster. It consists of a giant sealed glass tube marked with graduations from 0 to 100 and has at the low end a bulb containing liquid the color of pomegranate juice—or blood, depending on your imagination—that expands or contracts within the tube to indicate the level of danger. On top of the giant thermometer, a ball of fire burns for twenty-four hours straight even in steady rain. Before I came to Snowglobe, I would watch the weather disasters that hit its population on TV, but I've never experienced one myself.

"When did it jump to ninety-three? How?" Serin balks. "It was a slow climb to eighty."

"Yeah . . . It's the blackout in District 1 that's caused the spike," Hyang supplies from behind the wheel, her voice higher and brighter than usual, no doubt in consciousness of Serin, who's gracing us with her presence today. "Compound penalty," she continues in that tone that rubs me the wrong way. "The blackout is a direct consequence of our being wasteful and irresponsible with the electricity imported from the open world."

Snowglobe has a penalty system similar to what we had in school, where merits are deducted for every infraction committed. In our case, they include things like failure to return to the set by the end of the break, lingering behind privacy walls longer than is reasonable, and various other instances of willful or accidental dereliction of actorly duty, all of which push up the Disaster Meter's gauge. A single actor's minor infraction is a drop in the ocean, of course, but multiply the drop by whatever magnitude it takes to account for all of Snowglobe's actor-residents, and the meter ticks up appreciably until it eventually reaches the flash point of 100. Then, while the instrument burns to cinders and ashes, the live weather drawing on *News at 9* determines which seasonally appropriate natural disaster—drought, dust storm, extreme heat, wildfire, snowstorm, et cetera—will descend upon the community, and at what level of intensity. All this hangs on the fingertips of the weathercaster.

Meanwhile, outside the domed city, the rest of the world buzzes with anticipation of the fresh drama and pathos that this year's meteorological disaster will bring to the screen. Many gamble, betting on the type and severity of the disaster to be drawn. Those with personal ties to Snowglobe hope and pray that whatever the disaster, it won't be too unkind.

In any case, there's not been a year in which Snowglobe escaped such a disaster—not in recent memory, at least, and not with the community's increasingly indifferent attitude and habits toward energy conservation, which have rendered multiple summer blackouts a regular feature for many years.

Thankfully, weathercasters sometimes manage to draw rather fun and wonderful disasters, such as Cola Rain and Rose Petal Storm, the latter of which was simply spectacular by anyone's standard. But the opposite can also be true, like when Snowglobe was hit by screaming typhoons or ten days of driving rain. Those are the kinds of disasters that have wreaked serious havoc in the Snowglobe community.

"Please . . . Anything but boiling heat. I can't take it," Ongi begs, gathering his hands in prayer in the direction of the Disaster Meter glowing with the fire on top, alone in the dark. "Let us have Cola Rain again. Yes, I wish for Cola Rain," he murmurs. "And for everyone's safety."

I wish to meet my dad. I wish for Chobahm to be accepted into film school. I wish for Grandma to get well. None of my brother's birthday wishes ever come true. Not a single one of them. So what else can I do but wish that his wish would come true this time; that everyone, including him, will be unscathed by whatever disaster is unleashed. Under the dome, the world is eerie in its still darkness. It's seven more degrees until disaster.

# THE CUCKOO IN THE ROWBOAT

"S-snake! Snake!" Shinae screams, leaping into the air.

"Where? Where?"

Always the toughest of us, Somyung shakes her walking stick—a dead tree limb she found on the trail—at the ground. The beam of her headlamp dances wildly in the dark as she looks around in panic for the creature Shinae called out about. Up ahead, Hyang lets out a laugh.

"There are no snakes in these woods!" she assures us.

Shinae, drenched in sweat and annoyance, yells back, "How about a destination? Is there a destination in these woods?"

Dragged into a sort of forced march to a mystery destination at this hour, we can't stop complaining every few minutes. Simply existing in this weather is enough to make sweat start beading on our skin, and yet here we are, ascending a steep and thickly wooded trail.

"Come on, Ajumma! Are we there yet?" I snap for what feels like the hundredth time.

Our Discomfort Index has long surpassed 100, and I'm not

sure if any destination is worth this trek in this heat. When the trail finally opens up, I gasp in spite of myself. In front of us lies a lake sparkling under the stars on the flat mountaintop. We stand there a moment at the trail's end, taking in the beauty while sighing and murmuring with wonder, the steamy air that's been clinging to us like a hot, wet towel finally falling away.

Then we're crossing the warm sand to the water's edge, where we settle with folding chairs and roll-out mats we've lugged up the mountain. Setting down the basket full of provisions, Ongi takes out the thermos of iced coffee and turns on the portable radio.

According to the news crackling out of its speakers, beaches everywhere, and even the Central Pond in front of the SnowTower—where the weather and news broadcasts take place, and where we staged our exposé—are jam-packed with people desperately trying to cool off. The bars and restaurants in Districts 2 and 3 are at capacity with the overflow of customers from District 1 experiencing a blackout.

But this lake nestled atop this hill is all ours. I suppose no one else has come up with Hyang's crazy idea to scale a small mountain on this sweltering night. I snap back to attention as Shinae asks, "Who wants the last slice of watermelon?" inciting a chorus of "Me! Me! Me!"

The cool, gentle breeze blowing off the lake dries our sweat as we talk and laugh. The air is fragrant with chlorophyll. Every bite of watermelon tastes sweeter than the one before.

I pause as an odd rowboat turned upside down by the far edge of the lake catches my eye. Could it be hiding a camera?

Of course it could. So could the many squirrel nests among the tree limbs up above.

Frowning, I shake my head. Best not to think about how, or if, we're being monitored. In Snowglobe, the surveillance is constant, after all. I turn as Miryu suggests that we all switch off our headlamps and count backward from ten.

. . . four, three, two, one.

Everyone looks up at the sky. The Milky Way drifts languidly across the blue-black of the expanding universe—or that's the illusion we all buy into, anyway, thanks to Snowglobe's state-of-the-art technology. It's precisely the sky that Fran drew last night; he has been filling in the weathercaster void left by Haeri. I study the constellations. Is that Venus over there? Uranus?

Ongi is the first to come back to Earth.

"Let's go float on our backs," he says, gazing at the shimmering water. "It'll be like floating in the galaxy!"

In unison, we're springing to our feet, whooping and hooting with excitement—except for Hyang, who claims to be hydrophobic.

After the exposé, we made a Snowglobe bucket list. At the top of it is a trip to the beach, and since then, all of us, even Serin, have been taking thrice-weekly swim lessons at the local pool. Still, a night swim in open water warrants due caution, so we decide to take turns floating on the two inner tubes, which we inflate with our breath. Somyung and Shinae wade in first, tubes around their middles.

"We can paddle around while we wait," Ongi says, snatching me and Serin by our wrists and pulling us toward the beached rowboat. I hesitate for a moment, uncertain, before the three of us flip the thing over and slide it onto the water.

At Ongi's insistence, Serin and I teeter in first while he holds the rowboat stable. He then tosses in the oars and guides the vessel away from the shallows. I'm expecting him to hop in now since the water is already lapping at his thighs, but that's when he pushes away the rowboat with all his might.

"What are you doing?" I demand.

"Oppa . . . ?" Serin accuses.

But Ongi is already wading backward, grinning sheepishly.

"There you go," he says. "You two have some quality time together while I go beat Hyang in Omok. It's the championship match."

Aghast, I glance at Serin, who glances at me, and we reflexively look away from each other. My mind jumps to the night of the exposé, when she and I tumbled onto the studio's floor like a pair of battling beetles, blood leaking from my left brow bone and streaking her cream-colored suit. That was the last time we found ourselves in such close physical proximity to each other.

"Paddle, will you?" Serin's voice leaps out at me then.

"Huh?"

"Can't you see? The boat's spinning in circles. Paddle!"

Her bark stings me into action, and I'm doing as I'm told without meaning to, promptly dipping my oar in the water and pulling. The rowboat begins precariously zigging and zagging across the water. After a while, though, our strokes have somehow synchronized, and we're gliding on the moonlit and star-spangled galaxy of the placid lake. Up ahead, Miryu pauses her backstroke and watches us a moment before giving us a thumbs-up and swimming away. I couldn't really see her face, but she seemed to be smiling.

On the retreating shore, Hyang and Ongi sit perched on their folding chairs with the Omok table in between, their heads turned in our direction. Somyung and Shinae float lazily nearby in their tubes, bathing in the moonlight; but if the beams of their headlamps indicate anything, they're watching us, too. Everyone's studying us.

Serin and I keep paddling awhile in silence, the sound of our oars dipping and gently sloshing water filling the awkward air between us. Then we're in the middle of the lake. Serin lifts her oar out of the water and rests it across her lap.

"I saw Grandma yesterday," she says, looking right at me from where she's seated at the opposite end of the boat.

"Grandma?"

"Yeah, Grandma," she repeats, smiling up at the twinkling sky. "You do know that she was released on bail, don't you?"

I do. So by Grandma, she means Goh Maeryung. Our television grandma—and a key player in Director Cha's scheme to make Haeri the biggest star in Snowglobe. I see.

It was a few days ago that the woman was finally granted bail on account of her declining health. With the stress of the legal proceedings surrounding her and Director Cha taking a toll on her, the formerly imposing matriarch of the Goh family was looking notably her age when she entered the courtroom in her blue inmate uniform. But what is this Grandma business?

"So . . . how did you see her?" I say, trying to sound casual while setting aside the issue of the title for now.

With a heavy sigh, Serin drops her face to level an annoyed gaze at me, all traces of a smile gone.

"What do you mean how?" she says, squinting at me as if I've just asked her the dumbest question. "I visited Grandma at her house, of course."

This girl . . .

All right, then. I take the bait.

"Since when is she your grandma?"

She waits a long beat, reveling in my confusion as she studies my face. Then she says, "Grandma told me . . . that I am Sanghui's baby girl."

I just stare at her, struck dumb. Sanghui—that's Haeri's television mother and Maeryung's daughter. Even after Hyang, the other girls, and I unraveled most of the mysteries surrounding Haeri's family, the question of what happened to Sanghui's original child, the little girl she gave birth to, is one we've never been able to answer.

I don't know where the conversation is going, but I already don't like it. How can Serin be the girl Sanghui gave birth to? From the little information we've managed to gather, I know the girl ran off to the forbidden woods to avoid being replaced by one of us and hasn't been found until this moment.

Right?

Serin then recounts the story of the three-year-old Haeri, who fainted at a Halloween party when she was scared by a guest dressed up as a jack-o'-lantern. It's one I recall well, having watched it in the open world as a child myself—one of the most famous moments in the entirety of the show's run, in fact. Following the incident, little Haeri retreated into her shell and wouldn't be coaxed out by anyone. She lost her speech, as well as her angelic smile, neither of which would return until the following spring. Her face remained expressionless on Christmas Eve when her mom put a diamond bracelet around her tiny wrist, and even on Christmas morning when she unwrapped a toy that was all the rage among kids her age that year. And whenever she had a meltdown, even her grandmother, who the little girl adored more than anyone in the world, was helpless in putting a stop to it. Haeri just continued crying until she could cry no more.

"That girl was my replacement," Serin says, absently feeling the skin around her mouth with her fingertips. "The scar that I thought all my life I'd gained in the open world, I'd actually gotten it right here in Snowglobe, in the family home . . . Grandma says that I knocked over a boiling kettle when she looked away for a second." Her eyes fill with heartache and self-pity. "You probably get the picture now. I was promptly swapped out for my replacement, and as she struggled to adapt to my family and Snowglobe, I struggled to adapt to her family in the open world."

Meanwhile, she goes on, Serin's new mom in the open world had intuited that Serin wasn't hers. It made no sense that her baby girl would disappear into thin air one night—a −50°F thin air, no less—only to be returned to the family a few days later without explanation, save for a taut scar burnishing the skin around her mouth and nose. A year passed, but she didn't take to Serin, maintaining that the girl wasn't her daughter. Neighbors murmured their pity for the young mom whose mind had clearly splintered. Three more years passed, and then some more, but she never changed her belief . . .

"That's insane," I cut her off. "Most three-year-olds are

verbal. Are you really suggesting that neither you nor your replacement uttered a word to your new families about what had happened?"

"Temporary loss of speech—remember?" Serin counters. "Emotional trauma caused the girl to shut herself off from her surroundings. Just as it did me."

I'm still processing this information when her annoyed face morphs into one of sheer rancor, and she is back on the attack.

"Is it really so difficult for you to believe that I am the original Haeri?" she hisses. "Why don't you go ask my grandma yourself, then?"

"That's not what I'm talking about," I say. There was never such a thing as the original Haeri, I'm about to add. All of us, even Sanghui's daughter, were just pawns—clones—for Director Cha to sort through until she found the best one of us. The one she'd make her star.

"But that's what I'm talking about!" Serin fires back. "Can you imagine being repeatedly rejected by your own mom, who is incapable of loving you? I can. I experienced it firsthand, and for the better part of my life. And so did the other girl!"

Sanghui's wretched sobs echo in my ear then. How could I ever forget? It had been one of my first few days as Haeri. In the bathroom, waiting for Sanghui to touch up my face, I'd ended up witnessing her total breakdown.

*How is she my daughter?* she cried as Maeryung tried to placate her. *There was no such thing as my daughter to begin with, and you—you know it!*

"Maeryung told you all this yesterday?" I ask, blinking away the memory.

Her eyes suddenly pooling with tears, Serin nods weakly. Then she drops her head and proceeds to sob softly into her hands. Watching her shoulders shudder with each sob, I can't help but feel a pang of sympathy for her, or for the little girl she once was, who had to grow up without a mother's love— supposedly.

I'm reaching out an awkward hand to comfort her when, all of a sudden, bright beams of light shoot out from under the rowboat's hull and checker the air. Then the *clack!* of the slate echoes around the midnight lake.

So I was right. The rowboat did hold a camera. The beam of light, as well as the clacking noise, means it's briefly shut off for regular camera checkups and transmission of the footage— granting us actors one of our rare required breaks from surveillance. They happen periodically throughout our days, but randomly, so the freedom is brief. When the next slate begins, we'll be expected to be back in our places, ready to resume the scene.

"Ugh . . . Why now?" Serin grumbles, lifting her face.

I'm thoroughly mystified. Her face, tearstained though it is, is utterly devoid of the pain or sorrow I bore witness to just a few seconds ago.

"Were you just pretending to cry?" I say in disbelief.

*"Pretending?"* she repeats, looking at me with such contempt. "Why would I have to, when the mere sight of your face makes me want to cry?"

The weight of her hatred settles heavily into my chest, and I push it back with a weary sigh.

"Will you ever stop resenting me? Have you forgotten that you're the one who stuck that needle in my neck and then tossed me off to rot in the retirees' village with Hyang? I almost ended up living as a ghost, all so you could play at being Haeri!" I say, hearing myself getting worked up at the memory. "And have I ever blamed you for any of that?"

I have never, and she knows it. The thing is, Serin did what she had to, or at least, that's how I see it. If not me, it was going to be her languishing in that godforsaken place. Both she and I merely tried to survive the hell storm into which Cha Guibahng and his granddaughter, Director Cha, had thrown us. That's all. A drowning person clutching and trying to climb atop their neighbor has no conscious thought process—only instinct. What Serin and I did to each other had been driven by the same survival instinct, which is why I made up my mind not to loathe her.

"Let me tell you again, Jeon Chobahm," Serin says then. "I don't resent you. Not you, necessarily. But I do feel incredibly frustrated with—" Her voice is heating up again, and she pauses to draw in a long breath through her nose. "It's unfair," she resumes, finally breathing out. "That you alone were spared."

Spared? I'm not sure I understand, but the conviction in her voice is so final that it chills me.

"What are you talking about?"

"Don't you get it? Somyung was orphaned at thirteen, and Shinae had to grow up in that disastrous family, under a father who called her mother a whore and a slut because she couldn't explain where her pregnancy came from. The girl torn away from her family at three to replace me? No one has seen her since she ran off into the woods. Yeosu died. And there's me . . . but what about you?"

What about me? What about me? I dig my nails into the clammy palms of my hands and stare back at her, speechless. That's when the tight bitterness in her face relaxes into a kind of curiosity, and she says, almost with childlike wonder, "How come . . . you alone are whole?"

Whole . . .

Her eyes searching my face for an answer suddenly tug at my heart, and I finally understand what she means. My one and only mom, Jeon Heewoo. My grandmother, Jeon Wol, who I love more than anyone in the whole wide world. My twin brother and best friend Jeon Ongi. And of course, there's my dad, Yim Hahnyung, who sacrificed himself for Ongi and me when we were still in our mom's womb. My life has been free of the sort of tragedy Serin could appreciate. I've never been without love.

"Sure. We're all victims of Cha's scheme. But some of us suffered more than others," she says, and I can feel her resentment coming up again. "And yet, everyone falls all over themselves over you just because you led the so-called exposé. Do you think that's right?"

Do I think that's right . . . ? I don't know. I've never thought about it that way. It takes a long moment, but I manage to respond, "So what is it that Bae Serin wants?"

"I want you to feel as sad and miserable as you've made me feel," she replies without missing a beat. "I had just reclaimed the life that was rightfully mine—the life of Haeri—and you went and took it away from me. Now that I have nothing, it makes me want to go for what's yours, for what it's worth."

"So . . . ," I say, feigning composure as her words bore straight into my heart. "Are you about to push me into the lake and assume my identity or something? Like in a movie? And then what?"

"That'd be dumb," she says with a laugh. "Miryu over there would practically skip across the water and save you."

"Thanks," I deadpan. "That makes me feel so much better. So what are you going to do, then? What's your plan?"

She pulls in a deep breath, taking a slow look around the lake. In the distance, under the heavens spilling over with stars, my brother's and friends' headlamps move like fireflies.

"I'm going to try to take what you have," Serin says, an odd smile drifting across her lips. "Family, love, friendship . . . all those kinds of things."

A gentle breeze blows in and flutters through her hair. She tucks in the loose strands behind her ear, and the watch on her wrist catches my eye.

"That watch—"

"I brought it from Grandma's," she promptly cuts me off.

Anger buds in me. It was a gift to myself, the wristwatch. My first purchase with the first paycheck I'd ever earned as Haeri the weathercaster. And now she's stolen that, too.

"Anything you have," she says, her eyes lingering on Hyang and the gang frolicking on the shore in the distance. "I want to take it for myself."

"You know I won't sit back and watch that happen," I say through my shock. I can't let her have the last word.

She responds with a smug, unhurried smile, as if my opinion is of no consequence to her.

A breeze picks up across the lake. Trees lining the shore shake out their leaves, and an odd bird's nest among the branches is illuminated in the moonlight. A fake one, I'm sure—likely just one of the countless hidden camera props. But there have to be a few real ones among them, too, no? Maybe even a cuckoo's nest . . . And the thought takes me away.

Cuckoos. Brood parasites that lay eggs in other birds' nests and trick them into raising their young. As if that's not enough, when a cuckoo chick hatches, it pushes the host species' eggs out of the nest. Brutal. But that's just the way evolution has programmed the species to perpetuate itself. It's a natural instinct, neither evil nor good. If it inflicts harm on others, though, is it really—

Somewhere in the trees, a cuckoo breaks into an emphatic call, jolting me out of my thoughts. Serin, her eyes hard, is grinning at me, sitting perched on her rowboat seat like some kind of cuckoo herself. I reach for the hull and grip it fiercely. I won't be pushed out of my nest.

# HAERI'S HOUSE

On the car ride back home, Serin surprised everyone by expressing her desire to tag along with Shinae and me to go watch Somyung's biathlon training. She was always the most athletic of us, as well as a great shot, so it didn't come as a surprise when she announced her ambitions to train for the infamous competition—but Ongi, sitting by Serin as if a loyal pet, just beamed his patronizing smile of encouragement at me, making me want to slap him. Does he really believe that him tricking us into bobbing on the lake together in that rowboat has made all the difference? That we've finally struck a peace deal or something? He's an idiot if he falls for the sudden shift in Serin's attitude and behavior.

Back at home, Serin cozies up to Miryu at the sink, where she's washing the thermoses and cups we used on our trip.

"Can I help you with breakfast from now on?" she says with a shy smile on her face.

As for Miryu, she hasn't been able to find work, her infamy as a cold-blooded serial killer preceding her. Sadly, it doesn't look like she'll be able to land a real job anytime soon, though there have been a few lackluster offers from the calculating director-types hoping to boost their own ratings by casting her in their failing shows.

"Work? What do you need work for? You know I make more than enough to support us. Take a load off while you can—while you're here," Hyang had said one day. "Live a little. Or just relax. You deserve it."

From that day on, Miryu has taken it upon herself to earn her keep in other ways, and over the course of time, she discovered a latent talent for cooking.

"Why, of course, Serin," Miryu says, welcoming Serin's offer. "That'd be wonderful."

"Oh, I'm not good in the kitchen or anything," Serin demurs. "But I've been wanting to learn how to cook. From you, Miryu. I'm sorry I've never told you how much I appreciate you cooking for all of us."

"Aww . . . Thank you for telling me that," Miryu says with a bashful smile. She's still learning to accept that she's worthy of others' trust and kindness. "So . . . is there a particular dish you want to learn how to cook first? Should we start with it? Tomorrow?"

By the pantry, Hyang is emptying the picnic basket, unable to stop smiling at this heartwarming scene. This kind of interaction with Serin was unthinkable just a few hours ago.

Finishing her task, Hyang grabs me by the hand and pulls me to her room. She closes the door shut and asks in a giddy whisper, "What did you two talk about in the rowboat?"

What did we talk about in the rowboat? Where do I even begin?

"Oh, come on," Hyang presses, her eyes bright with curiosity. "I'm not going to get all choked up next week in the editing room, am I?"

"I don't know . . . ," I tell her. "We mostly talked between the slates, so no. I wouldn't get too excited as far as footage."

As I think back over my talk with Serin, I know that's an understatement. In fact, just as the light beaming from the second slate announced the end of the break, Serin dabbed some lake water under her eyes. And when filming resumed, she picked up the emotional intensity right where she had left it, in order to seamlessly resume the tale of her tragic fate as the original Haeri, disfigured and swapped out. And I . . . I just tried not to look too disgusted by it all.

At the height of her performance, Serin apologized to me for having resented me all this time. And how did I respond? By telling her off. I couldn't help it. Whatever she's up to, it was so utterly stupid of her, feeling the need to deceive Hyang, our director. Doesn't she know that Hyang's on our side no matter what? Serin, meanwhile, predictably stayed in character, her face arranged to look hurt and tragically misunderstood for the camera.

We paddled our way back to the shore in heavy silence. That was when it finally dawned on me. Serin *doesn't* know that Hyang is on our side. She doesn't know that it's okay for us, her included, to be who we are on and off camera because Hyang would never do us wrong. I do. I have absolute trust in Hyang, who spins the raw footage of our lives into a compelling narrative, and that is another luxury I have that turns Serin green with envy.

"What?" Back in the present, Hyang yelps her disappointment.

"Are you telling me that the conversation is lost in the ether for the rest of us?"

Sudden exhaustion crashes over me. I plunk myself down on her bed and stare at the ceiling.

"She wants to wipe the slate clean and become friends with you, Miryu, and all the rest," I tell her in a tired voice. And as I do, I feel sympathy for the enemy creeping back in despite everything. I'm sad for the girl's twisted fate, her lonely childhood deprived of a mother's love, and all the rest—I am. That is, if any of it is true.

"Did Serin really say that? She wants to wipe the slate clean and become friends with all of us?" Hyang says, incredulous.

"Basically," I confirm. "With all of us except me."

**The two-story red brick house—Haeri's house—is so familiar** to me it is like my own. I know it like the back of my hand, both as a longtime viewer and a short-time star of the TV show in which it was featured. Currently, its front steps are heaped with flowers and letters left by people mourning Yeosu's tragic death and the mysterious disappearance of the Haeri who came before her. The woods Haeri, as I call her.

Despite the details I've managed to gather about her, the girl who preceded Yeosu in our line of clones is still a mystery to me. All I'm certain of is that she ran away a little over three years ago, after finding out about Director Cha's plan to replace her. The last footage anyone has is of her entering the woods in Snowglobe's restricted zone, and then . . . nothing.

I think of the underground power plant I discovered shortly after my own arrival at Snowglobe, the secret one where the Yibonn force death row inmates and other rivals they "disappear" to produce the extra energy our city needs to function. I've always wondered if Haeri wound up there after running away, but I've never been able to investigate my theory. Not that I've forgotten about it. After our exposé, I made a promise to myself to find the missing Haeri, if she's alive, and bring her home safely. It's my way of atoning for the part I played in Director Cha's scheme. The willingness I showed when she first asked me to come to Snowglobe and keep her perfect show alive—a dream that, as an aspiring director, I also shared.

I sigh, snapping back to the present. I haven't been back to Haeri's house since before our exposé, but now I've come with a mission. I push open the gate left ajar and step into the front yard, noting with shock, the level of defacement on the once beloved property. The ornamental fruit trees and flower beds that had been painstakingly tended to by Goh Maeryung are ripped up and trashed, and spray-painted graffiti bleeds on the house's brick walls, deck, and broken windows, cursing the former occupants in red and black:

*BURN IN HELL!*

*You don't deserve this kind of paradise, you MONSTERS!*

Plenty of four-letter vulgarities are there, too, despite someone's unsuccessful effort to scrub them off.

With thick, dark curtains drawn over every window, the house appears all but condemned. According to intelligence leaked to the media by "insiders," when Maeryung's trial began, the surviving Goh clan fled to SnowTower in search of safety and relative privacy—as if privacy were even possible in Snowglobe. But soon afterward, Maeryung alone returned, having made up her mind not to cower. She was still the lawful owner of her property, whether people liked it or not.

I cross the yard and walk up the steps to the front door. The doorbell unit, too, has been brutally smashed in by angry mobs, I notice. I raise my knuckles and give the door a few determined knocks, only for it to swing lazily open on its hinges. I peek into the silent house, my heart quickening, and after a moment's hesitation, I slip into the foyer, absently wondering if this is breaking and entering, or trespassing. It's unlikely that Maeryung would even bother to call the cops on me, but I do brace myself for that possibility.

**"Can you please, like, edit out the whole of tomorrow morning's** footage?" I asked Hyang last night, shame rising inside me. An actor asking their director for such a favor is completely out of line, of course. It's collusion, a serious offense inviting serious consequences.

"You're kidding, right?" Hyang said, and as I hesitated to reply either way, her face grew serious. "You do know that there are people waiting for us to do something dumb like that, don't you?"

"I have to stop the cuckoo egg from hatching," I mumbled, shrinking into myself and turning away from her. "I swear I'll tell you everything tomorrow after I confirm some information."

Serin's claim that she is the Haeri carried by Sanghui is utterly ridiculous. No one, not a single person in Haeri's family or Director Cha, has even hinted as much. Not in court, and not in the news or infotainment shows where talking heads foam at the mouth speculating about our story. It simply can't be true, or evidence would have come out by now, right?

And even if it is, what is Maeryung up to then, letting Serin in on that bombshell of a secret now? And what does it matter which one of us is the true and veritable Haeri at this point? If my discoveries have taught me anything, it is that there is no one "real," or original, Haeri. We were all created as potential replacements for one another. All pieces in one woman's plot.

No, Maeryung's sudden disclosure can have only one purpose. To dump rocket fuel on Serin's burning rage against me—that's what it does.

Is Maeryung trying to lure Serin to her side using their mutual hatred for me, the destroyer of their lives?

I step into the living room. The same furniture is arranged in the same configuration I remember, but otherwise the place is in complete disarray. Dirty clothes, trash, and containers of old food are everywhere. A teapot and empty cups sit on the coffee table where I imagine Maeryung entertaining Serin yesterday. It is unthinkable that the perfectionist old lady, with her obsession for fashion, lifestyle, and home décor, has allowed her home to deteriorate like this. The parole she was granted for health reasons might be legit after all. Or she's lost all will to go on living.

"Hello . . . ? Is anybody home?" I call out tentatively.

The door to Maeryung's room is closed shut, and there are no signs of her anywhere else. But I'm hesitant to knock on her door, so I take a seat on the sofa for now. Could she possibly be in bed at eleven in the morning? A good actor knew no rest, the old lady liked to preach. But she is an actor without a show now, so . . .

With Cha Seol stripped of her director's license and no one else stepping up to helm the cursed show, the whole Goh family has been out of work. In a way, being unemployed might just be the cruelest punishment for the lifelong actress who doesn't know other modes of existence. There hasn't been a single case of actors being kicked out of Snowglobe due to the absence of a director. Even though the situation wasn't their fault, the Goh family could be forced out if they don't secure more roles soon.

I notice an unpleasant odor drifting in the air then. Scrunching up my nose, I look around the living room for the source, when a loud thud upstairs makes me jump. I leave the sofa and creep up the wooden steps, wincing at their squeaks and groans ricocheting through the still house. In the hallway upstairs, a sliver of light cuts through the shadows, and I follow it to Haeri's door.

It's been a while since I've seen this room, with its vibrant green walls. With a big breath through my nose, I take a step inside when something crunches underfoot. A bracelet. A few feet beyond is a rogue earring, and a few feet beyond that, a brooch lies glinting on the floor near the changing nook.

I cross the room to the changing nook, picking up the orphaned articles, and when I round the privacy wall, I'm only mildly shocked to see the disarray inside. Haeri's collection of sunglasses, watches, and jewelry is all over the counter and floor. Someone has gotten into her stuff, and it has to be Serin. It's only then that my mind leaps to the whimsical orca, the killer whale brooch, and with a gasp, I begin picking up the mess, looking for it. To my great relief, I soon find it inside the mother-of-pearl-inlay box I discover wedged between the counter and the wall.

The brooch was a gift from Bonwhe, the heir apparent to the Yibonn corporation, for Haeri's hundredth day at work as the weathercaster. He gave it to her—to me—on his studio visit that day when filming paused between the slates. In other words, the gift was off the record, and absolutely no one else knows of it. Otherwise, it would have been the first thing Serin snatched up.

I take out the brooch and gently close my fist around it, thinking of Yeosu, the intended recipient of this gift. I don't entirely know quite where I stand with the Young Master. It's only because of him and his lingering devotion to Yeosu that we have a show at all—but despite the help he's given me, I can't make myself trust him fully. He is a Yibonn, after all. Whatever was between him and Yeosu, his loyalty is to his family and their enterprise.

Still, it strikes me that at the time he gave me this piece of jewelry, Bonwhe didn't know Yeosu was dead, or that the Haeri in front of him was me, Yeosu's replacement. Yeosu never even got to see the brooch. And I'd hate for it to end up in Serin's possession. I empty out a soft velvet pouch and put the brooch in it.

I'll use it as a reminder of my mission—my true mission, and the reason I'm still in Snowglobe. No matter the obstacles, I'm going to find out what happened to the Haeri who came before Yeosu, the girl I knew as the "real" Haeri from TV.

I'm going to bring her home, so she can have her own

name, like the rest of us, and begin her journey of discovering who she really is.

It's probably the warm sun and stuffy air in the room, but I'm feeling suddenly heavy and tired. I'm rubbing at my eyes when light beams checker the air and a loud clack rings out, jolting me back to why I came here. I hustle out of the room and head back downstairs, where Maeryung's door is now open a crack. Holding my breath, I creep up to it and peer inside. Goh Maeryung lies limp in her bed, blood pooling red on the front of her white nightgown, a knife lodged in her chest. I find that I can't even scream.

# THE MURDER WITNESS

She stares at me with wild eyes, wheezing like a woman drowning. From the tips of her fingers dangling by the bedside, blood drips to the floor in regular intervals. Feeling numb, I begin moving toward the bed without realizing it.

Then terror finally breaks through my consciousness.

"The phone!" I gasp, shooting my eyes over to Maeryung's nightstand where I know the receiver sits by her lamp. But the nightstand is empty, holding nothing but her reading glasses. Did the phone get knocked to the floor? I rush over to search under the bed, when her weak, clammy hand takes hold of my wrist. I jump.

"I—" she croaks, looking up at me pleadingly.

"Don't move," I cut her off, blood thundering through my ears. "I'm calling for help."

But her grip around my wrist only tightens, and she fixes me with sinking eyes.

"I . . . ," she begins again, her voice dying in her throat.

I what? What does she want to say? Swallowing hard, I bring my ear close to her bloodless, quivering lips.

"I . . . m . . . sorry," she rasps.

Her words hit me like a gut punch. I pull back up and stare at her, feeling myself quake with the surge of overwhelming emotion that I can't even name. Tears start up in my eyes. I roughly wipe them away.

"Save your apology," I spit out bitterly, shaking her off. "Live, so you can apologize to Yeosu."

Turning away, I resume my search for the phone, but it's nowhere to be found, not in this room. I rush out to the living room. No luck there, either.

That's when her door slams shut behind me. I jerk around and gape at the closed door for a few disorienting moments, but there's no time to be distracted. It was probably just the wind that did it, and anyway, I need to call for help.

I run upstairs and continue trying to locate a phone, darting frantically from room to room. What are the odds that, in the house with a phone for every corner, none can be found now? Not even in Rhim's room, though when I was living here, she couldn't be without one even in the bathtub. I stand frozen in the second-floor hallway, panic and dread overtaking me.

Then like a miracle, the faint ringing of a phone begins drifting up the stairs from the ground floor. Jolted back to the present, I race downstairs toward the sound, across the living room and into the kitchen, where I pluck out the phone from the refrigerator, a cordless one that I recognize as having belonged to Rhim.

How did it get in the fridge? Again, questions rise in my mind, but I can't focus on them yet. I have to save Maeryung.

119. I punch in the Snowglobe emergency number with wildly shaking thumbs, already running back to Maeryung's room.

"One-one-nine. What's your emergency?" the dispatcher answers just as I throw open Maeryung's door.

All the way up to this point, I was prepared to say *Help! A woman has been stabbed in the chest! Come quick! She's dying!*

But now as I take in the scene before me, my mouth just falls open, and all I can do is make a noise of confusion.

The dispatcher repeats, "Hello . . . ? One-one-nine. What's your emergency?"

*Please send help!* She tried to kill herself, but I won't allow her to get off that easy. Not today!

"I . . . I'm so sorry," I finally stammer, my voice hollow. "I . . . I don't know how it happened, but . . . I seem to have dialed the wrong number . . . ? I'm really sorry. Bye!"

I hurry and cut the connection.


**I blink. I blink hard. Then I squeeze my eyes shut a moment and** pop them open, twice. But no matter what I do, the scene in front of me doesn't change. Goh Maeryung is gone. My ears ringing, I stare at the empty bed where pristine white sheets are stretched tight over the mattress as if by a professional maid. It was just minutes ago that I saw the Goh matriarch lying there, almost dead . . . wasn't it? I look down at the hardwood floor. Not a speck of blood.

But what about the image imprinted on my brain, of Maer-yung's blood dripping to the floor from her gray fingertips . . . ?

A sudden headache seizes me, and I press my fingers to my temples.

Jeon Chobahm . . . Was it just your mind playing tricks on you?

Then my eyes fall on my wrist, still streaked with Maer-yung's blood. With a cold drop of dread, I shake my head. No, it couldn't be.

**The journey back home is a haze. A few hours later, I lie in** Hyang's bed, shivering, as Miryu wets a hand towel and dabs at my forehead. She spots the blood on my wrist and cleans it up, then proceeds to carefully examine me from head to toe, making sure that I'm free of any acute injuries that would require urgent care.

"Is she feeling hot or cold?" Hyang asks anxiously, reaching for the fan—less energy-intensive than the air conditioning, I note. Turning it on, she sets it on oscillate as Miryu begins pelting her with questions.

"What happened to her?" Miryu asks, still at my bedside.

"I don't know," Hyang says with a shrug. "She showed up at my office looking like this."

The director's commons, situated between District 1 and District 2, might as well be a special district of its own, re-plete with a spacious, attractive greenspace frequently teem-ing with visitors and directors taking a midday break. Making the journey to Hyang's building had been a trial. As much as I tried to appear normal, I couldn't help but notice others' eyes on me. Their attention was almost enough to make me turn back.

Dropping her voice low, Hyang continues, "She had this look on her face like she'd just seen a ghost or something, and when she spoke, she didn't make any sense."

Miryu gazes at me, concerned, holding up my head with one hand and a cup of water to my lips with the other. I take a small sip, and the cool, clear liquid steadies me. They both tense when I sit up, but I wave away their protests, drawing a deep breath. My heart quickens as I share with them what I saw—or what I think I saw: Goh Maeryung stabbed in her bed, and her sudden vanishing in the following minutes.

Hyang's eyes bulge with disbelief. Miryu stares at me, grim-faced. Willing my pulse to calm, I look down at my wrist, which is now free of Maeryung's blood, the only evidence of what had happened. All other proof is gone, just as if it never existed. Did she really even grab my wrist?

*I . . . m . . . sorry—*

What else did she say? I try to summon her voice, but it only seems to recede further.

I searched everywhere inside and outside that house. All the closets—walk-in and regular—every mudroom, even the refrigerator/freezer, the pantry . . . I also went outside and scanned the alleys, but no. Goh Maeryung was nowhere to be found.

"How could it all have been my imagination? How about the blood? Could it be someone else's? Like . . . mine, possibly?" I'm rambling now, desperate to make sense of things. The more I try to recall anything, the more I find that I distrust my memory.

Hyang's pulling at her hair.

"I'll check the recording, of course," she says. "But they won't arrive until next week. So if Goh Maeryung indeed met that kind of ending, we'll just have to see it on the news first."

Miryu takes my hand and gives it a gentle squeeze.

"Get some rest for now," she says, and then, turning to Hyang, she nudges her back to work. Reluctantly, Hyang gets to her feet, promising to be back home at a reasonable hour, and with a carton from my favorite ice cream place.

**When it's just the two of us, Miryu turns back to me with a** saddish-looking smile on her face.

"So, what's on your mind?" she says. "You look like you have something to tell me."

I hesitate a moment.

"How . . . ," I finally begin, but I can't quite formulate the rest. As I stall, Miryu finds the words for me. "How did I do it nine times?" she asks.

I drop my eyes, the memory of the first real-life death I witnessed coming at me once again. Cooper's. His face twisting with bottomless terror just moments before he was swept clean out of the plane and into the frozen void—disposed of by Director Cha during my initial flight to Snowglobe. The image of his eyes flecking red with rupturing vessels flooded me with such vile horror that I couldn't even properly grieve his tragic end for the longest time.

*I'm . . . I'm sorry.*

The death I witnessed this time around wasn't any less horrific. The sight of Maeryung lying in a pool of her own blood stunned me so that it's only now that I begin to register its nauseating metallic smell. I'm shaking again.

"Stop reliving it," Miryu says firmly, taking my trembling hands in hers. "Banish it from your mind. It's possible, I promise."

"Banish it? What do you mean?"

"Listen to me carefully, Chobahm," she says, holding my gaze and edging closer. "You had nothing to do with whatever happened to Maeryung. Stop replaying it. You must."

Then the words just tumble out of my mouth. "How did you watch them die?"

"Watch them die?" she repeats after a moment. Pain settling in her eyes, she corrects me. "I killed the men in my show—and hid the bodies. That's not watching them die. Let's call murder a murder and get it over with." A bitter smile. "Yes, I see them everywhere and around the clock—even in my sleep, even when I'm surrounded by people I love. I can never forget, and that's just as it should be."

Then I'm recalling the murderous chill of that night when we met. The night of the raging snowstorm back in my home district, when Ongi and I found Miryu lying on the snow, bleeding from her head. I pulled her behind me on the sled to the clinic at the power plant, cold biting into my bones.

On TV, Miryu had simply come across as a psychopathic killer for whom hate or lust for revenge was never a prerequisite for the multiple murders she committed. One just had to be in the wrong place at the wrong time and capture her interest, and some weeks after that, they'd be dead. She was an addict, and killing was the only thing that satisfied her cravings. She had to get her fix—or so it was made to look on-screen.

"But Hyang says that you were thoroughly exploited by Cha Guibahng, your director. That you never killed anyone because it was what you wanted to do," I protest.

"Maybe so," she allows. "Still, it was my finger that pulled the trigger, and my hand that plunged the knife. Those are facts that will never change."

We're quiet for a few moments. I ask her, "Could you have done otherwise?"

She drops her eyes and lifts them back to me. With a big sigh, she says, "As I was reeling after the first murder, Cha Guibahng assured me that the guy had gotten what he deserved. That his death brought peace to several worthy actors. As long as I kept exterminating these vermin, he said, my show would go on." A pause. "And my family would be taken care of, including my sister."

Her pain knifes at my heart. Everyone in our settlement knew about her sister, who was said to be suffering a sickness of the heart. I remember our plant supervisor, a man I always hated, referring to her one day as the brain-dead girl. In the cafeteria a few hours later, my grandma accidentally dumped her lunch tray on his head.

Miryu lets go of my hand and draws back.

"Cha Guibahng won me over that day," she says. "Haeryu, my sister, was coming out of her fog with the medicine I was able to get her by doing his bidding. So what if I had blood on my hands? I was exterminating bad men, wasn't I? People who deserved it?" She shifts her gaze to the headboard. "That's how I survived in Snowglobe, telling myself that lie over and over. Until I couldn't anymore."

On the shelf of the headboard is a framed photo of her and

Hyang, taken by a kind bystander on the day of their reunion. In it, Hyang is Hyang, her smile uncomplicated, projecting nothing but unfettered joy. Next to her, the look on Miryu's face is harder to define. Her mouth is smiling, yes, but her eyes are like two pits of grief.

"I'm not saying that there aren't people without whom we'd all be better off," Miryu resumes. "Cha Guibahng, Cha Seol, Goh Maeryung, and so on . . . ." Another sigh. "But it is not our call to decide when their time on this earth ends, and it certainly wasn't mine."

I reach for her hands and take them in mine this time.

"Miryu . . . Let's move forward—you and me both," I say, trying to sound more chipper than I feel. "I swear I won't replay in my head what I saw today. I'm scared and frustrated, but I won't keep going back there and trying to piece together what happened—because truth will out, right? Just like how, in time, we all learned what a kind soul you are."

A wan smile on her face, Miryu nods weakly.


**A full week passes without word of Maeryung, during which** Miryu, Hyang, and I are on pins and needles every day, waiting for the unsettling news to break on the radio, on TV, or in the paper. But there's been nothing so far, not even the beginning of a rumor buzzing about in deep fan media. Then Hyang calls from her office today.

"I've just finished viewing last week's recordings. I saw what happened to Maeryung," she says.

As the director of our show, *You, Me, and Us,* Hyang gets access to the previous week's recordings, but only to the recordings pertaining to her cast. What this means is that if I had been in Maeryung's room when she'd vanished, Hyang could view the recording today, but not otherwise. She could only see where I'd been. And at the moment of the old lady's unsettling disappearance, I was running around the house, frantically looking for a phone. I wasn't in her room. So how did Hyang get to view the footage to even find out what happened to Maeryung?

"What? How?" I bark into the receiver.

"Goh Maeryung didn't kill herself," Hyang replies in a tone so cold that it makes my skin prick with goose bumps. "You, Jeon Chobahm, killed her."

# THE PREDICTABLE SCARLET LETTER

My heart slams against my chest and seizes there a moment. Then it begins to pound again, like a beast trying to escape its cage.

"What . . . what are you talking about?" I murmur.

Hyang's heart is pounding, too, if her wavering voice says anything.

"I have footage of you stabbing Maeryung."

It takes me a moment to register her words.

"That's not me," I say at last, and the empty chuckle I append makes me sound suspicious even to my own ears.

"I know," Hyang rushes to say. "But there's footage of it. And it's not fake."

As if I don't know it. A director can edit out unwanted scenes, but no one can create scenes that don't exist and edit them into footage. If that were possible, Miryu would never actually have had to carry out all the awful murders she executed.

"How do you know that the girl in the footage is me?" I demand.

Not that I think any of the girls would have done it. But the simple fact is that there are three other girls who look just like me in Snowglobe alone. We're so alike that even the system software that sorts out daily recordings based on face recognition technology counts me, Somyung, Shinae, and Serin as one face. One actor.

"Well," Hyang says, heaving a sigh. "The recording is exactly from the time and day you were at Maeryung's house, and the girl is dressed identical to you, and . . ."

"Identical?" I say, my voice high with incredulity. "I was just wearing blue jeans and a white T-shirt. Everyone has that outfit!"

"I know that, too. But there's more," Hyang explains. "It's what the girl does. She confronts Maeryung for stirring up Serin with made-up stories. Then she moves on to Yeosu's death, getting increasingly worked up, and when she finally lunges for the old lady with a knife in hand, she's shouting that it's time for payback."

A chill cascades down the back side of my body. My heart contracts so hard, it's as if it's trying to curl up into a ball. Confront Maeryung about stirring up Serin with stories? Demanding to pay for Yeosu's death? Who else among us is likely to do or say such things, if not me?

"And the next recording? What did you see in it?" I say.

"The slate goes off. There's no footage for another ten minutes," Hyang replies apologetically. "And the next available footage is of you bursting out of the house and showing up at my office door, looking like a deer in the headlights."

Half-formed thoughts begin to multiply and weave inside my head like spiderwebs. My brain is soon shrouded in a tangle of thick white silk. I try freeing one thought at a time, but it's impossible. I close my eyes. If I could only view the footage myself, maybe I could figure it out . . .

But access to recordings is strictly limited to directors. Even if Hyang wanted to share it with me, she couldn't.

"What are you still doing inside? The car is waiting for us. We need to get going or we'll be late." Serin's voice startles me then, and I whip around.

She stands poised at the doorway, looking lovely in a breezy lemon-colored summer dress suspended from her shoulders by two strings of tiny shells. Outside, a white limousine sent by Fran idles on the curb.

Fran. Amid everything else, I've almost forgotten. Today is Fran's special day.

Sweat slickens my palm. I can't ruin it. But neither can I let Serin know anything is wrong.

"Come on, Chobahm. We're going to be late," she adds in an extra-friendly tone that I know is manufactured for the camera, for Hyang, and ultimately, for the viewers.

From the receiver, Hyang's confused voice tinkles out into my ear, "I know that you, Jeon Chobahm, could never kill anyone. But if it isn't you in the footage, who the hell is it . . . ?"

Serin edges in, mouthing the words, "Who're you talking to?"

Then the chilling thought dawns on me. Could it be her . . . ?

*It's unfair. That you alone were spared.*

I stare at Serin, who stares back, studying my face intently. Did she . . . ? Did she do it?

*I'm going to try to take what you have.*

"Are you okay, Chobahm? Who're you talking to?" Serin asks in a hushed tone, brows scrunched in concern.

"No, it's nothing," I say with an awkward half laugh, half cough. "It's Hyang. She thinks she left her reading glasses at home." I turn back to the phone. "Sorry, Ajumma, but Serin and I have to go. Why don't you take another good look around?"

I set down the receiver and grin up at Serin, catching her squinting warily at me, her lips drawn tight. She immediately slaps on a smile and says, "Do you have the present?"

I murmur an affirmative and grab the wrapped gift sitting on the nightstand. Crossing the living room behind her, I can't help but notice the spring in her step today.

"Hey, Serin," I say.

"Hmm . . . ?" she responds blithely.

"Have you gone back to see Goh Maeryung again, since the last time we talked?"

I think I catch her eyes wavering for a split second. But then she replies, "No," with maddening simplicity before strolling out the door, causing me to want to snatch her back inside by her dress and grill her. I'm clenching my fists so hard that my nails dig into my palms. But I can't ruin the day. Not today of all days. I shimmy my feet into the dainty emerald heels Serin has laid out for me.

**"Oh, I haven't missed a single episode!"** enthuses the captain of the yacht, whose thick blond braids top the crown of her head like a laurel wreath. Serin beams graciously at her, and the captain ushers us aboard to the upper deck, where an intimate buffet table is set with champagne and fine hors d'oeuvres.

"We'll set sail as soon as a few more people arrive," the captain informs us. "In the meantime, please settle in and enjoy the refreshments."

Serin thanks the captain with another lovely smile. I follow suit, though I'm dying inside to be left alone with her so I can confront her with the question that's been burning a hole in my throat: *It's all your doing, isn't it, Bae Serin?*

If I speak it aloud, I know this party will dissolve into chaos. But for right now, the starry-eyed captain stands guard between such a disaster and me, as did the limousine driver. With a deep breath, I stifle my impulse to shout at Serin and cast my gaze upon the far distance where the shimmering sea meets the horizon, where the water is the deep sapphire color of Serin's shoe. It really is beautiful out here, I think just as the captain cries out in a jubilant greeting. I turn my head to see Bonwhe and his shadow, Assistant Yu, emerging onto the deck.

Serin bolts up from her seat, singing out, "Young Master!"

Bonwhe's eyes briefly acknowledge her before they settle on me.

"It's been a while," he says, and lets the faintest smile flit across his lips. Conspiratorial, one might call it. It's strange to think it's only been a month since I saw him last. Just before we moved out of the Yibonn estate, when I convinced him to give us our own show.

To take a chance on me. I wonder if he'll regret that soon.

In a summer suit, the Yibonn heir looks as impeccable as

ever. Does the boy even sweat? His flawless skin has a matte finish, as if today's scorcher has no effect on him. Running cool might just be the hallmark of Snowglobe royals after all.

Bonwhe and Assistant Yu settle at the table, and the captain announces from behind the helm almost as tall as she is, "Once again, welcome aboard, ladies and gentlemen! It is a pleasure to have you with me today. My name is Miho, and I'm the skipper who'll take you safely to our special destination—under a very special banner."

A few minutes later, the yacht is finally in motion, rolling over the gentle waves. Up above, an enormous wedding veil tied to the tip of the mast dances in the breeze against the perfect blue sky, its gauzy shadow dappling on the deck below. The banner Miho was referring to.

On the receding shore at our backs, the harbor is lively with spectators, many of whom have binoculars pressed over their eyes. Some sit elevated on makeshift lifeguard towers, dainty opera glasses in their hands. Clearly, today's ceremony is a supreme extravaganza even by Snowglobe's standards.

It must be the noonday sun, but sweat won't stop beading on my scalp. I'm busy trying to control the rivulets trickling down my temples and forehead—surreptitiously, I think—when Bonwhe extends his handkerchief to me across the table.

Caught by embarrassment, I mumble an excuse, but he just arches his brows and doesn't retract the offer. I know those brows, and that private look he's giving me. It's the same look he flashed me at the Christmas party last year when he thought that I was Yeosu, with whom he had a secret friendship. Today, though? He already knows that I'm not her. So why the brows?

"Thank you," Serin chirps then, and gently snatches the handkerchief. Turning to face me, she dabs the square along my hairline, muttering in my ear through a tight smile, "We're not trying to embarrass the Young Master, are we?"

As I let her blot the sweat off my face, a dreadful idea seizes me. This cuckoo chick . . . She is trying to blot me off, too, isn't she? With an involuntary gasp, I rear up and stare at her in horror. Serin pauses in action and stares right back at me a moment but then immediately resumes her smile.

"Don't worry, Chobahm. Your makeup's intact," she assures me playfully before turning to Bonwhe and his assistant to ask, "Isn't she even lovelier today?" A wink. "I did her makeup."

That much is true. This morning, Serin surprised me by offering to do my makeup, and though I had my misgivings, I took a chance and sat on the big chair in the living room as she worked on my face for close to an hour—with Hyang, Miryu, and Ongi in the audience making all kinds of approving faces and sounds. These two are finally getting along!

And though it was awkward to have her face bob up and down in my personal space, it didn't feel as intensely disagreeable as it does now; probably because I hadn't yet decided that Serin was the only person on this planet who could pull off stabbing Goh Maeryung while pretending to be me.

Grandma always taught me and Ongi to give everyone a fair chance, and that we should always get to know someone before passing judgment on them. But the fact that Serin is a cuckoo's chick is not influenced by my opinion, as far as I'm concerned. And what she did to push me out of the nest is beyond any treachery I could have dreamed of. To frame me for a murder and put me away . . . ?

I shudder to think of what the public's reaction will be if—when—the footage Hyang has goes live. Will she edit it out for me? But then, no matter what she does, Maeryung's death will be reported eventually.

If I don't figure out the truth, I'm doomed.

"Here we are, ladies and gentlemen!" Captain Miho's exuberant announcement brings me back. Our yacht is docking at today's venue, a massive cube of crystal-clear glass floating on the blue ocean. Inside it, I can see early arrivals in colorful cocktail attire already mingling, while servers in uniforms weave in and out of them with trays of drinks and finger food. In the distance, more yachts appear from all directions, each one of them featuring the same wedding veil flying from the tip of the mast.

Then the glass panels are sliding open on one side of the cube, and Serin and I step in first, followed by Bonwhe and his assistant. The glass floor is surprisingly grippy under my heels, I'm noting, when a school of shimmering fish swims gaily by beneath.

"This is the most amazing wedding venue ever!" Serin cries out, and Bonwhe laughs softly, infected by the pure delight in her voice.

Then the man of the day appears, resplendent in a white tuxedo.

# WHAT I SAW

"**Y**ou're here!" Fran calls out, beaming, striding over to us with his long legs. An almost identical version of our yacht's wedding veil/sail is draped over his shoulders, and despite everything, the sight of him makes me feel a little bit better. A former weathercaster and fan-favorite actor, he was one of the first—and only—friends I made while pretending to be Haeri and is one of the single good people I've met within Snowglobe. I've missed him more than I realized.

He addresses Bonwhe first, eyes shining with admiration.

"Thank you so much for coming, Young Master."

"It's a pleasure," Bonwhe says. "Congratulations."

Bonwhe extends his hand in a handshake, and Fran takes it with both hands.

"I'm the lucky one who gets to attend the event on behalf of the Yibonn," Bonwhe says, glancing at another yacht preparing to dock. Flying the Yibonn flag, the yacht is loaded with all kinds of shiny gifts for the happy couple. "But the president and the vice-president would like to send their congratulations, as well. Unfortunately, the president couldn't get the clear from her doctor to celebrate the day in person."

"That'd certainly have been our greatest honor, Young Master," Fran gushes with gratitude. "But the president's health is of the utmost importance."

All weddings are special and exciting in their own way, but today's wedding is more so because in Haeri's absence, Fran is filling in as the weathercaster currently serving the community. Hence the extra attention from the Yibonn. Watching Fran chatting with Bonwhe, I wonder if Serin or I would still be determining the weather each night if Serin hadn't stuck that needle in my neck, or if the girls and I hadn't marched into the studio with Hyang and revealed the truth about the Chas.

"So good to see you girls," Fran says, finally turning to me and Serin.

He makes a show of narrowing his eyes and looking at me and at Serin, and then back again. He says, "Is it just me, or is anyone else having a hard time telling you two apart—"

"Congratulations, dearest Fran!" Serin cries, cutting him off.

Launching herself at Fran, she throws her arms around him. Fran returns her enthusiasm, and the two rock from side to side in a tight embrace, gushing with joy.

"Is this Serin?" Fran asks me silently, pointing at Serin's back and mouthing the words. I play along and confirm it with a nod, and he closes his eyes and breathes her in, patting her back like a loving uncle.

"Thank you, Serin," he coos. "I'm so happy you're here."

Fran tying the knot today fills me with such joy that I could cry. But Serin is almost manic with it.

The investigation launched by our exposé revealed a lot of things to the world, including very unflattering things about Serin—because making sense of how Hyang and I came to form a pact required making sense of how I ended up in the retirees' village, which, in turn, required making sense of how Serin got to stick that needle in my neck, and so on and so forth. The press had a field day all this, needless to say; soon Serin was branded a vile and bloodless backstabber by most of the population.

*Whoa, watch out for that girl. She's nasty.*

*A bloodsucking wretch!*

All but Fran, that is. He has not once expressed his disapproval of Serin, not even right after it all came out. When he finally delivered on the promise he'd made me long ago of a pasta dinner at his place, he invited both me and Serin, and proudly handed each of us an invitation to his wedding at the end of the evening. No wonder Serin adores him. His kind compassion for her is genuine and exceptional, and I have to say that it does have a softening effect on her. She behaves for him.

"Did we tell you, Fran . . ." Serin begins as they finally break off the embrace. "Chobahm and I took your advice to heart, and we're now friends." She beams at him, still holding onto his hands. "You can confirm this on our show next week."

Fran grins, gushing that the news is the best wedding gift ever. Bonwhe glances dubiously at me, and I respond with a thin smile as next week's episodes begin playing in my head. Saturday's episode will show Serin's tearful apology in the rowboat, and Sunday's, my murder of Maeryung, Serin's grandma.

If Serin is a bloodsucking wretch for attacking me with a tiny needle, then what is Jeon Chobahm for murdering a grandma with a kitchen knife?

"Young Master!" another excited female voice goes up nearby. Jin Jinsuh, Fran's bride-to-be, races over in her wedding dress as magnificent as the sea. Her long raven waves bounce in the air behind her as the pearl pendant of her bow-tie-shaped necklace catches the sun.

She greets Bonwhe with due formality. Then, turning to Fran with a giddy smile, she draws his face toward hers with the tips of her long, slim fingers, and they rub their cheeks together in pure bliss. Fran is six foot four, but Jin Jinsuh is no slouch on the height front either, matching her partner almost inch for inch. Her dog, Manseh—meaning "Hurray"—who also has an imposing physical presence, is currently by her side, wagging its tail. The ten-year-old canine of the Sapsari breed is one of the most beloved characters in Snowglobe, in fact. Had it not been for the extraordinary bond between Manseh and Jinsuh keeping up her show's ratings, Jinsuh would have been kicked out of Snowglobe long ago, and there wouldn't have been a wedding today.

"It's so great to see you, Serin!" Jinsuh cries. Then, shifting her friendly eyes to me, she cries, "And you, too, Chobahm!"

"What?" Fran yelps with disbelief. "How did you tell them apart without even trying?"

"You do know that I have a keen eye," she replies, gazing lovingly into the eyes of her groom. "That's how I picked you out."

Fran gazes lovingly back at his bride. No amount of makeup can simulate the affection on his face. He always wears a lot, in order to mask the ravages of cancer, which he's now survived twice.

Watching them, I remind myself once more that I must keep my question locked away until after the wedding. I won't ruin Fran's special day, especially when he may not have too many days left to begin with, special or not.

**It may be the mood of the day set by the lovely occasion, or the** gorgeous venue bobbing lazily on the lulling sea. It's as if all the hundred or so wedding guests have decided to set aside their judgment of Serin and treat her as one of Fran's distinguished guests and colleagues, someone deserving of their grace and generosity. Serin, of course, reciprocates at least sevenfold, looking completely at home while socializing with everyone with such grace and ease, laughing and chatting, and really playing up the part of a perfect wedding guest—and a sane human being. She's hoping for an image overhaul inside and outside the venue, of course. Watching her in action takes me back to my early weeks in Snowglobe, when it was me desperate to inhabit Haeri—the girl I'd grown up watching. I look away, a sudden heaviness settling in my heart.

Physically, too, I'm feeling heavier, to the point where exchanging pleasantries and small talk requires a conscious effort. All I want to do is go back home and bury my head in my pillows. But I need to keep my eye on Serin.

The temperature inside the cubelike venue is pleasant, but recirculated air is recirculated air, and I suddenly find myself desperate for a fresh ocean breeze.

"Are you feeling all right?" a voice inquires then. I turn

my head to see a woman about Hyang's age staring intently at me from a wheelchair. With her flawless skin glowing almost alabaster against the deep emerald green of her short-sleeve suit, and with the loose dark hair framing her head bringing out the chiseled lines of her face, the woman gives off a strong local vibe—definitely a Snowglobian by birth.

"Oh . . . Yes, thank you," I respond, trying to smile. "It's just the air. It's . . . a bit stale, I think."

"Stale . . . ? The air?" the woman repeats in surprise, almost offended. Then, bunching her brows, she denies it. "No, it's not. It can't be. It has the same ventilation system as the dome itself."

I just stare at her, tripped up by the unexpected response.

"Have you never seen a woman in a wheelchair before?" she says after a moment, and that's when I realize that I'm staring at her thin, pale hands resting on the chrome wheel cranks of her chair.

"What . . . ? Oh, no," I rush to answer. "I mean, a good friend of mine uses one."

I'm talking about Suji, of course, my friend from home, who works at the post office in our small district. Except that her wheelchair is nothing like this woman's shiny throne.

I feel a sudden stab of guilt. I wonder how Suji is doing out there in the cold.

"And that good friend lives in the open world?" my conversation partner wants to know.

When I confirm, the woman shifts her gaze from me to take a slow look around the guests enjoying themselves.

"I heard that people like me are of little use in the open

world," she says. "And that whatever job we're lucky to secure, it pays peanuts."

Once again, I'm stumped for a response. She's not wrong. The open world is brutal, but since coming to Snowglobe, I sometimes forget how much so.

The woman gives a self-deprecating laugh and continues, "I'm not saying that the assessment is unfair—not necessarily. One's talent and value tend to be highly contextual, after all. Still . . . it's kinda funny."

"Funny?" I murmur dumbly.

"Yes, funny. As if able-bodied people are any less vulnerable to hypothermic death than your wheelchair-using friend in negative fifty degrees. As living creatures on this frozen planet, we all share that same fatal vulnerability outside the dome." She casts her eyes back toward the guests meandering around us. "So what if some of us are less mobile? That's just a minor inconvenience in the face of the huge existential threat we all must contend with. But people obsess over others' slight flaws and minor imperfections for the false sense of comfort it provides, especially those who are less secure in themselves." Another flutter of laughter. "As if anyone gets out of here alive."

Her words remind me of the plant supervisor back home, who would openly make fun of Miryu's sister for her condition. Was it a twisted attempt at guarding against his own insecurities? At feeling less vulnerable? I wrinkle my nose at the memory of his cruelty, as the woman, her hands still poised on the cranks of her wheelchair, watches me.

"There's nothing wrong with ventilation, by the way," she

declares. "You must be feeling poorly for another reason. So why don't you cut out early rather than try to please everyone?"

At this point, I'm thoroughly intrigued by this woman and her blunt way of speaking. Who is she?

"Did you design this venue?" I venture.

She hushes me with a pale index finger over her lips.

"Don't let anyone here get wind of it," she says in whispered tone. "They're all unapologetic extroverts—like the hosts themselves—and I'm already maxed out by their energy. I can't handle any questions."

So she is the brilliant architect behind today's stunning venue. A murmur of wonder escapes me. "Whoa . . ."

"See? You, too, are starstruck already," she says with a teasing grin and a shake of the head. "And that's my cue to get going."

"What? Wait! You can't miss the wedding," I protest.

"The lovely couple only invited me to be polite," she says, and holds out a business card. "Call me for your special-occasion needs. Friends and family discount—how about that?"

I take the card and give it a quick look. The chic, minimalist design befits the owner, but as for promoting her business—I'm not sure. No company name, no title, no address, no telephone number, and not even her name is found anywhere on it. Just a company logo on one side—two curved ladders resembling the structure of DNA—and on the other, a series of numbers: 9788936478292.

"What are these numbers?" I ask, looking up from the business card, but she's already halfway to the exit, her pale, sticklike arms pumping the wheelchair with surprising vigor.

*Call me for your special-occasion needs.*

I tuck the business card in my purse, wondering what special occasions in my life would require consulting such a massive talent.

Then I see Assistant Yu, Bonwhe's constant shadow, zeroing in on me through the crowd.

"Do you have a moment, Miss Chobahm?" she says.

"Sure," I reply, despite my body pleading otherwise.

Nodding briskly, she leads me across the crowded floor to a quiet corner. I glance around, half expecting her boss to be lurking somewhere nearby, but the Yibonn heir is nowhere to be found. We're alone.

"The board has approved the proposal," she informs me abruptly, and I turn back to face her. The proposal. There's only one such plan she can be referring to—the one involving potential weathercaster substitutes while Fran will be out on his honeymoon.

Before I can comment, Assistant Yu taps the heel of her shoe against the glass floor three times, and the floor panels in front of us slide open to reveal a clear staircase descending to a lower level. I blink, surprised, as she gestures for me to go ahead. Obediently, I begin down the stairs as she says, "The studio is already excited about the substitutes we've chosen."

I know what she's implying, of course. There has to be a reason she approached me.

"Let me guess," I say playfully. "They drew my name and Serin's name from the hat."

I'm expecting a chirp of a laugh and her confirmation, but no response comes. When I look back over my shoulder, she's gone. The opening, too, is gone, with the floor panels above having slid back in place, becoming a part of the seamless ceiling/screen currently displaying rippling blue water.

I'm marveling at the place's exquisite aesthetics and technology, temporarily forgetting about Assistant Yu and my unanswered question, when a familiar voice reaches me from below.

"Yes, but you and Serin are not the only ones we're considering," Bonwhe says.

# HERO'S END

Bonwhe smiles, acknowledging the surprise on my face.
"Sorry to pull you away from all the fun, but I thought this is a good place where we could talk privately," he says.

He's standing against a giant glass wall, beyond which a shoal of striped tropical fish swims by in glittering colors. I take a long look around. The lower level makes me feel like I've dropped into the sea in an all-glass elevator. Its walls, ceiling, and even the floor are glass, revealing the ocean beyond. *But what about the cameras?* I idly wonder before snatching a quick look around.

As if he's read my thoughts, Bonwhe speaks again, assuring me we're alone—no cameras. I give him a wary look, and he says, "Temporary structures, like this cube, tend to have blind spots everywhere because directors don't get to test them out beforehand. And by the time they get the footage and realize what cameras are needed and where, it's time to have the structure demolished."

"Fine," I concede. "But how do you know that this is a blind spot?"

"Because Mr. Yi Hyunoh approved the permit."

"Who's that?"

"My uncle. The youngest on my mother's side."

"So he slipped it to you that this is a blind spot?" I ask. Bonwhe's confession doesn't entirely surprise me. I recall learning in school that, in addition to media, the Yibonns have valuable connections in many Snowglobe industries, including, I guess, building and permitting. The thought peeves me.

*How many more blind spots do you know about as an almighty Yibonn?* I want to ask, but I decide to hold my peace.

Bonwhe doesn't answer my last question. He keeps talking as if I hadn't asked anything at all, describing how while Fran is off on his honeymoon next week, former weathercasters will take turns filling his spot on *News at 9*. "But there's a catch," he says. "You and Serin will step in as a pair."

"Why?" I say, hearing the note of protest in my voice. "What's the reason for the pair? Can Serin just do it alone? She'd be ecstatic."

"Ratings," he says matter-of-factly. "You and Serin together will boost viewership—there's no doubt about it. The network's already excited about scheduling you two to appear on the last day—to maximize the buildup."

The last livecast of the week. Sure, why not? That's just perfect, because it'd be immediately followed by the episode of *You, Me, and Us* in which Jeon Chobahm slays Goh Maeryung in cold blood.

Bonwhe continues in a semicorporate tone, "Everyone filling in has been contacted except Serin. I'll talk to her today."

I must make a face, because he cocks his head and studies me a moment.

"There's brunch tomorrow for the week's weathercasters, but attendance is not mandatory," he continues, but I'm not even listening to him at this point.

With a quick chuff of a laugh, I ask him, "So . . . why are you contacting me and Serin separately? What's the point of that?"

His eyes staring back at me catch the blue of the water. We're both silent, recalling the same moment, I'm sure of it.

*This is your chance to honor your promise to Yeosu. Let us take down Cha Seol, and I'll keep my promise to stay quiet about the mirrors.*

"I'm not saying that I don't trust you," he says, finally breaking the silence. "I just wanted to make sure we're still on the same page before you go on the livecast."

On the same page . . . of course.

Last Christmas, I stumbled through a hidden mirror doorway at the Yibonn's party. It whooshed me to a place as hellishly cold as the open world, where I discovered an underground power plant, run by death row prisoners the public believed to have been executed. Only, they hadn't. Rather than death, they'd been handed a different life sentence: an eternity producing the electricity Snowglobe needs to function.

The story the public knows about Snowglobe—that it sits on a bed of natural geothermal vents that keep it warm—is a lie. There is no natural warmth beneath the dome. I had uncovered the Yibonn's long-held secret hidden in the bowels of Snowglobe.

And Bonwhe is clearly still frightened I'll expose it, just like I did the truth about Haeri.

"I do not wish to go up against Yibonn," I tell him, looking him straight in the eye.

It sounded great in my head, but the absurdity of the statement suddenly strikes me. Twice rejected from film school and only seventeen years old. I do not wish to go up against Yibonn . . . As if I even could . . .

But Bonwhe doesn't laugh.

"You took over the broadcasting station in the SnowTower and called out your director in public," he says. "That's no trivial feat. I couldn't just sit back and hope that someone like you wouldn't try doing something heroic when given the stage again."

"Heroic?" I say, stifling a laugh. "I just wanted to reclaim myself and my identity, period. I had no interest in becoming someone's hero or exposing the underbelly of society."

Had I wanted to be a hero, I could have started at the power plant, confronting the obnoxious supervisor for his monopoly of the break room, for instance. But I was frightened of the possibility that he would dock my pay. Just as I feared my equally sheepish and fearful co-workers' lack of support. I'd seen it happen before—all the time. The pattern was that when an individual worker rose up against power, they ended up being disciplined—reeducated—before ultimately getting fired. So would it have been worth the trouble for me?

I didn't think so. At least, at the time.

"You haven't told anyone about what you saw . . . have you?" Bonwhe asks, his expression cautious.

I don't reply immediately. Even if I wanted to share what I witnessed, who would buy a story I can barely believe myself?

Hyang, who regularly has to fend off severe criticism that she bit the hand that fed her—her family? Miryu, who punishes herself every moment of the day with her past? Or Somyung and Shinae, who seem to have discovered what it's like to be alive, at last?

"I swear I haven't. And I won't," I tell him truthfully.

Bonwhe has no idea that my head's about to explode with my own problems. I couldn't stick my nose in the Yibonns' business even if I wanted to. I let out a long, trailing sigh without meaning to.

"You okay?" Bonwhe says, examining my face. Then, stepping closer, he lifts a hand and dabs off the sweat on my forehead with his shirt cuff.

"Don't. You'll get makeup on your cuff," I say, guiding his hand away, but he grabs my wrist and says point-blank, "What's bothering you?"

His eyes looking at me are now warm with concern. The cool insouciance, his default mode, has fallen away. That's when I become suddenly conscious of how close we're standing to each other, and my face flushes.

"What's bothering me?" I repeat indignantly, annoyed that my face is flushing. "Why do you care? Just a moment ago, you were making sure that I've kept my mouth shut, even warning me against being a hero."

"That's not what I'm talking about."

"There's nothing else to talk about, then."

He stares at me, frustrated. But his face softens again, and he lets out a low chuckle.

"What's funny?"

"What are you going to do now?" he says, and I can't quite place his tone. "Do you know that I can see through you?"

See through me? What is he talking about? I'm blushing again in spite of myself. And God! I can't stand the thought of him noticing it.

It's only when he lets out a pained breath, his face bunched in agony, that I realize I've lashed out and cuffed him in the ribs.

"See through me, huh?" I hear myself say, unable to stop. "You didn't even know that I wasn't Yeosu."

He takes a step back and stares at me. Seeing the hurt in his eyes, I'm finally remorseful, but I don't know what to do or say next.

In the silence that falls, Bonwhe slowly draws himself up, inhaling a long, stoic breath through his nose before gradually letting it out through his mouth. Holding me with his eyes, he rubs idly at his rib cage, where my blow connected with his side.

"I . . . I'm sorry for that, too," I apologize. "You know, growing up with a twin brother . . . I developed a quick fist."

He just stares at me for another long moment. Then, suddenly, his head tips back and he lets out a real laugh, with his eyes closing and the skin around them wrinkling and everything. It's been a while, but I've seen him laugh like that a few times. A school of a thousand silvery fish appears beyond the glass to our side, and they swim in circles before shimmering away.

"Jeon Chobahm," he says, leveling his eyes on me and switching to a serious tone, though his face still holds the residue of his laugh. "You're really not going to tell me what's going on?"

I glance away. He waits patiently as I hesitate.

"I think I'm caught in a trap," I tell him at last.

He raises a brow, urging me to go on, but I can't say any more for now, and I tell him so.

"Caught in a trap . . . ," he repeats softly, contemplating the expression.

We're quiet a moment, and then he says, "Can I share my expert opinion with you?"

"Your expert opinion?"

"Self-deception," he says, and glances off toward the infinite blue beyond the walls. "Lie to yourself. It's a survival trick. Deny your senses if you can't escape the realities that they tell you."

"That's ridiculous," I say, immediately offended by the idea. "And I'm sick of lies . . . upon lies upon lies."

**Back on the main level, the lighting intensifies.**

"And now! Let us welcome for the first time as husband and wife . . . ," intones Anchor Park from *News at 9,* today's master of ceremonies.

Music swells. Against the backdrop of gently breaking waves, the bride and groom walk down the aisle holding hands: Fran dressed in a splendid white tuxedo, and Jinsuh in a gorgeous, flowy blue wedding dress like the ocean. But it is the smiles they wear, ones of deep love and joy, that stick out most of all.

On the screens of the surrounding glass walls, a crustacean quartet is busy sawing at their string instruments with their prominent claws. Up on the screen of the ceiling, humpback whales jump and splash. Guests are jubilant—applauding, laughing, whooping, and whistling. Sadly, none of them are family or childhood friends of the couple. Those people will have to wait and catch the ceremony on TV, the same as the rest of humanity living outside Snowglobe.

A lavish reception follows. The banquet tables strain under the weight of all kinds of delicacies sourced from both the land and sea, but I have exactly zero appetite, my mind plagued by the image of Goh Maeryung dying in her bed. I close my eyes to blot it away, but then the image that swoops in is of Jeon Chobahm plunging a knife into Goh Maeryung's chest. The worst part of all this is that it's started to feel like I might have actually done it.

All I want to do is drag Serin back home by the neck of her pretty dress and interrogate her about the morning in question. I also want to ask Hyang for more details . . . and be reassured by Miryu that I'll be all right, that everything will be all right. Ugh. How long until those yachts return and carry us back to firm ground?

Fran, his face flushed and sweaty from dancing with Producer Yi, breaks off from the floor and heads over to the bar. Spotting me, he asks if I'm enjoying myself. I still can't figure out dancing—not that I particularly want to, anyway. But he's pulled away by another guest before I can form a reply.

I look back to the dance floor pulsing with beautiful people. It doesn't take long for me to spot Serin among them, laughing and shrieking joyfully with one dance partner after another, all the while consciously staying within Bonwhe's radius. She looks absolutely at peace with herself, in complete sync with the world around her; and in that moment, she is the girl who used to be the world's sweetheart.

I decide to hide out in a bathroom. That's what I did last year at the Christmas party when things got too overwhelming. This time, though, it's not because I'm terrified of giving myself away as a fake Haeri with two left feet. I just can't stand how lovely Serin is right now.

I speed walk to one of the exits, where I see another glass staircase leading downward, same as the one I descended to speak with Bonwhe. A peculiar odor—like that of rotting fish—drifts up powerfully and hits me in the nose.

# TEMPEST IN A TEAPOT

**Y**uck!

The stench only gets stronger with each descending step. I plug my nose with two fingers and inspect the glass stairs for cracks, wondering if seawater ever goes bad.

"Miss Chobahm!" someone calls brightly from behind.

I turn my head around to see a tall, skinny guy I don't recognize hurrying down toward me.

"Do you have a moment?" he says in a low voice, his eyes glittering. "We're setting up a surprise event for Fran and need your help."

"Oh, okay. Sure," I say. Even among the elaborately dressed crowd, he stands out. The feature I notice most about him is his eyebrows: he seems to have dyed them turquoise to fit the sea theme of the wedding. The bright, artificial color frames his intense green irises. They're mesmerizing.

He grins at my reply, and the gold pendant of his necklace hangs loosely and glints in the light.

"Let's go! We have to hurry before Fran sees us," he says, and takes the steps two at a time.

Downstairs, I'm having a hard time keeping up with the long-legged guy as he leads me through a series of hallways. But what about this stench? Doesn't he notice it?

"Do you smell that, too?" I finally have to ask, scrunching up my nose in disgust.

Glancing back at me, he replies as if it's nothing, "Oh, it's just the ocean."

As we pass the men's room, he amends his response with a laugh. "I suppose it's kind of strong today, I agree. There was a backflow in the gents', earlier, and I'm sure it doesn't help."

So that's what it is . . . ? Yuck, yuck, yuck. I cup a hand over my mouth and nose, but the damp funk just won't let up, even though we're nowhere near the offending bathroom now. In fact, the stink seems to have intensified, if anything.

Finally, we reach the hallway's end, my head throbbing with the briny stench. Bubbling on the other side of the thick glass wall we're facing is the deep blue sea, but when the man places a palm on the glass, a secret panel slides open, welcoming us into an airy bridal suite just beyond.

"You haven't been here, have you?" he says as my jaw drops.

This is a mermaid's room if there ever was one. There is a scalloped, cream-colored velvet sofa that resembles a half-open shell. In front of it is a matching coffee table, and up against the back wall are a vanity and a pearl-studded runway mirror, both illuminated softly by the conch-shaped light fixtures hanging from the domed ceiling.

I'm lost in the dreamy elegance of my surroundings when the panels slide shut behind me with a soft whir. Almost immediately after that, light beams cut through the air and *clack!* the slate goes off, signaling the start of a camera break.

"Oh, shoot!" the guy mutters under his breath. Then, turn-ing to me with a look of apology, he says, "I feel bad for even asking—but do you mind spending your break here? To help us with Fran's surprise?"

"Of course—I'd love to," I tell him, meaning it, and with a smile, he excuses himself to the fitting room.

Now that Hyang is my director, I'm not as desperate for the ten-minute breaks we get, though it doesn't mean that I don't feel protective of my alone time away from the camera. Once or twice, I've found myself stuck with intrusive types who have no boundaries whatsoever and corner you with all sorts of personal questions.

*Would you have chosen to live out your life as Haeri, if you hadn't suddenly found yourself in the retirees' village? Come on, you can be honest. We're off camera, you know?*

*Do you and Serin ever fight it out behind the camera? Tell me.*

Still, these questions are far easier to handle than frantic pleas for help:

*I was fired from my show last night. Can you please help? Maybe, like, go out with me? No . . . ? Then how about you punch me in the chin? Yes, that's it . . . that's it! Punch me in the chin, will you? Right here. Just a quick jab. Do it as soon as we start rolling. Please . . . I'll do anything!*

I glance warily up at the turquoise-eyebrow man as he emerges from the fitting room. What type is he? I wonder. Intrusive? Supplicant?

"Oh, well . . . ," the man says with a laugh and a shrug. "It turns out that our bride isn't here yet."

Then, reaching for the three-tiered bar cart, he picks up a

teapot and gestures for me to join him at the coffee table. Is he a bartender? There's something about him that's very smooth. Too smooth, perhaps. Slick.

"I'd imagine that it's not easy for a bride to sneak down here without her groom," I say, and he agrees with another disarming laugh.

I realize then that he's one of those people who are the same on and off camera. Most actors I've met start the break with a long, relaxing exhale. Their countenance changes immediately, their expressions returning to how they naturally are—for better or worse. I used to be like that when Cha Seol was my director.

"Try the sofa, Miss Chobahm," the guy says cheerfully, motioning with his chin. "I sat on it a little while ago, and let me tell you, it's like sinking into a cloud."

I take his suggestion and ease myself down on the plush cushion. Sad to say, but the image that enters my mind then is one of Serin turning green with envy when she finds out that only I got to sit on this beautiful sofa.

"You look tired. Have some tea," he suggests, pouring hot water into the glass teapot containing loose tea leaves. I thank him and inquire about his connection to the bride.

"Oh, we go way back," he says with a wistful smile, his green eyes twinkling. "She and I've been friends since before Snowglobe."

It's only then that I notice how the two give off similar vibes in the way that old friends do. They both have mellow and easygoing demeanors in defiance of their quite . . . angular physical features.

"This tea is just wonderful. It helps you relax and soothes you just the right amount," he says, holding out a steaming cup to me.

It sounds like exactly what I need. I take a small sip and hold it in my mouth for a moment before swallowing. He is right. The tea's wonderful. Its sweet, sweet aroma seems to travel throughout my whole body, and soon, I begin to feel drowsy . . . almost intoxicated. My vision dims as if twilight is slowly descending, and it feels as though every cell in my body is loosening in its place. Out of nowhere, the gentlest breeze blows against my skin, and I imagine myself being carried away like dandelion fluff. Erased. Dissolved into perfect bliss.

Through a haze, I watch as Jinsuh's turquoise-browed friend—what long fingernails he has—flips open the locket hanging from the necklace he's wearing, exposing a miniature clock face within.

*Tick-tock, tick-tock, tick-tock . . .*

The tiny clock ticks away with increasing volume; and just as it begins to grate on my nerves, it stops with a final *tock*. A moment later, my vision begins to sharpen again, but all my other senses remain dull, and it's kind of delicious. I want to stay in this state . . . Just a little bit longer. Then, poof!

The turquoise-eyebrow man is gone, and Serin appears in his place.

"Hi," she says.

I'd have jumped if I could, but it's like I've turned to stone—I can't move. I can barely breathe. In shock and confusion, I stare at her wide-eyed. Then the turquoise-eyebrow man's voice whispers in my ear.

*Who do you see in front of you?*

My pulse races. What is happening? I want to bolt up from the sofa, but I can't even blink. The voice repeats, *Who do you see in front of you? Name the person.*

Is this someone's twisted idea of a prank? I try to reply *What the hell is going on?* when my mouth begins to move on its own.

"Bae . . . Bae Serin. It's Serin in front of me," I hear myself say. What the hell?

This seems to satisfy the voice, which continues, *So it is true. Serin triggers the most intense fear in you.*

In front of me, Serin chimes in. "You're terrified of me? Why?"

She stares at me, grinning with such amusement. I refuse to answer this question. No, I will not answer it. I bite my lower lip so as not to make a sound, and pressure begins to build up in my throat. In a few moments, it's like a thousand needles trying to push their way through my skin. The voice warns, *The more you resist, the more it's going to hurt.*

I only resist harder. But it isn't long before my mouth drops open in absolute agony, and once again, I speak in spite of myself.

"Why am I terrified of you? Because you want me to be as miserable as you. You already killed Goh Maeryung and made it look like I murdered her—so you can ruin my life!"

All true, though normally, I'd never talk to Serin this way. The needles in my throat withdraw, and the voice resumes.

*Okay . . . Now that you began talking, why don't we bring in someone to whom you can tell everything?*

All of a sudden, Serin disappears in a cloud of smoke. In her place, another figure materializes. Tears rush to my eyes at the mere sight of her—the very person I've missed so much since coming to Snowglobe.

"Chobahm!" Mom cries, her eyes shining. Her face is exactly as I remember it, lined and worn from a life in the bitter cold.

She reaches for my chin and cups it in her hands, one of which still bears the scars of an accident at the plant. She almost lost her fingers between two wheels in motion when I was younger. Tenderly, she strokes my cheek. I can't feel her touch, but that's okay. The warmth of her smile blooming on her face is almost palpable.

"I miss you so much, Chobahm," Mom says tearfully. "I shouldn't have sent you off like that. If only I hadn't, you wouldn't have had to go through all that you went through . . . and you'd be here with us . . . at home."

I want to break down and sob my heart out. But I can't. And I mustn't. The idea of making her worry about me outweighs all my surging emotions. I swallow back the tears.

This disappoints the voice.

*Hmm . . . We're not completely honest with Mom, are we? We'll have to bring in someone who you feel more comfortable sharing your secrets with.*

There's an unintelligible chanting of some sort, and another cloud of smoke appears to replace Mom with Ongi this time.

"Why're you crying?" my twin brother says, eyes full of concern. He grabs my arm, but once again, I can't feel his touch. He's not real. The voice asks, *Who's in front of you now?*

Once again, I answer against my will.

"It's my brother. . . ."

Ongi raises his thumbs to my face to wipe away the tears,

but he's just a phantom. The tears stream down my cheeks and fall onto my lap in hot drips.

*Oh . . . so it's your twin brother, who we needed all along. Nice. Very nice.*

"Tell me, Chobahm," Ongi says in a tone so caring and gentle it's as if he's soothing a child. "Where did you go when you entered the mirror portal, and what did you see there?"

I draw up with shock. How does he know about the mirror portal?

Then it's as if ice crystals have replaced my blood and they're shredding at my veins. I scream in agony. The voice says, *Don't fight. Don't resist. Just reveal what you know. No more, no less.*

Predictably, my mouth drops open again and more words spill out:

"The mirror portal took me to an underground power plant. I saw prisoners working there—a guy with a heart tattoo under his eye. I recognized him. He was alive and breathing, working his wheel just like we used to at home . . . but the news said that he'd been executed. He was surrounded by other inmates, all dressed in uniform, just like him . . ."

*And . . . ?*

I want to sew my mouth shut, but it keeps moving against my will.

"It was so cold. Even though I was still inside Snowglobe, this sacred place powered by natural geothermal energy, there was no warmth there. It was just as freezing as the open world."

Ongi's eyes peer intensely into mine.

"So what is it that you learned?" he presses.

I'll keep my promise to stay quiet about the mirrors.

*No. Don't tell him.*

The tea leaves spinning and twirling inside the teapot don't dance on their own accord. What moves them is the current pushing them along.

*Come on. Your brother's waiting.*

The voice of the turquoise-eyebrow man is the current in the teapot, and me, the tea leaves.

"Snowglobe doesn't sit on a geothermal vent," I blurt, unable to stop. "Snowglobe is warm because of slave labor producing electricity in a secret plant. The idea that Snowglobe is blessed with abundant geothermal energy, and that those who live here need to earn the blessing by sharing their lives on television—"

Ongi patiently waits for me to finish up my thought, and despite myself, I do.

"—is just a big fat lie manufactured and perpetuated by the Yibonn family. The Yibonn have deceived us all along."

# THE PRICE OF MEMORY

**S**nowglobe is not naturally warm.

    Snowglobe doesn't have geothermal energy.

    Snowglobe is not blessed.

It was all a lie . . . made up by the Yibonn.

I shake with the enormity of the truth.

*You poor thing . . . Truth can be so unbearable.*

The voice speaks, soft and expressive.

*But you no longer have to carry that burden. The mirror portal, the underground plant, the slaves, the cold . . . unload it all onto someone now, onto your brother. Wipe your mind clean of the unbearable truth.*

Ongi's specter reaches his hand out to me as if he wants me to take it.

Wipe my mind clean of it? Yes, I wish I'd never seen what I saw! But what if the missing Haeri is there, at the underground plant? The Haeri who I stayed in Snowglobe to find? It seems like that's where people who are supposedly dead go. She could have found a mirror passageway after she ran into the woods and ended up in the plant, just like I did. And the only person who even knows about that possibility is me. Wiping my mind clean of all that I've found out would be the same as giving up on discovering the truth of her disappearance.

The one thing I've vowed not to do.

As if in a dream, I recall the words I spoke in the newsroom, the day I mounted the exposé against the Chas. I take responsibility for having been a willing participant in the cover-up while masquerading as Haeri, who I knew was dead.

*Are you going to take your brother's hand or what?*

The voice is asking, growing impatient.

Once again, I'm nodding against my will. I'm the tea leaves, and the voice is the water that carries me. Can I resist its force?

*Take his hand and forget what you saw!*

The voice demands, angry now.

*Take it now!*

Miryu once told me that if a person ever found themself in sleep paralysis, they could try snapping out of it by waking up their extremities. I focus all my concentration to the tips of my fingers and toes. All of a sudden, they burn as if someone is peeling back my nails, and I cry out in excruciating pain.

It's not real. I force myself to hang on to the thought, looking down at my hands. There are no nails torn ragged or raw nail beds prickling with blood. It's all in my head.

"Take my hand, Chobahm," Ongi pleads. "Unload your burden to me and be free."

The voice urges me along with it.

*Take his hand, and all your pain will go away!*

I scrape up the last of my strength and tell Ongi, "No, I won't . . . I will not ever do that to you."

Ongi's face falls, and he says, "Why is that?"

Because you're my brother, Jeon Ongi. My foolish brother who can't stop making wishes that will never come true. My crazy brother who stood up to Miryu when you thought I was in danger, even when you knew she could snap you in two like a twig. My idiotic brother who never once protested when Grandma gave me the bigger half of her fruit ration she'd smuggled home from the plant. And I am your sister, younger than you by ten minutes only because that's how long it took me to follow you out on the day we were born. I will never unload this burden onto you.

"It's okay, Chobahm," Ongi's phantom says.

It's uncanny how my mind projects these people with such accuracy. Serin's smirk couldn't be more annoying, and Ongi's smile couldn't be more earnest.

"Don't worry about me, Chobahm," he goes on. "As you've already figured out, I'm not even real—none of this is real. So just take my hand and end your suffering."

His words sink in. He's right. He's a product of my own mind, just like all of this. And my mind belongs to me.

"No!"

Something inside me seems to snap then. Ongi's phantom evaporates in waves, revealing the real figure in front of me. It's the turquoise-eyebrow man staring into my eyes, his face red with fury.

"Hurry up! We're running out of time!" he shouts. "When your brother offers his hand, you take it!!"

The pain is gone, but I still can't move a muscle. I wish desperately that I could lunge forward and rip out his turquoise eyebrows . . . but I can't even blink. I shoot daggers at him with my eyes, the only thing I can do. The look on the man's face turns quizzical then, and he cocks his head to one side.

"Is she coming back already?" he murmurs to himself, regarding me in disbelief. A moment later, he explodes with rage. "God damn it!" he shouts, and reaches for the teacup.

I realize that I need to say something, anything, that'd make him believe I'm still hallucinating, but with Ongi's phantom gone, my voice seems to have disappeared, too.

"Another sip won't hurt," the turquoise-eyebrow man says, holding up the teacup to my mouth. With the other hand, he peels back my eyelid and examines my pupil. "Hurry up and drink. It'll take longer to bring you back, but I'll deal with that later."

I'm panicking. I can't let him steal my memory, but I don't know if I can put up another fight. Then Bonwhe's cryptic words insert themselves into my mind.

*Lie to yourself. It's a survival trick. Deny your senses if you can't escape the realities that they tell you.*

I repeat these words in my head like a spell, and it begins to feel like I could let go of the truth after all. Heck yeah. Why not? I could totally unload this burden to someone else and be done with it. It'd be so easy. Suddenly, there's a cloud of smoke, and Ongi reappears before me, this time wearing a necklace with a locket dangling in the center. A familiar locket.

"Take my hand, Chobahm," he says, offering it to me.

His gesture unlocks my movement. I leap for the locket with everything I have. Ongi jumps back in surprise, his shape rapidly shifting into that of the turquoise-eyebrow man, but it's one moment too late. I've torn the necklace from his neck. As I fall to the floor with the locket clenched in my fist, the turquoise-eyebrow man jabs an urgent forefinger in my direction and bellows, a moment before the locket is closed, "May your memory be your curse!"

I'm on the floor gasping for breath as the last, sluggish tick-tock of the locket echoes around the room. *May your memory be your curse . . . ?* Did he just cast a spell on me?

"What the hell does that even mean?" I shout, or try to, glaring at the turquoise-eyebrow man, but I'm too weak to project any authority, and he just sneers at me. The air is ever so thick with the stench of rotting fish, and that's when I finally realize that he is the source. It's been him, all along. The walls flex and the room begins to spin around me. I close my eyes to the sound of him tut-tutting, "You foolish girl . . . You just have to choose the hard way, don't you?"

**My eyes pop open. Gasping, I sit up as if struck by a bolt of** lightning. Looking around the room in a half stupor, I slowly begin to remember where I am, and the velvety soft seat of the scallop shell sofa under me.

"Oh, you're up!" someone says brightly.

I blink my bleary eyes at the figure. It's Fran. He's wearing an azure shirt and a pair of white linen shorts, having changed out of his tuxedo. From the pearl vanity, Jinsuh, also having traded her wedding dress for elegant coastal attire, looks over at me.

"You should ride with us, Miss Chobahm. Everyone else has left," she says.

Their voices reach me as if from the bottom of the pool. There's pressure in my ears, and my head hurts.

"Is it all over already?" I say, my voice thick with sleep.

"Already?" Fran replies with a chuckle. "You've been sleeping for hours. At first, we thought you're probably exhausted and in need of a catnap, but you were out out—like, we could not wake you up."

Jinsuh, her flowing bridal hair in a neat updo now, wants to know, "How did you find the bridal suite, by the way?"

How . . . ?

The memory rushing back in, I spring to my feet and say, "Did he leave, too?"

Jinsuh just blinks at me.

"The turquoise-eyebrow man!" I cry with a rush of urgency. "Your best friend?"

Jinsuh and Fran exchange a perplexed glance before turning their gazes back to me, looking concerned now.

"There was a guest with dyed turquoise eyebrows today. He says he's your best friend?" I insist.

The couple exchange another confused glance.

Finally, Fran says, "Did you have a bad dream, Chobahm?"

A bad dream? The turquoise-eyebrow man was just a nightmare? That can't be.

But you no longer have to carry that burden. The mirror portal, the underground plant, the slaves, the cold . . . unload it all onto someone now, onto your brother. Wipe your mind clean of the unbearable truth.

A whiff of rotting fish visits me then, and then my heart squeezes hard, as if turning itself into a fist. Suddenly, I can't breathe.

In the vanity mirror behind Jinsuh, my face is turning blue.

"The mir . . . mirr . . ." I'm trying to get the words out, but my throat catches and I'm coughing. It feels like there are bugs crawling inside it, and the more I try to speak, the worse the tickle gets. In just a few moments, it's as if hundreds of crawling creatures have completely clogged my throat. I crumple to the floor, gasping for breath. Jinsuh rushes over and breaks my fall, her eyes wide with alarm.

*May your memory be your curse!*

The voice wouldn't stop ringing in my head. Before I can stop myself, I christen the couple's big day by vomiting gloriously on Jinsuh's gorgeous outfit.


**Inside the limo, Jinsuh is dressed in her wedding dress again,** her change of clothes having been ruined by me. She strokes Manseh's furry head as he admires the sunset through the window, his wet doggy nose pressed against the glass. Fran had to leave ahead of us for today's weathercast live, but Jinsuh waited until I felt up to driving.

"I'm so sorry, Miss Jinsuh," I murmur in embarrassment.

Pass out in the bridal suite for hours? Throw up on the bride's reception dress? What a guest I am.

"Just call me Jinjin," Jinsuh says with a warm smile.

*Jinjin Manseh,* or *Hooray, Jinjin,* is the name of her show, so her fans and friends alike call her Jinjin.

Jinsuh continues, "I'm actually super excited that I got to put on my wedding dress again. I think it's a shame to wear it once and then let it collect dust in the closet for the rest of your life."

Manseh licks Jinsuh's hand as if he approves of this opinion, and Jinsuh coos, "Oh, you thought so, too, didn't you, Manseh, sweetie? Didn't you?"

Manseh responds by panting. Then Jinsuh takes his front paw and pretends to speak for him in a made-up voice.

"I'm happy that Mommy is wearing that pretty dress again, because at home, she wears the same thing every single day."

The voice she does is every bit Manseh, and we all laugh.

We quiet down as we enter the roundabout with the Disaster Meter in the center. As the limo makes the circle, Manseh shifts in his seat to keep the burning instrument in good view, growling low at it. Then a few moments after we exit and merge onto our road, the canine explodes in a menacing, teeth-baring bark, his eyes glued to the meter receding in the distance. The driver heaves a heavy sigh. I shoot my eyes to the rearview mirror. Against the dark descending over the blood-red sunset, a fire burns fiercely at the tip of the Disaster Meter.

# RINGING IN THE YEAR'S DISASTER

Traffic halts. As if on cue, the cars around us empty as passengers leave their vehicles and spill out onto the street. Jinjin pops open the door, and Manseh exits the limo in a streak of fur. Jinjin and I hurry out and join the crowd gaping at the Disaster Meter.

The sight of it makes my stomach drop. Once again, the citizens of Snowglobe have done it. They've let the Disaster Meter creep all the way up to the flash point.

All of a sudden, the ball of fire burning at the tip of the meter explodes into a brilliant pillar of blazing light. It's followed by a heart-stopping *Boom! Boom!* that rends the air, and the single pillar splits into a dozen skinny beams that fall softly back to Earth in crackling parabolic trails. It's the spectacle heralding this year's disaster, kind of like an opening ceremony. All around us, sparks are falling like snowflakes, and people gaze up to the sky while holding up their palms, the look on their faces temporarily transformed to one of wonder.

Despite the circumstances, I, too, am mesmerized. I hold out a palm, and soon, a spark the size of a ping-pong ball lands on it with a tiny sizzle. I don't know what I expected, but the spark is crisp and cold against my skin, like a snowflake. A split second later, it has turned into a tiny plume of mist.

"Just my luck," Jinjin says then with a weary sigh, scooping up Manseh in her arms. "It had to be today, of all days . . . Isn't that right, Manseh?"

I look at her, and she forces a smile and tells me, "Fran has been a wreck about the drawing. He gets so upset when he draws a super storm or a deadly heat wave for the daily forecast, as if he's personally responsible for the luck of the draw."

And as luck would have it, the big drawing once again rests on his substituting shoulders. Last year, to his and the community's great relief, Fran happened to draw a storm of popcorn snow. Could his luck repeat this year?

The live disaster drawing is different from the nightly weather drawing. Unlike in normal news reports, its results are withheld from the public until disaster begins. In other words, only the weathercaster knows what meteorologic punishment is to befall the community when, for how long, or at what intensity, and so on, until the disaster officially hits, upon which the information is finally released. During the live drawing last year, however, everyone saw the involuntary relief flitting across Fran's face and knew that the year's disaster would be a relatively tame one.

Indeed, when popcorn began falling from the sky, most people were delighted. Barring the fact that a couple dozen lazy actors ended up in hospitals because they'd stuffed themselves full of the fluffy kernels gathering like snowdrifts outside during the whole disaster period, the disaster wasn't really disastrous at all.

"He's particularly anxious about this year's drawing, as if he might have used up all his good luck last year," Jinjin says, and Manseh showers her with kisses as if to cheer her up. I pet him on his adorable head.

"I'm sorry . . ." I tell her for lack of a better thing to say. "But I think most people know that whatever disaster is dealt this year, it's not Fran's doing. He has no control over it," I add lamely.

What I don't say is that Fran doesn't control anything. None of us do. The Disaster Meter and the penalty point system that feeds it—it's all by the Yibonns' design, like everything else in Snowglobe; and we've somehow been conned into accepting their arbitrary rules without question as if they're immutable, natural law.

"Thank you, Chobahm—you're right. But regardless of who's in control, people will get hurt," Jinjin says mournfully, running her fingers through Manseh's fur as he gazes up at her with pure affection. "I'm panicking, and I'm not even the one drawing. I don't know how Fran's dealing with the pressure right now."

She sighs a heavy sigh, and I join her, not knowing what else to say to this new bride worrying about her groom on their wedding night. The opening ceremony is over. The streets are emptying fast.

**"Thank god . . . You're finally home!" Hyang pounces almost as** soon as I step through the door. "Do you know what time it is? Were you out partying after the wedding? We have shit to deal with!"

As if I don't know. It's been a day, and Hyang has no idea. I have the impulse to snap back at her, but Miryu appears and gently chides Hyang, and the anger leaves me.

It's unusually quiet in the house. Miryu fills me in that Serin's at the afterparty, which is apparently being held on someone's yacht. Ongi, Somyung, and Shinae are enjoying a night out, complete with dinner and a movie. And here I am, plagued with troubles.

Hyang grabs me by the wrist and pulls me to the sofa.

"Sit," she says grimly. "We have a lot to talk about."

*You have no idea,* I think. Still, I let her go first. Every time I try to recall my encounter with the turquoise-eyebrow man, I'm overtaken by chest pains and shortness of breath as if my body is physically rebelling against the memory. It was definitely the case on my ride back home in the limo with Jinsuh, at least.

"I did nothing but pore over you girls' recordings in the office today," Hyang begins, and I feel a brief moment of relief. This is when she'll finally describe just how Serin managed to kill Maeryung and made it look like I did it.

But what she says next, I could never expect.

"While Goh Maeryung was dying in her bed, Somyung, Shinae, and Serin were all at home, in their rooms," Hyang says, staring at me intensely.

I just stare back at her, bewildered.

She continues, "Footage shows that it was you, Jeon Chobahm, who was at the Goh residence at the time in question. You are seen hurrying upstairs to hide in Haeri's changing nook—minutes before the murder took place."

"Hide?" I repeat, feeling a surge of dread. "No! I mean . . . yes! I did go in Haeri's changing nook but it wasn't to hide—"

"And in the next clip of footage"—Hyang cuts me off, as if my argument is not worth hearing—"you're seen racing out of Haeri's room to the kitchen downstairs, where you pluck a knife from the knife block on the counter. You go to Goh Maeryung's room. And you approach the old woman lying in her bed, ranting . . . 'Do you know, Goh Maeryung? That Serin wants my life now? This is all you people's fault! All of us were doomed, the moment you conceived the idea of us; and there's nothing in the world that you can do to undo what you did. But I was thinking . . . how about your blood? As dirty as it is, maybe it can pay for Yeosu's death? What do you think?'"

Hyang repeats the words so flawlessly, I know she's memorized them. The room begins to spin around me. I close my eyes.

The timeline doesn't make any sense. So, while I was in the changing nook and thus off camera, someone masquerading as me killed Goh Maeryung on camera. But how about footage of the real and actual Jeon Chobahm—me—discovering Goh Maeryung dying in her bed, calling 119, and then racing out of the house and frantically searching for the woman who suddenly vanished? Apparently, all that took place during the camera break, when the slate changed and no footage was rolling. As far as the recording is concerned, it never happened. Something cold and heavy settles into my stomach.

"Everyone will think that I killed Goh Maeryung," I murmur, my voice cracking.

"Beyond a shadow of doubt," Hyang agrees too emphatically.

When I open my eyes, she's staring at me with an odd expression on her face.

"So the footage will never be incorporated into the show," she declares. "Ever."

"What . . . are you saying?"

"I'm saying that I'm burying the problematic footage—for eternity. It'll never see the light of day."

Miryu reaches for Hyang's hand in a quiet gesture of support. Hyang takes my hand in her other one and squeezes it, perhaps to stop hers from shaking so badly.

"I'm your guardian before I'm your director," she says. "Frame you for murder? Over my dead body."

Editing rights lie solely in the hands of the directors. But said rights don't provide immunity from the law if a director is caught willfully disregarding a serious crime, such as a murder. Hyang is already in the crosshairs of certain viewers and directors who resent the fact that she was allowed to come out of retirement to helm our show. The tiniest misstep and she'll find herself back in that miserable village.

"You'll get in trouble—" I begin to protest, but Hyang won't have it.

"You're in no position to worry about me, do you understand that?" she says. "What we need to do now is find out who's behind all this."

"Who's behind all this?" I repeat absently. At once, something clicks in my mind, and—my promise to Bonwhe forgotten— I blurt, "It's the Yibonn."

Miryu stares at me, confused.

"What do you mean that the Yibonn is behind this?" she says.

"I . . . I accidentally discovered their secret—Snowglobe's secret," I explain. "I think they're trying to cast me out before I can reveal it. Or at least, ruin my reputation to the point where no one would believe me."

The more I think about it, the more certain I feel. The Yibonn saw for themselves what kind of power a girl idolized by society holds, thanks to our exposé. A girl like Haeri.

"What's the secret, then?" Hyang says, looking more grim than dubious.

I open my mouth to answer . . . but wait. What the heck is this smell? The air suddenly reeks of that familiar stench, the odor of rotting fish. I begin to dry-heave.

*May your memory be your curse!*

The turquoise-eyebrow man's voice echoing in my ear, my heart begins to clench inside my chest, as if being squeezed by an invisible fist.

"What's wrong, Chobahm?"

Miryu springs to her feet and catches me in her arms.

"I . . . I just . . . n-need a moment," I stammer.

Miryu and Hyang lay me on the sofa, as Somyung, Shinae, and Ongi burst in through the door, shouting, "The disaster drawing! It's happening now!"

Somyung snatches up the remote and turns on the TV.

"Ladies and gentlemen, the Disaster Meter finally reached one hundred this evening. Some of you were there, witnessing the event in real time . . ."

Fran addresses the viewers at home. He's wearing his white wedding tuxedo, the white wedding veil draped elegantly around his shoulders. His expression, though, is dark and heavy. It's not the face of a groom who's just married the love of his life.

Miryu and Hyang continue to monitor me as I try to manage my pain with slow, deep breaths. What the hell did that man do to me?

On the TV, Fran smiles, a forced and unnatural grin. He says, "Then let's get this drawing over with, shall we?"

The screen pans out to show a large, clear cylinder, even taller than Fran himself. Inside the cylinder, hundreds of gold postcards tumble about as if caught in a tornado. They are standard-issue prepaid disaster postcards, mailed out by the Yibonn to households all across the outer world in order to ensure democratic process in determining the next disaster.

On the disaster postcard that Fran drew last year, the sender had written: *If I'd be so lucky as to have my envelope drawn, I'd like a storm of popcorn snow to commence ten minutes after the drawing.*

Their request almost came true. But it took ten hours, not minutes, to prepare the popcorn storm, and Yibonn Media had to issue an official apology regarding the delay—along with a promise to upgrade the system in order to avert future inconveniences. This year, they've sworn to deliver the chosen disaster within an hour of its drawing.

"Oh man . . . This is so nerve-racking," Ongi says, twisting his hands together in front of his chest.

"Nerve-racking is right . . . ," Somyung agrees without looking away from the TV screen. "Never in my life have I cared so much about the drawing."

For all our emotional investment in these events as fans in the outer world, Snowglobe disasters have always been a sort of fiction affecting only the people on our TVs. But we are now those people on TV.

On the screen, Fran's flipping open the lid of the clear cylinder. Sticking a white-gloved hand inside, he immediately snatches up a golden postcard among the thousand flying madly about.

Some weathercasters purposefully drag out the process in favor of entertainment. They let the postcards slip through their fingers or pretend to miss the ones that practically stick to their gloves, making exaggerated expressions all the while. But Fran isn't playing that game. To him, the drawing is a somber event with potentially grave consequences for so many.

"Alrighty then . . . Let's find out what we've got here."

Without delay, Fran opens the envelope and begins reading aloud the identifying information written on the inside fold.

"This year's disaster was suggested by a viewer in the Ba-J-9 settlement."

He swiftly slides the postcard out of the envelope, and as per protocol, he reads it silently to himself as the camera zooms in on his face. Inside and outside Snowglobe, all eyes are on his face for the tiniest glimpse of what's to come. But the expression that soon registers on this face is . . . tough to interpret.

Fran doesn't look horrified . . . but he definitely doesn't look relieved, either.

# A RAT IN A TRAP

When he's done reading, Fran puts the postcard back in its envelope and locks it in the small safe beside the cylinder, designated just for this purpose. The disaster will officially be announced after it is delivered during the weather segment. If we can prepare for it, it's not a disaster, the Yibonn's founding president declared generations ago. In line with her decree, every disaster hits the community without warning and rages on until it is through.

"Let us now turn to tomorrow's forecast."

Fran gives nothing away regarding the disaster—not unless his enigmatic expression counts. Is he smiling or is he not? That question will almost certainly be the talk of the news media tomorrow, with pundits exploiting it from every possible angle.

"What? Is that it? You've gotta be kidding," Shinae huffs in disappointment as she looks to the rest of us. "I've got no clue. Anyone?"

No one says anything.

Meanwhile, the tightness in my chest has started to abate,

and I feel like I can breathe again. Hyang gestures for me to meet her in her room, when Shinae gasps, her eyes locked back on the TV screen. Everyone's head snaps back to the TV. Breaking news scrolls by at the bottom of the screen.

The network announces an upcoming show starring Goh Maeryung, currently on trial for her alleged involvement in the Goh Haeri project . . .

Director Jang Soohyun is appointed to lead the show . . .

"I guess her trial's finally coming to a close?" Somyung says, looking to the rest of us. "Wouldn't that be why the show's being revived? New material?"

Shinae pumps her fist in the air and lets out a whoop. "Yes! Finally! Here comes our money!"

Hyang, Miryu, and I glance nervously at each other. The knots in my neck and shoulders start to ache again. I have no idea what this new director's vision for Maeryung's show is—but if they are leading the program, that means they'll get access to all footage featuring Goh Maeryung. Including the tapes of Jeon Chobahm savagely stabbing her in the chest.

All last week, I was consumed by fear and worries of my visit to Goh Maeryung's house—where she, or her body, might be now, and just what it was that I saw on that day. But real trouble has only just begun. The Goh Maeryung show, when it resumes under the new director, will make everyone watch and believe that I killed the old lady. And if Hyang will have edited out the problematic footage from our own show like she said she would, she'll find herself in some real trouble, too.

I bolt up from the sofa, suddenly furious.

"Hey! Bambi!" Hyang yells, and reaches for me, but I'm

too fast. I'm already running up the stairs to Serin's room, almost knocking over Ongi. I slam open Serin's door and reach for the light switch, when Miryu's hand seizes my wrist.

"Slow down, Chobahm," she says, but how can I?

"I just need to check on one thing," I tell her, but Hyang has arrived. Together, they hold me back by both wrists.

"What is it that you need to check with in Serin's room, exactly?" Hyang says.

Ongi comes to stand by the door, too, looking upset.

"Whoa . . . What's going on? Why is everyone so excited?" With an awkward chuckle, he tries to pry me away from Hyang and Miryu, but they don't let go.

"You stay out of it, Jeon Ongi. This doesn't concern you, at all," I practically growl at him, wrenching myself free from Hyang.

Ongi doesn't take this well.

"Stay out of it?" he repeats in a pinched voice. "How can I stay out when you're acting so upset?"

"Stay out," I repeat, and that's where I should stop, but I don't. "Yes, I said stay out—since you'll side with Serin, anyway."

He stares at me as if I've just slapped him in the face. Meanwhile, Somyung and Shinae have joined us, and now everyone's staring at me in shocked silence. Their collective gaze begins to feel like a brick wall moving toward me, and suddenly, it's all too much.

"God! Please!" I cry out, clasping my head with both hands.

I have no doubt that the Yibonn is behind this somehow—but if they're pulling the strings, then who's my double? Does she, the double, know their master plan?

"I . . . I feel completely helpless," I say, my voice ragged. "I have to do something. Anything."

Ongi takes a step back, and Miryu finally lets go of my wrist.

"I can only imagine how you feel right now," Hyang says, her voice soft and conciliatory. She reaches for my hand and squeezes it. Then with a sigh, she says, "Listen . . . maybe you need to blow off some steam. I'll give you ten minutes. Scream, let it out—whatever you want. We can talk after."

Miryu turns for the door in silent approval of this idea. She nudges the others toward it, too, but Somyung resists, demanding to know what's going on. Stuck, Miryu looks to me for permission, and I just sigh.

It seems to be enough for her. With that, the four of them finally leave the room.

"Do whatever makes you feel better," Hyang says, dragging a chair to the open doorway and sitting down on it with her back to the hallway. "You have ten minutes. Go ahead. I'm here to make sure you do it safely."

That's when Ongi reappears behind her and stands by the chair, arms crossed in front of his chest.

"What are you still doing here? Let us be," Hyang tells him.

"Excuse me, but that's my little sister," he fires back, clearly offended.

Hyang says something sarcastic, and Ongi says something snide back. As the two of them start to go at it, I begin on Serin's closet, ransacking it for the same jeans and white T-shirt I wore on the day of my visit to Maeryung's home. Eventually, the pair's focus shifts back to me.

"Are you sure we should let her do this? Serin's going to be so upset," Ongi says, new agitation in his voice. Hyang scoffs.

"Weren't you the one who refused to leave your little sister's side or something just a minute ago?"

"I'm just worried. The two of them are already at each other's throats!"

"Let her be for ten minutes. Even a trapped rat has to blow off steam sometimes. Otherwise they'll lose it completely."

I continue rifling through Serin's stuff, mumbling to myself like someone who has long since lost it, indeed. Where the hell did you hide them, Bae Serin? Come on now . . . You did it. I know you did. You know you did. Come on . . . Come on . . .

Footage shows that at the time of her murder, Somyung, Shinae, and Serin were all home, in their rooms.

Serin was home? How could that be? She is my double. She staged the whole murder—she's working with the Yibonn to destroy my life. I'm sure of it!

I'm pulling out Serin's vanity drawer and dumping its contents on the floor when I notice an envelope affixed to its underside with layers of clear tape. I free the envelope the best I can with my trembling fingers and shake out a purple letter neatly folded in three.

Hyang murmurs her surprise. She must not have seen it before in all her directorial footage viewing.

"Serin's home!" Shinae's panicked voice alerts from the bottom of the stairs.

Hyang bolts up from her chair, hissing, "What perfect timing!" Then, grabbing Ongi, she shoves him out to the hallway. "Do something, On-man!"

"Wh . . . what? What do you want me to do?" Ongi stammers in feeble protest, but Hyang barks, "Play patty-cake, tic-tac-toe—I don't care! Buy us some time!"

Ongi hurries downstairs. I take a deep breath and open up the purple letter, my heart hammering in my chest.

> *Come to think of it, this is my first time ever writing to you.*
>
> *Your mother and I sat through the first episode of your show, though I'm not sure how much of it she actually caught as she seemed busier crying. It opened with the exposé, and seeing you wrestle with that girl named Jeon Chobahm sent chills down my spine, I have to say.*
>
> *You were only three when the accident happened. After it, your mother never accepted you as hers, and though I was heartbroken to see her push you away, I confess that a part of me was wary of you, too. How clever and manipulative you were even at that age. I tried my best to erase the thought, to see you as my little girl who just needed more love.*
>
> *But it turned out that your mother was right. You weren't ours. I regret having been so hard on her at times, blaming her for her inability to love and mother you. I'd been a fool who sided with a stranger's child, rather than his own wife.*
>
> *This first letter to you is likely be the last also, and I ask you not to write to us again. Let it be that we're dead to each other. We've chewed at each other's lives long enough.*
>
> > *Take care,*

The letter isn't signed, nor it is addressed to anyone, but it's clear to me that it's to Serin from the father who raised her.

"What's going on here?" Serin's voice quavers in the air then.

My heart jolts and I whip around to see her maneuver through the door past Hyang, casting a slow, bewildered glance around her plundered room. A card envelope, like a wedding invitation, is clutched in her hand. Behind Hyang in the hallway, Ongi and the other girls arrive in a panicked scramble.

Serin locks her eyes on me.

"What the hell are you doing in my room?" she demands in a barely contained growl.

I just stare back at her, frozen. Then her eyes shoot down to the purple paper in my hand. Her face falls, then twists, stuck between fury and humiliation.

"Give it!" she shrieks, leaping for me and snatching up the paper. "Are you insane, Jeon Chobahm?"

Then with wildly quaking hands, she carefully folds the letter back along its creased lines, as if the note of such cold rejection is precious to her.

"I see . . . ," I hear myself say.

"See what?" Serin snarls, glaring up from the letter.

It's out before I know it. "Your parents didn't love you, so you stole Haeri's life—to make up for the love you were denied. But then it all fell through, so now you're coming after mine!"

I'm shouting now, feeling unhinged. I watch as her eyes waver a moment, then steady, as if with a sudden awareness of the watchful cameras.

Ongi and Somyung are right behind us, ready to jump in

and break us up should we start attacking each other. Miryu is holding Shinae's hand, while Shinae is biting her lip so hard that she might be drawing blood. Hyang's staring at us coolly.

Serin leans in to bring her face inches from mine. Pinning me with her eyes, she hisses through clenched teeth, "Stop talking out of your ass. You know nothing about me."

"I'm going to ask you just once, so listen carefully," I say, standing my ground and holding her eyes, blood screaming in my ears. "Did you kill Goh Maeryung?"

Her face twists again with further disgust, and I can't help but note how strange it is—chilling really, to see a face identical to yours change expressions without your agency. It's like looking in the mirror and seeing it suddenly laugh and cry on its own.

"What kind of crap are you talking now?" she snarls, her wrath barely contained.

"You lured me to Goh Maeryung's with your story about you being Sanghui's baby. And when I took the bait and went to visit her, you killed Goh Maeryung and made it look like I did it in revenge for Yeosu. That's the crap I'm talking about."

Serin draws up and stares at me, stunned.

"You've finally gone insane, Jeon Chobahm, haven't you?" she says after a moment, her tone verging on awe.

"What did they promise you in exchange for that, for helping them frame me for the murder—"

She cuts me off with an abrupt, grotesque laugh—a cry, really. Then she levels a fierce gaze on me, her eyes wet with tears.

"She's my grandma . . . ," she snarls. "And I simply told

you what my grandma told me. That she was there when the accident happened. And that I would've made the best grand-daughter ever had it not been for—"

A look of sudden terror seizes her face then, and she jerks around to Hyang. Her whole body shaking, she asks, "Did something happen? . . . To my grandma?"

"She's gone," I supply for her.

Her wild eyes snap back to me, and she makes a pitiful noise, like a whimper.

"She died. Stabbed to death," I clarify for her to make her even more miserable.

A moment ticks by, and then the next thing I know, Serin is on me, screaming incoherent words. We wrestle on the floor in a scramble of limbs, both of us grabbing and pulling, until Ongi and Somyung manage to peel us apart.

"Don't touch me!" Serin shrieks savagely, shaking off Som-yung as if a vile thing.

Her face red, hair disheveled, and chest heaving, she throws us one last look of absolute hate before storming out of the room and down the stairs. A moment later, the front door slams shut with a thunderous crash.

We're all quiet a minute. Then Miryu says, "Is she headed to Goh Maeryung's?"

"It'll be for nothing," Hyang says, groaning and pulling at her hair in frustration. "Absolutely nothing."

"I'll follow her," Miryu says, already on the move, but Hyang snatches her in objection.

"No! The disaster will start anytime now!"

When the Disaster Meter hit 80, the Yibonn Media released

a special statement reassuring the community of its commitment to swift and timely delivery of the year's choice disaster as specified by the winning draw.

"That's exactly why I need to go," Miryu counters. "Serin might get caught in it."

Hyang can't argue this point. Miryu hurries out of the room.

# IN THE LION'S DEN

In Serin's room, Somyung, Shinae, and Ongi all stare at me in quiet disapproval, pressuring me for an explanation, but I just plop down on the edge of Serin's plush bed, suddenly drained of all energy. After a few minutes of silence, Hyang mercifully steps in and summarizes the situation for me— starting with the day I went to Maeryung's house and continuing from there. Watching my friends and brother listen to Hyang, their faces changing from confusion to outrage and everything in between, it almost feels like I'm reliving the past week.

In the end, Somyung mutters, shaking her head in disgust, "You'd think that the Yibonns, the family in charge of all of Snowglobe, would have better things to do than frame innocent girls for murder."

Shinae agrees, and then cocking her head to one side, she asks, "So just what is it that you know about the Yibonn that's making them so angry with you, Chobahm? What secret could they possibly be hiding?"

Her question makes all the things I'm keeping from her

rush to my mind, but I push the thoughts away with a hard squeeze of my eyes.

"I can't tell you," I hurry to declare. "Not just yet."

"What? Why?" Ongi balks predictably. "Please don't say it's to protect us—"

"Yes and no. Initially, it was to protect you, sure," I cut him off, and drop my head. "I kept the secret to myself because I didn't want to endanger or burden anyone with it. But then things started to snowball out of control, and now . . . it's hard to explain, but I physically can't talk about it." I swallow against the swell of nausea that arises as I remember the man with the turquoise brows, shouting at me. *May your memory be your curse!*

"I've been so arrogant," I continue. "I'm nothing without you guys—or Hyang and Miryu—but I convinced myself that I could handle everything on my own."

Also . . . no matter how hard I fought against the man at Fran's wedding, there have been times when I've wanted to wish everything I knew away. When it all felt too heavy. After all, I wasn't the one responsible for the Yibonn's decades of corruption—so how was it my responsibility to blow the whistle on their lies?

I wish that I hadn't seen anything. The thought strikes me hard. *Why, oh why did I have to run into that goddamned mirror?* I picture it in my head—me, at my first party inside Snowglobe, having no idea what I was running into—but almost as soon as the memory forms, the scent of rotting fish is suddenly right there again at my nose. Like clockwork, my heart begins to clench.

I feel sick. Here I am, begging my friends to believe that

I'm being framed, that the Yibonn are after me—and because of that man at the wedding, I can't tell them why. Tears of self-pity come to my eyes.

"It's okay," Ongi says gently, putting a hand on my shoulder. "We don't need a reason to believe you. We're always here for you."

"Ongi is right. We're always here for you," Somyung says, handing me a box of tissues. "After all, why they're after you is of little consequence to us. That they're after you is what bothers us."

Ugh . . . I don't deserve these kinds of friends. They believe me no matter what, even when I shouldn't be believed. The floodgate of tears bursts open at this thought, and I'm sobbing.

It's a few minutes before I can collect myself enough to reach for a tissue and blow my nose. Hyang murmurs that I'm coming back around.

"So . . . ," Somyung begins tentatively. "How about Goh Maeryung, then? Is she really dead?"

"No clue," Hyang responds. "There's been nothing in the news about her death or disappearance—or even a public sighting, so . . ." Frowning, she massages her temples with two fingers. "The biggest problem right now is that more than a few directors have likely already been viewing her footage."

What? My stomach turns over.

"There are a ton of unlucky directors in this city. Anyone fresh off a flop and looking for a chance to reinvent themself will have jumped at the chance to direct her show. The contenders will have been accessing her footage," Hyang continues. "Goh Maeryung's a big name, reviled or not. She could easily be their next meal ticket, you know?"

Shinae stops chewing her lip and says, "Then how come no one wanted to pick her up for so long? It's only today that her new director was announced."

"It's not that no director wanted to pick her up, but that the review board headed by Yi Bonshim, the VP, wouldn't pass their proposals—any proposal," Hyang answers.

"Any . . . ? Why . . . ?" Ongi says.

"Well, I don't know for certain, but I have to assume they were stalling. Waiting for the right footage to fall into their hands. The proper tapes to launch their show."

Shinae sighs. "Speaking of shows . . ."

From her cross-body bag, she rustles a card envelope bearing the Yibonn seal. It's identical to the one Serin was clutching when she stormed into the room. This one's addressed to Jeon Chobahm, though. Shinae slides out the card and begins reading it aloud for me.

"'We're so grateful to all of you who agreed to step back into the studio as temporary weathercasters. Please join us for a delightful luncheon prepared in your honor so we can properly show our appreciation—'" Shinae stops short and balls up the card with both hands.

Everyone looks to me.

*You foolish girl . . . You just have to choose the hard way, don't you?*

The burden I carry is the burden of the truth: the Yibonn's secret, that I, and only I, witnessed. Will Snowglobe's ruling family stop at ensuring that I'm thrown out of the society they welcomed me into? Or will they go all the way and make sure that I'm locked up six feet under, along with their secret?

**"Welcome, welcome, everyone. It's so great to see you all** here," sings the president of Yibonn Media, Yi Bonyung, breezing into the banquet room with a beatific smile on her face. Trailing in behind her are her daughter and VP, Bonshim, and grandson, Bonwhe, each wearing identical expressions of gratitude. All of us at the large, rectangular guest table—including me and Serin, who are seated next to each other—rise and receive the three.

"We apologize for the delay," the president says. "We were so intent on making sure that everything was perfect to welcome you today that things took longer than we'd anticipated."

Everyone at the table—with the exception of Serin and me, that is—is tingling with the excitement of stepping back into the spotlight for Fran after so many years away.

President Yi begins moving her way down the table, personally greeting each guest.

"Anastasia!" she crows ecstatically. "So wonderful to see you . . . How have you been?"

Anastasia, who was the weathercaster seven years ago, returns her energy, gushing on and on about the wonderful life she gets to live in Snowglobe thanks to the Yibonn corporation. You'd never guess that she was in tears just a few minutes ago, crying to her seatmate about how she hasn't seen her family in a decade because she is the only Snowglobian from her family. Like all former weathercasters, she was granted the unique privilege of permanent Snowglobe residency along with the position—even if her show is the least watched of all those produced within the dome, she'll never have her program canceled and be forced to leave. But that also means she'll never be able to visit her relatives in the outer world again.

Soon the president's in front of us.

"I just don't know how to begin to apologize to the two of you," she says to Serin and me, making a sincere face.

Meanwhile, the reporters and camera crew authorized by the Yibonn are in our faces, capturing every breath and microexpression.

The president continues, "All I can do right now is promise that, when the trial concludes, Yibonn Media will do everything in its power to make up for the loss and suffering you and your families had to endure all these years."

I have to admit, she puts on a good show. If I didn't know better, I'd almost believe she truly was the compassionate and benevolent icon she's pretending to be for the benefit of all around her—the guests, the camera, the butler, the master of ceremonies, the assistants, the bodyguards, et cetera. Then she says, "We're planning to visit your parents in the open world sometime soon, too, and deliver our most sincere apology in person."

Next to me, Serin's pupils enlarge, and the letter I saw in her room flashes before my eyes.

*This first letter to you is likely be the last also, and I ask you not to write to us again. Let it be that we're dead to each other. We've chewed at each other's lives long enough.*

But then she composes herself and puts on a quick smile, thanking the president for all her thoughtful kindness.

She didn't get caught in the disaster like we feared—in fact, it still hasn't arrived yet. Instead, Serin returned home safe and sound at dawn, escorted by Miryu. In the limo ride to the luncheon, she spoke to me exactly once, asking if I told anyone about the letter I'd dug up in her room.

"No," I told her, adding a tentative "Did you want me to?"

She just stared at me wordlessly a while before finally turning her face back to the window and muttering under her breath, "You just try . . . and I'll quarter you with my bare hands," which was just fine with me as it quashed any sense that, maybe, I should apologize to her for the things I said and did.

*Your parents didn't love you, so you stole Haeri's life—to make up for the love you were denied. But then it all fell through, so now you're coming after mine!*

We haven't exchanged another word since.

The president takes my hand in her silky smooth one that hasn't seen a day's work or blistering cold, and squeezes it with such faux sincerity.

"I heard that your grandmother's not doing well," she says. "So I was thinking . . . we'll have my doctor see her on our visit."

Just meeting her gaze has my heart beating like a cornered rat.

"How gracious of you, Madam President," I say, refocusing my eyes on her and trying my best to keep it together. But I know she can feel my trembling hand.

"Are you feeling okay, Ms. Chobahm?" the polished old

lady inquires, looking up from my hand and studying my eyes. Then leaning closer to my ear, she adds in a near whisper, "Do you need to take a break? Maybe you want to go check yourself in the . . . mirror?"

The obvious emphasis she puts on the word mirror jolts me, but there's no time to mull over its implication. The moment my thought jumps to the mirror, the stink of rotting fish rushes to my nose and I drop to the floor, a pain like my veins splitting open rushing through me. Urgent voices rise and fall all around me through the ringing in my ears. Assistant Yu's face hovers over me, and when she tries to sit me up, the touch of her hands is like hellfire.

**Ten minutes later, in the opulent bathroom of the tearoom,** I steady myself against one end of the gleaming trough sink, dry-heaving. Well, at least I didn't throw up on the president's outfit. That's better than my performance at the wedding.

"Wrap it up, will you?" Serin's voice comes in through the crack-opened door, bristling with irritation. "I really don't appreciate being stuck in here, staring at the walls."

It was Assistant Yu who carried me here to get some rest, but it is Serin who's been hanging behind, waiting for me to recover.

"No one asked you to stay," I shoot back. "In fact, please leave."

Serin responds with a withering sigh. "I'd love to. But think about it," she condescends immediately. "What would it look like if I returned by myself?"

"It's not like anyone thinks we're best friends anyway," I say.

But her retort doesn't come. I think that for once I've gotten the last word when I hear the president's voice cooing from behind the door. My heart jumps with fright.

"I know you're concerned about Miss Chobahm, but you're our guest, too, Miss Serin," the old lady says. "It'd make me feel so much better if you'd go back to the banquet room and enjoy yourself."

"Oh, but I couldn't, Madam President . . . ," Serin demurs with a little laugh.

Never would I have dreamed that I'd be praying for Serin's company one day, and yet here I am.

Serin swiftly abandons me for the banquet room. To think that I thought, even for a deranged moment, that she could be of any use to me.

Then the president strolls in, smiling richly.

"I knew you'd show up today, regardless of how you feel after the other day's ordeal," she says, crossing to the sink and checking her impeccable updo in the mirror with a few tilts of her head. "It's what got you in trouble in the first place, isn't it? You act recklessly, as though you're invulnerable, despite being powerless. But of course, I've been wanting to see you for myself. To see the effect of the hypnosis?"

"Why are you doing this to me?" I manage to say, my breaths quickening again. "Do you just like torturing me?"

Through the mirror, she locks her eyes on mine. Yi Bonyung and mirror. What a dreadful combo. I look away, bracing myself against the sink in anticipation of a bout of pain, which thoughts of the mirror seem to trigger.

"Oh, honey . . . I'd never kill you," she says in an openly insincere tone. "Death often transforms a useless good-for-nothing into a beloved martyr, inspiring fellow losers—excuse me, followers—to continue on their unfinished path. And who would want that?" A chuckle. "Therefore, you shall live."

"So that's why you're making me a murderer instead—to have the world turn against me."

"There you go," she chimes, letting her mouth stretch in a sinister smile. "It's just too bad you had to go digging where you shouldn't. It'd have served you better if you weren't so smart . . . Anyway, yes. Whatever you claim to know about us, people won't believe you."

Suddenly, I'm furious—more furious than terrified. The next thing I know, I'm snarling, "And what if keeping me alive comes back to bite you in the end?"

The words pour forth without a single thought. I know I'm being ridiculous, pathetic, completely reckless despite being powerless as she put it . . . but so what? So what? What else do I have? Plus, I'm beyond caring. Like a cornered rat, I continue, "I could show up in your bedroom one day and kill you in your sleep, and then your entire family. Have you thought about that?"

There's silence as she gazes at me with an elaborate pained look on her face. Then her expression changes to a smile, the kind a grandmother gives while dealing with her spoiled grandkid's elaborate birthday wishes.

"Well, so be it. Don't bother killing my grandson, though," she says. "He's about to get his anyway."

I stare at her, confused.

"What do you mean?" Really, what *does* she mean? "Are you going to punish Bonwhe?"

"If you were me, would you allow someone so foolish to

succeed you?" she replies, turning on the faucet and washing her hands with the peace and calm of someone with all the power in the world.

"Why?" I shout. "Why go to this length? What did he do so wrong?"

She doesn't answer right away. Shutting the water off, she turns to regard me with pity in her gaze.

"It's nothing personal, honey. But duty obliges, and I must maintain peace and order in our world." She grabs a hand towel on the floating shelf and dries her hands with it. "But you don't have to do anything. In fact, please do nothing, really. Don't try to escape the course I've already plotted for you, or attempt to plot your own course. Just follow where you're led." She reaches for my head and tucks the loose strands of hair behind my ear. "Remember. If you pose a threat to the system, your loved ones will go down—one by one. And whether they're my blood or yours matters not to me."

"Why did you kill Goh Maeryung, then? Why her?"

"The hag dared to try to blackmail me, wanting to recover her name. Her power. If only she'd stayed quiet, it'd have been Serin, not her, who ended up dead. But oh, well . . . It's not too shabby for a final act, all things considered. She ended up saving Serin's life."

"Me getting even with Serin—that was your initial scheme, then?"

She just smiles and turns for the door.

"Be careful with that mirror," she says. "It's live."

I flashback to the first surreal moment when my index finger dipped into that surface. And just like that, the stink immediately returns to saturate the air, and I collapse to the floor, where I writhe with agonizing pain. There's nothing more I can do or say. The president gazes down at me for a few seconds before rearranging her face into an impassive smile and strolling out of the bathroom.

# THE FUNERAL

When my mind finally returns to where I am—the banquet hall—the main dishes that I don't even remember have disappeared and dessert carts are rolling in, each loaded with an assortment of exquisite sweets and teas. Somehow, I sit through the remainder of the luncheon, not that I process any of it. My eyes keep drawing back to Bonwhe sitting diagonally across from me. Watching him chat casually with his neighbors at the table, I can tell that he's having a good time—without once letting his polite and proper mannerisms slip.

This is your chance to honor your promise to her.

He kept his promise to Yeosu, and now he'll have to pay for it. The price? His crown. But then what? What happens to an ousted heir?

I think of Yi Bonil, the president's firstborn son and the original heir apparent before he abdicated the seat to his sister Yi Bonshim, the current VP. It wasn't long afterward that he disappeared from the eyes of the world. A few months later, it came out that he'd been fighting an incurable illness for a long time, and soon after that, there was a state funeral. Only now, I wonder . . . did Yi Bonil really have an incurable illness?

It must be this thought that sets me off. Suddenly, the sound of people laughing and chirping begins to ricochet dizzyingly around me, and I'm panting for breath again. I can't breathe, let alone pretend that I'm okay. I excuse myself and hurry out of the banquet hall.

I shuffle down the hallway trying to catch my breath, when I spot a glass door up ahead, past the tearoom. Approaching, I push it open and step into an impeccably manicured courtyard. The air is fragrant with fresh summer greens, and I drink it in through my nose—until the thought hits me that it's all just recycled air trapped inside the dome. How I long to breathe fresh air again, the real fresh air outside the dome that goes anywhere it pleases.

"What are you doing here, all by yourself?" a voice inquires, and I jolt around to see Bonwhe standing behind me, arching his brow teasingly. "Sorry—did I startle you?"

"What? . . . No," I deny. "I'm just getting some fresh air. It's beautiful out." I hastily pretending to admire the garden. He draws next to me and joins me in gazing at the flowers and shrubs.

"So have you figured out what kind of trap you're caught in?" he asks.

But have a question to ask him.

"What you said to me the other day. What did you mean by it?"

*Lie to yourself. It's a survival trick. Deny your senses if you can't escape the realities that they tell you.*

"Accept what you can't change?" I ask. "Don't put up a losing fight and just go with the flow? Is that what you meant?"

If so, then it shares the same core message as his grand-mother's advice to me in the bathroom. Bonwhe looks at me quizzically, and I pounce. "Our conversation on the day of the exposé . . . Did you tell anyone about it?" There's accusation in my voice that I didn't intend, and I see defense go up in Bonwhe's eyes.

No one else but he and I should know what I said to him on that day, what eventually persuaded him into letting us do our exposé. The conversation was through the studio's hotline, which is strictly private. No media has ever got ahold of it, and no media ever will—or at least, that's what I've been told.

But then how does the president know? How does she know of Bonwhe's crime—that he allowed the exposé that brought down Haeri to go on? More than that, how does she know of my crime? She might have illegally accessed the foot-age somehow, of course, being the almighty president above the law. But there's also the possibility that Bonwhe himself could have come clean to her. After all, his role that day was that of an interim president.

Bonwhe glances up at the towering mansion behind us.

"I don't think it's a good idea to discuss such a thing here," he says in a low voice.

I have to agree. "Okay, then," I say, and head back inside. At the glass door, I pause and turn to him.

"Please watch yourself, Bonwhe," I tell him in a near whisper.

**The limo ride back home is uneventful and absolutely quiet,** owing to Serin's utter lack of concern for my physical or emotional state. For the majority of the ride, I gnaw at my lip, turning my questions over in my mind. Do I really think that Bonwhe could have told the president about our conversation? That he might be the one who threw me into hell?

When we roll into our street, though, these questions are acutely displaced by fresh trouble.

"What the hell . . . ," Serin mutters.

No sooner than she says it, camera flashes explode outside the tinted windows of our limousine. Jostling reporters bang on the windows and doors, shouting, "Did you hear of Cha Guibahng's passing? How do you feel about it? What do you have to say?"

Serin and I turn to each other, eyes wide with shock. Director Cha's grandfather? One of the masterminds behind the Goh Haeri project is dead? The next shouted question makes my stomach drop.

"Did you hear of Goh Maeryung's disappearance? Do you know anything about it?"

Rage rushes into Serin's eyes staring at me.

"What did you say yesterday . . . ?" she asks, holding me with her eyes as she reaches for the door lever. "Didn't you say that someone who looks an awful lot like you broke into Grandma's house and stabbed her to death?"

In panic, I swat her hand off the lever and hiss, "What are you doing?"

Serin draws back, looking at me like I'm some kind of pathetic idiot. Then a car screeches to a halt behind us, and we both whip around to see Hyang fly out of the driver's seat. She rushes for us through the gang of reporters and camerapeople, wielding an open umbrella in each hand like a pair of shields.

"Move! Move!" she shouts.

**In the living room, we watch as the windows' white curtains** light up with flashing cameras outside. Reporters' shouted requests drift through the windows relentlessly. Miryu, her face heavy with worry, brings us tea to help calm our frazzled nerves.

"The news broke back to back while you were away," she lets us know. "Of Cha Guibahng's death, first—result of his family's decision to withdraw life support—followed by Goh Maeryung's mysterious disappearance. Since no other information is available regarding her whereabouts, rumors are running rampant."

How will they feel when they learn I killed her? My mouth dries out. And thus the Yibonn's scheme to bring me down picks up speed.

Serin turns to me with a smirk and says, "So what are you going to do now?" which makes me want to slap her. But I turn my back to her and give Hyang a long look.

"Ajumma . . . ," I begin at last, feeling my throat tighten. "Goh Maeryung's murder footage—don't leave it out or try to doctor it in any way."

Hyang just stares at me, her face turning to stone. What other choice do I have? It's useless pretending that I could escape what Yibonn Media has planned out for me. My resistance is futile, and it will only hurt those I hold dear.

*Lie to yourself. It's a survival trick. Deny your senses if you can't escape the realities that they tell you.*

I should take the advice. It's all I've got right now.

**The next two days pass in a blur of camera flashes and eager** reporters. I don't emerge from the house again until Wednesday, even then remaining in a fog until a jerk in a sedan cuts us off without any signal. Hyang, in the passenger seat, flies into a rage. Rolling down her window, she sticks her head out and bares her teeth, screaming, "For god's sake, you idiot! If you want to kill yourself, go do it alone!"

Miryu reaches for the control, and Hyang's window begins to slide back up, forcing her to duck her head back in or get decapitated.

"Why?" Hyang protests. "They were in the wrong! You saw it!"

"You're way too wound up right now," Miryu calmly tells her.

"And you are being way too chill!" Hyang counters.

Miryu takes a stoic breath and tightens her grip on the steering wheel.

"For me, it's my enemy's death," she says. "But for you, it's your grandfather's."

She seems . . . sorry. Or, at least, sad that the situation must be so complicated.

"I told you, Jo Miryu, never to feel bad talking shit about him in front of me," Hyang fires back, turning her gaze forward and crossing her arms in front of her chest. "I continued referring to him as my grandfather because I knew it would make you feel guilty if I didn't, but I wrote him off completely long ago. I don't consider him blood—or a human being, for that matter."

I know she's telling the truth. The only reason Hyang finally agreed to attend Cha Guibahng's funeral today is Miryu's wish to confirm his death for herself. The director had loomed so large and darkly over much of her adult life that she couldn't believe he'd finally perished. When Miryu expressed this wish, Hyang picked up her car keys and promised that she'd open the coffin herself, if that was what needed to happen. But Miryu was reluctant to leave me home alone. So that's how I ended up tagging along with Miryu and Hyang to Cha Guibahng's funeral. It wouldn't hurt to bid my final goodbye to the man who'd had his filthy hand in bringing me into this world anyway. Or to have the chance to wish that he burns in hell for all of eternity.

Meanwhile, Hyang won't even look in my direction.

*Goh Maeryung's murder footage—don't leave it out or try to doctor it in any way.*

She'd balked hard at this suggestion, as I'd expected.

"I know how awful things look right now, but please . . . this is not how you go about solving it," she'd implored, to which I responded by threatening to report her to the authorities if she wouldn't listen to me. Hyang has since chosen the silent treatment.


**We arrive at the funeral.**

"Hyang!" Dr. Cha Sohm calls, hurrying toward us in her

solemn black dress. Tears in her eyes, she takes her sister's hands in hers and squeezes them wordlessly for a few moments. Then turning to Miryu and me, she murmurs a greeting, not quite able to conceal her surprise at seeing us here. I bow my head in return, and we make polite small talk centering on the scar on my face, which is healing itself to near invisibility, thanks to her.

In the Control Room on the day of the exposé, the technical director I was combating smashed a thick glass mug against my left brow bone, leaving a gash that required seven stitches later on. Sewing my face back up in the operating room, Dr. Sohm wouldn't stop apologizing to me for the awful trouble she'd gotten me into. Just like me, she'd been manipulated by Director Cha, her sister, who'd pressured her to perform plastic surgery on Serin—the girl she thought was the real and original Haeri. That's why she helped Serin with her plan to switch places with me. She believed I was a doppelganger stealing Serin's—the real Haeri's—life. She also offered apologies on behalf of her grandfather and her sister, though I told her not to waste her time—even if they'd apologized themselves, I wouldn't have accepted their empty words.

A short distance away, a clutch of guests steals glances at the three of us, whispering among themselves. The funeral is sparsely attended by family and loyal friends—fellow directors, mostly—and not at all suggestive of the grandeur and esteem the dead man had once enjoyed as the most decorated director in Snowglobe history.

"We're here to attend the burial," Miryu tells Dr. Sohm with a polite bow of her head. "And then we'll be on our way."

The noonday sun blazes down from the cloudless blue sky.

At the burial site, people are hand-digging Cha's grave, sweat pouring freely from their faces. Laboring among them is Cha Joonhyuk, his eldest son. In the near distance, reporters and camerapeople pace the perimeter, anxious for a chance at an exclusive scoop.

"Do you . . . maybe want to pitch in with the shoveling, too?" Dr. Sohm asks Hyang, almost apologetic. "I know we really don't have to do this, but . . . you know how Dad gets sometimes, fixating on certain ideals. Apparently, he feels this day is sacred. He wants everyone to commemorate Grandfather by helping to prepare the grave."

"Sure," Hyang responds with wholly unexpected receptivity. "I'll do my part in properly ushering him off to the next world."

She begins toward the grave, and the crowd begins buzzing.

"*Whoa* . . . She really is something else, isn't she? How dare she show up here?"

"Her sister can barely meet anyone's eyes at the hospital anymore. What makes her so proud of herself, strolling in here like she owns the world?"

Hyang ignores them. And in a way, she does own the world—or at least, their world. Directors can say whatever they want, whenever they want, free from the fear of having their words and action being broadcast for eternal entertainment or damnation. If they don't like how they look in something, they can just cut it out.

"Her grandfather taught her all wrong," another voice tut-tuts. "How dare she destroy another director—her own sister, no less."

Then it all happens in a blink. Hyang, picking up an idle shovel, makes for Cha Guibahng's coffin in a few quick strides and wedges the metal head under the lid, flinging it open. She shouts, "Grandpa, it's me—Hyang!"

Camera flashes fire all around the perimeter, capturing Hyang's manic smile.

"Whoa . . . ," she says in mock amazement. "Hospital life treated you pretty well, I see. I thought you'd look like shit—undead for years with tubes and hoses sticking out of you . . . but look at you! You look so fucking amazing, I can't stand it!" She raises the shovel overhead.

"WHAT THE HELL ARE YOU DOING?" Director Cha Joonhyuk booms from inside the grave in progress and stops her short. Throwing down his shovel in anger, Hyang's father plants his hands on the edge of the pit and leaps out, managing to hoist his chest up aboveground. From there, he tries to crawl out on his elbows, commando style, but he doesn't quite have the strength or coordination. The image that flashes in my mind is one of a helpless puppy I once saw on TV—whimpering and struggling mightily to climb over a pet gate.

In a few moments, the director falls back into the pit. His face beet-red with exertion and outrage, he screams up at his youngest daughter, veins like earthworms bulging in his neck and forehead, "YOU PUT DOWN THAT SHOVEL RIGHT NOW!"

Then a small ladder is hurriedly lowered into the hole, while a couple of impatient guests begin tugging at the fuming man's arms and shoulders in an attempt to heft him up aboveground—only to lose their grip at the last moment and fall back on their butts, sending Cha back into the hole in a harsh tumble. At this point, the whole situation is almost funny.

Meanwhile, a few others have restrained Hyang, pinning her arms behind her.

"Let go!" Hyang shrills, kicking her feet in the air. "I said, LET GO OF ME!"

Miryu springs for Hyang. When I follow suit a half beat later, it's as if I timed my action to the resounding *clack!* of the slate.

Then a shapely leg capped with a shiny black shoe appears in my path. Unable to stop in time, I trip over it and tumble down to the soft grass, which breaks my fall. What in the world . . . ?

I whip my head around to glare at the owner of the offending foot, but when I take them in, my thoughts blink to a stop. Cha Seol, my Director Cha, is standing over me, dressed in black from head to toe like her sister Dr. Sohm. Gazing dispassionately at the racket surrounding us, she tells me, "Stay out of our family matter." Then she lowers her amber eyes to me.

# HOW TO CHANGE THE WORLD

"**H**ow . . . how did you—" I stammer, squinting up at her from the grass.

"Apparently, even scum like me is allowed the chance to pay her last respects," Cha Seol supplies, uncrossing her arms and holding out her right wrist for my inspection. Clinging to it like a giant leech is an electronic monitoring bracelet issued to inmates like her who have been granted an emergency leave.

"How have you been?" she inquires, peering down at me.

*How have I been?* The ridiculous question sets me off all over again.

"You must be delighted to be here. Now you can blame it all on the dead man. Is that what you're planning to do? You were just a pawn in his schemes like I was in yours, right?" I respond, giving her my best impression of a bitter sneer. Behind her, the artificial sun festers in the artificial sky, casting a dark shadow on her face and shrouding her features.

An angry shout goes up at the pit then, followed by a roar of excited voices. I turn to the commotion and see a clutch of mourners around Cha Guibahng's coffin struggling to contain a flailing woman. It's Hyang, of course. Her loud, indignant voice soars above those of all her adversaries.

"Bury him? What? What a terrible waste of perfectly good grass!" she screams. "Just burn him! Burn him and lock up the ashes! Save the environment!"

The ruckus redirects the attention of everyone who's been watching us. Cha Seol turns her gaze back to me.

"Something happened to Maeryung," she says evenly. "I don't believe she has gone missing. Not for a second."

My breath catches, but I manage not to let it show.

"Do you know anything about it?" she says. The sun behind her is positively blinding. With my heart pounding and throat parched, it takes me a moment, but I reply, "What makes you think that I should know anything about it? And why should I tell you anything even if I did?"

"Because if something happened to Maeryung, you're not safe, either."

Has she caught on to what's going on? If so, how?

She holds my glare with her flaming eyes. They still manage to roar like a tiger's.

"The Yibonns merely suspended my license when they could have revoked it. Innocent until proven guilty is what they're claiming," she says, putting in a sour laugh. "In truth, they need me to maintain my director status."

"How so?" I snarl.

"You really don't know . . . ? Strip me of my director status, they'd have to issue me a temporary actor status until the case concludes—the same as all you girls."

I listen intently as she goes on. As an actor, Cha Seol explains, she would almost certainly be snatched up for a show—and not just any show but the first ever in the history of Snowglobe to feature a former director fallen from grace. Everyone would be tuning in. Who wouldn't want to hear her side of the grotesque scandal, straight from the horse's mouth?

"Such a show would expose what directors have been allowed to get away with all this time, which the Yibonn absolutely cannot allow," she continues. "People's unquestioning trust in a fair and equitable institution is what has sustained the current order for generations."

I should know that, and not just because Bonwhe himself told me—back when he thought of me as Yeosu.

What's kept Snowglobe peaceful and thriving all these years is our trust in the order's fairness and equity.

A breach in this trust would swiftly undermine the current social contract. People inside Snowglobe would be less willing to put their privacy on the line for a system that they perceive as corrupt, and then viewers in the open world would resent the fact that others got to live a life of warmth and privilege inside the dome for no good reason. It would be the beginning of the end for Snowglobe, or at least Snowglobe as we know it.

Cha Seol warns in a low voice, "The Yibonn group will eliminate anyone who poses a threat to their order. They always have."

I know that, too.

"You girls are a huge risk and liability to the order, in case you didn't know. What do you think your exposé did, if not raise doubt about this virtuous institution and its fair governance? Imagine how sick the Yibonn must feel, having to sit back and pretend that they were as fooled by me as everyone else, that they want only justice for the girls who've pulled back the curtain on their collective illusion . . . Allowing you to live here, and with every soul inside and outside Snowglobe cheering you on?"

"So what?" I snap. "What are you trying to say? That I should watch my back? As if I don't already know that."

But my dismissal falls flat even to my own ears. She is right, of course. Still, I can't let her know that. I double down and say, "What do you care about any of us anyway? Haeri— sure, I can understand. You needed her to be alive and well so your show could go on. But that's all over now. So what do you want from us?"

Unfazed, she calmly replies, "Be rational. Don't let emotion take over." A pause. "Don't miss your chance to change the world."

She said the same asinine thing when I visited her in jail to press her about Haeri's whereabouts, the Haeri who had supposedly disappeared into the woods one day: *All I wanted was to change the world. With you. With all of you.*

Just who does she think she is? Hate surges white from deep inside me, and I don't even realize that I'm tearing at the grass until it's fisted in my hands. I leap to my feet, gripping clumps of sod. I have the impulse to scream, to light into her at the top of my lungs, but the thought of hyena-like reporters salivating for just such a scene stops me cold. I do launch the muddy sod at her, though. I can't help it. Then I tell her, bearing down on each word, "Look at yourself. You can't even attend your grandfather's funeral without that ugly thing around your wrist. Change the world? Ha! You? . . . How dare you pull me—no, all of us—into your sick game?"

As if in emphasis, thousands of cicadas burst into a deafening screech just then. *How timely,* I think, when Cha Seol opens her mouth again.

"What does changing the world mean to you?" she says.

I grit my teeth. I don't know if I can take her crap for another instant.

"Let me tell you for the last time," I say, my voice turbulent with barely tamed anger. "I. Don't. Care."

"Heroes change the world to save others," she tells me. "But ordinary people change the world to save themselves."

For a moment, I'm thrown off guard. "What?" I breathe.

She continues, "To break through the limitations imposed on them, to save themselves and their loved ones from the jaws of the world. They step into hell for that heavenly cause: keeping themselves, and those they care about, alive. That's how ordinary people change the world." Her amber eyes take on a soft shine. "Change the world and save yourself. And that's how you'll save everyone else, too."

I'm twitching with anger, hate, fear, and every nameless emotion churning inside me.

"Are you goading me into taking on the Yibonn?"

She just stares at me, as if to say that the decision is mine. I shake my head.

"That'd just put more people in danger. Better just me than—"

"You're right." She cuts me off and sighs. "It's simplest just to give up and let them do what they want." She shifts her gaze to the far distance, unhurried, in control. "But don't think that things will continue to be bad tomorrow just because they were bad today. Tomorrow, things will be worse. You gave up on one thing today? Tomorrow, you'll be asked to give up two more, and the next day, three more, and before you know it, you'll have lost everything, even the ones you wanted to protect with your last breath."

I clench my teeth and squeeze my eyes shut. Something hot shoots through me from head to toe. I dig my heels into the grass and take in a deep breath. When I open my eyes, I'm somehow telling her, "I can't let that happen."


**Meanwhile, the tumult around the coffin has subsided. Cha Seol** takes a casual step away from me, conscious of the audience turning their attention back to the two of us.

"Whatever you held over Bonwhe to get your way that day," she says, her eyes on her blouse front now, flicking off dirt and loose grass with her hand. "I know you won't tell me what it was. Not that it looks like I'd have the time to ask, anyway."

A director noticing us alerts his friends with a jab of his elbow and a chin pointed in our direction. Cha Seol levels her gaze on me again, and rushes out the words in a near whisper, "Whatever ace is up your sleeve, play it, and go from there."

The ace up my sleeve. She means the secret I pressured Bonwhe with that day, when the deputy chief of Yibonn Media swooped in to put an end to our exposé. When I flashed it, it effectively stopped him in his tracks. My mind begins drifting to the mirror portals and to the underground power plant. The lie at the center of Snowglobe . . .

Just like that, the powerful stench returns, cutting through the grassy fragrance. Sourness pools in my mouth, and then I'm doubling over with agonizing pain.

*May your memory be your curse!*

The pain intensifies. I fall to my hands and knees and begin dry-heaving.

"Hey, Bambi!" Hyang shrieks with alarm and races over.

Seeing me in this shape mere feet away from Seol, Hyang is beside herself. I wave a weak hand to let her know that everything's fine, but she is already at her sister's throat. Snatching Seol by the collar, Hyang screams in her face—though with Seol being a good head taller than her, it means Hyang has to teeter on her tippy-toes to do so. "I told you not to lay a finger on her, didn't I?"

A hint of animation registers in Seol's stoic eyes.

"Come on, Hyang," the big sister says in a tired voice. "You're almost thirty-two now. Grow up and show some decorum for the guests, if not for yourself?"

This just infuriates Hyang further.

"Ha! Look who's talking," she snarls. "Who the hell do you think you are, giving me advice, you sociopath!"

Even in my state, I can't help but note how sibling squabbles remain the same, no matter the stages of life. Miryu, appearing from nowhere like she often does, pats my back as I wipe futilely at my chin, which is dripping with saliva and bile.

Seol slaps off Hyang's hand clutching at her blouse collar and turns her attention back to me.

"What's the matter, Chobahm? Are you sick?" she says.

"I don't know. This stench, though . . . It's like a bucket of rotting fish . . ."

"Rotting fish?"

I can't tell her anything more, of course. Not the hypnotist's turquoise eyebrows, or the mirror portals, or . . . anything else. And the moment I think about these things, I lurch forward with my hand over my mouth, my stomach heaving violently. Cha Seol turns to Miryu.

"Didn't you experience something like this before?" she says.

Miryu sucks in her breath.

"Do you think Chobahm has it . . . ?"

"It wouldn't surprise me."

By the coffin, Hyang's father, Director Cha Joonhyuk, seems to have taken center stage, shouting about the incredible disrespect displayed by his daughter and the younger generation to which she belongs. At the bellowing man's side, Dr. Sohm, Hyang's other sister, labors to calm him down. But the scene only sustains a handful of people's attention. Many more heads are turned in our direction now, and I can almost see their antennae twitching in the air, trying to catch the frequency of our conversations.

"I've got to go now and let them know the show's over," Cha Seol says hurriedly and makes to head for the coffin. "But take Chobahm to that clinic, will you?"

Miryu makes a face.

"What do you mean, the clinic?"

With a sly grin, Cha Seol replies, "You know what I'm

talking about. The clinic that only sees actors? The one that no director can find? The Mirage Clinic."

Then she continues on toward the crowd, disappearing into it. With the sour taste lingering in my mouth, a new question needles at me. Cha Seol—just what does she want to change the world for? What's in it for her?

# THE MIRAGE CLINIC

As we pull out of the cemetery, Hyang is hysterical, demanding that Miryu turn the car around immediately. Miryu ignores her until Hyang leans over to the driver's seat and seizes the steering wheel, jerking it one way. The car does a mad fishtail as Miryu wrestles with Hyang, but it doesn't take long for her to regain control of the vehicle. From the backseat, I leap for Hyang's arms and hold them behind the headrest of her seat.

"Are you nuts, Ajumma?" I yell. "Do you want to follow Cha Guibahng to hell? Is that what you're doing?"

It's not that I don't understand how she feels. Miryu just told us that she had also been hypnotized once—by her director, Hyang's grandfather himself.

It was on the day of her expulsion from Snowglobe. Miryu had a chillingly lucid dream on the train bound for home; every time she thought of Cha Guibahng, she felt so disoriented that she finally threw up all over the frozen gimbop dinner of Mr. Jo Woong, the train's engineer at the time.

Unlike me, though, Miryu had heard of the practice before via local urban legends involving directors fearful of their unsavory doings being exposed silencing actors through hypnotism before releasing them back into the outer world. She wondered if her own director, Cha Guibahng, had done the same to her.

Her suspicions proved true. After she returned home, whenever she thought of Snowglobe or her director, she'd immediately be seized by a debilitating headache and terrible hallucinations; and if she even thought about telling people of her years in Snowglobe, her stomach would lurch violently, preventing her from stringing together a coherent sentence. Preceding these events, there was always an intolerable odor, like that of mold infestation.

"I fell into a waking nightmare each time the smell came on," Miryu said.

So that explains the state I found her in at the clinic in my home district, when she got hit by Cooper's black limo. She had let out an agonized scream, clasping her head in pain every time I tried to talk to her about Snowglobe—her hypnotic trigger, apparently.

"So that's what he did to you? Put a hypnotic trigger in you that flares up and attacks you whenever you think of his dirty manipulation?" Hyang starts raging again. "Turn the car around!"

Her arms still pinned back by me, she kicks the glove compartment, taking her frustration out on the innocent plastic. "I'll give him what for, and I don't care if it's his corpse!"

"Come on, Hyang, you're not hearing me," Miryu says,

always so calm. "I couldn't even breathe when I so much as thought about thinking about Snowglobe before. But I'm back here and thriving! Do you get it? If I was cured, Chobahm can be too—we just need to figure out what it was that broke through my hypnotism."

In fact, on her flight back into Snowglobe after I invited her following the exposé, Miryu had another terrible hallucinatory episode in which she imagined that her plane crashed into the dome and burst into flames. When she came back to reality, however, she found herself in Snowglobe's Customs and Immigration office, mysteriously free of the sickness that had haunted her for so many years at the mere thought of the place.

"Can we focus on what's important right now?" Miryu pleads. "Getting Chobahm treatment?"

Hyang, unable to counter Miryu's point, falls to silent stewing, her breaths ragged with anger. Miryu glances at the dashboard clock and steps on the gas. I don't know much about the clinic she's taking me to—the Mirage Clinic. Miryu has just told me that it's a treatment center owned and operated by unlicensed doctors who only see actors, located at the opposite end of Snowglobe from the cemetery. According to her, the clinic is a local myth she first heard about a long time ago.

Judging by the fact that we're driving there now . . . I guess the rumors of its existence are true.

"Hey, Bambi." Hyang still won't look at me when she speaks. "What did you and Cha Seol talk about?"

I gaze at the dashboard clock, into the camera lens I know it hides. Do I still believe that Yibonn Media keeps its hands off raw recordings? No, I don't. Not anymore.

I need to be careful what I say.

"Nothing," I tell her, affecting a yawn as if the topic bores me.

To my surprise, Hyang doesn't pursue the question further. But then in another minute, her eyes still straight ahead on the road, she asks me, "Does your threat still stand? Would you still report me if I edited out the problematic footage?"

I contemplate this question for a moment.

"So did you, or did you not?" I ask her back.

*You, Me, and Us* airs on the weekends. If the scene in question doesn't air by Sunday, then the president will know that I, in league with Hyang, have defied her and resisted the path she has laid out for me.

Hyang turns around in her seat and levels a fierce gaze on me.

"Yes, I left it out," she says. "I will not incorporate it."

I have no response.

*Tomorrow, you'll be asked to give up two more, and the next day, three more, and before you know it, you'll have lost everything, even the ones you wanted to protect with your last breath.*

I do not want to provoke Yibonn, if I can help it. But can I really sit back and let them destroy me?


**"One adult, one minor, please,"** Miryu says, sliding money through the hole in the plexiglass window of the ticket office. "And could you tell me where today's special exhibit is?"

Behind the window, the ticket agent is cleaning his eyeglasses with a piece of cloth while I stand to Miryu's side, saying nothing, though inside my head, my thoughts are swirling. Rather than the clinic I was expecting, the building in front of me seems to be a museum of some kind—so different from the place I thought we were going that I almost wondered at first if we'd gotten lost until Miryu and Hyang stopped the car. When I tried to question them as I climbed out of it, they shushed me.

The Mirage Clinic. Is this part of the mirage?

The ticket agent looks up at Miryu, startling and dropping his glasses to the floor.

"Sure," he says. Without taking his eyes off Miryu, he pushes back his chair and, with a little grunt, reaches down for his spectacles. "Special exhibits are in Rooms 3 and 4," he continues. "Student discounts are available, and if you're a director, you can get a pass that lets you in all the exhibits."

Such perks for directors are commonplace in Snowglobe. Hyang produces her key to the editing office for the agent to examine, and he puts his glasses back on to verify the key's authenticity. Her identity confirmed, he passes it back and issues tickets.

"For those of you with regular passes, the entrance is on your left," the agent informs. "And for you, Director, with the special pass, the entrance is on your right. Enjoy!"

"Oh no . . ." Hyang pretends disappointment. "Only I get the special tour? Too bad!"

Miryu, forever meticulous, double-checks the special exhibits with the ticket agent, who kindly confirms Rooms 3 and 4.

"When you get there," he adds. "Make sure to pull on the lever and activate the air freshener!"

Huh? I'm wondering if I heard him right, when I catch a

fellow visitor, a woman, glancing back at us over her shoulder for a long moment before disappearing into the entrance on the left.

**Inside the museum is a crazy maze of hallways lined with count**less closed doors, each indistinguishable from the next but for the random number plaque they bear. Curious, I open a few at random. Behind each door is, of all things, a single toilet—I do a double take when I see the first one—featured in a special and unique environment. For instance, door number nine opens to a toilet in the middle of a boreal forest, while the neighboring door number thirty-seven opens to a toilet stuck frozen in the arctic.

It's not that I've forgotten our mission here, but these exhibits are so out of whack that I find myself rushing from one door to another, my thoughts of the clinic we've come in search of all but gone. Door number fifteen opens to a white porcelain toilet sitting on a green, checkered lawn, and door number forty-one to a polished silver metal toilet nestled in a bamboo grove. Some doors are marked with a red occupied sign above the door handles. A toilet museum. It really takes all kinds to make Snowglobe, I guess.

Then Miryu finally locates door number three and calls me over, and we step inside an exhibit where a jade toilet sits peacefully by an artificial waterfall twice as tall as me.

"You sit and be comfortable. I prefer standing," Miryu tells me, nudging me down on the celadon-hued throne. Though this toilet is only an exhibit, it's still surrounded by privacy walls that come up to my eyes, the same as all operating toilets in Snowglobe. When I settle, the small built-in screen in front of me comes to life, and a voice begins:

*"Welcome to the Jang Suho Museum's virtual tour. Together, we will explore the history and mission of our organization and the science and art of flush toilets, as well as how each exhibit was conceived and actualized . . ."*

The virtual tour begins with a montage of engineering and construction work.

*"The founder, Mr. Jang Suho, a Snowglobe director who had dedicated his life to entertainment, shifted his creative eye to the symbolism of flush toilets in the age of Snowglobe; what it means as the last remaining bastion of one's privacy . . ."*

Speaking of which, there's a camera still rolling in this room—I spotted it earlier, positioned on one of the walls. Though I know it can't record anything happening within these privacy walls, I still stretch my neck and peek warily over the stall to make sure of its angle.

Meanwhile, closed captions on the screen seem to have gone haywire. They don't match the voice-over at all. Currently, they're reading:

*Bend forward at the waist and bring your face close to the screen, as if expressing deep interest in what you're being shown. Your next message will appear when you're completely out of the camera's range.*

I do as the message says, saying out loud, "Oh, wow . . . who knew toilets could be so fascinating?"

Miryu crouches down by me and makes similar sounds of amazement. "So that's how they design the exhibits . . ."

The voice-over continues:

"Each unique exhibit comes with a scent designed to complement the specific environment featured. Please locate the hand lever and pull it down to activate the air freshener."

On the screen, closed captions throw up the next set of instructions:

GOOD JOB. MAINTAIN YOUR BODY POSITION WHILE RAISING YOUR HAND ONLY TO PULL DOWN THE LEVER. YOU WILL EXPERIENCE THE SENSATION OF FALLING THROUGH THE FLOOR. PLEASE REFRAIN FROM PRODUCING SOUNDS OF ALARM OR DISTRESS AS THIS WILL PREVENT YOU FROM MOVING ON TO THE NEXT STEP.

I pull down the lever, and immediately filling the air is a refreshing scent that brings to mind the image of cascading fresh water crashing onto rocks below. Closing my eyes, I'm inhaling the scent deeply into my lungs when the jade toilet begins a sudden, terrifying descent. Mother of god, this again? But remembering the instructions, I clench my back teeth together hard, so as not to scream.

A few seconds later, the ride comes to a merciful halt. I look around in a daze.

Is this the clinic . . . ?

With a free fall like that, I expected to find myself in some dark basement, but instead, my traveling throne sits parked on the edge of what appears to be an endless flower field under a flat blue sky. In awe, I get off the toilet and step among the flowers, the smell of fresh dirt and the sweet aroma of the various blooms rising pleasantly to my nose.

This is a real flower field . . .

But the comically flat and low-hanging sky overhead is fake—definitely fake—not that the projection on the Snowglobe dome I'm living under these days is the real thing, either.

The perfectly square horizon surrounding me, too, indicates with no uncertainty that this is an artificial space.

A honeybee buzzes by me and lands on a scarlet flower I can't name. Wait a minute. Is it a honeybee? Every honeybee I've seen in Snowglobe so far had a yellow-tipped abdomen . . .

"Hello!" a girl's voice calls then, and a figure shrouded in a bee veil approaches me, carrying an intimidating-looking beehive in their gloved hands.

"You're here for detox?" she says brightly.

"Uh . . . the Mirage Clinic—"

"Yup, code name Mirage Clinic. It's a detox treatment center."

The silver name tag over the breast pocket of her white lab coat reads WEDNESDAY. When I look up from the name tag, her eyes enlarge for a moment.

"Goh Haeri . . . ?" she murmurs in disbelief. "How—"

"I'm Jeon Chobahm."

"Oh . . . Of course!" she says, smiling wide. "Did you come down alone? They told me there would be two—"

That's when Miryu lands with a *thunk!* a few yards away in the flower field, somehow riding on a purple quartz toilet from the special exhibition Room 4. Wednesday's face lights up with recognition.


**The treatment center operates in the middle of the flower field,** in a square clearing bordered with three large apothecary cabinets with hundreds of palm-sized drawers stuffed full of bitter-smelling medicinal herbs.

"Most of our patients don't have time for tea," Wednesday

says, pouring hot water into glass mugs containing lemon slices and chunks of golden honeycomb she's just harvested. She has finally lost the beekeeper's veil, and I can see that she's not much older than me. From each of her heavily pierced ears hangs half a dozen hoops and barbells.

Wednesday continues, "It's so awesome that your director has your back and that you don't have to watch the clock like the rest of us," referring to my unauthorized escape from cameras. Meanwhile, said director must be getting a superb cultural edification on flush toilets while strolling through the vast museum all alone.

Wednesday explains to us that a big part of their responsibility here is to monitor and manage visitors' movements in order to ensure that actors and directors don't run into each other, as well as regularly update the list of actors working at the Yibonn mansion, both of which are crucial in the efforts to keep the operation a perfect secret.

"Thank you for the best tea I've ever had. It must be the fresh honeycomb," Miryu says, and Wednesday breaks into an ear-to-ear grin, blushing with pride. A moment later, though, she catches herself and clears her throat. Picking up her pen and clipboard with an official air, she turns to me.

"So let's get started with the intake," she says. "Name, age, and the duration of your residence in Snowglobe so far, please?"

"Jeon Chobahm, seventeen years old. Duration of residence is a little less than three months . . . since the exposé?"

Her pen still busily scratching down the information I supply, she moves on to the next question. "How did you learn about us?"

As I stall, Miryu answers for me, "Someone once told me during camera break: Flush down your trouble where the blind spots converge."

Flush down your trouble where the blind spots converge. What a clever riddle. Toilets are off-limits for camera. Then a museum of toilets is where blind spots converge. Go flush a toilet there and you'll be taken to the cure!

"It was Yi Healerb . . . the only friend I made during seven friendless years in Snowglobe," Miryu says, cracking a bitter smile. "I ended up losing his friendship but managed to hold on to his riddle."

Wednesday gazes sympathetically at Miryu for a moment. Then she straightens her lab coat and says brightly, "Well, I'm so happy that you found us. My name's Wednesday, your detox clinician. It isn't my real one, of course, just an alias after the day of the week I'm assigned to work as the clinician. Shall we begin, then?"

Putting down her clipboard, she leads me to the examination table. I'm about to hop on it, when the sky begins pulsing red, rinsing the flower field and everything it contains in an ominous crimson.

# THE REUNION

As the fake sky continues flashing red as if in mute warning, I look to Wednesday for a clue. Her face, which has been almost nonstop smiling until now, has turned grim and serious.

"It's an alarm for us to hurry," she says. "Quick, Miss Chobahm—hop yourself up on the table."

Doing as I'm told, I ask who's sending this alarm. Wednesday tells me it's the ticket agent aboveground, indicating that he, too, works for the clinic.

"Why do we need to hurry, though?" Miryu asks, standing guard by the table and scanning the flower field that has just begun to pulse green and red alternatively, in sync with the sky, which is pulsing blue and red now. "Like you said, our director is supportive of this visit."

"It doesn't happen too often . . ." Wednesday hesitates briefly. "But every once in a while, the Yibonn sends their spies to root around the museum for dirt. They never find anything, but we're definitely on their radar."

"So you have to watch out for the Yibonn more than you do directors," Miryu says.

Abruptly, the pulsing stops and the flat blue sky returns.

"Absolutely," Wednesday confirms. "Most directors can't be bothered with this place. The editing algorithm automatically skips over any footage containing actors sitting on toilets anywhere, so it'd be a determined director who goes back and pores over footage sourced from here, which then would be ninety percent useless anyway."

So we're not the only ones wary of the Yibonn, I'm realizing, when Wednesday shrugs and turns her attention back to me.

"Let's get this treatment star—" she's saying when the sky begins pulsing red again. Sighing with dismay, she declares, "We have to evacuate now." Then she takes off her lab coat and shoves it in a trunk she rolls out from under the table. "I apologize, but your treatment will have to wait," she continues, gathering the empty mugs and other clinic accoutrements and dumping them in the trunk. "I'll check with upstairs and see if we can reschedule it for as soon as tomorrow, okay?"

Wednesday continues busily emptying the clinic. I glance at Miryu, who's watching Wednesday, wearing a look on her face that I can't quite interpret. Then as Wednesday darts to the next cabinet, Miryu snatches Wednesday's wrist, stopping her in her tracks.

"I'm afraid we won't be able to return tomorrow," she says. "I'm certain that the Yibonn sent the spies today because they know Chobahm's here."

Wednesday gapes at Miryu, clearly alarmed.

"What? You mean they've tracked her to the museum?"

The sky stops pulsing red for the second time then, and the look on Wednesday's face morphs into one of dread.

Miryu lets go of Wednesday's wrist.

"I'm not telling you to risk yourself to help us," she says. "Just pleading."

Wednesday stares at Miryu, then at me. And I don't know if I'm imagining it, but her eyes seem to soften as she turns her gaze back to Miryu. She takes a long, slow breath, and when she closes the trunk shut, it is with grim determination.

"Thank your lucky star that today's Wednesday, Miss Chobahm," she says, and instructs me to hop back on the table.

Miryu and I watch as Wednesday moves deftly through treatment prep, the last of which involves taking out a small beehive from the cabinet under the table. Half a dozen disturbed bees of as many different stripes buzz and crawl around it. There are the usual yellow and black, but also white and black, blue and black, green and black, pink and black, and so on.

"So, most cases of hypnotism are triggered by what hypnotists refer to as a potion—meaning, they slip some sort of hallucinogen in your drink. Here, we undo its effect with bee venom therapy," Wednesday explains, carefully guiding a pink-striped bee crawling on the hive into a small, bell-shaped glass cup she's holding. As I note the bee's exceptionally long stinger, she continues. "Our flowers have been genetically engineered to produce concentrated levels of the antitoxins we're after, and these little guys have quickly adapted themselves to their food source."

She lifts my shirt hem to expose my stomach and places

three of the bee-containing cups around my belly button in a triangular formation. I glance up at her uneasily, and she promises me with a smile, "Oh, you will feel the stings."

Then, one by one, she gives the cups a gentle shake to agitate the bees inside, and each buzzing creature promptly responds by delivering its supposed cure—which is not at all a swift prick and a sting à la the flu shot, but more like a series of tiny jabs over a few long seconds. I grit my teeth, resisting the urge to cry out.

Finally removing the cups, Wednesday informs me, "You'll start feeling the effect of their venom—a sort of buzzing and prickling sensation all over your body. Let me know when you feel it in your fingers and toes."

In a short minute, said sensation begins spreading through me from my core like crackling electricity. Then the rotten-fish funk of the turquoise-eyebrow man suddenly rushes to my nose, and I lean my head out of the bed just in time to empty my stomach over the grass.

"Is this all part of the detox?" Miryu asks Wednesday, her hand on my shoulder to keep me on my side as I continue to retch.

A puzzled look on her face, Wednesday watches me a minute before rushing to the apothecary drawers in search of something.

"It's not supposed to be this quick, the throwing up," she replies. "It could be a rejection."

"Rejection?"

"Yes. It can happen if the initial toxin used is too potent."

I'm shivering now, suddenly drenched in cold sweat, as the turquoise-eyebrow man's curse echoes in my ear:

*You foolish girl . . . You just have to choose the hard way, don't you?*


**"*Chobahm . . .*" I hear someone desperately calling my name.**

I lift my heavy eyelids to see Miryu by the exam table on her knees, holding my hand. "Chobahm!" she cries. "Are you feeling better?"

"How long have I been out . . . ?"

"Just a few minutes—but that's long enough," Wednesday says, dabbing her sweaty forehead with her sleeve.

I glance down at my stomach where the three cups cling. From the bee stings under each cup, dark red blood is beading out.

"Wednesday quickly pumped you with a neutralizing agent and extracted contaminated blood," Miryu says.

Then Wednesday asks me, "What do you smell just before the attack? Is it some kind of rotting fish smell?"

I squeak a surprise.

"How did you know?"

"So it was Buhae . . . ," Wednesday mutters, biting her lip.

"Buhae? What's Buhae?"

"Buhae's a person. A hypnotist, one of the very best. We don't know much about them, but their name means 'rotting sea.' Everyone under their spell reports smelling the same stench," Wednesday replies, before continuing apologetically. "And there's no treatment that can completely undo their spell."

"Where can I find them?" Miryu wants to know, rising to her feet.

"No one knows. No one even knows who they are, or

what they actually look like. A handful of actors under their spell have come to the clinic for a cure, but their descriptions vary. Some have described Buhae as an old man with yellow eyes, and others a young woman with a forked tongue . . ." Wednesday trails off, shaking her head slowly.

*Or,* I think, *an amiable young man with turquoise eyebrows.*

"It's their signature move to invade the victims' consciousness in disguise like dreams. A talented hypnotist, for sure." She holds out a small blue pouch to me. "Take these pills. They can't be the ultimate cure for your case, but they'll help with the symptoms, the pain."

"But there's got to be a way to undo their conditioning," Miryu insists, taking the pouch for me.

"Yes, there is," Wednesday allows after a moment. "You have to find and confront your hypnotic trigger, whatever it is. The thing, or things, that when referenced, trigger your reaction. But the closer you get to your trigger, the more agonizing the reaction becomes . . . so only a few manage. And Buhae's talent is unrivaled."

We're silent. Then Miryu glances at me with a sudden look on her face.

"I guess I was lucky, after all, that I was trapped in that airplane," she says, appending a hollow chuckle. "Snowglobe was my trigger, so when I flew back into it, I must have been forced to confront it, regardless of any reaction."

"I'm sorry that I'm not much help," Wednesday apologizes, collecting the cups from my stomach. "We really have to hurry now, though. Pull up the flush valves, and the toilets will take you back upstairs. I'll find you as soon as I can."

"No," I object, slowly sitting up. "You put yourself in danger and stayed behind for us. We'll wait for you."

"Chobahm's right," Miryu agrees.

Wednesday looks like she's about to protest, but then a knowing smile comes over her face, and she says to Miryu, "You haven't changed a bit."

Miryu and I stare at her, puzzled, and Wednesday says, her eyes shining with pleasure, "We've met before . . . six years ago, so you probably don't remember me."

She gazes at Miryu for another moment. Then she resumes hurrying through the lab, picking up various apparatuses and hiding them while explaining, "There was a kid who I grew up with at the public orphanage in District Three. We were inseparable, having been admitted on the same day and being the same age . . . But then he was adopted by a young couple one day. I was sad for myself but happy for him, and we kept in touch. It wasn't too long thereafter that I started noticing these bruises on him. It turned out he was being abused by his adoptive parents."

Wednesday's voice grows tight with the memory.

"He threatened to report his adoptive parents to the authorities, but they just laughed in his face. Yup—the director was in on it, ignoring the abuse and editing out anything unsavory because the show centered on the couple's perfectly curated life."

A sigh.

"Being little kids and being orphans, we felt helpless. We didn't know anyone or how to reach out for help, so for a while, I just prayed daily that the couple would die and that my friend would return to the orphanage, and then—"

"You're the girl who showed up at my door . . . ?" Miryu's murmur cuts her off.

"Yes, ma'am," Wednesday confirms, grinning. "Your house was only two minutes away from the orphanage, on foot. Even as I kid, I'd heard all kinds of awful things about you."

Wednesday tried carefully planning the timing of her visit to Miryu's, so she could show up at her door during a camera break. But each time she attempted to visit, something always happened and derailed her plan. Eventually, she decided that she could wait no more. The abuse needed to stop yesterday. So she marched straight to Miryu's house while cameras were still rolling and asked Miryu to become her hired assassin.

Miryu turned down Wednesday's request and sent her home. It wasn't that the stone-cold killer suddenly couldn't find it in her to do the job, of course; but she wouldn't allow a thirteen-year-old girl to bear that kind of weight on her soul.

So Miryu bided her time, waiting for the perfect opportunity to present itself one day, and when it did, she paid a visit to the couple in question. She didn't kill them. She didn't have to, which she already knew. She merely showed up and let them know that they'd be next, should they even so much as lay a finger on the kid ever again. In other words, Miryu let her reputation do the heavy lifting for her. And that was that. The abuse was history.

"My friend and I had a strong suspicion that we had you to thank; and we wanted to, so badly, but you were never home after that," Wednesday says, bringing her story to a close.

"I made sure to stay out of sight. There was no reason for us to associate further," Miryu replies. Then a faint smile appears on her face as if remembering something, and she adds, "I did eat all the cookies you kept leaving at my door, though."

"You did?" Wednesday squeals with sudden joy. "My friend baked them all himself!"

Their delight is contagious, and I can't help but join in. "I'm so happy you two finally got to meet again—" when Wednesday pulls up the flush valve on my toilet, and *swoosh!* up into the fake sky I soar.

A few minutes later, I'm strolling out of the museum, feeling all warm and fuzzy inside at Wednesday's story. Hyang's standing under the awning, gazing up at the sky.

"Ajumma!" I call, and she turns to me with an odd look on her face.

I'm about to ask her what's wrong, but she supplies the answer with a finger pointed skyward. Countless bubbles fall softly from an unassuming sky. I gasp. I now understand what the second round of alarm was about down at the clinic.

The disaster is finally here.


**With the late-afternoon sun illuminating each falling bubble in a** rainbow of colors, it's a peaceful, delightful, and exquisitely ethereal beginning of a disaster. It's not the cola rain Ongi wished for, but Fran managed to draw a safe disaster once again.

Feeling giddy with relief, I run out to the parking lot, into the bubble rain, calling to Hyang, "Come on, Ajumma! Feel the rain on your skin!" But in the next instant, my feet slip out from under me and I land on my tailbone with a sharp cry.

"Jeez . . . Slow down, child!" Hyang chides as she makes her way over, but in a few seconds, her butt is on the asphalt, too.

I absently rub my hands on the slick ground, whizzing up two small mounds of soap foam without even trying. Then Miryu finally strolls out of the museum, stopping short when she sees us slipping and sliding in trails of bubbling soap suds.

"Are you two alr—" she begins to call, but the rest is swallowed up by a sudden, ear-ripping sound of tires screeching in the front parking lot. Then a deafening crash and the sound of shattering glass rend the air, and I curl up into a tight ball, hands over my ears.

A few disorienting moments pass. I lift a cautious head and look around, heart hammering. No imminent danger or tragedy here. Slowly, I get back up to my feet and begin crossing to the front of the building, doing a mix between an ice skater's slide and a penguin's waddle. Off to my side, Hyang and Miryu are doing the same, trails of soap suds bubbling behind them like comet tails.

When we finally round the corner, the scene that confronts us is one of absolute horror. The front end of a huge delivery truck is inside the ticket office, filling the mangled and twisted structure with black smoke.

Then Wednesday races out of the museum, stopping cold in her tracks as her eyes register the horrid scene. With a blood-curdling scream, she staggers to the ticket office that traps the earnest museum employee who let us in just an hour ago. He is now crumpled over in his seat, unconscious, covered in blood and chalky dust, and it is only as I take in Wednesday's cries that I understand. He's Wednesday's best friend from the orphanage, the grateful thirteen-year-old survivor of child abuse, who baked cookies for Miryu and left them at her door for a full year.

Across the slick ground getting slicker by the second, Wednesday crawls on all fours toward the ticket office. The faster she tries to move, the more her limbs slip from under her.

I was wrong, earlier. This is the real disaster. It's happening now.

# THE AMBITION THAT TURNED ON ME
## Cha Seol
### 24 YEARS AGO

". . . and presenting this year's full-ride scholarship is our honorary professor, Director Cha Guibahng . . ."

The thunderous applause erupting at the mention of Grandfather's name drowns out the rest of the announcement, which says: "Every year, the award goes to a freshman who entered the institute at the top of their class . . . this year's well-deserving recipient of the award, Miss Cha Seol!"

I rise from my seat and head up to the dais, shoulders back and chest up. I can feel everyone's eyes tracking me. Some are filled with pure admiration, and others with green envy, but most brim with something that falls in between the two. With every stride, I make a conscious effort to appear confident, invincible, not to be messed with. Over the next six years, I will show everyone—everyone—just how superior I am to all the rest, including those idiots who believe that I didn't win the award on my own merit, but with Grandfather's help.

"Congratulations on the job well done, Miss Cha Seol," says Grandfather in an official tone, but his eyes gazing into me shine with grandfatherly love and pride.

"Thank you, Director Cha," I reply, matching his tone. "I'll be sure to prove myself worthy of the honor."

Taking the glowing piece of paper, I climb down the dais and return to my seat. My neighbors—fellow freshmen with their dime-a-dozen talents—lean over from all directions to gawk at the award sitting on my lap.

"Can you share your essay, or at least your show proposal? I'm so curious just what kind of application essay gets one a top-of-the-class distinction," my seatmate to the right beseeches.

I have the impulse to respond with a question of my own: *And what use would that information be to you now?* which I suppress, of course. But really. She should have asked herself that question a long time ago.

Instead, I give a laugh that sounds smug even to my own ears and tell her, "Watch it on TV someday. I promise you that the network will pick up my proposal."

The show proposal I submitted as part of my application essay stars the Yibonn clan in the Yibonn mansion. It's a guaranteed slam dunk, of course, but no one has dared suggest it because no one has dared dream of it. Put the first family to work? In front of camera, no less? How dare you? So it was up to me.

*Brazen, bold,* and even *naïve* were some of the pejorative descriptions that distinguished members of the admission panel intentionally threw around in "praising" my proposal. It was obvious that they wanted to cut me down and the scale of my ambition in order to make themselves feel better about their chicken selves, while reminding me that the Yibonns weren't actors—as if I didn't know.

"Directors never act," they told me. "And the Yibonns? They are the directors of our world, our order, our social and economic system, and the like, which makes everything else possible."

For all their hand-wringing, I was too good to be denied; and in the end, no one received higher marks or more glowing feedback than me. But what does it mean when the praise came from such dullards?

Why does everyone so worship the Yibonns? How come they continue to sit on top of the world, and no one ever questions the legitimacy of their power? Take Yi Bonil, the doomed and violently dull heir, for instance. He has nothing on me. Absolutely nothing. And he is supposed to inherit—excuse me, direct—the world that has me in it? Him?

Before the awards ceremony, I make a special trip to the toy store and buy the bubble gun I promised Hyang this morning. On my way back home, I stop to see Mom at her workplace—a crammed and musty herbal pharmacy the size of a postage stamp. Why she neglects her family for this place, I'll never know.

"Seol, sweetie!" she greets me with surprise, which then swiftly gives way to concern. "Is everything all right? What's wrong?"

She holds a glass jar in her hand, inside of which pink-, green-, and powder-blue-striped insects fly about, buzzing noisily. Are they bees . . . ? If they are, they have the most intimidating stingers I've ever seen. I ask her about them—more as a way to make small talk than anything, but she turns oddly awkward, uncharacteristically fumbling over her words for some reason. But whatever. I have an agenda here.

"Mom . . . can we talk?" I say.

**I've been planning what I want to say to her all day.** It started with Hyang's epic temper tantrum this morning.

"But you promised that you'd be there!" she wailed, angry and sad. "I hate you! I hate you, Seol!"

Dad, busy packing Hyang's boxed lunch at the kitchen counter, stepped in for me. "Hyang, honey, it's not that your sister wants to miss your field day, but she has to attend the film school entrance ceremony today. She was admitted at the top of her class, isn't it amazing?"

I was thinking, what seven-year-olds know, let alone care, about such things? When, predictably, my baby sister shouts back "I was going to win my sack race today, too! I was going to show her how good I am at running, jumping, throwing, and . . . and—"

It was getting too hard to take, so I pulled out the big guns.

"Hey, Hyang—what if I get you the bubble gun this evening? You know—the one you've had your eyes on since the last time we went to the mall together?"

Ten minutes later, Hyang, red-nosed and puffy-eyed but finally smiling, willingly left for school, holding Dad's hand. Crisis averted, all right, but the whole thing has stirred the old resentment in me again.

As always, Hyang had been perfectly understanding this morning when Mom reminded her that she would have to miss her field day again because of the pharmacy. Hyang is used to Mom's absent mothering. In fact, she showers Mom with I-love-yous twenty times a day though Mom only spends time with her between dinner and bed.

I worry about her, my baby sister. She confuses me for her mom, and Mom for her big sister, which is why I'm visiting

Mom at the pharmacy today—to bring the issue to her attention, once and for all.

Mom listens to me without getting defensive, angry, or interrupting to voice her objection. She apologizes—sincerely. But I'm not mollified.

"If you're sorry, then at least try to get home on time, will you? Aren't you concerned that Hyang and Sohm spend too much time with Dad? What if they grow up to be weak and soft like him?" I say, hearing the barbs in my voice and hating it.

"Sweetie!" Mom balks, but what the hell.

"I know, Mom! You chose him, so I want to think that he can't be that bad, but—"

"We're getting a divorce."

Did someone just hit me on the head with a gong? I stare at her, dumbstruck.

Divorce?

Dad cannot live without Mom, that much I know. He loves her, truly and deeply, which is his only redeeming quality, in my opinion.

"I have to leave Snowglobe, sweetie," Mom says, looking at me with eyes filling with tears.

She's getting kicked out of Snowglobe? Why? As the immediate family of her director husband, she doesn't even have to worry about the viewership. I don't understand; and I'm as smart as her and Grandfather combined.

"Explain it to me in a way that makes sense," I demand.

Mom cups my face with her hands.

"I can't, sweetie," she says, her voice cracking. "Not yet."

What does she even mean? I'm suddenly angry.

"Mom," I begin, looking straight into her eyes. "If you leave Snowglobe now, we may never be able to see each other again. Even immediate family members can't just leave Snowglobe of their own will and then come back. And if I get kicked out of here one day, that'd still be to the retirees' village, not to the hell of the open world you're headed to."

Mom hangs her head. Then picking it back up, she gazes at me a long moment. There's so much pain in her eyes that I can barely hold them.

"I'm leaving so I can protect you girls," she says. "If they find out who I am . . . they'll destroy your lives."

"What do you mean, if they find out who you are?" I demand, furious now. "What have you been up to?"

She seems like she's about to cry, but then a resolute look comes over her face, and she reaches for my hand.

"Sweetie," she begins, composing herself. "Please know that there are people out there who want to change the world, make it a better place for everyone . . . just like you want to bring the Yibonn family in front of the camera. That's what I've been up to. I've been working to change the world. But the net is closing in, and I must run because . . . I'd never forgive myself if the price of change is you." Her hands squeezing mine are warm and soft, just like her amber eyes searching my face. "It may take time, but the world will change, and when we get together again—"

"Just stop!" I shout angrily, shaking her off. "Why would you change the world? Are you some kind of hero? And even if you are, what kind of hero abandons her kids?"

Then I'm storming out of the pharmacy, furious and equally confused. In my state, I forgot to grab Hyang's bubble gun, but who cares about such a thing anymore when your mom doesn't come home that evening, or the next, or the next, or ever. Not even Hyang.

And just like that, Mom left us—left Snowglobe. Hyang and Sohm didn't even get a goodbye.

I learned to cope with the loss by merging Mom's wish for a better world with mine. I wished that her wish would come true, for the world to change, so I could find her wherever she's holed up in the open world and tell her exactly what I think of her—that she's a coldhearted, selfish, completely insane, and irresponsible mother who never deserved us. I couldn't let the border be her excuse for abandoning us, for hiding from us.

It was about ten years later that I realized with some shock that my wish, my ambition, had turned rotten. A lot had happened in the meantime, such as my engagement to Yi Bonil that ended up being called off. A few months later, Bonil died of some terminal condition that was never defined for the public, and the cloud of mystery surrounding his sudden death restoked my fire to put cameras in the Yibonn mansion.

Yet each time I got close, new obstacles arose. "She'll never marry into the Yibonns with a charred face like that," Grandfather explained to me as he made the call to swap out the girl, years later.

She was only three. And that was when the reality of what I'd done hit me for the first time. I'd wanted multiple Haeris as insurance for the unexpected tragedies in life—illness, unavoidable accidents, what have you; and not for Grandfather or Goh Maeryung to consider the girls as mere inventory.

Then one day, it became clear to me that all they wanted

through the Goh Haeri project was to lift up their own names, nothing else. They didn't care about my mission. About my dream of having Haeri, an actress, marry into the Yibonns, so we could finally put cameras in that mansion.

Whenever I brought up how Haeri's marrying into the Yibonns might change the world by bringing the clan in front of the camera, Grandfather just laughed and said, "Seol, my sweetie, stop being a child. You know who we owe our wonderful life to, don't you?"

That Grandfather was such a small man inside was a huge disappointment, and I eventually told him as much. But then what about me? What was driving me and my "naïve" ideas? Sure, I wanted to prove that the Yibonns were no better than me, but that's a no-brainer. The real fire in my belly was my need to prove to myself that I can change the world without deserting my loved ones like you-know-who.

Mom . . . Had I set out to change the world for the ones I loved, like you once did, I wouldn't have been able to treat the girls as mere means to an end. I tried to change the world for me, and the price I was willing to pay was the lives of the girls.

**All that was then. Now, Chief Kim returns from the phone booth,** snickering and shaking his head.

"They're sending us another van," he says to the correction officers flanking me in the backseat. "This one's apparently going to have tire chains."

The correction officers revise their grip around my arms. I look out the van window, at the bubbles falling peacefully from the sky. Suddenly, I'm transported back to the past.

Seven-year-old Hyang armed with her bubble gun chases me, laughing and squealing as she runs into the bubble storm she's creating. She says, "I wish I could show Mom, too!"

Occasionally, I still wonder . . . *What if you'd stayed, Mom? What would life look like for me now?* But then I know. I'd have ended up exactly where I am now, led by my pride and arrogance. Even so, some part of me wants to beg . . . *Can you come back? Please? Come back and scold me. Come back and hug Hyang, pat Sohm on the shoulder. Come back and try again—change the world. Make it a little warmer, a little safer for those who deserve it.*

# PART 2

9788936478292

The surgeon disappears into the operating room where I know the ticket booth worker lies, promising to do her best. She doesn't offer us anything else, no less his chance of survival. When the doors swing closed, the three of us sit waiting on the bench in the hallway.

Outside, the world has been launched into sudden and total chaos. There are road wrecks everywhere and injured people screaming in agony. The air is filled with lights and sirens promising imminent rescue, but in the continuous unfolding of the disaster, traffic quickly comes to a standstill, trapping even the ambulances and police cruisers in it.

"Thank you so very much . . . I couldn't have brought Thursday here by myself," Wednesday says to Miryu with a bow of her head. Miryu rejects the credit, but we can clearly see the bruises and scrapes she sustained while transporting Thursday, Wednesday's aptly named friend, to the hospital on these slippery roads. Rivulets of blood dry on Wednesday's knees, too. She turns to me and says, "And many thanks to you, too, Miss Chobahm."

On our way to the hospital with Thursday, the bubble storm only got worse, and so did the traffic. We were going nowhere. A few hopeless minutes dripped by with nothing moving except the bubbles beating at the windshield. But then I remembered. There were tethered inner tubes still sitting in the trunk of our car! So we fashioned a makeshift pull-sled out of them and loaded Thursday on it. Then Miryu towed the sled to the closest hospital, the one in Snow-Tower, with Wednesday monitoring his vitals and me occasionally repositioning Thursday's legs so they didn't drag. As for Hyang, she stayed behind with the car. Two hours have passed since.

"Be right back," Miryu says, rising from the bench. "I'm just going to go make a quick phone call."

She's concerned about Hyang, who is probably still stuck in the road amid the actively unfolding mayhem. Wednesday, who seemed to have fallen into some kind of trance, flinches back to herself and focuses a surprised gaze on us. She thanks us once again and tries to send us home, but Miryu assures her that it will just be a minute before she returns.

"I owe her again," Wednesday murmurs, watching Miryu disappear down the crowded hallway.

"I doubt Miryu thinks so," I tell her.

*Clack!*

The slate goes off then. Cameras stop, but nobody takes a break. The halls are still overflowing with injured people who hobbled and crawled their way here in search of care, and right now, seeking medical attention is way more urgent than the ten minutes of free time. Similarly for medical staff, their sworn duty of care as medical personnel supersedes any rights they wish to exercise as Snowglobe actors.

The red light stays on above the operating room sign. Wednesday lets out a sigh.

"She's a good person," she says, picking back up the subject of Miryu. Then looking straight into me, she says, "She'd have had a very different life, had she been paired up with a different director. I personally think that her show was ridiculous."

What? She's seen her show? How? I thought Wednesday was a native of Snowglobe, born and raised here, and everyone knows Snowglobe locals don't get to watch the shows that are produced within the dome. As if registering my surprise, Wednesday says, "Yes, of course, I watched all the episodes," as if it's not a big deal. "Her show was the first I sought out at the film school's library when I was admitted."

"The film school . . . ?" I repeat, further surprised.

Wednesday gives a quick glance down the hall, which is bursting with all kinds of patients and staff. Then in a hushed voice, she says, "Weren't you curious how a detox therapist stays in the secret clinic all day long without anyone noticing my absence?"

Oh . . . ?

It's impossible for an average actor to hide from cameras all day long and not get in some serious trouble real fast. She'd have been found out a long time ago. Of course.

"Only those who are exempt from acting duty can become a detox therapist, such as immediate family members of directors or film school students," Wednesday explains.

Okay . . . but why would directors' families and film school students jeopardize their present and future by working for the detox clinic? When I express this doubt, Wednesday smiles and says, "Not all film school students are there to become directors. People like me are there for the cover, of course. When we join the secret operation, we sign an agreement that says we'll drop out of film school and leave Snowglobe forever at the first sign of someone keying in on our real identity."

I feel suddenly ashamed. I've seen people like her, but only on TV—people who do what they do with the full knowledge that it could destroy their path to success at any moment; people who put their whole lives on the line for a cause.

My heart swelling, I tell her how much I admire her courage and conviction, and she just stares at me a moment and says, "Why did you do what you did then?"

I stare back at her, not catching on.

"When you took over the studio with Somyung and Shinae and Hyang?" she explains. "All of you put your lives on the line."

"But that's different," I counter, and it's true. "There was no other choice. We had to put our lives on the line because . . ."

"My mom was a director," Wednesday says as I trail off, searching for the right words. Her voice is suddenly intense. "When her shows bombed one after another, she was torn from me and sent to the retirees' village. That was my first introduction to the cruel injustice of this place. Then years later, when I finally saw the system for what it was, and how eagerly it twisted and mangled people's lives in order to serve itself, I knew that something needed to change. Not that I had any idea how, of course."

"So you had no desire to become a director one day?"

"Nope," Wednesday says proudly. "I went to film school because of Thursday. He'd already been a student for a year, and he persuaded me to join him there to do my part in possibly changing the world."

Wednesday smiles faintly at the memory, and a new question pops into my mind.

"Who discovered the huge blind spot for the clinic? Who built the clinic?"

Wednesday is silent a moment. Then she sighs and makes an apologetic face.

"I'm so sorry. But that's a secret I can't tell anyone."

I murmur that it's fine, my curiosity only intensifying as I do. It was all so well-designed—the artificial sky in the underground section of the clinic appeared exactly like the sky trapping the Snowglobe community. And how was the air so fresh . . . ?

It has the same ventilation system as the dome itself.

That's when it strikes me. The mysterious woman at Fran's wedding! I dig through my purse and find the business card she gave me. The slate's going to clack any time now to signal the end of our break, so I hurry and present the card to Wednesday.

"Is this the person who built the clinic?" I ask with a rush of excitement.

Someone capable of actualizing a secret clinic might know a thing or two about the magic mirrors that the Yibonns use to travel, also. And even a family as almighty as them have to outsource sometimes . . . no?

"Who gave you this?" Wednesday asks me back, unable to hide her surprise.

"A woman I met at Fran Crown's wedding. She told me that she built the floating venue?"

And that's when it hits me.

"I'm fine . . . ," I murmur, standing up and patting myself down all over in disbelief. Then I'm gleefully shouting, "I'm fine! I'm fine!"

I was just thinking about the mirror—but it didn't trigger the hypnotic reaction! There's no stench of rotting fish up my nose or heart-twisting chest pain. I report this to Wednesday, and we rejoice in the news.

Shortly thereafter, Miryu returns, looking far more relaxed than when she left.

"I just talked to Shinae," she says. "Everyone's safe at home—and worried sick about us. I got an earful about how I need to get a car phone."

"How about Ajumma?"

"Hyang's still trapped in traffic. Shinae says she called from a nearby police barracks."

I'm about to express my own relief, but I start dry-heaving instead, a familiar, albeit belated, stench returning to my nostrils.

Looks like I'm not cured after all.


**I circle the hospital building twice before settling on a phone booth** in a relatively quiet corner. Picking up the receiver, I calm my breath and dial the number—9, 7, 8, 8, 9 . . . With this many digits, it really doesn't look like a phone number, but Wednesday convinced me to give it a try, adding with a knowing grin that it just might be the person I was looking for.

. . . 9, 2.

I press the last digit—the thirteenth—and as soon as my finger lifts off the number pad, someone picks up the call.

"Hello?" a voice says.

I stammer in confusion, thrown off by how quickly the call was picked up. From the coin slot, a hidden camera records me.

"Been waiting for your call," the voice says, which I now recognize as that of the woman in the wheelchair. "Can you come by my office now?"

"Now?" I glance at the clock in the hall. Its hands are ticking toward eleven p.m. "Where is your office?"

"On the outskirts of Snowglobe."

Whichever outskirts she might be referring to, it is far from SnowTower where I'm calling from. Outside the hospital, bubbles continue to dump from the sky, wreaking havoc on the world below. "Um . . . The weather's making travel kind of difficult right now . . . ?"

"If one is traveling on the road, that is."

"Pardon me?"

"You're in SnowTower, which is great."

How does she know . . . ?

"Take the elevator," she instructs. "Any elevator, in fact, and punch the number on the card for the floor."

The number? I flip over the card in my hand.

"A mirror will be waiting for you," she says.

"What?" is all I can muster, when the loathsome stench hits and the chest pain begins.

With a faint chuckle, she says, "I'll see you in a bit, then."

"Wait!" I squeak, breathing through the pain. "Tell me which floor—" But she's already hung up.

Frustrated, I examine the card in my hand. There's nothing else but the business logo—two ladders curved to form a circle—and the same old thirteen-digit number.

My breaths still ragged, I hobble toward the lobby's end where there's a squadron of elevators—eight, to be exact. I park myself on the periphery and scope for a chance to catch a ride in one by myself.

Meanwhile, the hospital's vast lobby has been turned into a sort of refugee camp swamped with bloody, wounded people sprawled on stretchers and makeshift beds. Loved ones sitting vigil are almost indistinguishable from the patients, bruised and banged up themselves and looking rattled to the core. The disaster must be intensifying outside. Near and far, lights and sirens haven't stopped, and the doors keep flying open with fresh arrivals as harried medical staff rush about.

It's a chaotic scene, and I feel a fresh sense of doom rising inside me, when my eyes catch an odd patch of stillness. Amid the crush and confusion, a woman sits in a fold-up chair reading a newspaper as if nothing's wrong in the world. But wait . . . Isn't she the woman who stole a shady glance at us at the toilet museum? Is this just coincidence?

As if noticing my gaze, she raises the newspaper and hides behind it—shadier still—but my attention is pulled away by the elevator's ding. The doors open and a full load of people pile out. When it's completely empty, I race to it and slip in through its closing doors.

9, 7, 8, 8, 9, 3, 6, 4 . . . I begin punching the numbers, feeling like some little kid unable to resist playing with buttons. SnowTower is a 204-story building, and the only floors open to the public are the first and the seventy-third, the latter being the hospital floor.

Breathing deeply, I press the final number. And that's when all the lights go out.

# OUT OF MY REACH

hat on earth? Was it all the button pushing that tripped up the wiring or something? My pulse begins to pound when a bright green light emits from the floor display over the doors, and the elevator suddenly rockets up through the shaft. I watch the nonsensical numbers flashing on the screen. 73 . . . 333, 7189, 284752, 3579301348 . . . Terrified, I grip the handrails with everything I have, my eyes stuck on the digits zipping madly on the display, not that I can keep up with them. I don't know how much time passes before the vessel's frightening ascension finally begins to slow, then, with a cheery ding, comes to a complete stop. By the floor display, I've arrived on the 9788936478292nd floor.

I take a few slow, deep breaths to calm my racing heart. When the doors finally slide open after what feels like an eternity, I hurry to escape, suddenly frightened.

But I've barely taken a single step when I glance down, and with a horrified shriek, I stumble back from the edge, losing my balance in the process and falling down onto the elevator floor. There's nothing waiting to receive me beyond it. In fact, the elevator seems to be suspended in the air outside the SnowTower. A chilling gust sweeps in and makes my hair stand on end. In a confused panic, I scoot backward and plaster myself against the elevator's far wall, my heart drumming in my ears.

Wait a second. My breath catches. In front of me . . . is that a mirror bobbing in the air? Yes, it is, the same frameless, oval mirror I saw leaning against the thousand-year-old tree in the restricted woods where I ran into Bonwhe back before I'd learned the truth about Haeri. On my hands and knees, I crawl toward the edge of the elevator and look down. Vehicles the size of small ants crawl along the roads in strings of yellow and red lights. Forget people. They're too small to be seen from this height. Another gust picks up, and the elevator sways in the empty air, making my stomach drop. I retreat from the edge and press my back up against the far wall, my eyes on the mirror bobbing in the air almost ten feet away.

*A mirror will be waiting for you.*

Am I supposed to just hurl myself through thin air to reach it, though? The mere thought of attempting such a feat makes me want to cry. Sure, if this woman really knows the truth about the mirrors and how they work, her insight could be incredibly valuable to me—a potential card to play against the Yibonn. But so what? There's no guarantee that she'll offer to help me.

I scream in frustration, which at least seems to drive away the nausea that's been lingering since the latest flare-up.

Shaking my head, I force myself to think. The woman in the wheelchair obviously has a connection to the detox clinic—but what could that mean? Whose side is she on? It's possible that my actions right here and now could set off a chain of events that could save me and change the world in the process; but it's also possible it is all just a trick.

"For Christ's sake!" I shout in sudden anger. "How about a heads-up if she was going to have me jump through these extreme hoops?"

I curse the uncaring woman's thoughtlessness, sizing up my distance to the mirror and calculating my odds of success. Each time I try to will myself to jump, though, I'm overcome with the image of Cooper Raffaeli free-falling from the airplane cargo through the frozen air, his mouth open in a mute cry.

My fingers and toes tingle, and my skin is damp with cold sweat.

"I can't do this . . ."

I know—I'll go back down to the ground floor and call the woman from there. Yes, I'll talk to her again and ask her to help. My decision made, I shuffle gingerly to the elevator's keypad. Closing the doors will help me feel so much better, I'm sure. But no matter how many times I press the close button, the damn doors won't move, and still the only source of light inside this metal box is the green backlit floor display stuck at 9788936478292!

I try the seventy-second floor for the medical center, as well as the first floor. Nothing. Frustration boiling over inside me, I jab my finger at any random buttons with rising violence. Nothing, predictably.

"Ha!" I finally let out a hollow laugh. "I see. It's set up so there's no other option but to jump for that mirror."

My strength leaves me, and I plop down on the floor in

front of the keypad. The world below is a slowly spinning kaleidoscope of twinkling lights. It's mesmerizing. So pretty. I could almost appreciate its beauty if not for my extreme circumstance. Then it hits me. Where are the bubbles?

The atmosphere is completely free of them, I realize. How odd. How extremely odd. Disasters never relent on the first day they're rolled out. But then boom! As if my thought has summoned them, bubbles begin to pour from the night sky.

Hanging on to the handrail with one hand, I edge toward the open doors and stick my other hand out in the air, catching a bubble on my open palm. I close my fingers on it, and it promptly pops, leaving behind a slippery film. But something feels . . . unsatisfactory, insubstantial, like it's not real or something.

I think back to the rainbow-colored foam I lathered up in the museum's parking lot just a few hours ago. The foam seemed unstoppable. And the moment I realize it, the same exact foam begins bubbling on my palm where the bubble has popped. That's when it clicks. All this is a trick of my mind . . . an illusion.

*You have to find and confront your hypnotic trigger . . . The thing, or things, that when referenced, trigger your reaction. But the closer you get to your trigger, the more agonizing the reaction becomes . . . so only a few manage.*

Only then do I properly comprehend Wednesday's meaning. Your hypnotic *trigger* . . . My trigger is mirrors, like the one I passed through to meet with Bonwhe in the forest—and the one in front of me now. The closer I get to it, the more intensely my mind tries to fight against it—like by creating an illusion of free-falling through thousands of feet to a messy death. The scene in front of me looks terrifying, but it isn't real—and if I manage to push through the fear, I should be able to break through my hypnosis once and for all.

Or can I? What if it's real, and I'm wrong?

Suspicions keep rising inside me, but I let go of the handrail and move to the center of the elevator. For a few deep breaths, I stare at the empty air ahead, or the illusion of it. Finally, I begin moving toward the edge, my heart pounding in my ears. Once I get there, I transfer my weight to one foot and try sticking the other out of the elevator. Holy crap. Where I expect my heel to swish through the nothingness, it's met with resistance. The empty air isn't empty at all. It's solid. Incredible. I try shifting more of my weight onto the foot.

"I'm not falling!" I cry with the exhilaration of relief, which I then use to push myself onward. Then I'm walking on air, into the night sky, my heart pounding. I try a little twirl, laughing out loud, giddy with the miracle of not having plunged to my death already. Of course—the world below isn't real, either. The real world is swept up in the bubble disaster right now, with roads jammed everywhere with pileups and emergency vehicles trying to get through. There wouldn't be these strings of headlights snaking peacefully through the city if what I was seeing reflected reality. But the moment I think this, the scene below changes to one that I've just recalled in my mind—one of the current disaster. It's as if I'm thinking it into existence!

Then there's the sound of the elevator doors sliding shut behind me. I flinch but will myself not to look back, terrified that if I confirm I don't even have that elevator to scramble back to in case something goes wrong, I'll change my mind.

I fix my eyes on the mirror up ahead and take another step forward, adrenaline shooting down to the tips of my toes once again.

It is then that the world suddenly begins to spin around me. What now? I close my eyes shut, bracing for the worst— whatever that might be. When I open my eyes again, I can't comprehend the scene in front of me.

Rather than hovering above the city, I'm now in a white room full of mirrors. From wall to wall and floor to ceiling, it's hundreds of mirrors, the same frameless oval as the one I was supposed to enter.

The illusion changed. Dammit! How am I supposed to find the real mirror among them all now? The most powerful hypnotist in all of Snowglobe . . . Buhae's notoriety doesn't come from nothing, I guess.

Not knowing what else to do, I reach tentatively for the nearest mirror, and its smooth, silvery surface cracks like a spiderweb at the moment of contact. I gasp and recoil, but my reflection in the cracked surface just stares out at me, wearing a chilling smile.

"Jeon Chobahm," my reflection says, "you don't actually believe that you can go up against Yibonn, do you?"

I whirl around reflexively, only to be confronted by another mirror and another me reflected in it. She stares at me with a look of such pity and exasperation.

"So what's your plan?" the me in the mirror wants to know. "Expose the secret power plant? Do you think the truth of the power system could bring down Yibonn? What harm has the lie really done to the people anyway?"

Then, all around me, all the other mirrors come to life

with hundreds of versions of me. In one, I'm sobbing with abandon; in another, I'm ranting furiously; in yet another, I'm cussing someone out, my face ugly with contempt.

"Don't you know that your stupidity is putting others in danger?"

I don't want to die. *I DON'T WANT TO!*

I put my hands over my ears and begin smashing the mirrors, kicking them one by one. The cracked and warped images they reflect explode in a rain of a million shards. But reflections are infinite, and a new one sprouts up just as soon as one breaks. Meanwhile, the voices from all the unbroken glass echo sharply around the room, growing progressively louder and more disorienting by the minute.

Collapsing to the floor, I mash my palms onto my ears, desperate to block out the cacophony, but it's no use. All around me, the sounds of my own whispers, sighs, giggles, shouts, shrieks, and sobs swarm and buzz. I bury my head between my knees and scream.

"Stop!" I cry, trying to drown it all out. "I can't just sit back and watch them take it all away!"

Then suddenly, all is quiet. A new wave of dread replacing the old, I lift my head and take a panicked look around. From the cracked and shattered mirrors, water trickles out—slowly at first, like rivulets of raindrops streaking down a windshield. In a short minute, though, they have turned into torrents pouring through bursting levees, and the room begins to flood at a rapid rate.

"It's all right," I tell myself, staggering up to my feet. "It's all an illusion anyway."

But water's already lapping at my waist. I spin around in

shock and feel the coldness seeping into my side. The clothes are soaking wet and damp as I hold them in my hands. How could this be an illusion, really?

That's when the familiar stench fills the room's dwindling air space, and an enormous wave barrels through the room. And this water? It's so intensely salty that it's almost bitter.

"H-help . . . ," I cry feebly between gulps of bitter water. But waves keep surging over me one after another, and I'm finally going under.

Air bubbles escape from my mouth and nose and crowd my view. I flail my limbs desperately, swallowing water into my stomach and lungs. Gradually, my frantic movements slow, my heartbeat turning sluggish. Is this how I go?

Random images parade through my mind then. The first one is of Wednesday crying out and crawling on all fours toward the crushed ticket office trapping Thursday. Then it's Mom, Grandma, and Ongi crawling on bloodied hands and knees toward my wet, cold body, their cheeks streaked with bloody tears that stream from their eyes. Behind them all, President Yi stands over them, wearing a rich smile of satisfaction.

*Before you know it, you'll have lost everything, even the ones you wanted to protect with your last breath.*

"No . . . I won't let her!"

I will not let her destroy my world.

Visualizing the last remaining pockets of air in my lungs, I marshal all my will and twitch my fingertips like I did when I was trying to break free of the hypnotic spell at the wedding. Then miracle of all miracles—I'm breathing underwater! Down below me, a single mirror stands shining on the floor, and I swim to it, thanking all the hours I've spent at the pool in the past months.

As I near the mirror, I'm once again stunned by what I see. According to my reflection, I'm not swimming at all, but standing erect on two feet. On firm ground, on a floor.

The water that surrounds me is an illusion, but the mirror is real.

The moment I realize it, all the water in the room lifts at once. I look around in awe. Behind me stands the SnowTower elevator that took me here. In front of me on the floor is a low table, and off in the corner, a giant vase lies shattered in a pool of water, surrounded by hundreds of cut flowers. Did I knock the vase over during my struggle with the illusion? My back is still wet. I turn my attention back to the mirror and, staring into the eyes of my reflection, I reach for it.

**As usual, it's dark inside the mirror. This time, though, I don't** have to accidentally bump into a button to trigger anything. The thing is already whooshing through some kind of tube as if being sucked out of the earth. Into the night sky saturated with bubbles, I soar, recalling the image of a Warring Age rocket ship launching into space. Up, I go, and higher still, until the glass curve of Snowglobe's dome swims into view and I'm sure I'll crash into it . . .

But then, at the last moment, the elevator slows smoothly instead of running into the glass, and I touch down into a room affixed to the topmost point of Snowglobe's famous dome on the other side, where the greatest architect-engineer of all time greets me.

# THE UNRECORDED HISTORY

"At last! What took you so long?" The moment I pass through the mirror connecting the elevator and the room, the woman in the wheelchair greets me, looking tired and more than a little baffled.

It was just after eleven p.m. when I got on the elevator, but the timepiece glinting around her pale wrist says it's almost five in the morning. I must have been lost in the illusion for quite some time.

"You have no idea what I went through to get here," I tell her, hearing the edge of grievance in my voice, but she's already gliding away across the floor.

This wheelchair of hers looks like the one I saw her use at Fran's wedding, except that it's automatic and seems to move without her doing anything at all. I've never seen an automatic wheelchair before—not in the open world or here in Snowglobe; and I'm still admiring it when the woman glances back for me, and her wheelchair magically slows as if attuned to her thoughts.

I catch up to the woman as she leads me to her office.

The space I'm in seems to be an observation chamber of sorts, dangling from the very topmost point of the dome, and my questions about it are endless. *What's up with the weird multi-digit number I punched in to get here? Why did the elevator refuse to take me back once I'd reached the floor with the mirror, even when I tried to close the door? Would it have descended again eventually if I hadn't moved?* She answers all of these, adding at the end that the floor I was on is a camera-blind spot—one that only she knows about—in SnowTower.

I bow my head and thank her.

"Thank me for what?" she says, frowning up at me.

"For making me push past my fears. Thanks to you and the elevator, I was forced to break through my trauma. I faced my trigger, and it worked."

It's true. The telltale smell of Buhae no longer rushes to my nose when I think of the mirror. The woman gives me a long, puzzled look but doesn't probe further.

She leads me through the hallway. At the end of it is a small, windowless room in warm neutral colors. There's a yellow armchair and a rectangular metal coffee table with rounded edges. A coat rack stands by the table, holding fur coats, of all things. If this is her office, it's underfurnished to the point where there's not even a TV. The woman points to the yellow armchair and gestures for me to have a seat.

"How did I get up here? Can the elevator fly on its own, like a rocket?" I ask her, easing down on the armchair.

The woman gives a little laugh in place of an answer and parks her wheelchair across the table from me.

"The tunnel—or portal, if you will—connecting my office to the top of SnowTower is built with the same glass panels covering Snowglobe. You weren't flying, though it may have looked like it—just traveling up the tunnel."

So it blends perfectly with the artificial sky above, making it invisible to anyone looking up. The same with her office's exterior walls, she explains.

"All right, but . . . where are we, exactly?" I ask her, still processing.

With a proud grin, she says, "See for yourself," and squeezes a corner of the table.

In the next instant, the whole tabletop turns on like a lighthouse beacon, illuminating the glass ceiling above with a column of intense white light and transforming it into a mirror.

I've seen this before. It was on the day of our escape from the retirees' village. The brilliant headlights of Hwang Sannah's truck did the same thing to the glass panels of that dome. I assumed it was a onetime trick, but it appears I was wrong . . .

Within Snowglobe, particular frequencies of light turns reflective surfaces into mirrors—and mirrors into doorways. I file away the information. Just when I think I've learned everything there is to know about this place, it keeps getting stranger.

Wide-eyed, I look at the woman. She just smiles and wheels over to the coatrack, where she picks up a fur coat and shrugs into it.

"You should dress for the weather," she says. "I made sure it's long enough to cover you from head to toe."

I'm confused.

"Are . . . are we going outside the dome?" I ask.

"Bingo," she says, raising the hood over her head and securing it in place with a built-in scarf.

"But one thick layer is no protection against the cold out-side," I tell her with an involuntary chuckle.

"Don't you fret," she says, and flings a small object in my direction like a throwing star, which I catch by reflex. "Put it on your bare skin. Right above your beating heart."

I glance down at the black, plastic heart-shaped thing in my hand, baffled.

"You want me to put this on?"

"Why, yes—the symbol of love. Love keeps you warm, don't you know?"

I blink at her, unsure of what she's getting at—until she taps her knuckles impatiently against the side of her wheel-chair and tells me to have faith in technology. I do as I'm told, pressing the plastic heart on my skin right above my heart, and it sticks like a patch. When I pick up the white fur coat from the rack, its near weightlessness surprises me. I could have sworn it was a coat made of some heavy animal fur, but under closer inspection, I see that the garment actually consists of hundreds of tiny, opalescent plastic tubes linked together.

"It's heat-generating technology," the woman informs me, beaming with pride or sarcasm, I'm not sure.

I return to my seat and the woman gently taps her fist against another corner, twice. A moment later, the patch of floor we're sitting on separates from the rest in a diamond shape, levitating in a slow twirl. My jaw drops once again, but before I can ask her what's happening, we're whooshing through the ceiling mirror to emerge outside—onto the dome top of Snowglobe.

Whoa . . .

The view from this lookout is so breathtaking that it takes

me a minute to register the harshness of the chill that greets us. Snowglobe curves outward below us, the lone refuge teeming with color and life amid snow-blasted mountain chains and windswept prairies. In the distance, the pale light of dawn breaks through the dark sky. Under the glass dome beneath my two feet, the sun also rises, poking through a thick fog.

I'm inhaling for another whoa when I realize that the thick fog blanketing the domed city under my feet is no fog at all but an enormous bubble cloud. The disaster.

Meanwhile, my eyelashes have bloomed with ice crystals, and the lining of my nose has frozen. I glance at the table's white temperature display. The current temperature is −38°C. Even in the summer, the early-morning hours in the open world are anything but warm.

"Here . . . I'll help you stay warmer," the woman says, and sweeps the silver tabletop with her hand, which seems to activate some kind of heat vents on the sides of the table.

"That's amazing . . . ," I murmur in appreciation.

"You wanted to know where we were?" the woman says. "You're in the field office of the designer-slash-architect-slash-engineer of the dome."

I look at her, amazed that I'm sitting in such an unbelievable space right now with such an unbelievable figure.

"Fancy a spot of tea?" the lady says then. "You should! You came all the way here."

Still speechless, I just watch her as she produces a tea set from the table's deep drawer. When she sets the teapot on the tabletop, the water inside begins to boil all on its own.

"Is this table making the water boil? How does it work?" I hear myself say at last.

"Batteries," she replies matter-of-factly, as if to say *What else?*

She pours the steaming hot tea into two cups. Behind her in the distance, the sun filters a fiery red through the thick clouds that have gathered.

"I hear that you asked Wednesday about me?" she says, sliding the teacup sloshing with black tea across the table to me.

*Who discovered the huge blind spot for the clinic? Who built the clinic?*

The lady takes a slow, careful sip of her tea, watching me amusedly over the brim of her teacup. Then she says in a mock teasing way, "What could possibly be going on in that brain of yours?"

I have so many questions, of course, and they all rush into a bottleneck in my mind.

"Um . . . ," I begin, struggling to pick one. Then it comes to me. "What should I call you? The business card you gave me didn't include a name or title?"

The lady draws back in her wheelchair and stares at me, a look of surprise on her face. Then she exclaims, shaking her head. "You're right! I was so afraid of Yibonn spies catching us together during our conversation that I forgot to even give you my name. The name's Ichae—Shin Ichae. Most people call me Chairman Shin even though I don't run the company, at least not publicly."

*Shin Ichae . . . Shin Ichae . . .* I roll the words around in my head a few times, but no memories come up. How have I never heard of her before? She has an office on the roof of Snowglobe and designs places like Fran's wedding venue, which was built to resemble Snowglobe itself. Surely that person should be legend, right?

"With your last name being Shin . . . You're not a Yibonn, so how do you know about the mirrors?"

Chairman Shin smiles and drops her gaze, taking another leisurely sip of her tea. Then she says, "Don't you want to know how I knew that you knew about the mirror first?"

She's right, of course. The prerequisite for her invitation was that I already knew how the mirrors worked.

She continues, "A few days after you and your friends exposed the Cha duo's atrocities on TV, the president herself came to visit me in my office."

"The president . . . ?"

She couldn't mean President Yi Bonyung, because everyone knows that the president had been hospitalized at the time following a significant stroke.

"Yes, President Yi Bonyung," Chairman Shin confirms. "She had come to personally deliver her orders, which were for me to delete from the system any and all biometric data connected to Jeon Chobahm."

I have no clue what system she's talking about. Still, it doesn't sound good. I stare at the chairman, feeling vaguely uneasy, and she explains. "The mirrors are a mode of transport exclusive to those few whose biometrics are registered within the designated system. Even among the Yibonns, it's only the president, the VP, and the heir who have access to it. The technology is coded to your DNA, irises, fingerprints, and so on."

Okay . . . *overwhelming.* Also, if this system is so exclusive, how was I, of all people, able to access it? I hope things will start making more sense as we go, but I can't help wondering, how is she privy to all this seemingly top-secret information? Who is she? What is her connection to the Yibonn?

I probe, "And . . . the president put such a vitally important system in the hands of an outsider?"

"The president didn't. We did: my family, my ancestors. We designed, engineered, and have been managing the system in question since the beginning."

"Your family?"

"Correct. The fact they leave out of more Snowglobe origin stories these days is that the founding president only came up with the vision, the idea of Snowglobe. A feat of imagination, for sure—but imagination alone doesn't get you very far. You have to have the brainpower to actualize the vision. Otherwise, it's just a pipe dream. And that's where my distant ancestors came in—to bridge that huge gap."

She pauses to let me absorb this. Then she continues, "The network of camera cables running through Snowglobe like veins through the human brain? The software algorithm that filters and sorts out recordings collected every second of every day? It's my family who put that in place and far more. We laid the foundation of Snowglobe."

She pauses again, studying me. On the far horizon, the sun has finally escaped the dark clouds, and the full force of its rays is silhouetting her shape.

"How come I never learned about you or your family in school?" I ask her. I'm torn between amazement and skepticism. "They teach us everything there is to know about the Yibonn family and their contributions, but nothing about those who made everything possible behind the scenes . . . Something's wrong about that, no?"

Chairman Shin withdraws her smile, and after a long moment, she finally answers, "There can only be one sun under the sky. That's what the founding president believed, and they weren't entirely wrong. My family's intellectual and technological prowess, if known to the public, would be impossible to ignore. We'd crowd out anyone who tried to compete."

"Are you saying that the founding president intentionally blotted your family out of Snowglobe history?"

"No, in fact. It was my family who proposed the idea to her."

"But why?"

Her eyes darken, and she replies, "Self-preservation, most likely. We didn't try to be another sun. The bargain my ancestors made was to opt out of history, and live quietly and peacefully as the operators and administrators of the system." A sigh. "But that didn't satisfy the president. Not only could she not allow another sun, but she couldn't allow the moon in the night sky, either."

Chairman Shin is living proof that her family wasn't purged by the founding Yibonns, at least not completely. Still, my heart pounds in my chest just imagining what she's going to say next.

"How did you survive?"

"Well, my ancestors were no dummies," she says flatly. "They had programmed the system so that the admin mode could only be accessed with the biometric data of the Shin member who created it. From recording and editing algorithms, to the mirror technology, they made sure that the Yibonns couldn't overtake the system with stolen data."

A proud look returning to her face, she points a finger to her chest and concludes, "All this is to say that without my inputting of my own biometric data into the system, President

Yi Bonyung cannot access squat. That is, my physical presence is a requirement. Without me, she can't sneak a look at a single recording, either."

I stare at her, the implications of all this reeling through my mind. And I'm not sure if I have stars in my eyes, but Chairman Shin raises her arms and does a little head bow as if she's a stage actor receiving applause at the end of a performance.

Then a new question pops into my mind. The Chairman just said the system could only be accessed with the DNA of the person who created it—but how is her genetic data identical to her ancestor's, the one who programmed the system? No two humans are genetically identical—not unless they are genetically engineered clones . . . like us born of the Goh Haeri project.

After some hesitation, I cautiously voice this query. Chairman Shin's face shifts into a long-suffering smile, one caught between grief and joy.

"The Goh Haeri project was not the first of its kind," she says, looking at me dead-on. "It's long precedented by a similar project, if you know what I mean."

Sitting before me is not just the descendant of Snowglobe's architect, but the architect herself. She has traveled through time and space in the form of her genetic clone. I freeze in place, a slow chill descending my spine.

# THE KEYS TO THE KINGDOM

"**Y**es. I'm a clone like you," Chairman Shin says. "While the Goh Haeri project concerned creating multiple copies of a genetically engineered being who had yet to exist, our family's case was far more straightforward. We just had to preserve a single, preexisting genetic code over the course of generations."

I'm shaking. Seconds thunder in my ears, just like when I first learned about the secret of my own existence.

"The point is, I'm the key to the Snowglobe system," the chairman goes on. "But unlike most keys, I'm organic—made of living tissue, and therefore prone to decay and death like all other living things on Earth. The president can't risk me dying and locking her out of her entire system, so she makes a spare, a copy, while I'm alive and well."

I squeak. She continues, "I am myself and all my predecessors all at once, if that makes sense, including my mother, who died immediately after showing me how to run and manage the system." Here, she casts her eyes down to her two inert legs. "And because our genetic data must be preserved at all costs, there's no escaping our genetic condition."

Out of the blue, tears start down my face.

"Why are you crying?" Chairman Shin says, looking at me bewildered.

After a while, I manage to choke out that I don't know, though that's not entirely true. I'm crying because of the sadness I feel for another life that began for the sole purpose of satisfying someone else's need.

We're both quiet a minute. Then I finally gather myself and ask her, "Is that how you were able to build the Mirage Clinic? Because the Yibonn won't touch you, anyway?"

The chairman snorts.

"What do you mean, the Yibonn won't touch me?"

"Because they need you to be alive in order to use your genetic data . . . ?"

She rests her chin in her hand and gazes down over District 3 under the dome.

"As we speak, there's a girl with my genetic data who's growing up in the Yibonn mansion. She is my ancestor, my descendant, and me all in one—the spare key."

She shifts her gaze back to me as I stare at her, speechless.

"A long time ago, my predecessor's predecessor—my grandmother, if you will—she tried leveraging her status as the key to the system in order to compete with President Yi Bonyung." A rueful sigh. "And guess what my immediate predecessor—my mother—did. The moment she was made privy to my grandmother's plan, she went straight to President Yi and told her everything; and surprise, surprise—Grandmother expired that night. It was many years before my mother realized what she'd done. The clinic is the result of her belated penitence."

Another sigh, longer than the first.

"Well," the chairman says. "For all her treacherous stupidity, it wasn't my mother's fault. I mean, she grew up in President Yi's care . . . basked in the president's affection and glory without ever questioning how she'd begun, why she'd begun—or *if* she'd begun, for that matter. President Yi was her mother and god rolled into one. I should know—I was once just like her. Anyhow . . . my life under the Yibonn is more like a candle in the wind. A far cry from being untouchable, so . . ." She hesitates for a moment before continuing. "When she asked, I had no choice but to do her bidding. I let the president access the conversation."

She flicks her eyes to me apologetically, but I don't think I'm following.

"What conversation?"

"The phone conversation between you and Yi Bonwhe in the studio, just before the exposé."

Oh . . .

That's how President Yi knew that I was in possession of her ugly secret—the truth about Snowglobe's mirrors, and the secret power plant they lead to. She pressured Chairman Shin into granting her access to my conversation with her grandson.

"I'm sorry," Chairman Shin apologizes.

*For what?* I want to ask. *For obeying the person who has the power to replace you with a spare?* She couldn't have done otherwise—I couldn't have done otherwise in her position, and I tell her so.

"For what it's worth, I obviously didn't delete your biometrics from the mirror system. It'll take work for the president to unravel those technical details, so . . . ." Chairman Shin allows a conspiratorial smile to finish her sentence.

"How did you register my information in the system, to begin with?"

"Because Goh Haeri's was registered," she replies. "On Christmas Eve last year, the mirror system sent out a security alarm, informing me of an unknown user whose genomic data matched that of Goh Haeri, but whose fingerprints and retina didn't."

She goes on to explain how biometric indicators commonly employed for authentication purposes can be altered intentionally or accidentally over the course of one's life—like via accidents including abrasions, burns, and transplants—and so as a countermeasure, the system was programmed to accommodate updates as needed. When the system asked her if she wanted to update the user's biometric identifiers on that day, she approved it.

"My assumption was that the Goh Haeri who'd used the mirror before and vanished had been brought back," she says.

"You mean the Haeri who disappeared into the woods?" I ask, feeling a jolt in my heart.

"Yes."

"So she did use the mirror? Why? How?"

"When we register the genetic info of anyone who is not a Yibonn, it means one thing," Chaiman Shin says, her voice turning cool. "That person is being sent to the underground power plant."

My pulse picks up. I knew it. I knew it! Of course the

Yibonn wouldn't just let Haeri go. If Haeri had told them what Cha Seol did to manipulate her show, they might have kept Haeri somewhere to use her to punish Cha Seol in case she ever became a true threat to their power. Somewhere like the underground plant.

"I have to find her," I say, my heart racing again. "I have to find her and everyone else locked up in the power plant, and get them to testify against the Yibonn. Expose the Yibonn's deception of their citizens all these years, while they've been sitting on their giant lie about the geothermal vent, exploiting everyone!"

Chairman Shin gazes at me, looking impressed.

"So you had figured it out," she says. "That Snowglobe is not powered by any natural miracle. There is no geothermal vent—it's just propaganda they peddle to keep people from asking where the energy really comes from."

I nod gravely.

She continues, "What the founding president was looking for when she founded Snowglobe was not some rare geothermal site but a completely uninhabited land where she could build an illicit subterranean power plant without anyone's scrutiny . . . Get it? The founder had already completed the power plant before my family got involved with the dome, so for the most part, it's always been off-limits to us. We know almost nothing about it, aside from that it exists."

I recall the gigantic glass tower deep below the surface, filled with sweaty prisoners spinning in their gearlike wheels like hamsters, unable to stop.

Chairman Shin explains that had her family built the power plant, it would have been automated, like most systems in Snowglobe. But the Yibonns built a power plant requiring human labor—allowing their family, not the Shins, to maintain absolute control of it, and cementing its status as their most vital secret. The power plant is, essentially, what legitimizes Snowglobe and the Yibonns' hold of it.

"Miss Chobahm," she says, her voice suddenly resolute. "Do what I'm unable to do for me. Go to the power plant and shut it down."

Shut it down.

That would freeze Snowglobe. It would expose the truth that Snowglobe is not some magical oasis, but rather a place built on the backs of others. And once that happens . . . all order could be lost. Chaos could take over the world.

A shiver running through me, my teeth begin to chatter.

"Chairman Shin, what do you think the world will look like when the power plant halts?"

"Here's my answer," she says after a moment, placing her right hand on the tabletop and making a tight fist. In the next moment, a pain so sharp and excruciating grips me in the chest, right where I'm wearing the plastic heart. It's as if a stake is being driven through my own heart. Breathless with pain, I drop to the floor.

"Breathe in . . . Breathe out . . ." Chairman Shin calmly advises. "Slowly and deeply. Come on, you can do it."

But I can't! I gasp for breath, with my heart rate suddenly so high that I'm scared it will explode.

"Don't be scared. What you're experiencing now is all part of the adjustment," Chairman Shin assures me as I stare at her from the floor, terrified and uncomprehending.

"The plastic patch on your chest," she explains, her voice with rising excitement. "It's a cardioverter! It turns up your heart rate to crank up your core temperature. You know how you get hot when you run? Same principle!"

My heart keeps racing as if it's about to kick out of my chest, but nevertheless her explanation has a comforting effect.

"How is this thing possible?" I manage in a minute, my voice hoarse from the strain I'm under.

"It's more than a cardioverter, in fact," Chairman Shin replies, grinning. "Heart rate, blood flow, respiration, digestion, et cetera, the device converts the body's energy output into electricity and stores it."

"Respiration . . . ? You mean it collects energy even as I breathe, and turns that into electricity?"

Chairman Shin runs her fingers through her faux-fur coat.

"Yes—and it uses that electricity to turn the clothes you're wearing into heatware, for instance. Though that ability is limited to performance fabric."

I stroke the faux fur of my coat. She's right. It's radiating significant heat.

"To bring down this dome and the Yibonn," Chairman Shin says, now gazing down at the world below, where morning unfolds. "I knew a revolutionary technology was required. Demolishing the current order wouldn't be worth it if our society devolves back to what it was like during the Warring Age."

So it was that she began secretly developing the cardioverter, she explains. And after years of blood, sweat, and tears, her invention was finally perfected, to the point where public adoption at last became viable. Disabled as she is, however, she first needed to find the right candidate who could help make her plan a reality—by shutting down the underground power plant for good and revealing the truth about Snowglobe's energy source.

A breeze flutters Chairman Shin's obsidian hair across her pale forehead.

"President Yi forcing me to access your conversation with the heir will go down in history as the pivotal moment that ushered in the end of the Yibonn regime. After all, that's how I found my future partner, Jeon Chobahm."

Partner . . . ?

"What do you say?" Chairman Shin plows on. "Would you join hands with me in bringing in a new world?"

I contemplate the question. If only this technology had been made available sooner . . . Dad would have survived the brutal cold exposure he'd sustained to save the people trapped in the stalled bus when Mom was pregnant with Ongi and me. In that world of Chairman Shin's, where ordinary people could take leisurely walks outside as if they lived in Snowglobe, he and Mom would have taken thousands of walks together, hand in hand. Tears well up at these thoughts, and my heart begins a slow pounding, but it is not the doing of the cardioverter.

There's nothing more to think about.

"It'd be my honor, Chairman Shin," I tell her, my heart swelling with the exhilaration of a journey beginning.

"Excellent!" she exclaims. "First, let's get some breakfast, and then we'll get you ready to head right over to the plant.

We'll need to be quick if we want to stay a step ahead of the cunning presi—" Reading my face, she draws up short. "Is everything okay?"

"I'm sorry . . . but I, I can't just leave."

"Why?" she demands. "Are you scared?"

"No! No!" I rush to deny. "But Miryu must be worried sick by now. I've been gone for hours and she has no idea where . . . and so must be Ongi and Hyang, and—"

Chairman Shin's great sigh of relief cuts me off.

"You can just call them," she says, as if it's a no-brainer. "Any time before you leave. And however many times you want!"

But that's not all. I tell her that the Yibonn has been following me since the museum, and that the president is sure to grow suspicious if I suddenly fall out of her radar like that.

*In fact, please do nothing, really. Don't try to escape the course I've already plotted for you, or attempt to plot your own course. Just follow where you're led.*

"If the president discovers that I've infiltrated the underground power plant, then everyone will pay the price—Ongi, Hyang, Miryu, Somyung, Shinae . . . and maybe even Serin," I continue breathlessly. "And of course, you, Chairman Shin, for disregarding her directive to delete me from the mirror system, among other things."

"And that is precisely why you need to head over right away—"

"Please let me find another way," I plead, but firmly. "Let me find a way to avoid the Yibonn's attention and get there safely."

Chairman Shin regards me warily. It is a long moment before she nods her acquiescence.

"I believe in you," she says, gazing into me with grave solemnity. "And in your commitment. But please remember: There won't be another chance for us."

# A MAN-MADE DISASTER

n the dressing room of the studio, Serin shoves a sheaf of
paper to me.

"Have you even read the script I wrote?" she accuses right
away.

I take the stack and skim the first few pages. They're crammed
with lines she carefully planned out for our upcoming joint
weather gig. I'm too tired to hide how tired I am.

"Just run the show, will you? I'll jump in when I see fit," I
tell her, which sets her off even more.

Snatching up the paper and throwing it on the floor, she
lashes out. "Do you think this is a joke? Jump in? Why? So
viewers will think that I'm hogging airtime?"

I haven't slept a wink since meeting with Chairman Shin
three days ago. Not that I haven't tried. It's just that my brain
won't shut off, and Serin's fighting words only heighten my
exhaustion.

I want to get Hyang's or Miryu's take on the mission I got
myself involved in, but Hyang is chained to her desk at work,

and Miryu has been sitting vigil at the hospital with Wednesday, caring for Thursday, who remains unconscious.

"Look. I'm too tired to argue right now, so leave me alone," I say, appending a sarcastic please.

She huffs, "You think I'm speaking to you because I enjoy it? This is work! Do you get it?! Work—"

Just then, the door eases open and Producer Yi Dahm walks into the dressing room, saving me from further harsh words. Serin swiftly banishes her scowl and begins picking up the pages strewn on the floor.

"Hello, girls—" Producer Yi chimes, forcing an awkward smile.

Color rises to my face at the memory of me, Somyung, and Hyang taking over Producer Yi's Control Room at gunpoint, but I return her greeting the best I can, smiling awkwardly in an unspoken acknowledgment of our fraught history.

Serin chirps her greeting, and Producer Yi marvels, "Whoa… I'm seriously hard pressed to tell who's who."

She isn't kidding. It was our new makeup artist/stylist, Goh Sanghui's replacement, who turned us into carbon copies of each other despite our protests to the contrary. I can still see her self-satisfied expression as she took a step back and assessed her work.

Pushing through my guilt and embarrassment, I apologize to the producer for the unpleasantness we'd caused in her Control Room the day of the exposé. It's far too little, too late, I know that, and I chastise myself for not saying sorry sooner. I saw her at Fran's wedding, and I could have apologized then, had everything not gone haywire for me with Buhae.

Producer Yi just casts her gaze out the wraparound

window where, on the other side of the glass, the bubble disaster rages on.

"Even the most overpriced bath bombs I own don't produce this many suds . . ." she muses with a sigh, completely ignoring my apology.

Serin and I turn our attention outside, too. Far below us, mounds of bubbling soap suds, mostly pink and purple with occasional clumps of yellow and green, collect on the streets like thunderheads forming on the ground.

"I've heard that the people in the raincoats and galoshes business are making a killing," Producer Yi continues. "Did you know that?"

I didn't, but it comes as no surprise. Who wants to walk around in soggy shoes and clothes?

"Needless to say, directors are ecstatic about all the chaos unfolding, as it injects drama into shows," she says. "In the open world, a sort of bubble mania is said to be sweeping through our youngest viewers who don't comprehend the gravity of the situation. They're apparently dying to visit the Bubble Kingdom, as they call it. I guess every cloud has a silver lining, wouldn't you say?"

I'm not sure what she's getting at, or how I'm supposed to react. Victims of the current disaster are already in the thousands, and even for those who haven't suffered physical injuries, hardly anyone is unaffected by it one way or another. As Serin and I stall for a response, the producer continues, "I'm telling you this so you don't stress yourselves out over the livecast—like Fran, you know?"

Serin and I share a glance. I get it now. Until the disaster ends, which will happen on the exact hour and day specified by the winner—the person whose disaster slip was chosen to begin with—the nightly weather segment includes news of it. And with the all-star lineup of past weathercasters filling in for Fran each night, *News at 9* has been drawing a massive audience, as if it hadn't been already.

"I was thinking," Producer Yi says, her eyes suddenly shining with a kind of giddiness, "that we'll finally reveal the winner tonight."

"Tonight?" Serin exclaims after a moment. "I assumed that Fran would do it when he comes back tomorrow?"

"That was the plan," Producer Yi says, grinning. "But people are getting real antsy about the delay now—and who can blame them? The reveal has always been on the first day of a disaster, but as you know, Fran being gone shook things up."

"I know!" Serin agrees with an emphatic nod.

"Plus, a surprise reveal tonight by you two? What a treat it's going to be for the viewers!" Producer Yi enthuses, looking from Serin to me; and all I can see in her eyes are sharply rising ratings charts. Two Haeris revealing the winner of this year's disaster. Producer Yi is not Producer Yi for nothing.

Eagerly, Serin and Producer Yi begin revising the script together. I steal a glance at the full-length mirror hanging on the wall, envisioning myself shutting down the underground power plant and cutting off the heat it supplies to Snowglobe.

But now's not the time. Not yet.

**"Ms. Chobahm—"** Serin calls in an overly sweet tone, while savagely kicking me in the ankle with her sharp-toed shoe. She gazes at me with smiling eyes, hate simmering just below their surface. The message in them is clear. *What the hell? Wake up!*

I put on a quick smile and call back, "Yes, Ms. Serin . . ."

With anxiety over the underground plant distracting me, I keep drifting in and out of the livecast. The lights in the studio are as harsh as ever, and the red letters glowing LIVE above the giant camera before us are no less intimidating than the last time.

Serin's shoe meets my ankle for the second time, and I almost cry out loud before remembering to deliver my line. "To all of you out there who've been waiting for this moment with bated breath . . . we're honored to be finally revealing this year's winner . . ."

Then Serin is unlocking the safe sitting on the stand between us and taking out the gold envelope.

"Would you, Ms. Chobahm?" Serin says, holding out the envelope to me.

"But I'd like you to, Ms. Serin," I say.

And we go through the motions of deferring the honor and privilege to one another before Serin pretends sweet surrender.

"The winner—the imaginative viewer who provided the idea for this year's disaster—is Miss Jung Ihyun in Ba-J-9," Serin announces. A bright smile for the camera, and then she proceeds to reading the postcard:

" 'Hello! My name is Jung Ihyun. I'm in fourth grade and I live in Ba-J-9. I got a bubble gun for my birthday yesterday, and it's so much fun . . .' "

From the awkward, but careful, handwriting that keeps slanting to the right, to the cartoonish bubbles hand-drawn in pink and purple crayons, I feel the nine-year-old viewer's innocence and wonder at the world. I picture her excitement and disbelief at the sight of bubbles dumping from the sky on the first day of the disaster, and her family's delight at the financial prize I know will accompany her win, which should be enough to provide economic relief for a full year.

Inevitably, there will be people with connections to Snowglobe who will resent the girl for her innocent idea that's causing so much grief and destruction in the community, but the majority of people will be happy for her. Just like we were for Suji when she won the contest some years ago. *Here comes the star of the year—Suji!*

" 'If I win, I'd like the disaster to begin about three days after the drawing . . . ,' " Serin continues reading. " 'Because my favorite part of any present is the anticipation, and so it would stretch out the fun part. Anyway, it'd be amazing to see a blizzard of bubbles in Snowglobe.' "

Amazing indeed. The untold number of victims so far, umbrella and rain gear makers rejoicing in skyrocketing sales, media people celebrating the boost in ratings, and even the nine-year-old winner are all just cogs moving inside the devious machination of the Yibonn. My blood begins to boil again at the thought, and as I remind myself that I'm on live TV, a new impulse comes to me. What's stopping me from telling the truth right here and now? Yeah, why not? Why not expose the Yibonn in all its atrocities? Isn't this the perfect stage?

But Producer Yi wouldn't just sit back and let me finish. Of course not. A push of a button by her would kill the camera.

*But please remember: There won't be another chance.*

No. I cannot ruin Chairman Shin's plan with a rash act. I calm my quickening breaths the best I can, when the earpiece transmits Producer Yi's flustered voice.

"Hi, girls . . . Looks like we've just received some breaking news? Um . . . we put it out on the ticker, but I think you guys should announce it to the viewers . . ."

I glance up at the live monitor to see myself standing next to Serin, whose smile freezes as she tracks the text scrolling along at the bottom of the screen.

BREAKING NEWS: PLANE CARRYING MR. YI BONWHE
GOES MISSING AFTER LOSING CONTACT WITH AIR
TRAFFIC CONTROL

What . . . ?

Producer Yi's voice rings in my ear like it's coming from the bottom of the ocean.

"Details are just coming in. I'll put them on the teleprompter . . . Serin? I want you to read."

A train of white letters appears on the prompter's black screen. I read them over and over, but I can't seem to make sense of them.

Then Serin says, "Um . . . one moment, folks . . . I'm told we have some breaking news . . ." The on-air calm she projects despite the distress she, too, must be under, is impressive. "Reports are coming in that the private jet carrying Mr. Yi Bonwhe has crashed on its way to outer-world district Ja-P-22 upon encountering bad weather. Authorities are still trying to reestablish contact with the pilot . . ."

I stare blankly at Serin in the monitor, my head buzzing.

"According to the Yibonn spokesperson, Mr. Yi Bonwhe was traveling to Ja-P-22 as part of Yibonn Media's corporate mission to visit the families affected by the Goh Haeri project and offer them an official apology . . . ," she continues, snatching a quick glance at me. "The accident took place in remote terrain leading to Ja-P-22, Miss Jeon Chobahm's settlement. Other personnel aboard included Mr. Yi Bonwhe's personal assistant, as well as his physician . . ."

This sucks the last breath out of me. The plane crashed on his way to visit my family . . . ? Even at the surface level, the association is unsettling. Is it truly an accident, or President Yi's doing?

*Remember. If you pose a threat to the system, your loved ones will go down—one by one. And whether they're my blood or yours matters not to me.*

But I didn't do anything! At least not yet. Has the president already found out that I met with Chairman Shin? And why Bonwhe, her own heir? Is this some sort of sick, preemptive warning? Like, *You better back off, right now?*

In the monitor, Serin's eyes have gone glassy. I take my eyes off the monitor and glance at her quavering next to me, my head blank. The winning postcard is still clutched in her hand, and I absently note seventeen days written on it in childish script. In the next moment, the meaning of it hits me. Seventeen days . . . is the duration of this year's disaster as requested by the nine-year-old winner in the open world. Her rationale? I read on—of course. March seventeenth is her birthday. In the margin is a quick note highlighted in yellow from the editing team, reminding us not to announce the duration.

I, too, used to send in those disaster ideas—every year without fail—until I was in the sixth grade. In fact, I used to spend significant mental resources trying to come up with the most extraordinary disaster idea no one had ever thought of, imagining that winning the lottery and having my idea come to life in Snowglobe would be just as fantastic as directing a show one day. Not once did I think about the consequences of my outrageous ideas, their possible effects on the real-life people living in Snowglobe. I shudder, suddenly deeply grateful that my disaster ideas were never given a chance to see the light of day.

Then I twitch again at the absurdity of it all. No one dares question the point of these disasters. No one realizes that we've been dancing to the Yibonn's mad drumbeats, or that we can stop. But I do.

# GONE

"**D**ear viewers—once again, we interrupt regular programming for this breaking news. The private jet headed to Ja-P-22 with Mr. Yi Bonwhe aboard crashed shortly after losing contact with air traffic control. The last communication with the pilot indicates that the plane was caught in a severe snowstorm still raging in the area. This is a developing story, and we will keep you updated as new information comes in," Serin finishes reading the prompter.

Through the earpiece, Producer Yi's instruction follows that we resume the weather drawing right away, her voice wavering with the effort of holding back the tears. Serin shoots me a panicked glance.

It's obvious that we're all reeling from the shock of this particular breaking news. Less obvious is that it has also thrown off Serin and me, and now neither of us seems to know how to gracefully regain our footing. Helplessly, I scan the grim faces of staff surrounding the set, conscious of the prolonged, heavy silence reigning in the studio. Such dead air would normally have triggered a heart attack in Producer Yi, but the current circumstances are anything but normal. She doesn't rush us.

*Please watch yourself, Bonwhe.*

If only I'd been a little less cryptic when warning him of President Yi's plans! Could I have stopped him from getting on that plane? But how? How was he to know his own relative would go to these lengths to punish him for our conversation the day of the exposé? How was I to know? Killing someone in a plane crash and blaming it on the eternally bad weather of the open world is so over the top, it's almost unbelievable. Isn't it?

But even if I'd somehow learned about the future crash and told him about it . . . if someone had warned me that my grandmother—my own blood—was going to try to kill me, would I have believed the messenger?

Stop! I will myself. Just stop! All of these are just excuses to justify my own shortcomings—my own inaction. I'm unraveling.

*Our conversation on the day of the exposé . . . Did you tell anyone about it?*

I'd asked Bonwhe that, but I didn't fully trust his answer. I was distrustful of him is more accurate. At my deepest core, I could never believe that he hadn't confided in his grandmother and told her everything of our phone call, including my knowledge of the secret power plant. On some level, I believed that we could never be true allies. Bonwhe was a Yibonn; and I told myself that I couldn't afford to care about a Yibonn when my own people's lives were on the line.

I'm too ashamed to even ask for forgiveness, not that there's time for it now.

Bonwhe's face continues to linger in my vision as a terrible memory intrudes—of Cooper tumbling violently through thin air thousands of feet above the glacier below. Something hot and painful rises from deep down in my core, and I'm suddenly wheezing and choking with tears on live TV.

Next to me, Serin watches me in distress. I grasp her shoulder for support, trying not to tremble, and she not only makes herself available but turns to actively hug me—before surreptitiously twisting away from the camera and muting her microphone.

"Yes, you should cry," she whispers. "The tragedy happened on Young Master's way to visit your family, after all."

When she pulls back, the glance she sneaks at me carries her meaning. *Behave well. People are watching you.* My blood growing cold, I picture President Yi watching me on TV right now, a rich little smile pressed on her lips at how gutted I am with terror and guilt over Bonwhe's "accident."

Jeon Chobahm. Get it together and manage your face—right now.

I gather myself and face the camera. Making my voice as appropriately professional as possible, I deliver my line.

"Then let us resume the weather drawing . . ."

Should I unravel with guilt or beg for Bonwhe's forgiveness, it will not be a public performance. President Yi will not break me.


**Outside the SnowTower, the bubble storm that raged all day** seems to be relenting, at last, giving plow trucks a fighting chance at a cleanup before the next big dump. The roads are slick with colorful, foaming slush. Traffic is bumper to bumper with cars and trucks hastily fitted with out-of-season snow chains and studded tires, their trunks and backseats stuffed with panic-purchased groceries and other necessities. On sidewalks, pedestrians sporting cleated galoshes gingerly navigate their next steps. As Serin and I wait for our ride on the curb, a few passersby notice us and do a double take. Serin drops her face and mutters, "Be there soon, my ass."

It's only been a few minutes, but I have to admit that Hyang couldn't come faster. Up ahead, a puppy out on a walk with its owner slips on the slick pavement and slides sideways into a nearby foam drift despite the spikes under his doggy boots. I drop my head, wishing to disappear, when a couple makes a beeline for us.

"I wish you'd picked better weather for tomorrow," the guy says with an edge of resentment he doesn't bother to hide. His girlfriend openly glares at me, her eyes red and swollen from crying.

"Personal apology to family . . . Was that your request?" she accuses.

I give her a blank stare.

She continues. "It's Cha Seol and Cha Guibahng who did what they did to you girls—not Mr. Bonwhe! Why should he . . ." She trails off, overcome with emotion. Her man squeezes her to him, shooting me a look.

"At least pray for decent weather for the search party," he says in a tone screaming that all this is my fault. I want to remind him we can't even control the weather in the open world.

"Let's get a taxi," Serin says to me, already waving her hand to hail one.

Hyang's car finally appears then.

"Sorry, we're late!" Miryu apologizes from behind the wheel. "There's a parking ban right now so we had to circle the block."

Serin and I practically dive into the backseat as another couple passing by is heard saying, "Did you watch the news? Did you see that Chobahm girl resuming the drawing as if she didn't have a care in the world?"

"I know—she is a piece of work, isn't she? The awful crash happened on his way to her family, for Christ's sake . . ."

It's not a gratuitous conversation they're having for my benefit. They didn't even see me, and it cuts deeper.

Slamming the car door shut, Serin tut-tuts, "See? Didn't I tell you to cry?"

From the passenger seat, Hyang lets out a languorous yawn, having pulled an all-nighter two nights in a row while editing tonight's episode of *You, Me, and Us,* which airs directly after *News at 9.* Behind us, a taxi blares its horn in a burst of impatience, and Miryu steps on the gas.

As we merge onto the road, I happen to glance up at the rearview mirror in time to see a black sedan pulling out from behind the taxi. It's the same black sedan that had been idling on the curb outside the SnowTower as Serin and I waited for Miryu and Hyang. It had been blinking its yellow emergency lights, and I remember wondering if that was why parking enforcement officers were letting it idle there for so long. The officers seemed suspiciously generous only toward that black sedan.

"I have something to tell you all," I say, my tone more

solemn than I intended. With the hypnotic spell I'd been subjected to overcome and the privacy of the car keeping my words protected, I can finally tell them how I got caught in the Yibonn's crosshairs. Only directors can view the unedited footage from their shows, meaning only Hyang will be privy to the recordings of what I'm about to admit after the fact.

It's now . . . or never. I take a long breath and continue, "Snowglobe's warmth doesn't come from a natural geothermal vent. It's a big fat lie by the Yibonn."

Miryu slams on the brakes, earning the ire of the driver behind us, who promptly lays on their horn. Hyang, who had opened her mouth wide for another loud, drawn-out yawn, turns around in her seat, her face contorted in shock.

"I'll fill you in on everything while we drive. It's a long story," I tell them.

In the cacophony of furiously blaring horns, Miryu puts the car back in gear, and soon I'm spilling it all: from the mirror and the underground power plant to Buhae's hypnosis. All the while, I know the pinhole camera hiding in the dashboard clock is recording everything. While the public believes that no one, not even the president, has access to an actor's footage apart from their director, I now know that she does. Which is why I'm leaving out the part about my meeting with Chairman Shin, and only talking about my plan to go shut down the underground plant that will expose the truth.

"What did you just say?" Hyang says as I finish my last sentence.

Miryu's eyes in the rearview mirror gaze at me worriedly. I repeat, "I'm going to go missing for a little while."

At the studio, I drew a twelve-inch-per-hour "bubble bomb" for tomorrow's weather, and my heart sank, feeling as though things couldn't get any worse. But when I saw that puppy being swallowed by a thick suds-drift outside, something tickled in my brain. The disastrous conditions might just prove an opportunity.

"By noon tomorrow, the city will have been inundated by huge drifts of suds heaping up everywhere, which will help me evade the cameras while I travel to the mirror. Then when I'm gone at the power plant and drop off the radar all together, we can blame it on the suds. Say I went missing in the disaster, or something."

I elaborate on the details of my plan to travel underground and switch off the power plant's main motor to cut off Snowglobe's heat supply.

"And where's this mirror?" Miryu wants to know, trying hard to stay focused on the road while processing all this.

I think about it. There are several that I've encountered, though most would be difficult, if not impossible, to access or to avoid the spy's attention. One in the Yibonn mansion, one in the SnowTower, one in Chairman Shin's field office, and the last one in . . .

"The forest—the restricted zone," I tell her.

In the distance beyond the city limits, the dense forest stands darkly against the domed backdrop, its treetops heavy with suds.

Hyang objects, "But you don't know what trouble you'll encounter once you get there. It's a ridiculously risky and irresponsible plan—"

"I'm going with you," Miryu declares.

"What?!" Hyang balks.

"I'm going with you, Chobahm—underground, above-ground, between ground, wherever."

Serin, who's been listening silently the whole time, finally speaks up.

"Hold on," she says, with an incredulous laugh. "You're not seriously scheming to bring down the Yibonn right now, are you?"

When I don't deny it, her jaw drops with astonishment. Turning to Miryu, she says, "So you weren't bullshitting when you told me that the president was watching her? I just thought it was a ridiculous story you pathetically came up with to make me forgive her for going through my room. I mean . . . who would imagine that the almighty Yibonn would bother with someone like her, much less frame her for a murder?"

Her tone makes me grit my teeth. Miryu had already given Serin a heads-up on my troubles—or at least tried to—when she brought Serin back home after she'd stormed out of the house following our epic fight in her room. Still, Serin isn't convinced. She pins me with her contemptuous eyes and demands, "And why, exactly, are you disclosing all this information now—with me in the audience? Since when did you trust me?"

*I don't,* I want to answer. It feels entirely surreal that I've come to the point where I find myself forced to seek her cooperation. Bae Serin's cooperation. Not that I foresee her offering it—not without some great big fuss, anyway.

"I . . . I need you to do me a favor while I'm underground," I begin.

She makes a face, which is as expected, but she doesn't immediately shoot down the request.

"What is it?" she says suspiciously.

"Can you be me while I'm gone?"

"What are you talking about?"

"I'll be lost in the disaster as you, Bae Serin. And you'll be Jeon Chobahm and stay here, under the president's radar."

Our car rolls to a stop at the light, and Hyang and Miryu twist in their seats to gape at me.

I continue, "Because feigning my disappearance will only work for so long. When Jeon Chobahm doesn't turn up after a while, the president will be sure to grow suspicious."

And that will put everyone I love in danger.

"Are you saying that Yibonn is tracking you around the clock? Even as we speak?" Serin says with a chuff of a disbelieving laugh.

"Yes. I believe so," I tell her, my eyes on the black sedan in the rearview mirror, which is aggressively weaving back into our lane.

We fall quiet. The light changes to green, and we turn onto the quiet residential block of our neighborhood, the black sedan still trailing behind us. The sedan's windows, tinted far beyond the legal limit, don't allow a glimpse inside.

"Why me, though?" Serin says, breaking the short silence, and she sounds genuinely curious. "Shinae or Somyung could do that job, too."

I open my mouth to answer when we see our street awash in the flashing red and blue lights of police cruisers parked outside our two-story home. Somyung and Ongi are talking to the officers in the front yard as Shinae looks on anxiously from the front steps. Miryu presses down on the brake when

Shinae spots our car and shoots a strong look of warning, shaking her head side to side ever so slightly.

"Is she telling us to run?" Serin wonders aloud—a moment too late.

Hyang's already swung her door open and stepped out of the car.

"Excuse me," she yells indignantly, striding over to the cruisers. "Can I help you?!"

A police officer with a somber expression pivots on his heels. Tipping his hat only slightly, he says, "Are you Director Cha Hyang?"

"Yes, I am," Hyang confirms. "What's the matter?"

"We need you to come with us for investigation," he says as two other officers step out of the shadows and flank her.

"What?! What investigation?" Hyang protests, outraged. "And do you have any idea what time it is?"

The severe-faced officer reaches down for the handcuffs dangling from his duty belt. He says, "Director Cha Hyang, you're under arrest on suspicion of abuse of editorial power."

Hyang's head snaps hard in my direction, and she throws me a wild look of disbelief.

# IN MY SHOES

The police officer explains that the crime report alleges intentional omission of some pivotal footage, relating to a very important scene in this week's episode of *You, Me, and Us*. I don't need to ask to know which scene they're talking about. I'm sure it's the one in which Jeon Chobahm stabs Goh Maeryung in bed.

But I didn't report Hyang. Yes, I did threaten to do so, but I'd never actually follow through on it. Returning Hyang's stare, I shake my head in denial. And somehow, that's enough. Hyang believes me. Summoning her righteous indignation, she begins bluffing away at the officer with renewed authority.

"Do you even know what you're talking about?! How would anyone even find out that a scene was falsified, even if it was?" she shrills.

*No one could know, except the president,* I'm thinking. The woman doesn't need to see the footage to know that it exists—because she's the one who orchestrated the murder.

Hyang continues, her voice rising another decibel, "Is it

your job to arrest innocent citizens left and right on baseless accusations? Is it? Is it?!"

The officer appears momentarily stumped.

"We . . . we've been dispatched on a report filed by Director Jang Soohyun," he allows after a moment.

"Director who?" Hyang says, narrowing her eyes.

"Director Jang, who's recently been put in charge of the Goh Maeryung show, and thus has access to relevant recordings," the officer clarifies. "She reported that some critical footage that should have been incorporated into this week's episode of *You, Me, and Us* has been intentionally left out."

Hands on her hips, Hyang opens her mouth to gather a response, but she can't quite manage one. Meanwhile, Somyung, Shinae, and Ongi have moved to stand behind Hyang, looking bewildered as they attempt to make sense of the situation.

Miryu steps in front of Hyang and takes over for her. "Look, Officer. It's only been minutes since the episode aired. That's not enough time for a police report or anything . . ."

Then a sneer flickers across the officer's face. He glances around at us before replying, "Didn't you argue about this yourselves on live TV—that directors should be held accountable for wrongdoings? The laws have been tightened since then."

As the other officers nod in agreement and support, he continues, "Directors and actors are finally equal in the eyes of the law. Please. Whether you're guilty or not, we need you to cooperate with law enforcement now."

I look around to see that a crowd has gathered, thanks to the police cruisers' dazzling light and sound display advertising a disturbance in our usually sleepy neighborhood. Beyond them in the near distance, the black sedan idles watchfully on the curb.

At once, Somyung, Shinae, and Ongi begin protesting the arrest, while Hyang tries to calm them. The officer isn't wrong. We did make a stance about directors and actors being treated equally, and we can't go against those words and make an exception for Hyang. Still, Miryu has a hard time accepting Hyang's arrest.

"You know it's a trap," she says to Hyang in a low voice. "They'll try to heap other charges on you and strip you of your director status."

With a sly grin, Hyang says, "Don't worry, babe. I'm squeaky clean—never even got so much as a traffic ticket," before following the officers to the cruisers.

Miryu starts for Hyang's car, insisting that she accompany her to the police station, but Serin stops her. Serin then whispers something to Miryu, and a moment later, Miryu swiftly turns and heads for the garage, to her own car. Somyung, Shinae, and Ongi rush after her. I move to follow them, but Serin grabs my hand and shoves me into Hyang's car, which is still idling at the curb with its doors wide open.

"What are you doing?" I shriek.

"Wake up, Jeon Chobahm!" she hisses. "What are we accomplishing by following Hyang to the police station like lemmings? You need to prepare yourself for the worst-case scenario!"

"What worst case?" I ask.

"What if Hyang gets fired from the show?" Serin replies tersely.

"What?"

"We'll get a new director, who'll review our recordings,

including that which we just produced in the car ride a minute ago. Once the Yibonn realize we know their secret, we're all screwed—including me!" Her fury boiling up anew, she grabs me by the shoulders, whisper-shouting, "How dare you suck me into this mess?! How dare you!"

I hate to admit it, but she's right. The last camera break was a while ago, so we're due for another soon. No matter what, I must prevent our conversation in the car ride from being made public—and probably this one, too. But how?

I look her in the eyes. "We need to destroy the car cameras before they transmit the footage during the next break."

She starts. "What? That's illegal—"

"If you don't want our conversation getting out, it's the only way," I interject. "We can come up with an excuse— make it look like an accident. But we have to do it. What do you say?"

Serin stares at me for a long time, seething with fury, her hands still gripping my shoulders. Then, just as I'm about to give up hope, she nods.

I feel a swell of relief. Then Ongi suddenly appears outside the car, knocking on the window and asking, "You're not coming?"

I roll down the window and tell him that Serin and I have some business to take care of, which prompts a dubious look from Ongi. He glances back and forth between me and Serin, contemplating my answer. Then he says, "Can I help?" which is maddening.

I picture him joining me and Serin in destroying all the cameras rolling in their hiding places in this car. No way. That would make him an accomplice.

"*Oppa*," I say then, which causes him to flinch and draw back. As he stares at me, disoriented, I follow up with a one-two punch. "Kim Seolwon, Yi Woon . . . You still remember them, don't you?"

"Yes . . . yes, of course," he says.

I've just invoked the names of the fake researchers Hyang and I played when we'd boarded his train on the way to find Somyung and Shinae. When we'd parted ways, Ongi had vowed to remember them, saying he hoped their paths would cross again someday.

"They asked me and Serin for a small favor. A tiny one, really. We'll get it done and catch up to you guys."

From Miryu's car, Shinae calls out to Ongi, her tone irritated. Reluctantly, he turns back to the garage, saying, "I'll call you guys when we get to the police station!"

A minute later, the police cruisers are finally rolling away, trailed by Miryu's car. The crowd slowly disperses, but the black sedan remains where it is, idling near the curb.

As nonchalantly as we can manage, Serin and I collect gardening shears, a hammer, a mallet, and other tools from the tool shed at the back of the house and bring them inside Hyang's car. In a few minutes, all six of the cameras within the vehicle are thoroughly smashed to pieces.

"You know . . . regarding my proposal. About you pretending to be me when I'm gone," I begin tentatively as we sit back and take stock of our handiwork, our breathing just returning to normal. "If it'd help you make a decision, I can tell you right now: if you help me, I'll help you—"

"Can you just shut up?" Serin cuts me off, holding up a

stray camera cable and snipping it clean through with her garden shears. "I swear I'm going to explode." Then throwing the garden shears down, she looks around the car and says, "Let's burn it to the ground."

"You can't be serious," I say with a laugh. "Right now? Right here in our neighborhood so everyone can see?!"

"Well, do you know how to drive?"

I just stare at her.

She continues, "We could drive it into the sea and ditch it there."

I frown an instant disapproval, ready to tell her that such a move would only draw the president's attention faster.

*Clack!*

Light beams shoot out of the lenses of the broken and mangled, but apparently undead, cameras around us and checker the car's dark interior.

". . . *Nooooo!*" Serin wails tragically. I stay silent but clench my fists. Dammit. We failed.

Half a minute later, she's screaming at me, "What are we going to do now? What if the Yibonn come after me, too, because of you?!"

I gather myself.

"I guess you have no choice but to help me defeat them, then."

"What?" she breathes, her eyes burning with fury and contempt. "I'd rather die by the hands of the Yibonn than see you act like some kind of hero," she growls through clenched teeth.

I scoff. "You hate me that much?"

"Yes," she rebuts immediately.

"Why?"

"Why? Why? Because everyone everywhere thinks that you're such a big deal, when I know you're not worthy of even a fraction of their love and attention. You're nothing special!"

"You can have all of that, Bae Serin. I'll give it all to you!"

With the slates changing and the cameras off, and Hyang and Miryu gone to the police station, now is the best time to broach the subject again. I go on. "Say I don't make it back from the underground plant . . . our show doesn't have to end. I'm nothing special—I admit it myself. But if you take my place while I'm gone and pretend to be me, you could go on living as me forever. As Jeon Chobahm, the girl who gets all the love and attention, regardless of her talent. I'll leave my legacy to you."

Serin's face, staring at me, seems to soften a bit, and she cocks her head to one side and looks me up and down a few times.

"Why wouldn't you make it back from the plant?" she wants to know, sounding hopeful. "Is the secret power plant such a dangerous place?"

The simple truth is that I don't know. No one knows. Even the genius architect of the Snowglobe dome herself, who also designed the mirror system, doesn't know much about its goings-on at the plant. I have a strong suspicion that the inmates working the wheels, including the man with the tiny heart tattoo under his eye who I saw during my first visit, are under some kind of hypnotic spells themselves. Behind their dazed eyes, there was no awareness or agency, no desire to escape their fate. What had happened to them? Did the Yibonn drug their drinking water? Poison the air they breathe?

There's no guarantee that I won't become one of them once I get there, and spend the rest of my life stuck inside one of those wheels, running to nowhere without a thought in my mind. I suppose it's also entirely possible that I'll be found out before I can accomplish anything and be banished, or killed, by the president. Which option is worse? I can't decide.

"Is that a real possibility? You not making it back?" Serin presses, her worry overshadowed by growing excitement.

I just shrug for now. In her dome-top office that day, Chairman Shin told me, *If you don't make it back after a reasonable time has passed, I'll go find you myself. Wheelchair and all—and that is a promise.*

I turned down the offer right then and there, because if something were to happen to Chairman Shin, our chance to overthrow the Yibonn would be lost forever. A foot soldier like me can be replaced, but never the chief—never the mastermind.

When a more reassuring answer doesn't come, Serin moves on to her next question.

"And what if you make it back? Then you get to be the hero, and I gain nothing?"

She waits for my answer, already looking disgusted.

"If I make it back," I begin, silencing my ego and reaching for her hand, "that'd mean the mission was a success. The age of the Yibonn will be over, and a new world will begin. Then . . ." I stall, struggling to finish my thought.

"Then what?" Serin presses with snotty impatience.

"It's quite simple. I'll come back as Serin, so you'll get the hero's return—and all the credit for bringing down the Yibonn. Be me for a while, and if I succeed in my mission, we can swap back when I return. You'll get all the glory."

It just came to me a moment ago—an irresistible offer Serin would be hard-pressed to turn down.

"You'd be Serin, the heroine who single-handedly shut down the secret power plant and exposed the ugly lie of Snowglobe, of the Yibonn. Imagine the love and respect that'd flood your way. It would be enough to last the rest of your life. No mere Haeri could achieve that."

Chairman Shin must know a thing or two about rewriting history, after all—what to embellish and what to mute, who to lionize and who to sacrifice . . .

As I reflect on these possibilities and all that lies ahead, a sudden, powerful terror comes up on me unawares, and I burst out sobbing. Serin jumps up with a shriek and stares at me with extreme annoyance.

# SWIMMING UNDERWATER—INCOGNITO

Sometimes, when you lie in bed at night, the dread that consumes you is triggered by the thought of waking up the next day only to repeat it all over again. The ceaseless routine of your so-called life. There's no hope for a better future, or even just a different one. You're spinning the hamster wheel in place, day in and day out until the day you die—unless you make it into Snowglobe, and everything changes. Or at least, that's what I used to think.

So no matter how exhausted I was at the end of another grueling day at the plant, I'd come home and open up my journal to record my reflections on the various TV shows I watched while toiling away at the wheel. I thought capturing any ideas and inspiration that spontaneously popped up during my work would be sure to benefit my future career as a show director. Often, just the sight of my densely packed notes was enough to fill me with new hope, a renewed purpose in life, but just as often, I found myself sinking into a pit of despair. Asking myself, *What does it matter anyway? I'll never get it.*

The weariness you wear like a second skin, the boredom

of repetition, the meager consolation of your favorite show, the vague and dwindling hope of making it to Snowglobe one day . . . On my lowest days, there seemed no point to any of this. At all. No experience was uniquely mine. Mom, Ongi, Suji, and even the man I most despised—our plant supervisor—lived the same unenchanted life, dreamed the same unenchanted dream. Why bother waking up tomorrow and going through the motions of living all over again, when the same exact living is already being done by countless others?

I wanted so badly to find a feeling, an experience, a script that called to me and me only. I wanted to make my mark in the world, to distinguish myself from all the rest. I wanted the name Jeon Chobahm to mean something.

But I was born as one of the Haeris, a Haeri who was at once singular and interchangeable. Did I so desperately itch for a unique and extraordinary life because I'd somehow intuited the truth of my identity? Oh, how I'd loathed my life—my world—that could have been anyone's.

I'd like to think that the particular itch was uniquely mine, uniquely Jeon Chobahm's, though I'm probably wrong.

Anyway . . . the chance to scratch that itch is finally here in front of me. I'll go shut down the plant, and then Chairman Shin's cardioverter will liberate us from the wheels and cameras. I'll forever be remembered as Chairman Shin's partner who peeled back the hideous deceit of the Yibonn. I'll leave the kind of mark I always imagined.

That is, I would, if it weren't for my deal with Serin. Thanks to our swapped identities, the truth of my actions will be hidden from the world. To the rest of the population, Serin will be the one who emerges from the underground, while Cho-bahm stays home. I'm giving up my name for a chance to save the world, because for all its intolerable monotony, boredom, and general ugliness, it is where my loved ones live.

*To save themselves and their loved ones from the jaws of the world. They step into hell . . . surprising their own selves. That's how ordinary people change the world.*

Serin will do better than fine, living the rest of her life as me, as Jeon Chobahm. And all that is great, because it's for the best. But then why am I feeling so sad? Perhaps Serin and I have more in common than I want to admit. A thought that annoys the hell out of me all over again.

"What now?! Why are you crying?" Serin finally says as I loudly suck back in the snot running from my nose. I wipe the tears off my face with a quick sweep of my hand.

"Hey, Bae Serin . . . ," I begin. "Do you know how long I've . . . I've . . ." But I break out sobbing again, overwhelmed by another rush of emotion.

"What? Speak, girl!" she demands impatiently, thoroughly irritated. "You changed your mind, is that it?"

"No!" I rush to deny. "No, I haven't, and I won't! . . . But you were right. I've been a complete brat, ignorant of all the blessings in my world when you and others had it so much worse. So I'm going to go out there and protect it."

I don't want to exist as a hero in a world where there is no Mom, Grandma, or Ongi to be proud of me. Without Som-yung and Shinae to look back on our epic adventures with, or without Hyang and Miryu to rejoice with in the new, free, and borderless world one day, life would be so empty. But that's what happens if I go to the power plant as myself rather than Serin. If the president realizes what I'm doing, she won't hesitate to kill everyone I love—she's already proven it.

Bonwhe's gone. I'll forever regret holding back my gratitude for his friendship. I don't want to repeat the same big mistake.

"I get it," Serin says, regarding me coldly. "It kills you to think there's a chance that I'd be living as a hero who saved the world, while enjoying the fruits of your ultimate sacrifice. Am I right? So why don't you ask Somyung or Shinae instead?"

"There's no one more dedicated to the role than you," I tell her promptly. "You're the most committed actor I know. You even erased your fingerprints to become me, remember?"

Serin's fingers on her lap curl in on themselves ever so slightly.

When Serin succeeded in banishing me to the retirees' village, a big obstacle still remained between her and the life as Haeri she always desired: the weather balls were programmed to respond to my fingerprints only. For Serin, who was even going around Director Cha's back to slip into Haeri's role, this was a real problem—but not one she couldn't solve. Once I was out of the way, she held on to an actively boiling teakettle, literally burning off her fingerprints. She then reported this unfortunate accident to Producer Yi Dahm, who had no choice but to arrange for the reprogramming of weatherballs using Serin's altered fingerprints. It is when this detail surfaced on *News at 9*'s in-depth reporting that Serin's reputation went from tragic to terrifying.

I watch Serin as she runs through a series of calculations.

"So if you don't make it back, it's Serin in the obituaries," she says after a while, lifting her eyes to me. Her tone is so casual and bright that it sounds almost pleased. "Jeon Cho-bahm's death would devastate the world, whereas Bae Serin's would devastate no one, which minimizes the total pain and suffering . . . How about that? It all works out so neatly." She looks at me as if expecting me to agree with her. "It's a deal! I live as Jeon Chobahm if you don't survive. And if you do, I get all the credit."

"Yes."

"But how do I trust that you won't stab me in the back?"

"I won't," I promise, fighting the urge to add *I'm not like you.*

Nonetheless, Serin throws me a look that makes me think that I might have said it aloud after all. Then her face softens to a smirk and she lets out a little laugh, as if to let me know that she appreciates my self-restraint.

"You can't walk back on your words—got it?" she says, offering her hand in a handshake.

"Worry about yourself," I reply, taking her hand.

Then we're moving on to planning our next step in the newly termed Operation Identity Swap. Serin, ever shrewd, contributes some good ideas that I couldn't have come up with on my own.

Once we're through, I race into the house and phone Chairman Shin. But just as I'm informing her of my decision to head underground tomorrow, the light beams appear from all corners of the room, signaling the end of the camera break. A moment later, I'm returning the receiver to the cradle, beating the slate in the nick of time. Cameras resume. I casually pick the receiver back up and call the taxi.

When Serin and I finally join the rest of the crew at the police station, we're told that Hyang's not allowed visitors other than her lawyer. Still, we spend the night on the floor in a sort of peaceful protest. At daybreak, around six a.m., we return home, except Ongi and Somyung, who stay put.

It doesn't even take a full minute after we cross the threshold for Miryu to say, "I'll go find her a good lawyer."

"Let me go with you, Miryu. Leave around nine?" I say, adding that I want to head to the pool for a quick swim anyway, to clear my head and reset after the eventful night. Miryu expresses her concern that the exercise might be too much for me to handle, but Serin chimes in to say that she'd love to go with me. All is as scripted. We're setting the stage for the identity swap.

Meanwhile, Shinae, reclining on the sofa, is understandably skeptical.

"You two are going to the pool? Just the two of you?" she says, squinting her sleepy eyes at us, clearly wondering, *Since when?* As far as she knows, we've barely spoken to each other since the last epic blowup in Serin's room.

Serin playfully cuffs me on the arm and tells Shinae, "Jeon Chobahm here finally apologized to me yesterday. I said it was about time."

As good as an actor as she is, she sounds far from convincing. But Shinae is too exhausted to probe further. She smiles and accepts the answer with a yawn.

"Alrighty, girls . . . ," she drawls. "Remember. United we stand, divided we fall . . ."

She rolls onto her side and promptly falls asleep. As I turn toward the door, I direct a thought her way.

*Sweet dreams, Shinae. I'll see you soon.*

On our bus ride to the pool, Serin and I don't exchange a single word. It's all part of our act designed to show the viewers that, yes, we agreed to a truce, but our relationship is as awkward and volatile as always.

**It's early in the morning, but you wouldn't know it by the num-**ber of people crowding the pool's locker room, many of whom steal curious glances at us as we walk in.

Inside our stall, Serin and I get changed into our swimsuits.

"What? You brought that swimsuit, too?" I scoff, making a show of being offended, which cues Serin for her line.

"Do you have a problem with it? Between Hyang's arrest and our trip to the police station, I didn't have the time to unpack my swim bag from yesterday—so it's the same suit two days in a row for me," she says.

Chatter builds up in the far end of the locker room. I peek over the stall and see people in various stages of undress trickling over to the big TV screen mounted on the wall, which currently shows President Yi Bonyung addressing the world from her home office. She's wearing all black and a grim expression.

"The snowstorm continues to tear through the area around the crash site," she says, and pauses to bite down on her quivering lip. In a moment, she gathers herself and continues, "Search and Rescue's drone cameras have sent back footage that confirmed the fatal crash . . ."

The screen cuts to the very footage, which, through fuzzy

and halting static, clearly shows the horribly twisted remains of a plane scattered and half-buried in a bleak, blizzard-swept landscape. I feel empty as I stare at the Yibonn logo painted on the plane's severed wing poking out of the snow, when the screen cuts back to the president.

"We've verified that there are no distress signals coming from the wreckage."

Low cries and murmurs of grief sweep through the locker room. Someone begins to sob. The president continues, "In order to ensure safety of the crew, the Yibonn Media Group has decided to suspend the recovery effort until the weather clears . . ."

I look around the locker room. Written on the face of everyone riveted by the screen is abiding trust and admiration for their president, the head of our world. She is the picture of a valiant leader who, even in the face of the most disorienting grief, keeps herself together and does what's right.

"It is truly regretful that I find myself relaying this tragic news when everyone's already devastated by the disaster that's been sweeping through our community for a whole week . . ." Her eyes moisten again.

I wring my trembling hands together to steady them. The hypocrisy of her pretending to mourn the people who she killed herself sickens me.

A brief press conference follows. People won't stop looking back over at me and Serin, who at this point have finished putting on our identical swimsuits, identical swim caps, and identical swim goggles. As if being clones is not enough. Serin ignores them and nudges me out of the locker room.

The pool is full of people despite a bubble bomb warning in effect. It's day six of the disaster, after all, and an increasing number of people are losing their patience and voluntarily braving the onslaught of suds.

I understand their motivation. Those with low show ratings often are the most willing to expose themselves to any disaster's danger and drama. Because what could be worse than getting kicked out of Snowglobe, where you have to live the rest of your life in a permanent disaster?

Serin and I choose a lane and dive into the pool. There's no camera underwater, and we take advantage of the fact, pretending to practice our diving skills while occasionally popping above the surface for breaths. We do that for a while, and to finish our workout, we position ourselves at the opposite ends of the pool, where we push off the walls and swim the entire length of the lane underwater.

Then Serin exits the water and walks the length of the deck over to my end of the pool.

"Hey, Serin," she says, still catching her breath. "I'm going to head out. I want to stop by the police station and get Ongi and Somyung some breakfast before joining Miryu."

I hoist myself out of the water and sit on the deck.

"I can take care of bringing Somyung and Ongi oppa food, if you want," I say, putting a gratuitous emphasis on *oppa* à la the real Serin, which triggers an involuntary smirk to flicker across her face. "That way, I could let them have a rest for a little while, too."

The real Serin stares skeptically at me for a moment before letting out a huff of a laugh.

"Sure, Serin. You go do that," she allows generously. "You go do that for your oppa. Oh man . . . You've started to sound like a member of the family—do you know that?"

Hmm . . . okay. The response is well within the general flow of our script, I suppose—but what's up with the extra snark? She needs to remember that she's pretending to be me here, Chobahm. I don't ever sound so snarky and sarcastic . . . or do I? I'm feeling attacked all of a sudden.

"What's that supposed to mean?" I snap, with what I admit is not-totally-fake hostility. Serin-impersonating-Chobahm responds with further snark. I, impersonating Serin, say something back even ruder . . . and on and on until we argue our way into the lockers. There, I, Serin, finally lash out for the benefit of the cameras and any witnesses around.

"If you hate me so much, how about I just disappear?"

Such a signature Serin move, I congratulate myself privately. It's odd, how well we know one another's weaknesses. Then I turn up my volume and intensity to reiterate, "How about I disappear from your sight, Jeon Chobahm?! That'd make you happy, wouldn't it?!"

We're laying the groundwork for our next move, of course, which is for me, Serin, to wander off into the disaster and fall off the radar.

Just then, the muffled sound of sirens filters into the locker room. Someone turns up the TV volume, and the morning news anchor's grim tone fills the room.

*"A severe weather warning is in full effect for all areas of Snow-globe. Please stay home and do not travel unless absolutely necessary. If you're outside, please seek shelter . . ."*

On the TV screen, the time-lapse video of weather radar

crawls a nauseating green and purple all over Snowglobe. I'm not sure if it's the sight of it or the thought of what's to come, but I'm feeling suddenly queasy when Serin's hand reaches through the gap between our stalls and taps me on the shoulder. She is either wishing me good luck or reminding me to get going.

# RETURN OF THE SHOW

Exiting the pool complex, Serin and I stalk angrily in opposite directions down the street without a word. Overhead, storm clouds cluster over a brooding sky, already dumping soap bubbles on the landscape below. On the streets, mounds of colorful, foaming soap suds multiply and grow tall like some clouds themselves wherever bubbles are unleashed en masse. I, now clad in Serin's favorite summer dress, head over to the police station as per the plan.

"*Oppa!*" I call out to Ongi, arriving at the lobby.

Although I mostly came here to bide my time until the soap mounds grow massive enough that I can travel behind them without detection, I also can't resist the chance to see Ongi and Somyung again, maybe for the last time.

*Is that a real possibility? You not making it back?*

I push away the anxiety and premature grief gathering inside me again and mewl to Ongi, doing my best imitation of Serin.

"Oppaaa—you must be so tired. I'll take over while you two go grab a bite to eat," I suggest without giving Somyung so much as a glance. I don't ask after Hyang, either, forcing back the Jeon Chobahm that wants to surface. I know how to do it. It's just like when I had to hide myself behind Haeri on the screen.

Thankfully, neither Ongi or Somyung seems to suspect anything, their current states of exhaustion and stress no doubt working in my favor. Yawning, Somyung informs me that she and Ongi have already had breakfast at the police barracks.

"We sure could use a break, though. If you're still all right to take over for a while?" she says.

"Nope. Can't do—sorry," I reply snottily, glancing away from her eyes, which are rimmed red with fatigue. "If you don't need to eat, I have to be somewhere else."

Somyung just rolls her eyes shut and tilts her head back against the wall, as if she expected nothing less. And I, Serin, stand my ground and remain silent to show that her opinion means nothing to me.

Ongi is gazing warily out the window, at the weather unfolding in real time. The bubbles are coming down in mad droves now, reducing visibility to near nothing. From my backpack, I take out two pairs of rubber-soled boots and hand them to Ongi, along with my umbrella.

"Here, oppa. Take these shoes and umbrella."

"Oh, great! Thanks, Serin . . . You still have a pair for yourself?"

"I don't need any. I'm taking a taxi."

"Then let me hail one for you."

Ongi walks me out of the police station. He opens the umbrella and holds it up for us, tilting it heavily toward me. I'm amused. I never imagined that my brother, the eternal prankster of the family as far as I'm concerned, could be so considerate, dependable, caring, and . . . so oppa-like around a different audience. Suddenly, the tip of my nose begins to ache like I'm about to tear up or something, but that would just be over-the-top ridiculous. I flare my nostrils and inhale the morning air, blinking my eyes fast to pull back the tears.

*Is that a real possibility? You not making it back?*

Mercifully, a taxi pulls over. I hurry into the backseat, muttering directions quietly to the driver. Leaning back, I look up at Ongi standing by the open door, forcing my face into the brightest smile I can muster.

"Alrighty, then . . ." I say. "See you at home."

Ongi swiftly closes his umbrella and, before I can react, thrusts himself into the backseat, half sitting on my lap.

"Slide over a bit, would you? I'm going with you," he says, pulling the door shut as I stare at him, speechless. "I feel gross. I'll shower at home and then come back."

"Wha-what . . . ?" I stammer, scrambling. "But I'm . . . I'm not headed straight home."

"Really? I guess I'll take a detour, then."

"What? Why?"

But Ongi's already talking to the driver.

"Thank you for picking us up, sir. Could you take us to . . ." He looks to me. "Where did you say you were going?"

"How about Somyung?" I protest, stalling to regain my balance. "What would she think if you just abandoned her here?"

"Oh, I'm sure she'll be fine. She's in a safe place, after all. I'll tell her that I had to save a runaway teen."

As I fumble, he looks me straight in the eye and says, "It's written all over your face, Serin. You're not going home, are you?"

What in the world? Is he determined to sabotage the plan, or what?!

I don't know what to say. Before I can stop him, we're riding together toward the city limits, to a hostel located on the edge of the restricted zone. My destination.

The Baekjae Hostel is a shabby, run-down accommodation patronized by burned-out actors seeking to recharge, away from the hubbub of daily living. On the more macabre side of things, the forest sprawling behind the hostel has also attracted evildoers attempting to pull off the perfect crime. Actual bodies have been found there. That's why the Baekjae Hostel became one of the most dramatic places in Snowglobe, making it the perfect destination for all drama queens, including Serin.

The windshield wipers are on full speed, but they're helpless against the ceaseless barrage of bubbles coming down in clumps. The taxi driver, who's been white-knuckling the wheel with his nose pressed to the windshield up until this point, sighs and lets off the gas.

"Sorry, folks. This is as far as I can go," he says, pulling off to the side and turning off the engine.

The few fellow motorists who have been crawling along this remote, pothole-laden road seem to have come to the same conclusion. I thank the driver for trying, and I tell him I'll walk the rest of our way.

"Are you sure? It's accumulating fast," the driver says, concerned.

Ongi sides with the driver.

"The plow truck should come back to do another sweep soon. Why don't we wait in here until it does? It won't be long."

Another sweep? Meaning they'd clear the road of suds? That'd be the end of my plan.

"Oppa—you stay safely in the car," I say. "That way, I won't have to worry about you falling through an open manhole or something."

Ugh. I cringe internally at this last comment, which was so incredibly Jeon Chobahm. Without delay, I pop open the door and step out into the chest-high suds, only to have Ongi follow me out like a lost puppy.

"What are you doing?" I demand, attempting to keep my voice light.

Ongi opens up the umbrella and holds it over my head.

"Oppa vowed to be on your side, no matter what—remember?"

Gaah! A devoted oppa indeed, and yet he doesn't even recognize his own twin sister. A bitter taste fills my mouth.

"Then do what you want," I say, almost spitting it out. I don't sound like Serin at all now—but I can't help it. I'll just have to lose him in the growing suds.

We slog toward the hostel and the lurking forest beyond. Are we getting any closer? In the chaos of driving bubbles and increasingly impeding suds, I can't keep track of our progress.

"We're going to be separated in this mess," Ongi says. All of a sudden, he hooks his arm through mine and squeezes me against him.

I think I might have flinched, but I stifle any further reflex. Biting back the snippy comeback that would no doubt give me away, I force a smile and tell him, "You're so sweet to me, oppa—but don't you think it upsets Chobahm?"

"Upsets?" Ongi says, and pauses briefly, as if considering the point for the first time. You don't even care, do you? Then he says, "If she is upset, then it's too bad."

I feel my blood beginning to simmer.

He continues, "What's important is that you, Serin, are kept happy enough that you don't bother to resent Chobahm any longer."

This stops me in my tracks. I stare at him, confused. Ongi just smiles his open smile at me and nudges me onward with a pull of his hooked arm. We continue wordlessly toward our destination for another twenty minutes or so.

By the time we finally hit the hostel's parking lot, the suds are up to my neck. All around us, the world whizzes and bubbles with suds of iridescent green and purple, and I briefly wonder if we've somehow been transported inside a peculiar and complicated piece of abstract art.

Cupping my hands around my mouth and nose and creating an air pocket, I put my face in the suds. I can breathe in this manner—no problem—though the bitter taste of soap in my mouth is another matter. I lift my face and spit a few times to get rid of the unpleasant taste, when a loud *clack!* issues from the vehicles stranded in the hostel's grounds.

My heart thuds. The cameras are off—meaning the time has come for me to enact my escape. It's now or never.

The original plan was for me to check into the hostel before sneaking off to the forest, so as to leave behind the appropriate footage. But heading straight there may not be a bad idea after all. I don't want to risk losing my bearings in the storm and becoming so disoriented that I can't find the mirror passageway—not to mention, the more soap bubbles I inhale, the more tempting it seems to get out of here as fast as possible.

Turning to Ongi, I say, "Now that you've gotten me here safe, you should go back home. I . . . I just want to lie low for a little while. Be alone. I hope you understand, oppa."

The suds are foaming at our chins now, but he's still keeping his grip on the umbrella, which he pointlessly holds over my head.

"Come on, Jeon Chobahm," he says then, looking at me dead-on.

All my facial muscles freeze. We stare at each other for a moment.

"What?" I manage to breathe out, with a desperate little laugh. "What are you talking about?"

"You're making this oppa real sad, do you know that?" he says. "What am I? Chopped liver? Why didn't you tell me what you've been going through?"

My head has gone blank. I don't know how to respond.

He continues, "Why would you struggle all alone? When you have me, your big brother? Couldn't you reach out to me? Tell me where you're going or why, in case there's anything I could do to help? Jeez . . . it's not that difficult!"

*Shoot* . . . When did my oblivious big brother become so . . . perceptive?

I feel tears start to come on. Violently, I rub my eyes, which further drives the soap suds into my eyeballs.

"Gosh, it stings!" I cry out, trying to rub away the suds with a relatively dry part of my hand. "This is all your fault,

Jeon Ongi! I should be out of this storm by now!" I accuse fatally, giving myself away.

He tut-tuts in patronizing disapproval, the way he always did growing up, and I know he's seen right through me. I stare at him helplessly, and he holds out a travel-size package of wet wipes, like the kind restaurants tend to give out to messy customers.

He says, "So tell me again how I should just stay home and get out of your way."

I just stand there, stubbornly ignoring the wipes, and with a monumental sigh, he pulls out a wipe and wipes my eyes for me, clearly reveling in the role of the older, wiser oppa.

"When you brought up 'Dr. Kim Seolwon' and 'Dr. Yi Woon,'" he says, making air quotes with his fingers, "I knew you were up to something again." A chuckle of incredulity. "Like I didn't realize it was you . . ."

"You knew it was us? Since when?"

"How could I not know?" he says, exasperated. "We've been blood since before birth." His expression turning triumphant, he adds, "Hey, I only recognized you the moment you stepped into the police station because I'm your big brother. I bet Somyung has no idea."

There's nothing I can do but let out a huff of laughter. This kid . . .

"Okay, fine," I concede. "But you still have to go."

But Ongi won't listen. He follows me to the edge of the forest, bugging me with one question after another until I crack and give him the gist of my plan, minus the deal I struck with Serin.

"So I need you to go home and tell everyone that I'm

staying—no, Serin's staying at the hostel for a few days," I tell him. "Tell them I needed some time off. Anything more, Jeon Chobahm should be able to fill in."

Ongi glances at the hostel parking lot, where cameras are still paused. He says, "I'll go with you, then. Follow you to the—"

"Absolutely not," I cut him off. "Not that you'd be able to anyway. The mirrors won't recognize your biometrics."

Ongi pretends to consider this a moment.

"Then you can't go, either," he says, grabbing my wrist. I slide out of his grip easily, as we're both slick with soap suds.

Meanwhile, my wristwatch, which thankfully is waterproof, indicates less than two minutes before the cameras resume. Shifting my gaze back to Ongi and peering into his eyes, I remind him, "Don't you remember? I was born after you because I was watching your back?"

Ongi gives a laugh and an incredulous "What?" as if he hasn't heard this a hundred times before.

I continue, "So why don't you stay back and cover for me this time?"

I take off my soggy backpack and fish out my coin purse containing Chairman Shin's business card. Holding it out to him, I say, "Here. Inside, you'll find my emergency contact."

Ongi gives me a long look. Then, reluctantly, he snatches the coin purse and hangs it from his neck by its long strap.

He says, "So when will you be back?"

*I don't know* is the honest answer, but that wouldn't help me right now.

"In two days, I think. Or maybe three."

His face twists with outrage.

"What?! Three days to go flip a freaking switch?!"

"It was a generous estimate, okay? I'll likely be back much sooner."

As long as I don't turn into a soulless zombie inside the glass tower, that is.

"If you're not back in three days—max—then I'll literally smash into that mirror thingy and go find you myself, and that is a promise," Ongi says, looking at me intensely, his chest rising and falling. I want to roll my eyes at how dramatic he's being when he suddenly steps in and puts his arms around me for a tight hug. I reflexively tense—before hugging him back.

"Please don't smash the mirror and trap me in it forever, you silly," I tell him.

"Shut up," he says. "Be safe."

"I'll be back before you know it."

"You'd better."

The deeper I move into the forest, the more the suds wane like an outgoing tide. I guess without the cameras to witness and record their effect, even a disaster can't be bothered to try too hard. Relieved, I begin trudging through the thick underbrush in earnest, frequently checking the compass to make sure I'm headed in the direction advised by Chairman Shin. Before long, I'm running, covered in a slick mixture of sweat and suds residue, and just when my legs begin to feel like two columns of lead, I spot the gleam of the large oval mirror leaning against the giant tree trunk.

# RETURNED FROM THE APOCALYPSE

**H**unching my shoulders, I tiptoe through the undergrowth toward the mirror. No signs of other humans or human activity. That is, unless you count the absence of the rocking chair or the fire pit that stood in this area when I met with Bonwhe. All evidence of them has been cleared—thoroughly scrubbed off—as if in a silent declaration that they will never be needed again.

*Your last letter read a lot like a farewell, and I was pretty worried.*

Memories of the day, Bonwhe's tender face, keep rising in my mind. I try to combat them by glancing off to the clear sky above the treetops. Toward the center of town, bubbles, far from where I am, continue pouring down as if determined to bury the world.

Is Ongi safely back in the hostel lobby, waiting for the plow truck? How about Miryu? It must be rough getting to the lawyer's office in this weather. At least Hyang should be safe at the police station where she is detained. And this last thought sobers me up all over again. If Hyang is convicted and imprisoned, then *You, Me, and Us* will be assigned a new director, who then will have access to our conversation in the car, which Serin and I failed to destroy. I have to move fast before President Yi puts one of her cronies in the position.

I take the heart-shaped cardioverter and the heat suit out of the backpack. Peeling off my sweat and soap-drenched clothes, I wipe dry a patch of skin over my heart and press the plastic shape against it. Next is the heat suit, a black hoodie-and-tights combo that has the substance and texture of a sturdy garbage bag for all its elegant appeal. Finally, I pull on the hood and cinch the built-in scarf around my neck, and I'm ready.

I reach for the mirror, dipping my fingertips into the anxious face of my own reflection. Then I'm in it, engulfed in dimensionless dark. But I've been here before, so I steady my breath and wait for my eyes to adjust. In a few moments, the tall gearshift and the dashboard materialize before me in the darkness. I pull back the shifter and push the large button in the center, recalling Chairman Shin's instructions. Immediately, the vessel begins plummeting through the abyss, and in a few moments, I've arrived. I look out the mirror and find myself in a narrow hallway paneled with dark wood planks.

Raising my knuckles to the cardioverter, I give it three solid taps. In the next instant, the same sharp pain like a stake boring into my chest seizes me, and then my heart's accelerating at a terrifying pace. No need to panic, though, I remind myself. Everything's working as it should. I take a few big breaths and adjust to my new physiology. Then, finally, I'm flinging myself through the glass and out into the hallway.

*It's cold as hell here* is my first thought. Thankfully, Chairman Shin's heat suit seems to be kicking into gear, converting my rapid heartbeat into thermal energy, though just enough to keep me alive and functioning for now.

I begin down the dark hallway, following the row of dim lightbulbs overhead. Meanwhile, my artificially enhanced heart rate seems to go through cycles of dips and spikes, which makes me feel dizzy and weak one moment, then supercharged with energy the next. But I push forward, and it isn't long before I reach the end of the hallway, where an enormous cave opens up and the familiar glass tower rises massively in it.

The Gearwheels Tower, as I've termed it in my mind, looks like a cylinder made of different-sized wheels stacked and configured like the inner workings of a giant mechanical clock. They spin dizzyingly inside the tower itself, each powered by a huffing and puffing human, their glazed eyes peering at nothing.

Even as I stand there gaping, the monstrous cold continues working its teeth through my heat suit. And with my own irregular heartbeat beginning to have a real effect on me, I'm feeling half drunk. I must hurry. I begin circling the glass tower, looking for a projector like the one Chairman Shin told me about. The last time I found myself here, I failed to notice anything else in my panicked desperation to catch the eye of the tattooed prisoner inside. This time it's different, and I almost surprise myself by spotting the black projector lying on the floor not even halfway around the tower.

Without a second's delay, I crouch down and switch on the projector. Brilliant white light explodes onto the tower's glass wall and—as I guessed—turns it into a mirror, on which I see my amazed reflection. Everything so far has been just as the chairman described. But what awaits me beyond this point, whatever evil is being perpetrated beyond these glass walls, no one knows.

Fear and doubt plague me again. Could the air inside be infused with some kind of hallucinogenic gas? How will the inmates react to me, if they even wake up from their stupor? Will I end up one of them?

The projector's light begins to dim, and along with it, the mirrored patch. I've no more time to hesitate. Now or never. I hurl myself through the mirror.

**Hot, humid air engulfs me. I'm standing just inside the glass** tower, facing all those gears of gleaming metal spinning nauseatingly before me. From the inside, the glass tower is thickly opaque, and I can't see anything beyond.

I look around, trying to get my bearings, when I notice a little girl staring at me from inside her wheel, mouth open in astonishment. Six or seven at most, she is wearing a pair of tattered pants and a faded sky-blue T-shirt with a yellow smiley face fading into pixels.

What in the world? What is a little girl doing down here?

I stare back at her in bewilderment, and the girl hops out of her small-sized wheel and scampers over to me. I turn off the cardioverter with three hard taps of my knuckles, and my heart immediately decelerates, which only puts further stress on my body, already straining from the mad swing in temperatures. But I marshal my focus and raise an awkward hand. "Hey . . . Hi?"

The little girl stops dead in her tracks. Eyes suddenly enlarged, she looks at me as if seeing a ghost. Then she screams,

"Team Leader!" Sucking in another breath, she repeats, "SUPERVISOR! SUPERVISOR!"

Her voice is ridiculously loud for someone so small. But no one working the wheels seems to hear her through their extreme focus—or trance.

"Stay back!" someone shouts. Suddenly, a man with long, sleek hair woven into three braids that trail down his back bolts out from behind one of the wheels. His sun-kissed, light-colored hair and elfin ears jump out at me.

"Joon . . . ?" I murmur in shock.

No way this is the man I'm thinking of—the former star whose unique charm had viewers everywhere swooning? Anastacia's eternal soulmate? Could it really be him?

A onetime actor in Snowglobe like me, Joon was condemned to death for threatening to kill his director. Still, the love between him and his beloved, Anastasia, persevered until the end. In fact, it was because of their tragic love story that Anastasia would one day rise to the position of weathercaster.

"Orderlies!" Joon shouts, snatching at the little girl and pulling her back behind him. "Orderlies!" he repeats, fixing me in place with his eyes and covering his mouth and nose with the sleeve of his faded blue inmate's shirt.

Then three figures dressed in white coveralls, goggles, and masks charge out from behind the wheels toward me, looking exactly like the staff working in the hyperbaric unit at the SnowTower medical center.

"No! Wait!" I cry, but someone's gloved hand clamps a mask over my face. There's a sharp sting in my upper arm, and then my eyelids drop shut.

**When I come to, I'm lying in an all-white room featuring paper** birch panels. My old clothes are gone, and I'm now wearing a faded blue inmate uniform, just like they are. Beyond the oversized plate glass framing the near wall is some sort of secondary room, where Joon sits stiffly on the windowsill and watches me. Next to him, a woman presses her face to the glass and cries out in an anguished voice, muffled by the barrier between us, "Hey, Wisher! Are you okay?!"

*Wisher? Is that a name? Why is she calling me that?* Joon, his eyes narrowing to slits, opens his mouth and asks through the speaker, his voice clearer than the woman's, "How did you get back in here, and without your coveralls?"

I stare at them blankly. After a few moments, the woman, all worked up for some reason, starts pleading to me, "Teacher told us . . . that . . . that you ran off as soon as she brought you aboveground. She left again this morning in search of you, saying that she couldn't rest until she finds and brings back your remains."

What? Who's Wisher, and who's this Teacher?

The woman continues, "What happened aboveground? What—" But Joon stops her with a raised palm.

"Slow down, Healer," he tells her. "Was there anything else unusual with Wisher, other than signs of the virus?"

Signs of the virus? What virus? And if they think I'm Wisher, whoever that is, that means they must be confusing me with someone—a girl who looked exactly like me. The woods Haeri. My guess was right—she's down here. Or at least, she was. But why is her name different? And where is she now?

"There was absolutely nothing else unusual with her," she says. "Her temperature, too—it was only slightly elevated when we first took it, but normal on all subsequent measurements."

Furtively, I bring a hand to my chest and feel for the cardioverter. Its hard plastic surface presses back at my fingertips under the thin cotton of the uniform. If this woman checked me over, she must have noticed it . . . but why is she keeping my secret?

"Hmm . . . ," Joon says, still gazing at me warily. "It doesn't make sense that she would be unaffected after such a prolonged exposure aboveground." But then the look on his face takes on a strangely hopeful quality, and he asks me, "Tell us, Wisher, how did you make it back from the wasteland in one piece, and without protection of an antiviral suit? Don't leave out a thing."

The wasteland? What wasteland? Do they mean the outer world—the frozen tundra beyond the dome? They certainly can't be talking about Snowglobe. Judging by appearances, at least, it's a paradise, not a wasteland.

I stare at them in utter bewilderment, and the woman lets out a fresh groan. "Oh no . . . ," she says. "Did you . . . lose your memory again, Wisher?"

My perplexity only deepens the more she speaks. Viruses . . . memory loss . . . what planet are they living on?

"I'm from Snowglobe. You know about Snowglobe, don't you?" I try.

Their brows arch in confusion.

"Snowglobe . . . ?" the woman repeats after a moment. "Is

that what you call it—Snowglobe? Your survival strategy? Is that a code name or something?"

Meanwhile, Joon seems to have no idea what to even make of the word. These people can't be serious. They really don't know what Snowglobe is . . . ? But how? Every person in the world knows about Snowglobe, unless they live in complete, television-less isolation. The tattooed man I saw had originally been incarcerated in Snowglobe, after all. And Joon . . . He was one of its most sought-after stars! Hurriedly, I run through a list of shows, directors, actors, the Yibonn, President Yi, and anything else Snowglobe, but the confusion and concern in their faces only grow more pronounced with each new term I throw out.

Joon, keeping his suspicious eyes on me, tips his head sideways and tells the woman in a hushed voice, "She's definitely been exposed to the virus."

It is then that the horrible realization dawns in my mind. When a death row inmate gets sent down here . . . they aren't just locked away from the rest of the world. Their memory must be wiped clean. Buhae's voice echoes in my head then. *May your memory be your curse!*

Suddenly, the door flies open behind Joon and Healer, and someone urgently reports, "Sky's passed out!"

As soon as I recognize the newcomer, my mind goes blank. Impossible. In disbelief, I shake my head and look again, certain I'm mistaken. Because the person standing to my back . . . is supposed to be dead.

Bonwhe. The heir to the Yibonn fortune is alive—and dressed in a faded blue inmate uniform.

# THE FORTRESS

"What?!" Joon barks, and bolts out of the room, pushing past Bonwhe.

Is it really him standing in the doorway? But how . . . ? Why . . . ? My heart begins a slow pounding. I'm staring at the figure in the doorway with open shock and confusion, when I sense Healer watching me with narrowed eyes, her head cocked to one side and arms crossed in front of her chest. I quickly glance away—but the sight of Bonwhe is like a magnet, and my eyes are drawn back to him almost immediately.

Finally, Healer turns her attention back to Bonwhe.

"So what were Sky's symptoms leading to this?" she asks Bonwhe.

"Dry cough and mild fever for a couple of hours."

"Damn! The brief exposure is all it took? That means that Wisher here is definitely in danger . . . but then how come she herself is not symptomatic?"

They swivel their heads and regard me warily. His face in

this moment is blank, containing neither the tenderness he reserved for Yeosu or the playful mischief he revealed to me on occasions. Nevertheless, it is still his, I'm sure of it. The voice, the features, the way he carries himself . . . they all belong to the Yi Bonwhe I know. Absolutely.

*The private jet carrying Mr. Yi Bonwhe has crashed on its way to outer-world district Ja-P-22 upon encountering bad weather. Authorities are still trying to reestablish contact with the pilot . . .*

Then a possibility dawns on me. Was it all faked?

The sense of hope and relief I feel at this thought is instantly eclipsed by my horror at the president's cruelty. She would throw away her own heir—her grandson—as a tool to manipulate the public against me and the other Haeris rather than risk her own secrets coming out. And the worst part of it all is that I feel so hopelessly powerless against her. Tears surge to my eyes, and I hunch over in a desperate attempt to hide them.

Healer then shrieks through the glass, "Wisher! Are you okay?!"

"Yes, yes . . . ," I rush to reply, afraid she'll take my emotion as evidence of whatever virus they're talking about. "I'm just feeling weak, I guess. I haven't eaten anything in a while—I'm starving, in fact."

"Starving?" Healer says, laughing with relief. "That's good! Having an appetite is always a good sign."

Turning to Bonwhe, she says, "Hey, rookie—can you bring her dinner? There should be some leftovers in the kitchen."

"Certainly," Bonwhe replies.

"And get a name, will you, before the name Rookie sticks?

Pick anything you want—just make sure that it's not already taken by someone else."

Rookie? So prisoners have to get new names when they're brought down here . . . meaning they don't even remember their own names? Which would mean . . .

My heart stops. That would mean that Haeri, upon her arrival here, would have gotten a new name, too—such as Wisher. But that still doesn't answer the question of where she is now . . .

The answer comes to me at once. The surface. If they think I'm Wisher, that must be because the original Wisher, also known as Haeri, is gone.

I've missed her.

**With a chuckle and a promise to get himself a name, Bonwhe** takes his leave. I'm gazing helplessly at the door closing behind Healer when she drags her stool closer to the plate glass and stares at me intently, her expression stern.

"You done messing with me?" she hisses out of the blue.

What? I blink. Isn't she on my side? She checked me for signs of the virus, meaning she must have seen my cardioverter, but she withheld the knowledge of it from Joon. Is she just realizing that I'm not Wisher after all?

My heart picking up again, I search her face for clues, and it only seems to make her angrier. In fact, she looks like a ticked-off lion in this moment, with her thick, unruly hair hanging in a frizzy, unstyled mane about her face.

"Hey!" the lion suddenly roars, making me jump. "Boss told me that you'd gone to the surface with Teacher. So I figured you wanted to go ahead and die already . . . but even so . . . Even so! Where was my goodbye?" She pauses for a breath, her eyes fixed on me. "I thought, and thought, and thought about it, and I still don't get it! Kids these days have no manners . . . How could you just disappear like that?! Don't you know I was worried sick?"

I just stare at her, speechless.

"Days passed, but Teacher didn't return—I started getting my hopes up that the outside world might have recovered from the virus that killed off the rest of humanity, that it might have become habitable again. And when Teacher showed up the other day with a new rescue, saying that you'd run off . . . my stomach did a free fall. Can you imagine? No, really—can you imagine?"

She looks at me with sorrowful eyes.

"I'm . . . I'm sorry?" I stammer, compelled by the heartbreak on her face.

She doesn't seem satisfied. "And what's up with the plastic toy on your chest? It wouldn't come off, so I tried my best to sanitize the shit out of it for now."

I run through a quick summary of what I've gleaned so far. The Haeri who disappeared into the forest was living here under the name of Wisher. One day, she left with this Teacher figure for the outside world— aboveground—and disappeared there. Now everyone seems to think that I'm her, returned from the viral apocalypse.

Then I guess I'll have to pretend to be Wisher while getting my bearings here. Insisting on lecturing these people about Snowglobe or my mission here would only complicate things.

But then what if this Wisher girl returns? And what about

the challenge of playing a girl I know nothing about? Stepping into Haeri's shoes was child's play compared to this, seeing as how I'd followed her life on TV for years and years and years. I knew her inside and out, but this girl is a mystery to me.

First things first, though. I need to tame this agitated lion in front of me. She and Wisher were clearly close, close enough that she was willing to cover for me about the cardioverter. So coming clean to her about my identity and pleading for her help and cooperation would probably backfire.

As I fumble over my thoughts, the lion leans closer toward the plate glass, her hands clasping the edge of the counter and her shoulders hunched to her ears. Throwing a quick glance left and right, she says to me in a low whisper, "I can tell that you have something you're reluctant to share with Joon. Whatever it is, share with me now—so I can help you."

Despite the lion vibe, her eyes are almost beseeching.

"Healer . . . ," I say after a long moment.

"Yes, Wisher," she answers eagerly, her gaze twinkling with expectation. "What is it? Tell me."

"Are you scared of the world outside?"

Her shoulders sag. Frowning, she draws back.

But I press, "Are you scared to leave this place and go aboveground?"

She gives me a long look, as if considering the question.

"Of course I am scared of leaving this fortress!" she says, finally. "Aren't you? Aren't you scared of going outside, aboveground, contracting the virus and dying, like the rest of humanity?"

So that's the story they've been told.

"Healer . . . ," I say, feeling pity rising inside me.

Where do I begin with the truth? I pause and take a deep breath before continuing.

"You want to know how I survived the world outside and returned unscathed? The answer is simple. The world is just fine. There's no killer virus, no deadly contagion—"

"What are you talking about?" she says, alarm and suspicion creeping back into her face. I can read her thoughts clearly: *Oh god—she is so infected.*

I hold her eyes, trying my best to look as healthy and alert as I can, and tell her, "Humanity is not dead, and none of you—I mean, none of us—have to be locked away in here and be exploited."

The lion's mouth drops open in an O.

"Locked away? Exploited?" she repeats after a moment, incredulous.

"Yes. We're working the wheels because—"

The lion bursts out laughing, cutting me off.

"Sure—I get it," she says, letting her laugh fade. "It sucks being locked in here because the world outside has gone to hell. But calling the power production essential for maintaining our life exploitation is completely off-base. I understand that it's not a paradise, but it's certainly not the worst—and you know that."

"No—that's not why we're turning the wheels! You're not creating your own power, you're being used!" I push back, nearly yelling with frustration.

"Are you claiming . . . ," she says as I heave a great sigh, "that Teacher has us locked in here for no reason?"

Someone knocks on the door then.

I lower my voice to a whisper-yell and rush out the words, "We have to get out of here! All of us!" If no one spins the wheels, this secret power plant will stop, revealing the truth itself—that there's no magical geothermal energy beneath Snowglobe.

The lion rears up, staring at me with a strange expression on her face. Then the door behind her swings open and Bonwhe reappears, calling to Healer.

"Ms. Knife is looking for you to relieve her at the wheel," he says.

Healer quickly fixes her face and gets to her feet, flicking a wary glance at me.

"I'm coming," she says, and heads out.

Bonwhe's eyes shift to me then, and he says, "Oh, right—your food! Be right back."

"Yi Bonwhe!" I'm calling out before I can think.

His head snaps and we stare at each other a moment.

"What?" he says finally, giving me an arched brow.

I don't know what he means by this, but it's not what I expected.

"Bonwhe . . . ?" I try again, stunned.

"What's Bonwhe?" he wants to know. "Is that a name?"

*What? Don't you know your name?* I want to shout, but . . .

"Don't you know me?" I'm asking instead.

"I do," he replies flatly after a moment, moving to the plate glass divider running between us. "Everyone's talking about you, Wisher. You're the girl who disappeared into the world during a mission with Teacher. But here you are now—you're back."

I just stare at him.

He continues. "Oh, me? Haven't decided on a name yet. It's only my third day here. I'm a rescue, of course. A fresh arrival."

"You were . . . rescued?" I say, my voice rasping. "From where?"

He tells me that Teacher found him on her most recent mission out in the world, and though prolonged exposure to the virus erased his memory, he feels outrageously lucky to have survived the plague that killed off ninety-nine percent of humanity.

"Down here, we're at least together," he tells me cheerily. "That makes things less terrifying."

"So you like it down here?" I ask him, feeling my heart sink with infinite terror and hopelessness.

Nodding eagerly, he goes on to tell me that the fortress is the planet's last remaining sanctuary for humanity, where over a hundred survivors rescued from the ruins of the world run the plant to generate light and electricity needed for subsistence. Sure, it's not an easy or posh life by any stretch of the imagination, but at least it's life, relative to what the undead are enduring outside these walls.

It's like he's reciting a paragraph of a textbook. As I stare at him, dread growing inside me, the eggheaded look on his face slowly changes to one of mild admiration, and he tells me, "I heard that you were one of the very first rescues brought into the fortress."

Wisher was one of the very first rescues? That would make this place only three years old or so, which it can't be, because according to Chairman Shin's timeline, the plant was built even before Snowglobe was, to provide heat for the domed city to come.

Bonwhe cracks a smile and continues, "By the way, I'm thrilled to join you and everyone else down here—"

"Jo Yeosu!" I blurt, my mind swirling again with confusion. "Don't you remember her?"

Bonwhe's smile retreats. He studies me a moment. Then, with a shrug, he says, "Who's that?"

My knees buckle. Bonwhe's memory, too, has been wiped out in the service of maintaining the lie of Snowglobe. "Never mind," I mumble, giving up. "Forget it. I'm glad you're thrilled to be here."

We lapse into silence, him lingering on the other side of the partition, me avoiding his gaze. As I let my mind drift, I think back to Hwang Sannah, who helped me and Hyang escape the retirees' village all those months ago.

*Don't feel like you owe her anything. Sannah has her own towering hatred of Snowglobe!*

The Yibonn have played with an untold number of lives, including those of the death row inmates kept down here. And who's to say that among those death row inmates, there aren't innocent people such as Sannah who have been wrongfully accused and convicted by the crooked system? And how about the little girl in the fraying baby-blue T-shirt? In what universe could she be a hideous criminal punishable by death?

Cha Seol, who scammed the world with her clone scheme, is sitting in jail at this very moment, waiting for her punishment. Meanwhile, the president and her evil corporation still lord it over us, on a pedestal of endless worship and gratitude.

The rage bubbling up inside me is worse than ever. I must switch off this place and expose the truth, and it will not bother me one bit if Serin gets all the credit for it.

**I expect Bonwhe to leave me alone, but even though I maintain** my silence, he never does. After a brief silence, I ask, "So when do you think I'll be out of quarantine?"

As if on cue, the door flies open behind him, and the lion returns, her chaotic mane astir.

"Your test came back negative, Wisher!" she says, sounding both confused and excited. "Come on out! Let's get you some food first."

She instructs Bonwhe to take me to the cafeteria and hurries back to the floor where her wheel awaits.

Led out of the isolation room, I finally get my first glimpse of the larger structure I've found myself in. The isolation room sits at the bottom of a vast, tree-trunk-like hollow. From what I can count, the structure comprises about twenty-five ringlike levels. The first five rings make up the wraparound production floors, where wheels turn in perpetuity. Above them, additional floors composed of interlocking hexagonal cells rise tightly in a honeycomb structure—an area that can't be seen from outside this power plant. They seem to hold the plant's living quarters, as well as other non-work-related facilities. The twenty floors above the five-story Wheel Tower are connected by escalators that run continuously between them.

I follow Bonwhe up the escalators and through the ascending levels, turning my head to take it all in. The hexagonal cells are wide open to the central atrium I'm walking up, without any exterior walls or doors, so that the activities going on inside are open for viewing. The cells' purposes appear to range the full spectrum of a vibrant and self-sustained community, from small-scale agriculture, gardening, and kitchen to cafeteria, recreation, and so on.

Many of these cells have wood floors and sleeping mats, some currently occupied by tired figures at rest. Even these cells, though, are wide open for view, the only half measure of privacy the clotheslines that are strung across the gaps. Some blankets and inmate uniforms hang from the lines.

"I don't mean to complain, but it'll take me some time to get used to not having any privacy," Bonwhe says, as if tracking my thoughts.

I make a noise of agreement and idly look down over the side of the escalator at the hollow. In the center of the first floor sits what appears to be a well. A well, of course. A survival fortress would need a dependable source of water, wouldn't it?

Meanwhile, Bonwhe points out a few of his favorite cells, which include a board game cell and a sort of retro movie theater operated with a home projector, where residents can enjoy movies from the Warring Age.

"Isn't it weird that a structure of this scale even exists?" I lead cautiously. "I can't help but wonder—like, isn't it a bit excessive to hide it all underground? I mean, it almost feels more like a slave colony than a refuge, right?"

There, I said it.

Bonwhe doesn't express an opinion—at least, not right away. He takes a slow glance around at the stacks of cells surrounding us, as if admiring the view.

Then he says, "That's what makes Teacher a great prophet. When everyone else laughed off the signs of the approaching apocalypse, Teacher kept faith and invested their great fortune in building the fortress. I don't know if I could have had the conviction."

I swallow hard, feeling my stomach turn. Though I've had my suspicion from the beginning, it's clear now that this Teacher figure Bonwhe's referring to is President Yi—posing as some kind of messiah both above and underground. I want to vomit.

# THE TOMB OF THE FOOLISH AND SAD

We arrive at the cafeteria on the seventeenth floor, which holds a grand total of four four-seater tables. All cells being uniform in size, the place obviously can't accommodate the entire population, which explains why there is one on every other floor.

Bonwhe scrapes up the cold vegetable porridge left in the vat and pours it into a wooden bowl for me, which he brings over to the table where I'm sitting. I thank him and dip my spoon into the bowl.

"Protein gummy?" he says, holding out in his palm a red, squishy-looking thing the size of an earplug.

Protein gummy? Is that what it is?

I turn it down politely. It sounded like he was only asking to be polite, after all.

He says, "You probably don't need it anyway since you're off the production floor for now."

Then he promptly pops the gummy into his mouth, joking about how newbies like him always have to perform a chore of some kind or another during breaks. He rises to his feet and bids me a quick goodbye before hurrying off.

Left alone, I begin shoveling the porridge into my mouth without tasting it. I'm too busy looking around, trying furtively to figure out just where the central motor might be hiding in this godforsaken place. Unlike in all the normal power plants in the open world where it sits proudly in the middle of the production floor, the central motor of this plant is apparently tucked away in the bowels somewhere, like the dirty secret that it is.

I'm just spooning the last of the porridge into my mouth when Bonwhe returns, telling me that he and I need to go see someone named Sky who's sick in bed.

"It's Joon the team leader's order. He wants you to reassure Sky that you're perfectly fine and healthy—that you didn't contract the virus."

I follow him down to the twelfth floor, to a residential cell whose open entrance features yet another clothesline sagging with laundry. Pushing the towels and clothes to either side as if drawing back a curtain, Bonwhe nudges me through. Inside the sparse cell, the same little girl I saw earlier is tucked in a faded blue sleeping bag, her eyes bulging with alarm at the sight of me.

She lets out an earsplitting cry. Plugging her nose with one hand and covering her mouth with the other, she disappears completely into her sleeping bag.

"Go away, virus! Go away!" she shouts from inside her cocoon.

So this is Sky.

"Rookie oppa! Make her leave! Please—!"

Another terror-stricken scream. The little girl must be, pound for pound, the loudest screamer in the world, I'm thinking, when she guardedly pokes her head out of the sleeping bag and glares at me, still desperately clutching at her nose and mouth with her grimy hands. Tucked under her chin is the big, balding head of a raggedy stuffed bear. The thing looks ancient. Ancient and mangy. Where did she even get it?

"It's okay, Sky," Bonwhe assures her in a tone of such ease and confidence that I almost forget that he's a newcomer to this place. "Wisher's test came back negative. She's perfectly healthy."

Sky's brows go up in disbelief, and she briefly contemplates this. But then she lets her brows drop and narrows her eyes at me.

"That's a lie, and I don't believe it," she says. "Wisher wasn't even wearing a protective suit. Anyone who ever does that comes back dead." She pauses to force out a few dramatic coughs. "I'm really sick . . . ," she resumes in a whimpering voice, looking to Bonwhe with helpless puppy eyes and sweeping the hair on her forehead to one side, inviting him to feel her high temperature for himself. "What if I died like this?"

Bonwhe lets a moment tick by. Then he leans in to me and whispers, "She left us no choice . . . ," as he grabs my hand and interlocks his fingers with mine. Sky's eyes just about pop out of their sockets.

"No—!" she cries, her hands shooting back to her mouth and nose. "You can't do that, rookie oppa!"

But Bonwhe puts his arm around my shoulders now and presses me against him.

"Wisher's perfectly fine—squeaky clean," he reassures Sky, all smiles. "So you're perfectly fine, too."

Sky still doesn't buy it. She stares intensely at us for another half minute, looking appalled and full of suspicion. Her eyes firmly on us, she tries for another forced cough, but I can tell that her heart's not in it this time.

Just then, a booming voice rings up from the hollow and summons Bonwhe.

"Sorry—I've gotta go," Bonwhe says to me. Turning to leave, he adds with a wink, "Get back in Sky's good graces, will you?"

He's gone before I can protest. Just how did I find myself tasked with babysitting all the way out here, when I have so much on my plate already? The porridge souring in my stomach, I heave a sigh and turn back to Sky. To my surprise, she has crawled partially out of her sleeping bag. She's still staring at me suspiciously, clutching her sad old bear so tightly that it looks like she's choking it to death—but it's progress.

"You're really clean, Wisher?" she says without easing her guard.

"Yes, honey. Why would I lie?"

"Then why are you acting so weird?"

"What, honey?"

"I don't know what it is, but something's very different about you."

My spine tingles under her sharp scrutiny. I think back to my initial encounter with her among the spinning wheels.

*Hey . . . hi?*

I cringe internally.

"Wha-what are you talking about, kiddo? How do I seem different?" I respond, already feeling as if I'm digging a hole.

*"Kiddo?"* she repeats indignantly. "Kiddo?! I'm not a kid! I'm Sky! Sky—who sees everything from up above!"

Incredulous, I stare at the girl. Then a small, involuntary laugh escapes me at her antics. She reminds me of my kid cousin back in the open world who'll soon be turning seven. At this thought, my confidence returns. Holding her with my eyes, I move in closer and sit across from her on the floor.

"Alrighty, then, Sky who sees everything . . . ," I begin. "Then do you also know—"

"Of course I do!" She cuts me off.

"What? I haven't even finished my sentence!"

Sky regards me coolly.

"The switch for the central motor," I try again. "Do you know where it is?"

How old is this Sky girl? By the size of her, she's about six or seven years old—but she speaks and acts far older than that. Sky lifts her chin and tilts her head back to gaze smugly down at me for a second. Then she says, "It's down at the bottom of the well. Uncle Knife told me that he saw it when he fell in."

"You mean Aunt Knife?" I repeat, recalling the woman who came to the cafeteria cell after I finished the bowl of porridge. Bonwhe explained to me that her badass name was chosen to honor her mad knife skills, adding that he, too, would like to come up with a name for himself that speaks to something cool about him.

"Yes, of course . . . It's Aunt Knife." She nods and gives me a cocky look. "I was testing you. Your brain doesn't seem that damaged, I guess."

Is she testing me? Ha! I can't help but feel a bit annoyed—but I let it go. If I hadn't met Ms. Knife earlier, this kiddo would have gotten me.

"You are right. Aunt Knife fell into"—I recall the gaping mouth of the well I saw from the escalator and press on—"the well on the first floor, right?"

Sky shoots me a frustrated look. It's fair enough for her to test me—I must look foolish to her right now.

"Yes, the cremating well," she says sharply.

My heart skips a beat. The cremating well? The cremating well? What kind of well is for cremating bodies? Composing myself, I follow up.

"And did Aunt Knife really tell you that? That she saw the switch to the central motor inside the well?"

"Of course she didn't tell me that. I overheard it. Grown-ups talk about all kinds of things around me because they think I don't understand."

Ugh . . . can I really trust this source? My confidence in her intel waning sharply, I ask her again, "Are you sure, Sky, that you're remembering it right?"

"I have a mind like a steel trap. I remember everything, including the lullabies my mom sang to me before I was even born."

"Right . . . right," I say after a beat, trying to sound sincere.

For all my lingering doubt, I decide to take a leap of faith and investigate her lead. It's not like I have a better choice. Plus, no one in their right mind would want to visit a cremating well on purpose—which might make it a prime location in which to stow a secret.

"Of course I remember everything!" Sky erupts again. "You know what else? I remember you and Teacher tiptoeing out of this place in the middle of the night exactly seventeen nights ago."

I draw back, trying to place this new piece of information in the puzzle of my mind, when a sudden twinkle comes into her eyes and Sky says, "So did you see the sky when you went out? The real sky?"

She stares at me full of expectation, waiting for my reply. As I stall, scrambling for the right answer, she loses her patience. Scowling, Sky jabs a skinny finger up toward her cell's ceiling, from which hangs a round, fraying quilt, its blue color so faded I can barely tell that it was blue to begin with.

"Is it really that color?" she wants to know.

The realization breaks through my mind then. Sky was . . . she was . . . born here. Born to a death row inmate and raised here all her life!

I'm staring at her in shock without realizing it, when she cocks her head to one side.

"Why are you looking at me like that?" she says.

Quickly, I fix my face.

"No, Sky—the real sky is at least ten times more blue and beautiful!" I tell her, which is a lie, of course, since it's always gray and never blue outside Snowglobe. But what does it matter. I continue, really hamming it up for the little girl who has never seen it. "At sunset, it turns a magical pink and purple; but depending on the day, it can burn an intense crimson."

Sky is riveted, and it's as if she's listening to the most amazing tale of adventure and romance.

"How about the clouds? The moon?" she wants to know, her voice dreamy now. This is where I can be a bit more honest, I suppose. I describe the real sky of the open world faithfully, highlighting the dramatic beauty of a dark storm swirling overhead, and the marble enchantment of the moonlight shining through high clouds on a calm, purple night.

"I want to see all of that someday, too . . . ," Sky says through a sigh, her eyelids heavy with sleep.

"How about we say good night for now," I suggest. "I'll tell you more about the outside world tomorrow."

I push myself up to a low squat, steadying myself on Sky's sleeping bag. My pulse quickens as I lose my balance and step forward, inadvertently treading on the place where I expect her feet to be tucked. But instead of the bony ridge of her toes, I encounter something softer and meatier, and it stops me short. Sky instantly becomes alert, and she shoots me a look.

"Please hurry and leave," she says, giving her sleeping bag a sharp upward tug. "I'm going to sleep."

Odd.

I wish her sweet dreams and take my leave. Stepping out of her cell and closing the sorry excuse of her privacy veil, I catch Sky, her eyes closed, singing herself and her mangy old teddy bear to sleep.

*Mama's gone oyster picking,*
*Baby is left all alone at home,*

*But with the waves singing her a lullaby,*
*Baby falls asleep,*
*With her head on her arms . . .*

**Judging by the faint chimes of a grandfather clock ringing up** from the ground floor, it's eleven o'clock. Not that time has much meaning inside the power plant. Day or night, the wheels never stop turning.

Still, for me, time poses an issue—in that there's no good time for me to sneak into the well that supposedly houses the central motor. Sitting in the middle of the ground floor, the well is surrounded by dozens of wheels operated by as many workers, with as many sets of eyes watching at any given moment. My only hope is that the workers, in their trance, will not notice me climb into the well.

But first, I need to find out which one is Wisher's cell without arousing suspicion.

Back in the cafeteria, I sit alone at an empty table, chewing over my problems. Meanwhile, the first shift has gone to bed until tomorrow morning. While they're resting, the second shifts takes on the duties of cooking and crop tending for the third shift.

"Hey . . . how come you're off the hook for work, still?" a voice says teasingly. "Didn't you test negative?"

Turning to the voice, I suck in a gasp. The man with the pink heart tattoo under his eye—the criminal I saw on my first trip through the mirrors—looms over me, his arms loaded with blue inmate uniforms.

"Come help me," he says, gesturing with his head toward the escalator.

News of his execution aired on TV. Little did I dream at the time that I'd see him again in this life, let alone take orders from him.

"Uh . . . o . . . kay," I say, gathering myself and hurrying after him. "I'm coming, sir . . ."

He stops dead in his tracks and turns to regard me quizzically.

"Sir? You playing games with me?"

What's wrong with sir? I don't recall his name, but I do recall his age at the time of his death, which was thirty-three, a whole lot older than me. I just blink at him, and he lets out a laugh and motions for me to hurry.

"You finally tired of playing the seniority card or what, Wisher?" he says as we get on the escalator. "Sir . . . ? Ha! Are you sure you're feeling all right?"

I see.

"Well," I begin, praying to hit the right note this time. "I figured that I should be more sensitive to my elders' need for respect, because . . . you know . . . you're thirty-three years old and practically ancient, after all. It's best to keep down resentment and prevent revolt."

We hold each other's stare, quiet a moment. Then all of sudden, he erupts in a laugh, shaking his head from side to side. I laugh with him, relieved to find out that Wisher's personality may not stray far from my own.

"By the way . . . ," he says, letting his laugh trail off. "Is that true?"

"What's true?"

Taking a quick glance around, he lowers his voice to a near whisper and says, "That there's no killer virus raging aboveground? That there's no plague?"

*You want to know how I survived the world outside and returned unscathed? The answer is simple. The world is just fine. There's no killer virus, no deadly contagion—*

I guess the lion passed my word to him.

"What else did you hear?" I ask him by way of an answer.

He takes another furtive glance around before whispering, "That you said we need to get out of here. All of us."

Who else did the lion tell? I wonder. And how will the rest of the people down here react to the truth? With shock, I suppose, at first—but surely once they realize there truly isn't a plague, they'll rejoice, right? They'll ditch the wheels and race out of this place, and then the central motor will grind to a halt, which in turn will bring down the curtains on Snowglobe's secret.

I'm privately smiling, my heart swelling at this imagined chain of events.

Then the guy says, "I can't wait for Teacher's next visit, so we can confirm it with her. When she was here two days ago, though, she didn't hint at any such news. In fact, it was the usual gloom and doom—with there being no hope in the outside world and all."

He stares at me, waiting for my response. Dammit. Looks like my fantasy isn't going to come about so easily. His conviction that only Teacher speaks the truth bothers me to no end.

"Do you still trust Teacher?" I hear myself say.

"What?"

"Obviously, Teacher lied to us. I'm the living proof that the world is . . . just fine. It hasn't been devoured by a killer vir—"

His hearty laugh cuts me off.

"Are you still pulling my leg?" he says, searching my face for a moment before shaking his head and laughing again. "You are, aren't you?"

I just stare at him, and he continues, "You forgot the sickness? We saw its effects with our own eyes, on a real person! There's no room for a lie—by Teacher or anyone!"

Now what is he talking about? What sickness could he possibly have seen? The confusion or disturbance in my face must be clear.

"I'm not saying that I don't believe you," he says softly, his tone reminding me of a well-meaning adult talking to a small child. "But you do know that you must guard against any negative thoughts about this place, because once they take hold of you, then it's just a matter of time before they drive you insane."

Over the escalator's railing, he glances warily down at Joon, who's supervising the production floors.

"Be careful with Boss," he warns. "He's already suspicious of you being clean. He'll pounce on you, for sure, if you start telling people strange things."

# WHAT THE ASHES HIDE

It turns out that the tattoo man is a gifted talker. Throughout our trek up the escalators and beyond, he seamlessly moves from one topic of conversation to another, and in that time I glean a couple more valuable facts: The man goes by the name of Heart down here, naturally, and Wisher is chill with everyone, even with Joon, the rather tense and edgy team leader.

Then we're finally arriving at the laundromat. Entering the cell, Heart croons, "And how's our rookie doing?"

Bonwhe's standing in a large trough of some kind, stepping on a mess of light blue pants and shirts that are soaking in the soapy water, a book in his hand. Looking up from the pages, he smiles. Heart and I load our laundry and join Bonwhe in the trough.

I glance at Bonwhe's book cover. It's a fantasy novel from the Warring Age, the same exact one Hyang was reading on the threadbare sofa of her home in the retirees' village back when I was first shipped out there, in fact.

We're all quiet for a while, immersed in reading or our

own thoughts, letting our legs do the work. To be frank, I'm quite amazed at the standard of living down here. From the escalators to the cafeterias, laundromats, gardens, theaters, rec rooms, libraries, and so on—how do these people believe that this is a survival fortress put together in a rush? Why does everyone just accept the story in which they were rescued from the world by Teacher, and never once wonder if Teacher could be holding them prisoner down here?

Then Bonwhe breaks the silence.

"So who's this Captain person?"

"You'll soon get to meet Captain," Heart says, lowering his own book, another romance from the Warring Age. "If Teacher's primary duty is going out on quests to search for a habitable land free of the virus, Captain's is to procure supplies for the family, which is just as important." Then, cupping a hand over one side of his mouth, he adds in a confidential tone, "Though, unlike Teacher, Captain lacks in character."

Heart's openness invites further questions, and Bonwhe doesn't waste the opportunity.

"When was the last time the well was fired?" he asks. "I heard that it's an incinerator."

Heart's face grows instantly somber, and he says, "On my first day here." He goes on to recount the story.

When Teacher brought Heart down here, he was a blank slate. He didn't even remember his own name—a consequence of suffering the nasty virus that had wiped out ninety-nine percent of humanity aboveground, according to Teacher. He was introduced to his new family, who received him with a round of welcoming applause. But just as Heart opened his mouth to express his gratitude, a single voice piped up.

"I believe in Teacher and everything Teacher has to tell us about the world," the person was saying. "But I'm haunted by this recurring dream where the world is just fine, not at all devastated or horrid, but peaceful . . . and even beautiful. I wish to confirm with my own two eyes that the world has ended."

So the fool got his wish. Teacher and Captain accompanied him out of the fortress. There being only two sets of protective suits, the doubter emerged into the world without wearing one. And the next day, Teacher and Captain returned, carrying a vacuum-sealed bag in which the fool's desiccated body rested like a piece of driftwood. Having long been protected inside the walls of the fortress, the fool's pristine immune system couldn't handle the virus's assault—not even for a day, Teacher explained.

His contaminated body was incinerated in the well. And it was when the acrid smell of burning flesh finally began to fade in the air that Heart fully accepted the fact of his incredible luck. He was a survivor of the plague. That was about six months ago.

"It wasn't the first time, either. I'm told there had been three similar incidents prior to that one I witnessed," Heart continues sadly. "Apparently, people had gone up to check the world out for themselves—and died, of course."

"Did they have the same kind of dreams?" Bonwhe is curious.

Heart shakes his head no.

"Dreams are a reflection of your subconscious mind," he replies with a sigh. "Life in the fortress can feel stifling at times, but it's important that we don't let our feelings take over. Those fools obviously did, and if you ask me, it's their own fault. Don't be too alarmed when you see the next fool volunteer to go up and die—and don't think that it couldn't be you, rookie."

Bonwhe gives an uncomfortable chuckle and assures Heart that it won't happen. I just nod gravely, hiding my shock while pretending old familiarity with these tragic tales.

I wonder who this Captain figure might be, if Teacher is the president. Then it strikes me: The VP. A natural pair; salt and pepper.

These "fools" didn't even make it outside, and I'm sure of it. It's not at all difficult to picture President Yi jabbing these people in the neck with lethal injections as soon as they hit the glass walkway leading out of here.

I excuse myself for a bathroom break and leave the laundromat. I need to get a move on before the treacherous Teacher and Captain and whoever else return and find me. I want Sky to see her namesake for herself.

**Back in Sky's cell, the little girl is snoring gently. Her choke hold** on her stuffed bear has loosened in her sleep, and the mangy thing lies free by her face now. I tiptoe over and lift it, vowing to return it in its original condition just as soon as I'm done with it.

I find no joy in borrowing her treasured companion without her permission, but I couldn't find another thing of a greater value in this place, so it's the bear.

Covering the thing with blue uniform pants that I took from someone's clothesline, I take the escalators all the way down to the ground floor. Dozens of residents working the graveyard shift are turning the wheels, their fish eyes focused on nothing. I casually make my way toward the massive stone well sitting in the middle of the hollow, occasionally stretching my arms this way and that to see if anyone will notice me from inside the wheels. And no one does. Encouraged, I try bolder moves, such as jumping up and down in place and swinging my arms wildly. Still, no one even flinches, and I arrive at my target without so much as a stink eye.

An acrid smell wafts up thickly from the well, a gruesome reminder of its function. I lean over its gaping mouth and peer down. A bottomless void. When I lean back, I notice the intimidatingly long chain snaking from the well's bucket, suggesting the chamber's depth.

If Sky's right, way down at the bottom is the motor. It'd be great to confirm this with the Knife lady, but as a first-shift worker, she's already gone to bed.

Steeling myself, I drop Sky's stuffed bear into the well's gaping mouth.

"Oh no!" I cry, looking around in fake panic. "Sky's stuffie fell into the well!"

My frankly pathetic performance still gets no one's attention, but I continue with the act anyway. "Welp . . . I have no choice but to climb in and get it."

I look around again, amazed at how smoothly things are going for me right now. Apart from the wheels and the zombie workers inside them, it's only the well and the currently empty isolation room and the attached observation room on this floor. I feel a stab of exhilaration when the door of the observation room suddenly swings open and Bonwhe walks out to me, a mop in his hand.

"What are you doing there?" he says.

"Uh . . . I . . ." It takes me a moment to recover. "I dropped Sky's teddy bear and it fell into the well."

"What? How?"

"H-how?" I stammer. "I guess I don't know?"

It's true. I didn't think it through—at least not to that degree of detail.

"Don't worry about it," I tell him, moving to the bucket. "I'll take care of it."

"Wait . . . You're not going to climb in," he says, looking at me like I'm crazy. "For a stuffed bear?"

The strong smell wafting up the well seems to intensify then.

"I told you—I dropped Sky's teddy. You probably don't know what a big deal that is," I tell him, one foot in the bucket. "She's going to raise holy hell if she finds out."

Bonwhe opens his mouth to protest, but I've already seated myself in the bucket now, tossing myself into the well as the rattle of the chain ricochets deafeningly around me. This isn't how I pictured the ride at all, but the chain was apparently not secured to the pulley. At all. My stomach floating inside me, I can't even scream.

Then, abruptly, the bucket jerks to a violent stop. I gasp again, my mind finally catching up to my body. But then in the next moment, I find the bucket descending again, slowly and in control this time. My heart pounding, I pitch my head back and squint up. Far above, Bonwhe's silhouette is dark against the bright opening. He seems to be working the pulley for me, thank goodness. I'd have died if the bucket touched down. The thought sends a fresh jolt up my spine, and I fiercely grip the bucket.

Recovering my equilibrium and awash with gratitude, I gaze up again at his shape, and the irony hits me that the amnesiac Bonwhe is helping me to expose his family's great big sham. He'll probably resent me if, or when, his memory returns.

About a minute later, the bucket touches down softly, stirring up a thick cloud of dust that sends me into a coughing fit. I cover my mouth and nose the best I can and, narrowing my eyes to slits, look around the dusty murk surrounding me. It's close to black here, with light barely reaching all this way down. Plus, it's damp and cold. Shit, it's cold.

Warily, I climb out of the bucket. A pile of dust buries my ankles, and I move one foot in front of another, careful not to disturb it, my arms stretched out in front of me. It takes about twenty paces before my groping hands finally touch the cold wall. I steady myself against it and continue moving along the stone contour. I may be imagining it, but it seems that the well is far wider at the bottom.

Every so often, my feet bump against something buried in the dust, quickening my pulse with the hope that I've stumbled upon the motor; but when I bend down to inspect it, whatever it is just disintegrates at the touch of my fingers.

I don't know how long I've been groping in the dark, but it's been a while. I'm getting impatient. Impatient and angry. Sky must have told a lie about the motor being down here. Shit, shit, shit.

I'm thinking about jerking the chain to signal to Bonwhe to pull me back up, when I remember. I have to find that goddamned teddy bear! Cursing myself, I take a huge breath and hold it, resigned to the idea that I'll just have to breathe in some thick dust and hope it doesn't permanently damage my lungs. Then, bending down to the floor, I begin sweeping my hands through the dust in search of the godforsaken thing.

Though my mouth is clamped shut and I'm barely even breathing through my nose, the cloud of dust that rises up all around me finds its way into me, and soon there's no way that I can ignore the taste in my mouth. I stand back up, three-quarters blind and sick to my stomach, spitting and gagging, when I see light breaking through the dust on the floor. Dim, but it's light, nonetheless.

My eyes widening, I get right back down in the dust on all fours and begin frantically sweeping, digging the dust bed right down to the hard floor, at which point bright light floods up into the well. The well's floor is not of stone but of thick glass!

But before I can even try to consider the possible implications of this discovery, the second discovery hits me in the face. Beneath the glass floor is a dizzying web of clear electrical cables, each glowing with the optical fibers pulsing with light inside.

What in the world? I gaze at the scene, astonished and bewildered. If I let my eyes drift, it's like gazing at a distant galaxy, and I briefly forget where I am and what I'm doing here—until another coughing fit snaps me back.

I lower my face to the glass floor for a better look. Some cables glow more intensely than others, I note, when a pattern on the surface of a particularly dim cable catches my eye. A series of letters and numbers. *Sa . . . D, 13?*

My heart skips. I sweep away the fine dust settling back down on the glass and scrutinize the letters on the neighboring cables.

Ra-U-98
Ra-L-2
Ja-B-54
Ja-R-121
Da-Q-19

Every one of them is a settlement in the open world. Then is each cable transmitting the settlements' daily quota of electricity to Snowglobe? The subscription fee for the programs produced in the dome?

I'm sweeping the dusty floor with my whole arms now, unsure of what exactly I'm looking for. Then my hand hits upon a small depression. My heart jolting, I move directly over it and clean off the dust to find a hooklike handle carved into the floor. And just beneath it glows what appears to be a utility panel with rows of switches, all lit red.

If this is the central motor, it's not what I expected it to look like. This just looks like a breaker panel . . . and why should there be a breaker panel here?

Then a thought occurs to me. Does this power plant even have a central motor . . . or is it running on something else?

A significant amount of electricity is pulled daily from the open world in the name of subscription fees, and yet we're told it's what's needed for the actors' day-to-day use. But could Snowglobe have been secretly siphoning an unlimited amount of electricity for heat as well? Does this power plant even produce power, or is its only function to transmit stolen electricity?

My heart pounds in my ears. I grip the hook-handle and pull it with all my might, but it doesn't even budge. Then I remember the bucket. I drag it over and hook its chain onto the handle on the floor. The length is just right, as if it's been waiting for this moment.

Straightening up, I take a step back but my foot trips over something, and I glance down. A crumbling human skeleton, half of its rib cage and skull still buried under the dust, is set aglow in the light coming through the glass floor.

The cremating well . . . This isn't dust. It's the ashes of people who tried to escape this prison. . . .

I knew none of the people who perished here, and yet breathless grief takes over me. They died without even re-membering their own names; and even in death, their ashes are being used to cover up Snowglobe's sins, literally. Tears surge. I take in a breath, inhaling each and every one of the faceless people into my soul.

Even the fate I wished on my former director is not bad enough for Yi Bonyung. Everyone alive shall witness the pun-ishment she will be dealt. When the moment comes, I will show no mercy.

I wipe my tears away and double-check the connection be-tween the bucket's chain and the hook-handle. Then I give the chain a heavy tug, signaling to Bonwhe to switch on the pulley.

*And what kind of punishment does he deserve?* I'm thinking. Is he a victim in this, or a villain? I'm still turning it over when I see his tiny silhouette move to drag the cover over the well, closing it shut. He doesn't return.

# SAVE YOU FROM OUR SINS

## Yi Bonwhe

Mom beams with pride, leading me into the bathroom. Inside, a new full-size mirror greets me, adorned with a large gold ribbon at the top. Then Grandmother appears behind me and says, "Happy fourteenth, my boy! Go on—try the mirror."

I'm frankly exhausted from the party that went on for too long, but I stifle my yawn and do what I'm told.

I reach for the mirror, and my fingertips dip right through its silvery surface.

*What . . . ?*

Mom and Grandmother let out a joint coo of delight. Then Grandmother gently squeezes my shoulder, her eyes fixed on me in the mirror.

"Remain extra-conscious of the public eye as you move up through the ranks—from heir, to VP, and then to president, ultimately. Never forget that we're the symbol of virtuousness and integrity in our society," she says.

Act like a leader even when you're alone in your bedroom, et cetera, et cetera. A speech she'll never tire of giving me.

I take in a deep breath and then let it out in small, sur-
reptitious increments, so as not to come across as heaving a
sigh, which is what I really want to do. But code of conduct
dictates that a Yibonn heir should refrain from such behavior.
An heir's heavy sigh is bound to make people around him
uneasy and anxious, providing fodder for speculation that all
is not well in the dynasty.

*So what is this mirror before me?*

As if reading these thoughts, Grandma pats me on my
shoulder and says, "The mirror elevator is freedom."

Then Mom, too, puts a gentle hand on my shoulder.

"It's a portal to a private space to which only the three of
us have access. There you can be yourself, free from public
scrutiny," she says.

I feel a sudden pulse of excitement at this, but then Grandma
warns, "But the portal will also introduce you to certain hidden realities—secrets that you've been protected from. And as
with all such things, these truths might occasionally feel like a
burden to bear alone for the rest of your life."

"Is it imperative that I learn those secr—"

"Yes, of course," she replies impatiently. "Bonwhe, my
boy . . . Don't forget. You're the future president of the Yibonn, tasked to lead the world."

A heavy feeling settles in my chest. Am I cut out for such a
task? Holding back sighs when others are around, doing what
I'm told without complaint, and pinching off any curiosity
regarding my own personal interests and preferences are the
only things I'm good at.

Once again, Grandma grips my shoulder.

"Now . . . let's see if our Bonwhe has what it takes," she

suggests with a bland smile. "I've been waiting to see your judgment and intellect in action."

Mom, suddenly looking as stiff and nervous as she did on the morning of my first midterms, takes my hand and squeezes it. Then she warns, "What you're about to see may be difficult to accept. But be strong. I believe in you."

It is then, inside the mirror moving at a soul-stripping speed, that I first learn about the underground power plant.

**"Hi, everyone! Today, I'd like to introduce a new member to our** family!" Mom says, her voice high with excitement.

We're standing in a hall surrounded by towering stacks of gearwheels, before an assembly of people. None of them are remotely familiar to me, let alone family. Why is Mom introducing me as their relative? And wait . . . I blink as I take in the gearwheels rising up around us. The people spinning the wheels have zero interest in my presence. My brain's still thawing from our freezing walk through the dark, subzero corridor leading to this place. My movements feel sluggish and uncoordinated, and I can barely bring my eyes to focus. I only half hear Mom explain to the assembly that my regret-table cognitive impairment is due to prolonged exposure to some virus. The whole front row takes a furtive step back, but then a welcoming shout goes up, and everyone cheers.

I think about the revelation Mom told me on our way down here. Snowglobe's heat is supplied by the sweat of these people?

It feels like the ground under my feet is buckling.

"Teacher! I have something to say." A voice breaks through

the lingering smatter of applause, and a man walks toward the front in big, confident strides. A long scar runs from his chin to his cheek on one side of the face.

"Hi, rookie. I'm Knife," he says to me, smiling. "They call me that for the scar on my face, see? We pick what we're called here. I assume that you forgot your name, too?" Then he turns to Mom and says, "Teacher, I've lately been having these disturbing dreams where my face gets slashed; and often, you appear in it—"

"I, too, often dream of our family," Mom says, briskly cutting him off. Fixing him with a sharp look, she smiles stiffly and nods her head a few times as if to say, *That's enough.*

"And I saw this boy, too," the man says, pointing at me. "In my dream."

Mom's smile freezes, and so does my heart.

"And do you know what else I also saw—excuse me, remembered?" the man continues with sudden intensity. "Everything! Including the face of the president of the Yibonn fucking Media Group!"

He pulls a handful of red gummies that look like earplugs from his prison pants pocket and throws them angrily on the floor.

"Take us out of here before things get ugly," he growls, stepping to her.

Mom takes a step back and shoots a glance at the assembly. Mutiny brews right before her eyes, though all around the hall, the wheels keep on turning, with no one inside them aware of what's happening.

Then a woman rushes to the front.

"Teacher, forgive me!" she cries. "It's all my fault. I failed as a team leader. I should have been more attuned to our family's well-being!"

Mom, regarding her with disdain, demands, "How about the special supplies I gave you? Did you distribute the pills to everyone?"

"Of course, Teacher!" the woman assures her in a tearful voice. "Distributed every last bit of them!"

Mom breathes out a small sigh of relief, but the man called Knife isn't done.

"It's not just me," he resumes angrily. "Others have begun to remember, too! Our memories are returning, slowly but surely!"

A few hoots of support go up above the assembly, as well as noises of shock and confusion. Then some people begin breaking from the rows and moving to the front in a show of solidarity with Knife.

"Please! Everyone! Please calm down and . . . ," Mom says, straining to remain calm herself as more people push forward. She takes another step back, stealing a nervous glance at the large grandfather clock. That's when the first chime of midnight tolls. *Diiiiiiiiiiiiing—*

As if this is their cue, all the workers inside the wheels slow their pace. The clock keeps chiming.

*Ding—*

*Ding—*

*Ding—*

One by one, the sweaty, exhausted workers step out of the wheels. In the hall, the faces of Knife and all the rest suddenly twist in agony. It's as if the sound of the chimes is physically affecting them—as if the noise has triggered some kind of reaction.

*Ding*—

*Ding*—

"I'm parched . . . ," someone cries.

"Wa-water!" another pleads.

Workers scattered on the upper levels begin migrating downstairs in small groups. The clocks keep chiming. I watch in horror as down below, one person after another stumbles toward the central well and jumps into its gaping mouth, crying of thirst.

My blood runs cold. That well isn't for water. Mom told me about it on the way down—it's an incinerator. Which means . . .

"They're all going to die!" I cry, turning to Mom in horror, but she simply looks on, as if all is as it should be. That's when I understand with a chilling sense of doom.

This is no accident. She's doing this on purpose.

Not knowing what else to do, I move to start for the well, to stop this madness somehow, but Mom harshly yanks me back. Her face close to mine, she yells, "Don't interfere. They should have been dead a long time ago!"

A wrenching cry peals out in the air, the cry of a little kid. We both whip our heads in the direction. A woman hobbles for the well while a little girl clings desperately to her leg.

"Mamaaaaa! Stop!" the little girl cries out in terror. "Stooooooop, please, Mamaaaaaaa! Don't gooooooo!"

But the woman doesn't even seem to hear her. As if possessed, she continues lurching for the well, dragging her leg saddled with her little girl. I shake off Mom and rush to the girl, and just as the woman climbs up on the well, I pry the girl off.

With the girl screaming and kicking in my arms, I try to stop as many as I can from hurling themselves into the pit of death, but it's all in vain. The few I manage to briefly hold back overpower me with inhuman strength, driven by their strange, unnatural thirst.

"No!" I shout in horror. "Please! Stop!"

Then everyone's gone. In the dreadful silence that has descended, the only sound is that of the little girl's agonized sobs and my own heavy breathing. Tears stream off my chin.

## "Bonwhe," Grandmother calls to me, but I don't look up.

In her library, surrounded by shelves of books and rare treasures, the horror of yesterday is still all I can see. My hands tremble with the sense memory of restraining the orphaned girl by her shuddering shoulders.

"You are to perform countless difficult duties from here forth," Grandmother says in a tone so solemn it's almost pious. "I'd love to live my life while doing nothing but noble and elegant things, too. But alas, that's not in the cards for us—no, sweetie. Not for me, not for you, not for any one of us Yibonns, who are called to keep this world in peace and balance."

Her words! I don't know if I can take it anymore. I squeeze my head between my two hands.

Shaking her head in disapproval, she plows on. "When it comes to strategic management of the underground power plant, regular and timely replacement of workers is key. It prevents any of the residents from getting too . . . curious, like the man you saw yesterday. So what you did—interrupting the purging process and saving that little girl—equates to a failure."

She pauses to let that hang in the air.

"Luck was on your side, though," she continues at last, her tone softening slightly. "That little girl you saved? It turns out that she's immune to hypnosis. So basically, you saved a future hypnotist from dying along with her useless mom. For that, you get bonus points."

I remain quiet. I have nothing to add.

Grandma moves in and lifts my chin with her hand. Peering into my eyes, she says, "It's up to you, though, whether you accept the failing grade and give up your position, or take the bonus points and try again. Which do you choose?"

I know that the question is in form only. There's no choice here.

"I'll try again, Grandmother," I reply dutifully.

"Are you sure?" she says after a moment, making an elaborate surprised face. "Are you willing to commit your life to our business—and all the bad and ugly bits that come with the good?"

"If I don't take on the responsibility, then Ichae would have to," I hear myself say. "Just like Mom had to step up when Uncle opted out."

"Ichae?" Grandmother says after a moment, sounding genuinely surprised this time.

Ichae. The girl who moved in one day when I was a kid. She's been living with us for some years now, but I seldom see her. Neither Grandmother nor Mom has ever provided me with a remotely satisfying explanation to justify her sudden appearance, but one thing I'm certain of is that she is a critically important person to them, to us.

"Why, I'm glad to know my little Bonwhe grew up to be such a mature and responsible young man thanks to Ichae," Grandmother says with a laugh.

Yi Bonwhe. I curse the name in my head, the name that will continue to determine the course of my life.

**Six days later, Mom hands me a present, congratulating me on** my squeaking by the first Yibonn heir test. It's a fountain pen engraved with my name, Yi Bonwhe.

"New residents are moving in today—a whole lot of them. I'll probably have to stay down there for a month," Mom tells me. "I've hired an assistant to help me with smoother transitions between batches from here on out. And we're going to ramp up hypnosis and thought control to tighten security and make sure revolts like the one you witnessed don't keep happening."

It hurts to breathe in, as if the air is nothing but toxic gas.

**The underground power plant is a necessary evil, I convinced** myself then. Ever since, that conviction has sustained me all this time with its daily inoculation of poison. Still, it doesn't protect me from shame, which I tried to dull by turning my attention to Yeosu. Caring for her helped me pretend that I might have a shred of decency left intact in me. In that sense, I used to wonder whether it was my selfish need to make myself feel better that drove my compassion for Yeosu, after all.

Then you showed up.

*It's an honor to finally meet you. I'm Goh Haeri.*

*Finally?*

*I meant to say . . . that it's nice to* finally introduce myself *to you as the new weather presenter.*

A familiar face indeed. But those eyes? I'd never met them before. Little did I know that you were about to turn my world upside down.


**"Now, don't screw this up,"** Mom warns me as we head down to the plant for the second time. "Prove that you've learned your lesson, and that you've got what it takes."

It's been a few years since I failed the initial test, and since then I haven't been allowed to set foot underground again. Fail this second chance, and I'll forever be dismissed as the heir.

"Dear family . . . !" Mom booms into the megaphone as we stand before the family once more. The faces I'm looking at are different, but their situation is the same. It makes me sick. "Please join me in welcoming our new rescue!"

From the front row, the same little girl I saved from the well openly stares up at me, her eyes alive with recognition. Against her side, she squeezes a mangy old stuffed bear as if it's her last remaining treasure. I pretend to scratch my face and raise a finger to my lips, signaling to her to remain quiet. The kid responds in kind, furtively nodding her head, her bright eyes fixed on mine. A smart one.

Can I save you again? Not just from death this time, but also from the injustice and the evil done by my family?

# PART 3

# THE PENTHOUSE

When I open my eyes again, I'm lying not at the bottom of the well but on the floor of a residential cell. What happened? Did I black out? How did I get out? I remember the pounding headache, and the overwhelming smell of soot and ashes that almost registered as a taste in my mouth. I remember frantically yanking at the hook-handle, again and again without result. I remember cursing Bonwhe for his inexplicable betrayal. I remember imagining what dreadful interrogation I'd have to face even if I got out of this well alive. I remember climbing inside the bucket, shaking the chain futilely, letting my eyes go out of focus as they rested on the tangled network of cables below me, glowing like a galaxy. I remember thinking of the people enslaved at the wheels in the open world, who would go on living and dying that way because I failed in my mission, and I remember the weight of my defeat, far heavier than the lid I couldn't lift, crushing me.

Then: nothing. Until now.

A shadow moves beyond the privacy veil of the sagging clothesline.

"I can't find it!" Sky squawks, and my heart jumps to my throat.

Shoot! Her teddy bear! But before I can blink, the clothes are pushed aside and Sky enters the room.

"Did you see a treasure hiding in here, Wisher?" she says.

As I make a noise of incomprehension, my eyes dart to the thing squeezed against her chest. Incredibly, it's the bear. Yes, I remember holding it in my arms in the bucket. But . . . I stare at it in disbelief. It doesn't appear ashy or sooty . . . just sad, old, and mangy-looking, as always. But how?

"Uncle Heart and I are playing treasure hunt, but I haven't found anything so far. Not a single prize!" Sky complains.

"What?" I reply stupidly. "Uh . . . I don't think there's any here either?"

Sky pulls a face and stomps out of the room through the veil of clothes. In my confusion, I follow her out.

I'm poking through this room and that—not that I even know what treasure I'm looking for—when I feel a tap on my shoulder.

"Are you looking for me?" a familiar voice says, and I swing around. There stands Bonwhe, looking tense.

"What happened?" I blurt out before I can think. "How did you get me out of the well?"

Bonwhe smiles thinly and whispers. "Fortunately, you passed out inside the bucket. So I pulled you up while Joon was away. Then I put you in a cart full of laundry and brought you to my cell. But we can't talk here." Pausing, he glances left and right, then reaches for my pants pocket and jams something in it.

"The top floor," he says. "Meet me there. I'll explain everything."

I slide my hand into the pocket and feel for the object he shoved in there. Is it a key?

**The twenty-fifth floor is the only floor I've discovered in this** place that has a locked door. The section of the escalator leading to it is different from the rest—entirely covered with a wooden arch, presumably for privacy since there are no weather events to worry about down here. The floor's design also deviates from what's typical, a continuous ring like a donut or coiled snake, rather than a honeycomb.

*What's the significance?* I wonder as I slide the key into the keyhole and twist it. Easing the door open, I step into a spacious, clutter-free room. My eyes widen with astonishment as I take a long, slow look around. There's a plush round rug on the floor, an elegant chaise lounge with an adjustable back, a huge built-in wardrobe that could easily hold at least ten people, a tea cabinet displaying perfectly curated tea sets, and so on. In other words, the room is completely out of place in this underground prison.

I don't know why, but I make a beeline to the closet and marvel at the assortment of clothes and linens tucked away inside it. Shutting it, I slowly move through the donut-shaped room, noting the luxury bathroom and shower, the pillowy bed, the stylish floor lamp, the carved dining room table, and even the writing desk.

Then it dawns on me. All this must be for Teacher and

Captain. I let out an incredulous laugh. They won't shortchange themselves on comfort or luxury, of course. Not even down here in this hell.

A bitter taste flooding my mouth, I turn for the door, and the sight of Bonwhe standing there startles me.

"Hey . . . ," he says, and tries for a smile.

I'm looking for a sign of guilt, of apology in his eyes when he calls me "Chobahm."

I just stare at him, feeling like I've been struck.

"I'm sorry I lied to you."

What? He never lost his memory? Before I can stop myself, I'm blurting out the next thing that comes to me.

"Why did you lock me in the well?" I ask. "Is it because you realized I found the switch?"

"I had no other choice. Not at the time," he says. He tells me how while I was poking around at the bottom of the well, Joon was looking for Wisher to investigate her return further. When Bonwhe saw Joon rushing down to the ground floor to ask if anyone had seen Wisher, he covered the well with the wooden lid. Then Bonwhe told Joon he had seen Wisher upstairs and lured him away from the well.

"So you did it to help me, is what you're saying," I reply, noting the edge in my voice.

"Did you really think that I meant to lock you in there?" he replies, sounding appalled.

When I don't answer, he lets out a chuckle—one loud enough to make me reach for his mouth and cover it.

"Keep it down, will you?" I hiss. "What if someone hears us? I have so much to ask you still!"

Bonwhe plucks my hand off his mouth and returns it to my side.

"No one can hear us through these walls," he assures, tapping his knuckles on the wall behind him. "A lot went into soundproofing this room."

"Is that so? Then answer me," I say, feeling my questions, which I've had to contain since the first time I saw him down here, rising fast. "Why are you down here? And if you're a supposed rescue from the surface like the rest of these people, how is your memory intact? The whole world is crushed by the news of your death—the plane crash? How dare you deceive everyone like this!"

"Are you disappointed that I'm alive?" he says after a moment, looking at me with a wounded expression.

What? What kind of question is that? I open my mouth to ask him, but as I stare at him, irritated, a lump begins to swell in my throat. My nose stings, and my eyes get all hot. And before I know it, tears have started. There's no use trying to stop them now.

"I . . . ," I say, choking on tears. "I had to . . . had to tell the world that . . . your plane went down on your way to apologize to my family!"

I'm sobbing at this point, everything boiling up inside me again. Then Bonwhe's wrapping his arms around me in a gentle hug; and even through our uniforms' fabric, I can feel his warmth and the slight flutter of his hands. I try pushing him away, but he pulls me closer, and I know for sure now that he's shaking, too.

"I'm sorry," he says, and his voice wavers. "I didn't know that my grandmother's punishment for me would be used against you, too."

"Don't," I manage to choke out.

*Don't bother killing my grandson, though. He's about to get his, anyway.*

"I knew you were in danger," I continue through tears. "And I didn't even warn you properly. You took a risk for me, and I failed to do the same for you."

Bonwhe draws back slightly and wipes the tears on my face with his shirt sleeve.

"I didn't need you to," he says softly. "I don't need you to."

He draws me back in, and we stand there a while, silent but for my muffled sobbing.

Finally I pull away and stare at him, saying, "Don't you want to know why I'm here?" I'm biting the inside of my lip so hard that a metallic taste begins to fill my mouth. "I've come to shut down this place—everything. I'm going to find the central motor and turn it off. Then it'll be all over—the great lie of Snowglobe, the Yibonn's legacy . . . everything."

*I'm going to destroy your family, even though you stuck up for me every time it mattered.*

"What I'm about to do will destroy your life—your present, past, and the future. Everyone will curse you and your family, and you'll have to live with it. And do you know what else? I don't even feel bad about it. I'm doing what must be done."

Bonwhe's silent. I glance away. I can't bear to look him in the eye.

"Such honesty . . . You could have lied, you know," he says, leaning in and resting his head lightly on my shoulder.

"You know I'm not like that," I say, sniffling. "I've always been a straight shooter, and you should know that by now."

He lifts his head leans back slightly to look me in the eyes.

"Then I'll be honest, too. You say that I took a risk for you, but I was only trying to keep my promise to Yeosu," he says. "So I want to stick up for you this time, Chobahm. If you will accept my help, that is."

I frown. Did he hear a word I said?

"What are you up to now?" I say, giving him a hard look. This makes him laugh.

"Stick up for me—do you even know what you're saying? You're offering to help me to destroy you and your family, do you realize that?"

"Consider it a chance for me to pay penance."

"Penance?"

"Yes, penance . . . for all the time I've spent doing nothing, when I knew what my family was doing was wrong. To tell you the truth, though, I'm as much in the dark as you are when it comes to the nitty-gritty of this operation. I'm supposed to be training to run it, but the first time my mom took me down here, I . . . failed my test. But still . . . I'm offering you my help, such as it is."

"So you have known about this place," I say. "All along, you've known."

"Not my whole life, but . . . long enough to be implicated," he replies.

"Then why should I trust you now, or believe anything you promise?"

"I don't need you to trust me."

I blink. "What?"

"And I don't need you to feel bad for me, either. I should already be dead by the hands of my own grandmother, remember? Whether it's prison or hell that I'm headed to, it doesn't bother me."

Maybe it doesn't, but just why is it that his answer bothers me so much?

Before ever discovering the truth of my birth—before President Yi ever threatened to kill me if I revealed her secret—I, too, had accepted life as it came to me. I believed there was no right or wrong in the game of life. One could only play the cards they were dealt to the best of their ability.

It turns out, though, that isn't true. There is right and wrong, and some people have been dealt impossible cards to play. There are clone girls exclusively created to be used and discarded by those in charge, and there are those born to achieve a task they never agreed to, even if the task is ensuring the continuation of the Snowglobe order. For them, life was a rigged game from day one, and they are condemned to their prescribed ending.

Then there's a sudden metallic scrape, the sound of a sliding key. My eyes jump to Bonwhe's, and we shoot across the room to the huge closet.

I peek through the slit in the doors, my heart racing. Joon's entering the room, trailed by another figure whose face I can't make out past the bulk of Joon's body. Carefully locking the door behind them, Joon double-checks, then triple-checks that the lock is engaged.

"Have you eaten yet?" Joon says to the figure, definitely female, who's now studying the mirror hanging on the back of the door. I still can't see her face, or that of her reflection.

"Would you like me to have the kitchens prepare some food for you, Captain?"

Jesus Christ. Captain's back, already?

The figure is dressed in white overalls, which I imagine to be the "survival suit" Joon mentioned earlier. "No need," she says, studying herself in the mirror. "I'm going back out tonight."

Wait. I know that voice. It's not the president's, and it's not the VP's, either. But I swear I recognize it.

"Tonight?" Joon expresses his surprise. "But you need a day of rest, Captain—no? Please forgive me if I'm overstepping, but I'm concerned that you might be pushing yourself too hard."

"I already told you," Captain says, sounding irritated. "I found a deserted store. It's stocked full of supplies our family needs. How do you expect me to rest?"

Spinning around, she runs her long fingers through her cascading onyx waves. Inside the closet, my mouth drops open, and I clap both hands over my mouth so as not to scream.

*You do know that I have a keen eye. . . . That's how I picked you out.*

*Just call me Jinjin.*

Jin Jinsuh, the ocean bride who swore her everlasting love for Fran in the floating glass cube. She strides across the floor to the chaise lounge and plops herself down on it, frowning and fanning herself with her hands in disapproval of the damp underground air.

Jin Jinsuh is in league with the Yibonns? It can't be!

"As always, Captain, I'm humbled by your tireless sacrifice for our family," Joon offers solemnly, bowing his head in a show of further respect, as if she's the queen and he's a royal guard. "Well, then . . . Would you need about four days' worth of supplies this time, Captain?"

"Uh-huh," Jinsuh replies smugly, fishing a small cardboard box from her suit pocket. Opening the box, she holds it out for Joon's inspection.

"The highlight of my excursion," she says.

White pills in blister packs?

Joon just looks at her, uncomprehending, and she lets out a trill of laughter.

"Vitamin D," she declares triumphantly. "The store had a pharmacy in it. There were signs of previous small-scale looting, but luckily, I was able to find a big stash of these pills in the back."

She pushes the box to Joon, whose face is bright with excitement now.

"This is amazing!" he exclaims, taking the box. "Thank you, thank you so much, Captain!"

Jinsuh rises from the chair and strolls over to the cabinets, where she selects a single key from the heavy bunch jangling from her hip.

"You have no idea how thrilled I was to find them. Artificial light's good enough for plants, but not so much for humans' vitamin D synthesis." Unlocking a cabinet, she produces a document from it. "Let's see," she says, running her eyes across the page, which is packed with dense text. "We can do two pills per person," she declares after a moment, looking satisfied. Then, shifting her gaze back to Joon, she asks, "By the way, is everyone behaving? Does anyone need a one-on-one session with me?"

Joon's bright expression darkens, and he hesitates a moment before saying, "There is one person, Captain . . . Wisher appears to need your help."

Jinsuh blinks at Joon, looking bewildered.

"And how do you expect me to help her?" she says finally, raking back her snaking locks with an air of impatience. "She's still missing, isn't she?"

"Uh . . . yes, Captain, I'm sorry that I forgot to mention . . . she came back yesterday."

"What?" Jinsuh breathes sharply. "Who came back yesterday?"

"Uh . . . Wisher, Captain . . . and she's not right," Joon says, cowering. "She's been babbling nonsense about many things . . . including this place called Snowball? Snowglobe? Anyway, she looks fine on the outside, but it's obvious that the virus has taken over her. She needs your urgent attention, Capt—"

"Where is she now?! Bring her to me right this moment!" Jinsuh demands, and the anger flashing in her eyes might as well be the edge of a sword slicing through my chest. I press my hands over my clenching heart.

# THE SUSPICION

Joon hurries out the door, and Jinsuh plops back down on the chaise, seething.

What do I do now?

Terrified, I turn to Bonwhe, searching his eyes as if I'll find my answer there. He takes my hands in his and squeezes them gently, mouthing a silent message—*"I will . . . get out . . . distraction . . ."*

Wait. What?

I shake my head from side to side in a vehement disapproval of his suggestion—No! What would Jinsuh do if she saw him emerge from this closet to appear in this room? Would she consider it normal, since he's Yibonn, or would she jump to search the rest of the closet and learn what he might have been doing in there?

The door flies open then, and a high, excited voice calls, "Captain!"

Suddenly, Sky's running into the room, clutching the mangy old stuffed bear to her chest. Who let her up here?

Jinsuh, springing to her feet, opens her arms wide.

"Sky!" Jinsuh sings, and scoops up the little girl barreling into her chest.

The rearing height of Jinsuh makes Sky look even tinier.

"How was your trip?" Sky asks Jinsuh, her face the happiest I've seen.

"It was great, sweetie!" Jinsuh replies. "Have you been a good girl while I was gone? I hope you've been eating, little one—and taking your protein gummies, especially."

"Yuck." Sky makes a face. "I hate protein gummies."

"I thought my Sky wanted to grow as tall and strong as this Captain," Jinsuh says. "And do you know how good protein gummies are for your brain development, too? For your memory?"

"Do I have to be tall to become a captain?"

Sky's innocent query amuses Jinsuh. She lets out a laugh and gazes at the ceiling for a long moment, a sisterly smile on her face.

"Of course you do!" she says at last. "You have to be tall and strong to be my successor!"

Sky makes another face, and Jinsuh chuckles, putting her down. Then she pulls something out of her pants pocket—a plastic wristwatch for kids.

Sky gasps.

"Is that for me?"

"Why, yes! Captain always keeps her promises. And do you know what? I'll keep my promise to take you out into the world, too—as soon as you're old enough."

"But you said that when I turned six," Sky argues. "Then

you said it again when I turned seven, and then again on my last birthday."

"And that's still not old enough, girlie," Jinsuh replies, smiling and fastening the band of the watch around Sky's tiny wrist. "You will grow up to be an amazing person, someone invaluable in this fortress, and in the whole wide world. Mark this captain's word."

The two gaze into each other's eyes, smiling. Then Sky's pulling at Jinsuh's arm, saying, "Help me find treasures, Captain. Uncle Heart hid them for me to find, and I've only found one so far!"

Jinsuh makes a disappointed face.

"I'm sorry, Sky," she says. "Captain has to take care of some business."

But Sky doesn't give up so easily, and they engage in brief negotiation before Jinsuh acquiesces. The two leave the room, hand in hand.

Bonwhe and I remain in the closet for another minute before cautiously stepping out.

"Let's go back to the well—we're running out of time! We need to shut this place down now," I say, growing desperate. I feel shaky all over. I didn't expect Captain to come back so soon, much less to be Jinsuh herself. If she catches me, any chance I have of executing my plan is done for.

"No—the well's too exposed," Bonwhe argues. "Let's go to my cell for now."


**As soon as we make it back down from the twenty-fifth floor,** we see Joon up ahead, barking at people to go find Wisher.

Bonwhe snatches my hand and pulls me into the closest cell, the library. Crouched behind the shelves, I ask Bonwhe in a whisper, "Did you know that Jin Jinsuh was working for the president?"

"No," he says, frowning in distaste. "I wasn't faking my congratulations at the wedding."

"Do you think she really loves Fran?"

And the moment the question leaves my mouth, it strikes me: The man with the turquoise eyebrows who put the spell on me. Could it be . . .

No one even knows who they are, or what they actually look like . . . Some have described Buhae as an old man with yellow eyes, and others a young woman with a forked tongue . . .

"Jin Jinsuh is Buhae, the hypnotist . . . ," I murmur to myself.

This explains the over-the-top extravagance of the wedding. It wasn't just because of Fran, a beloved former weather-caster, that they got such an exclusive setup—but because of the bride's intimate connection to the Yibonn, to the president, who must have tasked Chairman Shin with the one-of-a-kind venue.

It all makes sense now. That "memory" in everyone's mind of the virus they witnessed must have been put there by Buhae. Buhae, the most powerful hypnotist in all of Snowglobe, has been running the power plant for the Yibonn through mind control.

Jolting back to the present, I turn to Bonwhe. I can't focus on this now. The most important thing is shutting down this plant—everything else, I can sift through later.

"There's a breaker panel down in the well—where I expected the control switch to be. Do you know what it connects to? Or have you heard of any others like it, especially in a place that's easier to access?"

Bonwhe shakes his head gravely.

Shit.

Then a thought comes to me. A bomb!

"What about dynamite or another kind of explosive?" I ask Bonwhe, feeling a pulse of excitement. "We'll drop it into the well! Maybe by blowing the panel up, we can disrupt the flow of power to Snowglobe."

He looks at me a moment. Then he says, "I doubt it. They wouldn't keep anything like that down here. Something so powerful it could blow up the bunker glass? It would annihilate this place."

"Exactly. Whether it's the panel that controls the energy or something else, if we destroy this power plant, we'll likely destroy the source of the electricity flow, too. But we'd have to evacuate everyone beforehand—"

"Everyone here has been brainwashed to believe that the virus will kill them the moment they step outside. They'll never leave—not as long as they believe the story Teacher told them, which only Teacher can undo."

Dammit. The captives' diamond-hard trust in their captor is the obstacle looming larger than the well I want to destroy.

I curse. "So even if we somehow manage to subdue Joon and Jin Jinsuh, we couldn't convince any of the prisoners to flee with us."

"Correct," Bonwhe confirms. "The family wouldn't side with us."

Sliding a hand into his pants pocket, he produces two protein gummies and holds them out in his palm.

"We'll need to get rid of these first," he says.

"What do you mean?"

"On my first two days here, Joon personally delivered these to me three times a day, making sure that I put them in my mouth while he watched. I only actually swallowed the gummies a couple times, and each time, I felt very strange after . . . like my brain was full of sludge." He picks up a gummy and squishes it gently between his fingers. "I'd had my own theories already, watching people working the wheels. They'd be lost in a trance through the whole shift, but then when the clock struck the final hour of each shift, a light switched back on behind their eyes and they'd come off the wheels . . . even though every one of them will tell you that they felt the most alive while working."

"Are the gummies some kind of drug?" I ask.

"For sure," he says.

"But then how come no one has caught on to that fact? Has no one else felt off like you did on your first try?"

"I don't know," Bonwhe replies helplessly. "But the gummies are promoted as extra protein that helps with muscle recovery at the end of a hard day, so maybe the belief helps them dismiss any off feeling? Or it may be that they just got used to the sensation over time—who knows."

"Unbelievable," I murmur. "So that's how they're held hostage down here. . . . The gummies dull their pain and perceptions, and hypnosis convinces them there's an apocalypse waiting for them aboveground."

"Hypnosis?" Bonwhe says, looking to me for explanation.

I take a breath. "Jin Jinsuh . . . I think she's also a hypnotist, known as Buhae. She hypnotized me at Fran's wedding. Immersive hallucinations are her specialty."

I'd hallucinated drowning in a flash flood caused by water bursting out of hundreds of shattering mirrors. For the people trapped in here, it's the terrifying false memory of a world devastated by the virus. At this information, Bonwhe lets out a long sigh of defeat.

"Where are the gummies?" I ask Bonwhe with a rush of urgency. "Do you know where they're stored? Maybe if we destroy them, we can weaken the Yibonn's hold on these people."

"I've finally narrowed it down to a few possible places . . . Been looking for them myself since I arrived," he says. "The next purge is near. We have to find the gummies and trash them so they can't be given out—"

Purge? What's he talking about? I want to ask, but then there are colliding voices and the sound of shuffling feet outside, and someone's saying, "How about in here? Did you look in the library?"

My heart thuds, and in the next moment, Heart's standing over us, his brows lifting in surprise. He stares at me a moment, his gaze shifting between me and Bonwhe. Then, without taking his eyes off me, he shouts over his shoulder, "She's in here, Captain! I found Wisher!"

No . . .

As I sit there frozen with Bonwhe beside me, Jin Jinsuh appears, towing Sky behind her.

"Oh my, Wisher! It's so good to see you again," she croons,

smiling a sinister smile. "Come. Tell me all about your adventure."

I get up and follow her out of the library. When I glance back at Bonwhe, his eyes say, *I'll get the gummies.*

**In her room, Jinsuh yields the chaise to me and sits on the** square ottoman.

"Let's see . . . ," she begins, tapping her index finger against her cheek in a show of recollection. "You've been gone for a while. How long were you aboveground, exactly?"

"A little over two weeks, Captain," I say, holding her eyes. "Seventeen days, to be exact."

*Oh, please, please, please . . . let Sky's memory be correct.*

"Seventeen days . . . ," she repeats, nodding slowly. "That's a long time, girlie."

I look away from her eyes, feeling my heart rate pick up.

"So let's hear it," she continues. "What did you learn on your first trip up top?"

Those eyes . . . All of a sudden, my heart's beating so furiously that it feels like it's burning. I'm breathing in through my nose, trying to slow my heart somehow, when she pushes impatiently up to her feet.

"What?" she says, towering over me. "Do you think we need some tea?"

She strides over to the tea cabinet, her long onyx waves rippling down her back.

I wipe my sweaty palms on the supple leather of the chair, but noticing they're quaking, I quickly sit on them.

*You know what else? I remember you and Teacher tiptoeing out of this place in the middle of the night exactly seventeen nights ago.*

I hadn't thought about it until now, but if Sky is right, that means Wisher's absence from this place coincides with . . . I gasp, a terrible revelation dawning on me. I yank my hands from under my seat and clap them over my mouth before I can stop myself, causing Jinsuh's eyes to leap to me from the cabinets.

"What's the matter?" she says sharply.

"Nothing, Captain."

Narrowing her eyes, she studies my face. I swear we both can hear my heart drumming madly in my chest. How did I not think of it before?

*As dirty as it is, maybe it can pay for Yeosu's death?*

A huge wave of nausea crashes over me. The girl who stabbed Goh Maeryung in bed was . . . Wisher!

Jinsuh turns away and reaches for a perfume bottle on the counter.

"Oh, I just love how this smells. I got it on my most recent trip to the surface," she says, spritzing her hair with it and inhaling deeply, closing her eyes. A moment later, her eyes pop open again, and she treats me to another unsettling smile as she tousles her hair.

The smell wafting from her hair is like a blow to my nose. It's the reek of rotting fish, worse than ever. My eyes go out of focus; around me, everything begins to grow blurry except for Jin Jinsuh's intense obsidian gaze.

The awful stench that had preceded the hypnotic torture session . . . I'd first noticed it in all its overpowering intensity when I met the turquoise-eyebrow man at the wedding.

I think I understand now. The smell itself must have hallucinogenic properties, and Jinsuh deploys it to prep her victims. Under its influence, the victim sees not Jinsuh but someone else conjured up by her—in my case, the turquoise-eyebrow man.

On her wedding day, it was during an impeccably timed camera break when the turquoise-eyebrow man lured me to the bridal suite and put the hypnotic spell on me, meaning no recording of the event exists. Had it been outside the break, there would have been a recording, though not of the turquoise-eyebrow man but of the bride in her blue wedding dress—since cameras don't hallucinate. So who tipped her off on the timing of the break? It must have been President Yi, of course.

Jinsuh's pushing a teacup over to me.

"Here. Try it. It's the most prized tea among my collection."

I murmur a feeble thank-you and take the cup, my hands trembling wildly. Drinking this tea would, once again, make me answer all her questions truthfully—including that I'm Jeon Chobahm, and that I'm here on a mission to shut down this place.

Jinsuh positions herself before me on the ottoman and refocuses her eyes on me.

"Haeri," she calls, and my heart clutches. "I thought you were supposed to be dead already."

Her eyes fixing me, I'm unable to look away.

"I really don't get it, though . . . ," she continues. "That the president let you go is one thing, but that she did so without letting me know first is awfully strange, if you ask me . . .

and she let you back in here with your memory intact? What was she thinking? What if you ran your big mouth when you returned?" A pause. Then her face hardens, and so does her voice. "I'm told that you've already brought up Snowglobe?"

My heart pounds as her onyx waves lift and begin dancing wildly in the air around her face, coming for me. .

# THE VIRUS AT LARGE

Jin Jinsuh tips her teacup to her lips.

"Why aren't you drinking?" she chides.

"It's still a bit too hot for me."

Think of something, Jeon Chobahm! Think of something! If she finds out who you are, it's all over!

"Fine," Jinsuh allows, and smirks like someone who has all the time in the world. "There's no hurry."

"I assumed . . . ," I begin, squeezing my toes together in my shoes. "I assumed that you already knew why President Yi didn't erase my memory, Captain."

Jinsuh's smirk vanishes and her brows go up. Good, good.

I continue, "But since she apparently didn't . . . The president told me that I might be needed again—depending on how Jeon Chobahm does from here on out."

Her mouth opens, but before she can say anything, I'm rushing back in with another surprise.

"I saw your wedding, Captain."

She draws back a little, frowning.

"You did?"

"Yes, Captain. It made all the news everywhere, of course—you couldn't get away from it, even if you wanted to. I loved it. What a gorgeous wedding, Captain!"

Watching her face soften, I go on, "President Yi promised me that I could lead a life as full as yours—just as long as I pull my weight around here."

At this, Jinsuh's long, wavy locks, which have been slithering in the air toward me, stop dead. I breathe a sigh of relief. Her illusions—I can break them, if I disrupt her focus.

"President Yi promised you that?" Jinsuh says, her voice jumping a register.

I nod to confirm, and a look of agitation flares across her face. Crossing her arms, she says, "Did you and President Yi meet often to have these . . . conversations?"

She's trying to sound casual, but I can hear the distress in her voice.

"Yes, Captain," I tell her, straightening my back and lifting my chin slightly to hold her eyes square. My silent message is clear: *I've been recruited. You and I play for the same team now, so don't you question me.*

Taking a quick sip of her tea, she glances at me over the brim of her teacup. I can't stop now.

"Whenever President Yi summoned me, she encouraged me to ask any questions I had about the operation so she could better educate me. That's also when I learned about why Goh Maeryung had to be sacrificed in place of Bae Serin, as well as why we're letting Jeon Chobahm be for now . . . which was particularly interesting to hear—"

Jinsuh slams her teacup down on the table, making hot tea spill all over her hand. Then she's suddenly on her feet, shouting, "You have no talent, and you weren't even born here! President Yi promised you a life like mine? For what? Just for being a double for Jeon Chobahm?!" Bending down at her waist, she brings her face inches from mine, her eyes burning with anger. I can smell the tea on her breath. A long moment ticks by before she straightens back up.

"What else?" she says, trying to compose herself. "Did the president promise to make you an assistant captain or something?"

I remain silent, not confirming or denying anything. This pours more fuel onto Jinsuh's fury, of course.

"Then why would she tell me that I'm ready to run the whole place myself?" she's shouting again, talking more to herself than me now. "How dare she send you back down here without saying a word to me about it? She knows I've already chosen Sky as my successor!"

She's seething with anger now. I let her rant as I connect the dots. So she means for Sky to take her place one day— Sky, born and raised to become a loyal servant of the Yibonn. That must be why she's the only child down here. I wonder if Jinsuh could have walked the same path. If she, too, grew up in this underground hell.

Then someone's rapping at the door. In the next instant, it flies open and Joon tumbles in, looking terrified.

"Captain, there's been an accident in the kitchen—" he reports, reflexively covering his mouth and nose with both hands, overcome with the foul stench filling the room.

Jinsuh screams, "What are you doing?! Can't you see that I'm in a meeting?"

With an apologetic face, Joon plows on. "The rookie burned

our entire supply of protein gummies . . . Supposedly he was helping Knife with the porridge she was making, but . . ."

He trails off, dropping his head. Jinsuh, bubbling with fury, can't even speak, and the room grows terribly quiet for a few moments. Then her sudden, shrill, and agitated laugh breaks the silence.

"Wisher returns out of the blue, and the rookie causes an accident . . . What's next?" she says, leveling a sharp gaze on me, her eyes full of suspicion and resentment.

I try my best to appear at ease as she continues with her stare, impatiently raking through her long, wavy locks with her skinny fingers.

Joon glances uneasily up at her a few times before finally working up the courage to inquire, "How should we deal with the situation, Captain? Everyone will feel the full brunt of the physical labor without the protein gumm—"

"Relax!" Jinsuh shouts him down. "The warehouse has stacks of them, and it's not that far from here."

"Do you mean that you're going back out right away, Captain?" Joon asks.

"What else am I going to do?" she spits. "You said that all the gummies are gone, burnt to smoke!"

I want to shake Joon. Jinsuh's not going to some warehouse. She's going to President Yi, of course. Once they meet, Jinsuh will tell her about me, and the president will know that Jeon Chobahm is down here, at the center of her secret.

Glaring at me, she orders Joon, "Lock her up in the isolation room and keep a close eye on her."

Lock her up. Not kill her. It seems like whether I'm Jeon

Chobahm or Wisher, she still cannot touch me without her boss's approval.

Joon murmurs his confusion. "Pardon me, Captain . . . ?"

Jinsuh sighs heavily.

"What I'm saying is," she tells him in an openly condescending tone and cadence, "have someone else keep an eye on Wisher in the isolation room while you distribute vitamin D to the family. It's not the same as the protein gummies, but it'll help them get through the day. Got it?"

This is not good. Not good at all. I don't know what those pills she brought down here are made of, but considering how they're using the protein gummies, I bet they're not vitamin D.

"Why the isolation room, Captain?!" I protest, bolting up from the chaise; but Jinsuh forces me back down and clamps her hand over my mouth, the powerful reek of rotting fish instantly debilitating me. I look on helplessly as she turns to Joon and shouts more commands before brushing past him and out of the room. I know that when she returns, it will be with the president's order to eliminate Jeon Chobahm. Still, I can't seem to lift a finger to save myself as Joon takes me away.


**"Can anyone hear me?! Please let me out!"**

Locked in the isolation room, I kick and scream for help until my energy runs out. Then I collapse to the floor and let the tears run. I can't believe it. How did it come to this? What's going to happen to me now? Another mini-eternity goes by, and I find myself full-on sobbing and gasping for breath, racked with fear, hopelessness, and despair, when a quiet voice calls out, "Wisher—"

I look up, trying to place the source of the voice. It's Healer, calling to me from the observation room, on the other side of the plate glass. My eyes light up with hope, and she quickly gestures for me to keep quiet.

"What are you doing here?" I ask her in a whisper.

"Diver begged me to come and help you calm down— she'd been on watch duty and said it was absolute torture for her to listen to you in here."

"Where's the rookie? What happened to him?"

"He's on the top floor. Under watch," she replies. "Captain wasn't happy with him for destroying our gummy supply. You can't lock the top floor from the outside, so like, six people are watching him instead of one."

Shit.

With a quick glance over her shoulder, she continues, "So the rookie burned all the gummies . . . but what about you? Why did Captain lock you up in here, Wisher? She's not Teacher! She has no authority to—"

"Healer, do you remember what I said about the world yesterday?"

*Humanity is not dead, and none of you—I mean, none of us— have to be locked away in here and be exploited.*

Healer nods, a guilty look coming over her face.

"Is that why you're being punished?" she says, letting out a sigh. "I swear I only told Heart . . . I should have known he's got a pair of loose lips on him!"

"Yes," I tell her. "Yes, Healer—I'm being punished because I know the truth. And she's going to have me disappear."

Healer's eyes grow wide with horror, and she shakes out her lion mane.

"What are you talking about?" she says. "Captain can't make such decisions without Teacher, and you know Teacher loves us all like her flock, and she'd never—ever—approve such a thing. You know that, don't you?"

"Healer," I begin. "Just this once . . . can you trust me more than you trust Teacher?"

I stare at her pleadingly, summoning her trust in Wisher.

Healer stares back at me, looking troubled and torn. After a long moment, she lets out a groan, squeezing her eyes shut and ruffling her hair in anguish.

"Please help me out of here," I plead again.

There's no time. I need to either get away from this place before Jinsuh and the president come back for me, or destroy it altogether. But locked in here, I can't do either. I can't do anything.

"They added another padlock on the door," Healer says, at last, looking at me apologetically. "And Boss has the keys, of course."

"Where's Boss?"

"He's distributing vitamin D pills."

Dread surges through me. I'm about to cry out my despair when I catch sight of the power outlet on the wall behind Healer, and a sudden idea sparks. It's a long shot, but what if . . .

"Healer!" I say suddenly. "Can you sneak the beam projector out of the theater cell for me?"

**It takes much longer than I anticipated, but Healer pulls off her** task. Returning to the intake room with the smuggled projector, she follows my instructions to plug it into the wall and turn it on, full blast, toward the plate glass separating us. In a few moments, the glass begins to glow, becoming reflective and silvery before her eyes.

"It's turning into a mirror . . . ," Healer murmurs in disbelief. "Like the one that Captain and Teacher use to access the outer world."

The mirror is complete now, but with my side of the glass remaining clear, I can see Healer staring warily at it.

"Healer . . . ," I call.

With a firm nod, Healer reaches for me, her hand slicing through the glass like a hot knife through butter. I grasp it immediately, and with a grunt, Healer pulls me to her. Then I'm on the other side, in the observation room with Healer, who stares at me in amazement.

Now I know. I can get to the other side of the well bottom in the same way.

"Can you meet me at the well in ten?"

"The well?" she asks. "The incinerator well?"

"Yes," I confirm. "You just need to pull me back up in the bucket when I signal you."

"What? Are you saying that you'll be down in the well? What for? Are you nuts?"

I give her a wink and tell her, "You just think about what you want to do when you get out of this . . . fortress."

She gazes at me for a moment longer, then turns and gives the door two measured knocks with her knuckles. A moment later, the door of the observation room opens ever so slowly.

Standing outside is a woman who must be the Diver person she mentioned earlier. She's facing away from us, her eyes nervously scanning the hallway as she holds the door open. Silently, I slip out of the intake room and cross the floor to hide behind the grandfather clock that stands in the corridor, the beam projector tucked under my elbow.

I peek toward the center of the ground floor, where I know the well lies. What the hell? Where's the bucket? Rather than being coiled beside the well like usual, the bucket chain is stretching up—all the way to the eighth floor, where Joon is currently doling out Captain's vitamin D pills. A dozen people wait in line for their turn.

What in the world? What's the bucket doing up there? It's as if someone purposefully moved it to sabotage my plan.

That's exactly what they've done. Jin Jinsuh must have already calculated the risk of a scenario in which I am not Wisher, and is protecting against every possible outcome. Shit, shit, shit.

"Are you hiding from Boss?" a voice whispers, causing me to nearly leap out of my skin.

I turn to see Heart standing in a sweaty uniform, pushing a cart full of gray laundry. Why does this man keep popping up everywhere?

Meanwhile, Diver, who's now facing Healer through the open door of the intake room, seems to have finally realized that it wasn't Healer she's let out of the observation room.

"Wisher's gotten out!" she screams, looking for me desperately.

I snatch Heart by his uniform shirt and plead to him, "Help!"

If he is surprised at all, he doesn't show it. He simply shoves me into the cart and piles laundry on top of me, then drives the cart to the escalator.

"You can hide in my cell for now," he whispers through the clothes. Giving me a wink, he lifts his head higher, and we set off.

**A few minutes later, I'm in his cell on the nineteenth floor, sur-**rounded by piles of uniforms to be mended. I murmur my thanks, and he lets me know that Healer instructed him to wait for me outside and help me with whatever I need.

"This is the first time she's asked me for a favor, ever," he adds, a smile stretching over his face, and his ears turning the same shade of deep pink as his tattoo. It's almost sweet.

"Anyway," he says, regrouping. "You stay here. Be a church mouse and don't make a peep. As long as me and Healer are looking out for you, even Captain won't find you."

"Thank you, Heart. You're amazing."

"You're damn right, I'm amazing," Heart says in a playful tone, though he can't completely hide the tension underlying his speech. This must be stressful for him, too. "But I'm just paying back the kindness you showed me when I first got here and struggled to fit in, Wisher."

Leaving the cell, he turns around and adjusts the pants and towels drying on the clothesline so they provide maximum coverage.

I choose a large pile of uniforms and bury myself in it for further protection. Safely tucked beneath the fabric, I finally have the space to contemplate the new and unfortunate development Jinsuh has presented me with.

How am I supposed to get to the bottom of the well without the bucket?

I rack my brain for a solution, but no matter how desperately I scramble for an answer, none appear. Is this when I throw in the towel, at last? Abort the plan and flee this place, accept my defeat? But even if I make it out, I know I won't be saving myself—not really. For me, there is no escape. It's either I die here, or I die back in Snowglobe at the hands of the Yibonns.

"What did Uncle Heart mean? Why is he hiding you from Captain?" a muffled voice pipes up. In front of me, Sky's little face pokes in through the mess of uniforms. I shriek and sit up.

"Holy cow! What are you doing here, Sky?!"

"I wanted to ask Uncle Heart something, so I came here," she replies. "But then I saw him talking to you, and I hid."

As I stare at her, speechless, she frowns and squints her eyes.

"But what was Uncle Heart saying to you earlier?" she says. "Why would Captain mess with you?"

We both jump as beyond the cell we're in, the megaphone crackles loudly to life.

"Code Red. Code Red," Joon's urgent voice informs. "Family member Wisher has escaped the isolation room and is at large. Again, Wisher has escaped the isolation room and is at large."

*God damn it,* I think as Joon's voice continues. "She has been retested and was found positive for the virus . . ."

Meanwhile, panic explodes in Sky's eyes fixing me. She begins to hyperventilate, clutching at her mouth and nose with her shaking little hands.

Holding her gaze with my own terrified eyes, I shake my head from side to side, slowly.

"That's a lie, Sky," I tell her in the calmest, most trust-worthy tone I can muster. Even as I do, a small part of me wants to just lie back and give up.

Why? Why should I try to calm her? What is putting out this fire going to do? After this, there will be another one, and then another . . . At this point, it seems not a matter of if I'll be caught, but when.

Joon's voice is urging again, "Please, anyone not at the wheels at the moment—drop what you're doing and search for Wisher immediately. I repeat—drop what you're doing and search for Wisher immediately. We must find and isolate her. The safety and well-being of our family depends on it . . ."

A siren wails, and Sky opens her little mouth to pierce the air with her scream.

# A NEW FAMILY MEMBER

It's clear that I have no chance. The odds are stacked so heavily against me that I'm done for. I should just give up. Surrender. And yet one's survival instinct is a powerful thing, and it drives me to lunge for Sky and press a firm hand over her mouth, stifling the rest of her scream.

"I'm not infected!" I hiss through the wail of the siren.

Sky struggles against me in the heap of uniforms.

"I don't have a fever, and I don't have a cough! I'm healthier than you!" I explain, but Sky doesn't appear to hear me at all, instead continuing to fight.

"Okay, Sky! That's enough!"

We glare at each other, both panting. I keep my hand over her mouth just in case.

"Don't start screaming again until I get to another cell, okay?" I rumble. "If I get caught in here, Heart will be in trouble. You don't want that, do you?"

This seems to give her pause. Sky finally lets her body relax.

"You're going to be quiet," I order, giving her a firm look.

She nods, angling her eyes up at me pleadingly. Very slowly, carefully, as if defusing a bomb, I lift my hand from her mouth, staring intensely into her eyes. A moment ticks by as we hold each other in silence. Then a sudden vicious change comes over her face, and she leaps forward, grabbing blue pants and shirts from the pile and flinging them at me.

Oh, man . . . I really don't need this kid to act this way right now. I stiffen up, ready to fight back—until I hear noises from outside our cell, and I understand what she's doing. Clever. My pulse picking up, I lay myself back in the pile and close my eyes shut as Sky continues to fling stuff on top of me.

A few moments have passed when I hear the privacy veil parting violently. My eyes pop open with fresh panic, but through the gaps in the layers of fabric she's hidden me with, I can see Sky's face light up.

"Aunt Knife!" she cries.

"Sky! Was it you screaming, just now?" Knife says.

Sky's breaths quicken again, and I wonder if she'll sell me out. I close my eyes again, bracing myself for all that's to come.

"Me? No," I hear Sky reply instead. "I'm just hiding in here because I'm so scared."

I feel a surge of relief as Knife replies, "Come, Sky. It's not good to be by yourself right now."

"N-no! What if the virus finds me? I'm going to continue hiding in here!"

Knife considers this a moment.

"Okay, sweetie," she relents with a sigh. "Don't make a peep, though—got it? I honestly think you'll be safer in here, but just in case Wisher finds you, stay as far away from her as possible and scream for help, all right?"

"I will, I promise!"

Knife heads out, closing the privacy veil behind her.

Half a minute later, Sky lifts the shirts and pants covering my head.

"What did you mean . . . that you're healthier than me?" she asks me, looking at me steady. I stare back at her, my emotions a knot in my chest. You Baby Captain . . . Does it really matter now?

"It's a long story, Sky," I tell her with a sigh. "It has to do with the gummies and protein, and . . . and how they make you sleepy and stuff."

It's not much of an answer, but it's the best I can do. Plus, I'm trying to work out how many seconds it would take for me to get caught if I bolted out of here. Probably ten. Fifteen at most. A new wave of hopelessness pulls me under.

"Oh, right," Sky says then, as if remembering something. Digging through a neighboring pile of uniforms, she pulls out a chunk wrapped in a yellowing piece of cloth.

"Take some before you go," she says, undoing the cloth and opening the bundle.

Inside are dozens of neatly stacked red protein gummies.

My mouth drops open.

"Where did you find these?"

"Teacher and Captain say that they're brain food," she confesses proudly. "But I'm already plenty smart."

She grabs five of the gummies with her little hands and presses them toward me.

"Here. It's my present to you—for being nice to Uncle Heart."

"Are they your rations you've been saving?"

"Shh . . . You can't tell anyone, okay?"

The look on her face turning sad, she continues. "Everyone would be mad at me if they found out that I haven't been taking them, that I haven't been listening to the grown-ups."

"So why haven't you been taking them? I'm not mad— I'm . . . I'm just curious."

Sky hesitates briefly. Then she says, "They help me remember Mom's face too vividly. They're too good for brains, you know."

"What do you mean?" I ask her, my heart already aching.

"You know how Uncle Heart's always complaining about the gummies while whining about how he misses real protein from real meat? I don't miss real meat because I've never had any. But Mom's face is different. I remember her—which makes me miss her all the more."

There are no words I can offer that will soothe her grief. I know that because my own dad exists only in a handful of photos. Still, I try.

"You must have lots of great memories of your mom. Which one stands out to you the most?"

"The one where she leaves me," Sky says.

I frown, confused. "What, honey?"

Sky nods. "I remember all the aunts and uncles leaving with her, too."

My stomach plunges. I'm getting a bad feeling about this memory. "Leaving?" I ask. "Leaving for where?"

Her eyes go remote, as if she's recalling the exact scene from the past.

"It was the day the team leader made an announcement . . . when Teacher brought back the special pills," Sky says. "I remember what she told us. She said, *Living in this underground cave, our bodies can't synthesize vitamin D from the sun. Fortunately, Teacher has secured vitamin D pills for us. Every member of the family will be given two. These pills are a gift from Teacher, who loves us and who wants us to continue holding on to our hope of returning to the world one day—so take them with deep gratitude.*"

Sky sounds like a little kid who's only repeating what's been fed to her, which she is.

"Vitamin D pills?" I ask. At once, Jinsuh's voice echoes in my head.

*The store had a pharmacy in it. There were signs of previous small-scale looting, but luckily, I was able to find a big stash . . .* We can do two pills per person.

Apart from the variations relating to who procured the pills—Teacher or Captain—what Sky is saying checks out.

"Team Leader gave us the pills and made sure each of us swallowed them," Sky continues, her teary eyes clouded with the memory of the day. "And when the grandfather clock struck midnight . . . everyone ran to the well, complaining of thirst. Everyone but me." A pause. "It was so scary. I clung to Mom and cried, begging her to stop, but she just kept moving to the well." Sky wipes her tears with the sleeve of her inmate uniform, customized by Heart. "They all fell in. Even Uncle Knife, who I told you about. The well burned all night long, and five nights later, you and new rescues were brought in."

"When I was brought in . . . ," I murmur with a sinking feeling. "That was about three years ago."

I recall a comment Bonwhe made to me when I arrived, about how Wisher was one of the oldest residents in the plant. I'd thought it was odd at the time, but what if what he said is true? What if Wisher is one of the oldest rescues down here . . . because the workers who lived here prior to her were all killed to make room for new ones?

Sky confirms my statement with a nod, causing fresh tears to drop heavily on the front of her shirt.

My heart clenching, I gaze into Sky's face, my own eyes threatening to fill with tears. She was barely five three years ago . . . Can I trust her memory?

"I even remember what you were wearing on your first day," Sky says then, as if sensing my doubt. "It was red, and you told me it was called a dress—don't you remember?"

A red dress. This, too, checks out. In the last recording of her, the Haeri who ran into the woods is seen wearing a red dress.

*You have no talent, and you weren't even born here!*

Sky's remarkable memory. Is this the kind of talent Jinsuh was referring to? Are the protein gummies she had been exposed to in utero responsible for her steel-trap memory?

I don't dwell on it for long. If Sky's right, then the fact that the Captain brought in a new batch of vitamin D pills likely means the Yibonn are gearing up for another purge. And when the incineration is complete, a new cohort of death row inmates, the "rescues," will be brought in until Buhae's spell begins to wear off and the new rescues, too, start itching for a life outside these walls. Then the Yibonn will gear up again for the next purge.

Haeri—or Wisher—was one of the rescues brought in with the previous batch. The same group that's now about to be replaced.

It hits me like a slap. That must be why the incinerator well is so big. It's not just a tool meant for disposing of one wayward prisoner at a time—but a whole population. It's a mass grave.

"Have you told anyone?" I ask.

"Yes. I told Captain. Captain told me not to be so sad because she was going to be my mom and dad now."

"Did you tell anyone else?" I press.

"I told you, and you told me that I just had a bad dream—remember?"

"Oh . . ."

So no one believed you.

I push away the pile of uniforms covering my lap and find her little hand. Despite all the layers of clothes, her skin is cold.

"Joon is handing out the same pills right now," I tell her.

Little does he know that he's acting as the leader of a suicide pact.

"No . . . ," Sky murmurs, terror moving in her seen-it-all eyes. "Then Uncle Heart will also—"

"No, he won't. We're going to stop this, you and me."

"You and me?"

"Yes, Sky."

She considers this a moment. Then hesitating, she says, "I'm scared of Teacher, Wisher."

I keep my surprise to myself.

"I'm scared of Teacher, too—like, super terrified," I tell her after giving it a beat. "But I promise you, Sky—we'll do this together, and I will show you the sky that is blue, scarlet, snowy, and all kinds of beautiful. The real sky outside this place."

A faint smile appears on her sad face. After a moment, she says, "I think I like you more now that you're weird." Then she plucks a soft gel pill, different from both the protein gummies and the round vitamin D pills, from the bundle and hands it to me. "I was going to give it to Uncle Heart today along with the gummies, but I want you to have it. You need it to beat Teacher and save everyone for me."

I pinch the pill between my thumb and forefinger and hold it up to the light. It's filled with some kind of liquid. Clear like tears.

"What's this?" I ask Sky.

"I saw Captain give it to you before you left with Teacher on the mission—remember? She said it would make you healthy and strong for a new adventure."

Healthy and strong? Could it be a pill that brings back memories? Puzzled, I look from the pill to Sky, who interprets my glance the wrong way.

"I didn't steal it!" she protests suddenly. "After you left, they were just sitting on Captain's desk, so I tried one . . . and then I pocketed just one more for later."

I'm about to tell her how reckless and dangerous it is to put strange pills in her mouth like that, when the siren halts and the megaphone comes back on.

"Family, I have great news!" Joon cries rapturously. "Teacher is back!"

God damn it.

Teacher is back looking for Jeon Chobahm, of course.

There's a further crackle, followed by a sudden, loud screeching noise that rips at my eardrums. Then a new voice begins, "I'd like to thank our family for all the thoughts and prayers that made my safe and fruitful return possible."

I recognize that voice . . . full of smug vanity and self-possession. It's not the president's but that of her daughter, Yi Bonshim, the VP. So this is where she comes whenever the media claims she's disappeared on another getaway with her latest fling. The supposedly shallow, eternally immature vice-president has actually been running and overseeing the power plant for her own mother this whole time.

"Dearest family," Bonshim croons. "I cannot wait to share with you my latest findings and consequent renewed hope for our future, but the pleasure will have to wait. First, we must resolve the imminent threat to our community posed by a contaminated person at large."

A true descendant of one of the most charismatic and gifted orators in history, the VP pauses for a breath before continuing with her eloquent lies. "I understand the overwhelming confusion and uncertainty you all must be feeling right now, but I encourage you to remember how much worse it must be for our newest rescue I'm about to introduce to all of you . . ."

She's bringing in a lone rescue just before the purge? What could that mean?

Sky creeps to the edge of the cell to survey the situation

for me. Returning a minute later, she reports that everyone's attention is on Teacher and the rescue she's brought in, on the first floor, and that no one seems to be looking for me at the moment.

"Welcome to your new home," the VP says. "How about a quick hello to your new family?"

There's another brief, earsplitting feedback noise as she extends the megaphone to the new rescue. Then the rescue's hoarse, uncertain voice says, "Where am I?"

"Oh, there's no need to be scared," the VP reassures them, a smile in her voice. "A powerful virus wiped out most of humanity, but you survived. And I rescued you and brought you down here, remember?"

The VP's kind explanation doesn't seem to impress the new rescue, however, who responds, "What crap are you talking about now?"

There's a long moment of awkward silence, and then the VP forces a shrill and uncomfortable laugh before quickly redirecting.

"Well . . . Why don't you introduce yourself to the family?" she says, plowing forward.

The new rescue heaves a great big sigh of annoyance.

"Woman . . . what new family? I don't even know who I am," the rescue mutters almost to herself, but it echoes across the whole of the fortress through the megaphone.

I recognize her stinging sarcasm a microsecond before I do her voice.

"Ajumma?" I murmur, stupefied.

The exhausted rasp in the rescue's voice is new, but it's

undoubtably Hyang's. Kicking away the layers of clothes surrounding me, I scramble up to my feet when Sky snatches my arm and pulls me back.

"Don't go!" she pleads. "Teacher will get you!"

But there's no time to explain anything to her. I shake off Sky's childish grip and race out of the room. Way down below on the first floor, the VP's head snaps up, and she nails me with her eyes that recognize me instantly despite the distance, a grin of sharp satisfaction breaking across her face.

All around the hall, wheels continue to spin, their collective whir growing into a killing roar in my ears that drowns out the sound of my own pounding heart. These wheels . . . They will never stop spinning—not so long as this plant exists.

"Dear family!" the VP cries out triumphantly, "The infected member seems to be turning herself in!"

My terrified paralysis breaks as I notice scrums of people closing in on me from both sides of the hallway, some awkwardly holding open large blankets as if ready to throw them over me.

Snapping back to myself, I growl, "That's right, I'm crawling with disease . . . so back off, or I'll spit in your face. I'll walk down on my own."

# THE WISH OF THE LIVING DEAD

A human biological weapon, I make my way down to the first floor. People cover their faces with rags and shirt sleeves, shuffling warily away from me, but the look in their eyes is more than just terror. There's genuine concern and pity for me, too—for Wisher.

On the first floor, the VP is grinning beneath her clear plastic mask, the rest of her body encased in her ridiculous costume of a survival suit. She jeers, "I knew you'd crawl out of your hidey-hole."

By her side, Hyang frowns with further confusion under her identical plastic mask, looking back and forth between the VP and me. A few feet behind them is Joon, also wearing a mask. A hermetic body bag lies wrinkled at his feet like a freshly shed snakeskin.

"Let her go," I hiss, glaring at the VP.

Keeping her eyes on me, the VP raises the megaphone to her face.

"Dear family," she sings. "I now will administer to Wisher the last dose of the antiviral we have left!"

Behind her, Joon begins to draw a clear yellow liquid into a syringe.

"As we all know, some people can have fatal reactions to it," the VP continues, turning down the cheer in her voice. "So let's all pray that Wisher isn't one of them!"

She switches off the megaphone and takes the syringe from Joon.

I take a quick step and grab Hyang's hand, which she wrenches away from me immediately, looking appalled.

"Who do you think you are?" she says. "Do not touch me!"

"Ajumma?" I murmur in shock, and she makes her face even scarier.

"Ajum . . . what?! What did you just call me?" she huffs. "Kids these days . . . Did the virus destroy your good sense, too?"

I'm staring back at her speechless, dread surging inside me, when Joon leaps for me and throws me to the floor.

"Ajumma!" I scream, my face squished between the floor and Joon's chest. "Hyang! Cha Hyang!"

Hyang doesn't react to her name. Meanwhile, Joon's straddling my legs and tying my hands behind my back. I kick and scream to no avail, and then the VP's kneeling by my side, the syringe in her hand.

"Cut the crap. Be still," she says, sounding tired and annoyed.

I thrash again, raging with fury, raging with terror, raging with despair, but ultimately, raging with sorrow at the knowledge that this is it for me. This is where my story ends. I'm just beginning to accept it when a new voice enters the scene.

"Maybe I can help?" it says.

Joon turns his face to the voice, only to be met with a

flying teapot that shatters when it collides with his nose. With a sharp cry, Joon pitches to the floor, but the VP is right there, ready to plunge the needle into my neck. I stiffen, but a moment later, the VP lets out a surprised cry. The next thing I know, she's on the floor too, squeezing her empty, syringeless hand with her other one, crying out in agony. Someone has kicked the syringe out of her grip.

Then Bonwhe's pulling me up to my feet.

"How did you escape from the top floor?" I murmur at him, too stunned to think of anything else to say.

"My guards were distracted. Thanks to you drawing all the attention to yourself," he replies.

Then the VP's voice screeches in the air, "Yi Bonwhe!" She fixes her son a with death stare. "What are you doing?!"

"Yi Bonwhe?" he repeats blankly. "Who are you talking to? I haven't picked a name yet."

Shrieks and murmurs sweep through the crowd. I tense as a handful of brave souls break from the crowd and barrel toward us, armed with kitchen utensils and crying, "Teacher! Are you okay? You've gone insane, rookie!"

The VP scrambles up to her feet and switches on the megaphone.

"Stop!" she orders the people. "Your safety comes first! Step back!"

Then, switching off the megaphone, she hisses at Bonwhe through clenched teeth, "Are you crazy?! Do you want to end up like your uncle?!"

But Bonwhe isn't fazed.

"I told you, Mother," he replies without missing a beat, "that you'd regret sparing me."

What happens next is truly unbelievable.

The VP produces a gun from inside her survival suit and points it at Bonwhe.

"And I told you," she says, "that I'd have to do what I'd have to do, if push came to shove." Her hand, looking angry and swollen from her son's kick a minute ago, trembles slightly. "I beg you, son. Don't make me do this. I don't want to be that mom . . ." She swallows. "Who kills her own baby."

Bonwhe stares at her, jaw clenched. Then in the next microsecond, he's stepped to her in one quick stride to grab her gun by its barrel, which he shoves into his chest.

"What are you waiting for?" he says, glaring at her. "You're used to killing. It's not that different."

"But you're my son!" she squawks.

"And those people you murdered? They were someone's children, too."

The VP's eyes, which are glaring back at Bonwhe, begin to redden. Then Bonwhe's jerking the gun up and pressing its muzzle to his neck.

"Shoot," he demands. "It's only fair that these people see what the benevolent Teacher is all about. They need to know what they can expect to happen if they step out of line, too."

After a moment, the VP responds bitterly, "They're trash on borrowed time."

Bonwhe doesn't say anything, as if her remark isn't even worthy of his response. He just continues to stare her down, his chest rising and falling. An intense minute ticks by, with all eyes in the fortress on the dueling mother and son—with the exception of those belonging to the people currently trapped inside the wheels, that is.

Then finally, the VP breaks off her stare.

"Let's stop—this is ridiculous," she says.

For a few more seconds, Bonwhe keeps his eyes on his mother—and his grip on the gun. But then he, too, allows the tension to go out of his eyes. He lets go of the barrel. The VP withdraws her gun—only to raise it at me this time. Then the clap of the firing gun thunders through the cave, followed by another.

The next thing I know, the VP has crumpled to the floor, screaming in agony. Blood gushes out of her thigh, and her hand, hit by the bullet, loosens its grip on the gun.

"Chobahm, are you okay?!"

It takes me a moment to recognize my real name, so used to being Wisher have I become. Someone's anguished cry reaches me, muffled as if traveling across a great distance. Feeling numb, I pat myself down. The VP's bullet seems to have missed me?

When I look up from my hands, I see a figure running out to me from between two wheels. It's . . . Somyung. Trailed by Miryu, who is then trailed by . . . Ongi. Miryu's searching eyes stop dead on Hyang, and she races to her, calling her name.

Behind her, Ongi's squawking his astonishment.

"What?! What are you doing down here, Hyang?!"

I blink at the incomprehensible scene.

Meanwhile, chaos has taken over the fortress, with people everywhere scurrying in all directions, shrieking and gasping and screaming at the horror of contaminated intruders not even wearing survival suits.

"Who the hell are these people?" Hyang wonders aloud,

sounding sick and tired of finding herself swept up in yet another wave of confusion.

Then Somyung tells me, "News is going viral that Director Cha Hyang took her own life while in custody because of her shame and guilt over having tried to cover up Jeon Chobahm's murder. When we heard it, we knew something was wrong."

"How did you guys get down here?" I finally murmur, swimming in shock. "How did you find the mirror—"

"Your emergency contact—who do you think? Chairman Shin!" Ongi supplies, and flashes the business card I'd given him.

I stretch my neck and look around for Chairman Shin, and Ongi explains, "She's holding the elevator for us in case President Yi shows up—but it looks like we were late to the party, anyway."

What?

I look around in a daze. A short distance from us, Bonwhe is kneeling on the floor, holding his bleeding mom on his lap. Somyung trains her rifle on his back.

"No!" I cry, finally snapping back. "He's on our side!"

Somyung and Ongi throw me a puzzled look.

"Bonwhe, sweetie . . ." the VP is rasping, lifting a weak hand and pointing at us. "See? When order is threatened, screw-ups like them rise up with guns and violence. For the sake of greater peace and stability for all, we can't afford to weep over necessary sacrifices. Leave that to ordinary people. I beg you, sweetie . . . Don't be on the wrong side of history." She lifts her good hand and cups Bonwhe's cheek. "I believe in you, sweetie. You'll make a fine president, just as good as any before you."

"We're the screw-ups, Mom," Bonwhe says, his voice tight. "And that's why they're rising up against us."

Hyang bursts out complaining then. "For crying out loud, why is everyone being so dramatic? Do you people even know each other?"

Miryu shoots me a look of confusion.

"Ajumma doesn't recognize us," I tell her after a moment. "The Yibonn wiped her memory."

Miryu stares at me, stunned, and then at Hyang.

I'm about to explain further, but Somyung's flustered voice cuts me off. "What do we do about these people?"

I follow her gaze and see a sizable mob closing in on us, everyone shielding their face with a rag. Somyung raises her rifle in their direction.

"Don't hurt them," I tell her. "They're being used, too."

At the front of the mob is Knife.

"How have you all survived without the survival suits?" she demands, shifting her wary eyes to me. "And you, too, Wisher . . . How are you perfectly fine? You're supposed to have the virus!"

The chef's knife she's clutching in one hand is intimidating, but the look in her eyes is more of confusion than hostility. I snatch up the megaphone at my feet and shout into it.

"Listen, everyone! The world isn't over! There's no killer virus out there! It's a lie—a giant scam! Teacher and Captain erased your memory and replaced it with a false memory of a devastating virus—to exploit your labor and hide their secrets!"

More people are moving down to the ground floor now.

Meanwhile, second-shift workers are as oblivious as ever inside the wheels they spin.

"I don't have the power to restore your memory," I continue into the megaphone. "Nor can I prove to you that I'm telling you the truth. But take a look around you . . . Look at your fellow family members inside the wheels now who haven't so much as flinched through the siren, or while intruders broke in and shots were fired! Why do you think that is?"

This seems to have an impact on some of the people in the mob, who pause and contemplate the wheels.

"Wisher!" a cry comes, and Sky fights her way over through the mob on her little legs, the mangy old bear squished under her arm.

"I'm going to say something, too!" she yells, finally reaching me. "You said we'd do this together, Wisher!"

I regard her a moment, the only witness who has lived through it all. I hand over the megaphone to her, and she squeezes it between her two little hands and raises it to her mouth. Pulling in a large breath, she shouts into it, "Aunts and uncles! Teacher is a scary person!"

As the aunts and uncles listen on in shock, she recalls the story she told me—of the countless deaths she has witnessed.

At one point, a confused and angry voice pipes up, questioning the validity of her story. But Sky quickly silences them with a detailed account of the questioner's state upon their arrival to the fortress as she remembers it—including what they were wearing, the length of their hair, and even whether they were wearing socks. Everyone's silent.

Then Knife drops her kitchen knife, which clangs loudly to the floor.

"So what now?" she says. "What are we trying to accomplish—"

"We're going to get out of here and see the real sky!" Sky supplies the answer with a rush of exuberance. Turning to Uncle Heart, who's standing by the wheels, she shouts, "Taste real meat!"

Beaming, she goes on. "Aunt Knife, you're going to put your knife skills to work and make all kinds of meat dishes for Uncle Heart! And Aunt Diver—you're going to dive for real in the ocean! And Aunt Violet, you said that you couldn't forget the taste of ice cream. Don't! I want to taste it, too—ice cream!"

Sky is on a roll. Finally, Knife pulls down the cloth covering her face and says to Heart, "Hey, so you want to get out of here and eat some meat or what? I'll cook."

Heart snatches off the cloth covering his mouth and says, "Hell yeah! I go wherever our tiny captain goes!"

Just then, a loud thud comes from the isolation room. Miryu rushes to investigate, and when she opens the door, Healer tumbles out of it.

"Ouch . . . ," Healer whimpers, but she is smiling, having listened to our conversations. "Isn't there another group who needs to be included in this conversation?" she accuses, still all smiles. "Free the wheel workers, won't you? They have no idea what's going on."

Hope buds in my chest. Against all odds, we've done it. We're about to grind the wheels of injustice—all the wheels of injustice—to a halt, at last. That's when the heart-stopping sound of a gunshot explodes through the cave, and someone slams me to the floor, shielding me with their body just as another blast erupts in the air. A few seconds later, the person's agonized moan is hot in my ear. It's Ongi's.

Panic shooting through me, I scramble up to my elbow, and my heart drops once more to see Ongi roll feebly off my back onto the floor beside me. A short distance away, Joon lies inert on the floor in a growing pool of bright blood seeping out of his skull, his eyes wide open and lifeless. By his hand is a gun.

"Jeon Ongi?"

Somyung's trembling voice calls out, and my eyes snap to her. She's standing just a few feet away, her rifle pointed at Joon. Everything is blurry through my teary eyes.

I look back down at Ongi. Blood pulses out of his side at a frightening rate, but on his face is a weak grin.

"Well . . . ," he rasps as I gape at him, breathless. "You can't say that I never have your back."

# THANK YOU

His eyes twitch closed.

"Nooooo!"

I pitch sideways to the floor with my brother across my lap. Miryu flies to my side and tears Ongi off me.

"No! Don't!" I scream, hysterical.

"It's okay, Chobahm. I got him," she says calmly.

Then she lays Ongi flat on the floor and checks for his breathing and pulse. I take my wildly trembling hands and press them futilely against the hole on his side.

"No . . . Ongi, no . . . ," I murmur incoherently, feeling numb.

"He has a pulse," Miryu says.

"We need to get him to a hospital! Now!" I demand.

Suddenly, Bonwhe's next to me.

"Hospitals are too risky," he says.

"What?"

"What do you think the president is doing right now? She knows you're here, and that someone is holding the elevator.

She must have stationed squads and snipers outside all the mirror portals to catch us if we try to escape."

"Then are we all dead as soon as we get out of here?!"

"I'm not saying that. I'm saying that it's going to be a difficult journey to the hospital."

"So what are you suggesting? If we don't do anything, Ongi's going to . . ."

I can't even finish the thought.

"I can treat him for now," Healer says then, and instructs Heart to fetch the supplies and the gurney from the clinic cell.

I watch Heart run up the escalators, tears blurring my vision once again.

"I'll keep him alive—I promise," Healer says, taking my hand in hers.

And that's when it finally comes to me. Healer. Of course. Shaking out her lion mane, the brave woman asks for more volunteers.

"Can someone help me at the clinic? Heart's heart is always in the right place, but he's kinda squeamish, so I may need more support," she says.

I bolt upright, but Somyung stays me. "We need you here," she says.

A hand shoots up in the air then. I feel my stomach drop as Hyang says, "I'll go. I don't know the kid, but I'd feel much better helping out than just sitting here."

I turn and regard her, the look on my face identical to the expressions Somyung and Shinae are wearing. Hyang's memory is destroyed—she doesn't remember Ongi, or any of us, as she says—and I feel terrible for her. But there's a twinge of something else, too, which I'm hard-pressed to articulate. An irrational sense of anger or betrayal.

"Why are you all looking at me like that?" Hyang says, narrowing her eyes at us as if sensing our collective grievance.

Then Heart returns with the gurney, and Ongi is carefully lifted onto it. Healer, Heart, and Hyang begin rushing Ongi to the clinic cell, and I move to follow them.

"Have you forgotten why you're here?" Somyung says, snatching my arm. "Finish what you set out to accomplish. They'll take good care of Ongi."

I look around the floor. All eyes are on me now, including Sky's and Knife's, the hope that buoyed their spirit only a few minutes ago now dwindling.

Then a low, unpleasant laugh erupts, and we all turn to it.

"Why all this struggle?" the VP says, sitting slouched against the stone well. "You're all going to die, regardless."

She levels a vicious gaze on me, a grotesque grin on her face. It only makes me grow cold with fury. Shaking off the thought of snipers waiting for us at the portals, I pick up the megaphone. We may not survive, but the truth will.

"Go free your friends, everyone!" I shout into the megaphone. "Pull them out of their wheels, and destroy the wheels altogether! We'll smash this place into pieces so no one can be imprisoned in here—ever again!"

I ask Knife for her knife, which she hands to me without question. A few people are already at the wheels, pulling their friends out of the spinning cages and their stupor. Then, together, they start attacking the wheels with whatever they can get their hands on—chairs, tables, trash cans, et cetera. But real damage begins only when someone thinks to wedge an object between the gears, causing them to grind to a halt. Rapidly, others follow suit. Everything turns into a tool of destruction—blankets, wadded-up uniforms, pots and pans . . . until gradually, wheel by wheel, their hellish prison begins to shut down.

I cross to the mostly unconscious VP, trying to pull the flashlight from her belt. But my fingers, which have been trembling wildly since Ongi was shot, might as well be rubber. I fumble until Miryu silently swoops in to help me, just as she always does.

"Miryu . . . I have a favor to ask," I begin, pushing through my fear and doubt. Pulling down the neck of my shirt to expose the cardioverter on my chest, I continue, "Help me remove this. The damned thing won't come off no matter how hard I pull on it."

Miryu glances down at the cardioverter and looks back at me, puzzled.

"It's a cardioverter—" I begin to explain, but she cuts me off.

"I know what it is. Chairman Shin gave one to each of us when we came down here," she says, and pulls down her own shirt neck to show me the plastic heart clinging to the skin of her chest like a barnacle. "Why? Why do you want to take it off?"

Thank god for Chairman Shin. Because of her, I don't have to explain every detail of my plan. Somyung joins us then, and I start to tell her and Miryu what I saw beneath the bottom of the well, when the VP lets out a sudden, strangled laugh and slumps farther on the floor.

"You might be able to shut this place down for a little

while," she spits, choking on her cough. "But bring it down for good? Who do you think you are? This is our world and it's untouchable."

From the clinic cell, Heart's calling for help. Bonwhe volunteers, moving his quickly declining mother into the isolation room and locking her in.

The VP's sinister comment has disturbed me more than I want to admit. I take a long, steadying breath and continue with Miryu.

"Only a bomb can destroy the well, which we don't have. But we know that a tremendous amount of electricity travels underneath the glass at the bottom . . ." I pause and tap the cardioverter on my chest three times to make sure it still works properly. It responds immediately with a painful squeeze of my heart, followed by a spike in my heart rate that renders me drenched in sweat in just a few moments. I stop it with additional taps. Breathing hard, I resume. "We'll stick the cardioverter on the power breaker and overload it—until it blows up."

Somyung is skeptical.

"Will that really work?" she asks.

Miryu answers for me. "I think it will . . . Let me try."

She sticks Knife's knife into her waistband and takes the flashlight from me. Then her eyes flick to the bucket, and she asks me, "So the glass bottom should turn into a mirror portal if I shine this light on it, correct?"

"Wait!" I say, clutching at her arm. There's something I haven't told her. "You could die."

"I know," she says with perfect composure. "It's risky, and I'm the only one who deserves to face it."

Somyung and I stare at her grimly.

"Listen—Chobahm. Somyung. At the end of the day, humans are a selfish species. You'd be surprised at how few would be willing to give up warmth and comfort even when they learn that it comes at the expense of someone else's suffering."

Somyung and I are silent.

Miryu continues, "This place must be burned to ashes before human selfishness can get the better of us. And if that requires one person putting everything on the line, it's worth it. It's a small price for me to pay: one killer to make up for nine murders."

"But, Miryu . . . ," Somyung begins, and trails off, already defeated.

We both know that Miryu's mind is made up, and neither of us can change it.

"If something happens to one of you down here," Miryu continues, "I'd have to count that as my tenth murder. So please don't let that happen. Let me go take care of things."

I want to hold her back, but I feel my strength leaving me.

"Miryu . . . ," I plead without exactly knowing what I'm pleading for.

"Your exposé taught me things. I owe you girls for showing me what real courage is," Miryu tells us. "And now I get to dream about a borderless world—a dream that I know will come true so long as you survive."

She smiles, dropping her head as her eyes begin to fill with tears.

"These past months have been the happiest summer I ever had. Thank you . . . If I die here, it will be the best kind of ending for me—perhaps too good for a serial killer—so I want you to be happy for me."

She seems to consider this last remark a moment. When she resumes, her tone's brighter. "Yeah . . . ," she says, smiling again. "Be excited and happy for me. That'd make things less awkward when I return without a scratch, you know what I mean?"

She lets out a little laugh, which makes me ache more.

From a few feet away, Hyang watches us with the curiosity of a stranger. But her eyes are wet, too, I notice.

"For god's sake," she mutters. "What's with the tear fest . . ."

Miryu gazes at Hyang, tears finally brimming over the soft arches of her smiling eyes.

"Can you see me off?" Miryu asks Hyang, who has her back to us now, drying her eyes.

Hyang swings around on her feet and says, "You talking to me?"

Miryu nods a yes. And though Hyang makes an elaborate face of annoyance and bewilderment, she is already on her way.

"Just hold my hand as I climb into that bucket," Miryu tells Hyang, holding out her hand and nodding toward the bucket, which in the chaos has tumbled down from the higher floors and now rests on the ground level again. Hyang grabs it stiffly, and Miryu takes a few moments gazing at their held hands. Then her watery eyes shift up to Hyang's face, and she says, "Can I ask you to do one more thing for me?"

I'm not sure what I expected, but Hyang simply nods.

"You don't have to be happy all the time," Miryu tells her. "Not that it is even possible." A laugh. "But I want you to not be alone. Be with those who you can be yourself with. Live your life the way you want it. Your life is not for show, and you don't have to prove your worth to anyone, or anything. I wish you a very long life full of happiness, surrounded by those who you love and love you back. And when you become a tired old sack of a woman many, many decades from now, then come find me."

Hyang's eyes are full of tears again.

"Got it," she says, her voice cracking. "So go do what you gotta do and come back in one piece."

Then Miryu climbs into the bucket. Somyung and I, our red faces slick with tears and snot, station ourselves at the well's huge crank. Hyang, also crying, quietly joins us.

"As soon as you stick the cardioverter on the breaker and activate it, shake the chain. Hard!" I tell Miryu, trying to hold it together for her. "We'll pull you up as fast as we can, okay?"

"Of course—don't worry," Miryu assures us, and then, with a last smile and a thumbs-up, she begins riding the bucket down into the dark of the well. The three of us continue turning the crank, each stifling the sobs that push up in our throats. We must stay focused.

In a minute, the chain slackens. Miryu's bucket has touched down. We leave the crank and rush around its gaping mouth to peer intensely down into the murk, barely breathing. A minute ticks by, and the black void seems to begin to glow—almost imperceptibly at first, but in a few moments, there's no doubt; the faint light seeping from its depth rapidly intensifies. We fly back to the crank, watching the chain like three hawks, terrified of missing even the tiniest movement. Finally, the chain shakes and jangles.

"Pull!" I cry.

We work the crank handle with every ounce of our strength. Heart, Sky, and Knife have joined us by now, and they're frantically pulling at the chain, trying in vain to force the pulley by hand. We're all pushing and pulling, grunting, shouting, and crying, "Hurry! Pull faster!" when all of a sudden, white light explodes out of the well. A second later, a distant rumble grows in the depths, sending a tremor up from the earth. Heart scoops up Sky, and they retreat with Knife.

Blood pounding in my head, I keep turning the crank with everything I have. In less than a minute, there's another flash of light more intense and disorienting than the last; the next thing I know, I'm thrashing against Somyung and Hyang as they tear me off the crank and drag me away from the well, all of us shouting, crying, and screaming. We're no more than a dozen feet away when a roaring hellfire erupts out of the well, sending jets of sparks and ashes high up in the air.

# THE FINAL COUNTDOWN

'm not sure how much time has passed. The towering blaze has finally died off, and gloom descends throughout the cavernous space where the wheels have been destroyed or otherwise rendered motionless. Here and there, emergency lights turn on, their photoluminescent batteries requiring no electricity. There are smatters of coughing.

"She's actually done it . . . ," I murmur, my voice hollow, and Somyung nods next to me, tears streaming down her face.

*Miryu . . . You've done it. Just as you wanted, we'll always be there for each other, whenever we remember you.*

A few feet off, Hyang sits on the floor, gazing emptily at the well, which puffs black clouds of acrid smoke. Tears have carved paths down each of her sooty cheeks.

Then another kaboom comes from deep inside the well, and someone shouts, *"Watch out!"* as sparks and ashes fly out once more. A fresh wave of chaos tears through the fortress, with panicking people scrambling for the nearest cover.

"We have to get out of here!" Somyung shouts.

Sky bursts out crying in Heart's arms, the top of her left hand glistening pink with raw, burned skin. "It hurts, Uncle . . . ," she gasps out between coughing and crying.

"Hang in there, little captain," Heart comforts her, forcing a smile. "We'll get the hell out of here and take you to a doctor—first thing."

As if coming out of a trance, Hyang takes off her clear plastic mask and puts it over Sky's face. It's too big on Sky, but it's better than nothing.

"Ms. Chobahm!" I start at the sound of my real name. It's Chairman Shin in her wheelchair, fighting her way to me through panicking people scurrying in the opposite direction. She must have left her post at the elevator when she heard the bomb go off.

"Chairman Shin!" I hurry over to her, shouting. "We have to evacuate!"

"That's why I'm here!" she replies. "I felt the explosion all the way at the elevator!"

A dark look coming over her face, she glances around at all the people scurrying aimlessly with terror.

"There are way more prisoners down here than I thought," she says. "The elevator can only take five people at once!"

"We'll just have to evacuate five at a time, then," Bonwhe says, showing up from nowhere. "If we move quick and stay calm, we should all be able to get out safely."

He looks disbelievingly from Chairman Shin to me and then back again. From her wheelchair, Chairman Shin gazes up at the Yibonn heir, visibly shaken, and I rush to tell her that he's on our side. She accepts this quietly and doesn't ask me to elaborate. If anything, it's Bonwhe who seems more perturbed at seeing Chairman Shin down here than the other way around.

Returning to herself, Chairman Shin cracks a bitter smile and tells Bonwhe, "Obviously, I'm older than her. The Ichae you're thinking of is at the mansion."

*The Ichae you're thinking of.* It sends a shiver down my spine, the reminder that all this time, Bonwhe has been living with Chairman Shin's clone. Bonwhe seems to accept her explanation, nodding along when I remind him that we need to go, though not without effort.

"Fine," he says at last. "Let's clear out of here first. Then, though, I want to hear everything."

He moves to herd the panicking crowd, and I ask him, "What about Ongi?"

"Don't worry. He's all set," he says, and though it isn't much, I believe him.

Then he murmurs to himself, "Where to evacuate to, when all the mirrors are surrounded . . ."

"I know a place," Chairman Shin says, inserting herself. We both turn to her. Focusing on me, she continues, "You've been there, Ms. Chobahm. The blind spot at the SnowTower."

Oh . . .

Where I overcame Buhae's hypnotic spell. The portal to Chairman Shin's office.

"What is this place?" Bonwhe wants to know.

"There's a small blind spot inside the tower," Chairman Shin supplies, beating me to it. "Either the mirror or the regular elevator will get you there, but it requires punching in a special code that I randomly program."

"But the mirrors don't have buttons," Bonwhe says.

Chairman Shin pulls a business card from her shirt pocket and hands it to him.

"Press the emergency button as soon as you step in the mirror," she says. "Then move the shifter clockwise according to the number written on the card."

Bonwhe studies the card a moment.

Chairman Shin continues, "When you get to the blind spot, use one of the regular elevators to get to the first floor, and continue on from there. Even President Yi wouldn't think of that evacuation route."

"Okay, that's great," I say. "Chairman Shin, you should go through first and head up the elevator route. I'll stay behind here and direct people—"

"No, Miss Chobahm. You and I have to do something together."

I look at her, puzzled, and she steals a quick glance at Bonwhe before explaining to me in a hushed voice, "You and I will go after the president. We can't let her get away."

Bonwhe hears all this anyway and says, "Let me go with you, then. I know where Grandmother would—"

"I don't trust a Yibonn." Chairman Shin cuts him off, staring at him coldly. "I'm sorry," she adds, but it's clear she doesn't mean it. She watches Bonwhe as he drops his gaze and stares at the ground, defeated. Then, letting her voice grow warm and confidential, she tells him, "But I'll trust that you will successfully evacuate these people."

Bonwhe gives her a heavy nod.

"Thanks," he says after a moment. "Let me tell you where the secret bunker is in the Yibonn mansion, in case Grandmother hides there."

**I'm saying goodbye to Somyung, making her promise me that she** will get Ongi to an operating room, when Heart carries Sky and her mangy old bear over.

"Sky says she has something to tell you, Wisher," he says.

The little girl's face is a mess of tears and sooty ash, and it breaks my heart all over again. Sniffling, she pushes her singed bear to me and asks me to unzip its back, where I see a zipper parts its fur. When I do, I find the beam projector hiding in it. I look at her, stupefied.

"I picked it up for you . . . ," she says, trying for a smile even as she nurses her burned hand.

"It's exactly what I need. Thanks, Sky," I tell her.

I turn to Chairman Shin and ask her if we can take Sky to the hospital before heading over to the Yibonn mansion. The chairman hesitates, but in the end, she agrees to it.

"Have the man come with her as her guardian, then," she says, meaning Heart. "I don't have time to check her in and all that."

Heart readily agrees. All our preparations made, Sky, Heart, Chairman Shin, and I leave Bonwhe and the rest to gather the evacuees and flee, heading out of the burning plant and down the long hallway toward the mirror. I shiver as we pass out of the plant and into the abrupt cold, rubbing my arms. When we reach the mirror, we slip through its surface one by one. On the other side, Chairman Shin presses the red button, and the whole inside of the chamber we're standing in begins to pulse white. The chairman maneuvers the shifter with great care and precision. Six o'clock. Then two o'clock. Back to six . . .

Whoa . . .

Under her clear face mask, Sky's little mouth drops open

with amazement. She's still coughing, but she seems to have forgotten the pain in her charred hand, if momentarily. I stroke her hair. This brave little girl. She has carried so much . . .

Suddenly, my thoughts break off, and I'm coughing. Mildly at first, but it quickly grows into a dramatic, full-blown, breathless hacking, and I can't seem to stop. There's a tightness in my chest, where my cardioverter is strapped, that seems to be intensifying. Then Heart breaks out in a coughing fit of his own.

"Little Captain," he chokes out. "What's the first thing you want to do when we get out?"

Forcing a smile at Sky, who's watching him worriedly, he surreptitiously wraps a rag around Sky's blackened hand, which is oozing horrible stuff.

"See the big blue sky!" Sky replies, her face brightening again. "The sky as awesome as me!"

Meanwhile, Chairman Shin presses the emergency button for the second time, and when the pulsing white light stops, she announces, "Here we go."

"Be ready," I tell Heart and Sky between coughs. "This thing flies—"

But the mirror's already moving at an insane speed, whisking us up, up, up. In a short minute, we arrive at the blind spot at the SnowTower, all of us, except Chairman Shin, still hacking away.

Chairman Shin gets out first. Heart staggers behind her, carrying Sky. Finally, I step out, noticing Heart's shirt back curiously drenched in sweat.

Light pours in through the massive glass panels of the SnowTower.

"Look, Sky!" I tell her, pointing out the glass. "It's the sky!"

I look back to Sky, expecting to see her captivated little face; but what I see instead is Heart folding at the knees and pitching forward to the floor with Sky still in his arms. His forehead hits the hard marble with a horrible, resounding thud that stops my heart. On the floor, from under the safety of Heart's arching torso, Sky blinks at me in confusion, her head miraculously resting on the cushion of Heart's big hand, which he's reflexively placed to protect her.

"Wisher . . . what is Uncle Heart doing?" Sky says.

Her voice snapping me back, my eyes leap to Heart. He's sweating profusely. So much so that the entirety of his blue cotton uniform is drenched with it, turned a much deeper shade of blue. Where his body touches the floor, puddles are quickly growing. I drop to my knees and turn him over, and even with my trembling hands, it doesn't take any effort—his oddly weightless body simply flops over to one side like some kind of driftwood. Wide-open eyes stare emptily out of a face that I'm hard-pressed to recognize as his anymore. It's . . . it's mummified. Horribly shriveled up and desiccated. Completely sapped of life.

Chairman Shin gasps, "All the moisture in his body has been squeezed out of him. He's completely dehydrated."

Shaking with horror and shock, I put my hand over his eyes and close them, and his skin feels and sounds like dead leaves.

"Uncle . . . ," Sky cries out in the feeblest voice dying in her throat.

Then I notice with fresh dread that she is sweating profusely, too, with patches of wet spots appearing on her shirt and pants.

"No!" I cry, and scoop her up, forcing her face away from Heart's body.

"Wisher . . . What's happening to Uncle?" she asks, her voice barely audible now.

I murmur something incoherent as her sweat drenches my own uniform.

"Wisher . . . ," Sky croaks. "Am I dying?"

"No . . ."

"You're lying . . . I'm all-seeing Sky," she squeezes out, turning her tired gaze out the windows. "So pretty . . ."

Liquid continues trickling out of her eyes, nose, and mouth and seeping out of her skin. She feels even lighter now—as light as a cloud. A tiny puff of cloud like baby breath, floating high in the otherwise cloudless blue sky.

"Hang tight, Sky," I plead through tears. "You have to see the sunset. It's just going to be a little while . . ." I turn to the chairman, desperate. "What's happening to her?"

She breathes out the tiniest sigh as her eyelids flutter shut. Outside the SnowTower, clouds drift away in Snowglobe's blue, blue sky. So peaceful.

"These people . . . ," Chairman Shin says. "The president must have drugged them so that in the event they ever escaped the underground plant, they'd expire. She could have tainted their food or water with a certain substance or organism that stays dormant until activated by exposure to a particular environment. I'm guessing that the extreme cold they were exposed to during the short walk to the mirror might have acted as a trigger. Oh god . . ."

The VP's sniggering face flashes before me then.

*Why all this struggle? You're all going to die regardless.*

Tears fall from my eyes and drop onto Sky's face.

*I saw Captain gave it to you before you left with Teacher on the mission—remember? She said it would make you healthy and strong for a new adventure.*

An idea strikes me as I recall Sky's words. I wondered if the gel pill she stole was an antidote to the memory loss the plant workers experienced, but what if it's really meant to cure this . . . exposure sickness? Frantically, I fish the pill out of my pants pocket and push it past Sky's dry, bleaching lips. Chairman Shin moves to my side in her wheelchair.

"It looks like you're okay, Ms. Chobahm," she says, relief in her voice.

"But how?" I ask. "I ate the same food and drank the same water as the rest of them . . ."

"The severity of the reaction probably depends on the dose. Your exposure to it was much shorter than theirs."

If that's true, then the final countdown will begin for Healer, Knife, and everyone else as soon as they evacuate the plant. They're all going to die . . .

My words stick in my throat. I focus on moving Sky's tiny, listless body onto Chairman's Shin's lap.

"What are you doing?!" she says, gaping at me.

"I have to tell everyone else to stay put for now," I tell her, turning to race back for the mirror. "The other prisoners. I can't let them die. Take Sky to the hospital, please!"

Without waiting for her to respond, I reach for the mirror, my fingers inches away from the glass, when my heart jolts violently inside my chest and I drop to the floor, screaming in agony. A short distance away, Chairman Shin watches me in her wheelchair, radiating extreme annoyance. She pushes Sky off her lap onto the cold, hard floor as if flicking away a dead fly and begins cruising toward me in her wheelchair. I choke back a scream of horror as I watch the little girl fall to the ground, limp.

"Where do you think you're going? I told you that I need you to get the president with me," she admonishes angrily, letting her wheelchair roll to a stop. "Are you really going to ruin our plan for a basket full of human trash?"

What did she just call them? Who is this person?

I want to ask her, but the pain is too strong. It's all I can do to writhe on the ground in agony. Sky—I have to save Sky and everyone else down there . . .

Looking on, she says, "I'll make you a hero of the new world, Miss Chobahm. You just do what I tell you. It's really that easy." She pauses to give me a chilling grin. "Isn't it electrifying? To think that you're finally going to live a life you could have only dreamed of? A life in which everyone knows your name?"

I scrape up every last ounce of strength left in me and shift onto my elbows, shooting her a look of pure hatred. Anger flares up all over again across Chairman Shin's face, and when she squeezes the armrests of her wheelchair with extra force, my heart instantly twists inside my rib cage. Despite my rage, there's nothing I can do but dissolve into another cry of agony.

# A WHOLE NEW WORLD

"**Y**ou're finally up," Chairman Shin says, her tone bright with excitement. With great effort, I swivel my head on my stiff neck to look around. I'm in a cream-colored space with no windows—Chairman Shin's dome-top office. And . . . am I sitting in a wheelchair? My arms are lying on the chair's armrests, and my feet are neatly arranged on the footrest. I can't seem to move a muscle from my neck down—not even to lift a finger. Slowly, memory returns.

I remember Chairman Shin driving me all the way here by controlling the cardioverter strapped to my chest, forcing me to climb into this wheelchair like I was some kind of dog under the control of a shock collar.

*Stop resisting gravity,* I remember her chiding me. *Why cry over things you cannot affect? You're just making things unnecessarily miserable for yourself.*

Then my heart rate jumped yet again, and I passed out.

I thrash my head back and forth—the only part of my body I can seem to move—to see if I can generate some kind of momentum that way and get out of this chair, but my back seems to be glued to the seat.

"What are you doing to me?!" I say, glaring at her fiercely.

She gives me a tight smile.

"Once again, I'll show you—rather than try to explain everything," she replies, rolling past me and out of the room.

Where did things go so terribly wrong?

I replay our past encounters—meeting her at the wedding, the talk in her dome-top office, the plan we formed there, to shut down the underground plant and free the people trapped inside.

*What do you say? Would you join hands with me in bringing in a new world?*

As I relive these moments in my head, Chairman Shin returns, stationing herself on the other side of the low table.

"Fun fact—they banned automatic wheelchairs like mine in Snowglobe because they said manual ones are more dramatic," she tells me out of the blue. "Same goes for the banning of cellphones, which had been ubiquitous in the Warring Age. Everyone thinks the rules are designed to create better entertainment—the more calls that are missed and the greater the failure of communication and connection between people . . . the better TV." A snort. Reaching down, she grabs a pristine white plate with steak on it from her lap and places it on the table. "But that's just conspiracy," she continues. "In truth, it's all for them, the Yibonn. They want frequent failure of communication and connection among the people because it slows spreading of ideas and philosophies that could pose a threat to their power, if allowed to go viral. Those in power instinctively fear citizen organizations."

She swipes a corner of the tabletop with a finger as if flicking an invisible switch, and a well-marbled steak topped with a knob of golden butter begins sizzling. My mind jumps back to Sky's excited plea.

*Aunt Knife, you're going to put your knife skills to work and make all kinds of meat dishes for Uncle Heart!*

The smell of cooking flesh rising to my nose, Heart's face begins to mummify in my mind, and that's when I finally remember.

"Where's Sky?!" I cry, my voice fraying with panic. "Is she alive? What did you do with her?"

From the glowing digital display in the near corner of the table, I can tell it's 11:42 a.m. Two hours since we left the power plant.

"What about everyone else?" I ask, increasingly desperate, when she doesn't answer. "Did the rest of the inmates evacuate safely?"

Chairman Shin just shrugs.

"Let them take care of themselves," she says after a moment as if none of it is her business. "You just focus on our mission, Miss Chobahm. The important one."

She gives me a long, steady look.

"And what's that?" I manage to growl, feeling like I'm about to combust with rage. The pain in my chest is so intense it's like my ribs are splitting.

What could be more important than saving the lives of people trapped underground?

"Don't play dumb," she says. "Dispatching the super-villain, of course. Isn't that what a superhero does? Fate is on our side, too, apparently. An unexpected snowstorm is keeping President Yi from fleeing Snowglobe."

She flicks her eyes to the digital time display glowing white in the corner.

"When you destroyed the underground power plant, you cut off the stream of energy to Snowglobe. The heat is dying. By now . . . journalists, the most driven ones at least, must have infiltrated the Yibonn mansion to try to find an explanation. I'm so curious to learn which lucky journalist will get to capture and record the historic moment—the moment where the hero gets the villain. Whoever they are, they're going to have their minute of fame, for sure."

My heart rate surges again, and I break out sweating. In the next moment, I'm panting as if I'm running up a steep hill. Chairman Shin flares her nostrils and inhales the smell of the steak deep into her lungs, smiling.

"You're feeling it now, aren't you?" she says. "I don't know if you've noticed, but you're cooking this steak. With the energy your heart's producing, to be precise. And look at you—all you're doing is sitting back in a wheelchair!"

Making her eyes big and opening her mouth in an expression of awe, she stares at me as if waiting for me to do the same. But I'm too weak to respond in any way.

"Isn't it just incredible? This new way of harvesting energy?" she resumes, practically singing now. "Imagine a world where everyone wears a cardioverter. We'll all be free from the beastly cold and the burden of labor! Of course, the average person's life span will be halved due to heart failure, among other side effects, but that's nothing. The benefit of this new technology is so goddamned attractive that no one will think twice about the trade-off!"

"Are . . . you . . . insane?" I manage to rasp.

Chairman Shin draws back, looking genuinely surprised—maybe a bit hurt. Frowning, she considers me a moment before throwing back her head and letting out a hoot of laughter.

"You know what?" she says at last, retraining her gaze on me. "Some people might react the same way as you just did—a lot of people, perhaps, and I guess that shouldn't be shocking, considering how the Yibonn turned the entire population into brainless addicts glued to their wretched screens for some stupid shows. How scary would my invention sound to those simpletons who can't see, let alone think, beyond their screens? *What? Pay for shows with my life now?*" '

She lets out a sigh, shaking her head. Picking up a fork in one hand and a steak knife in the other, she gazes at me a moment. Then suddenly, she thrusts the knife at me, saying, "And that's why I need you, Miss Chobahm."

Grinning again, she lowers the knife and drives the tines of her fork into the meat, flipping it over.

She resumes, "Add to your existing celebrity as a victim-slash-hero of the Goh Haeri scandal, the epic achievement of destroying the almighty Yibonn and rescuing her fellow suffering beings from their evil grip—all with the direction of a genius architect and engineer behind the scenes, of course . . . I can't think of a more fantastic PR person than you for my cause."

Her eyes take on a solemn shine then, and she lifts her knife aloft in her clenched fist. "I can just imagine you saying it. 'Without the cardioverter technology, it would have been impossible to bring down the Yibonn,'" she intones. "'It is this invention of the amazing Chairman Shin that delivered us from further suffering in the hands of the evil corporation. Every man, woman, child, and dog, for that matter, will be fitted with the technology—and we'll free ourselves from the yoke of the cold and hard labor—forever after!'"

Grinning with all her teeth now, she refocuses her eyes on me.

"How did you like it?" she says, back in her normal register and tone. "I think the speech is at least as good as any of President Yi's clearly ghostwritten New Year speeches—excuse me, soon-to-be-former president. I'm still polishing up my own remarks, but rest assured they'll blow yours out of the water."

Revising her grip on the fork and knife, she finally cuts into the steak.

"Why . . . why should people trade their lives just to make your vision a reality?" I say.

Her face snapping up from the plate, she says, "What now?"

"In that world of yours, we'd be preparing to die as soon as we were born," I say. "We'd have to cram far more goodbyes into our shortened lives. Yes, we'd become hardier to the cold, but at what cost?"

Chairman Shin, sliding the plate of steak to me across the table, glides to my side in her silent wheelchair.

"Don't worry, Miss Chobahm," she says, and her voice is different now, soft and conciliatory. "People like you and me will never have to function as our own power plants."

She cuts a piece of steak and holds it up to my mouth on her fork.

"Because the invalids, the useless, the dumb, and so on . . . those people will create the energy we need—for us, so people like us can focus our brains and energy on further advancing the world through technological innovations."

I take the bite of steak—then spit it right back at her as hard as I can. Pathetically, I'm so weak that it just falls on my lap.

Marshaling the last ounce of power left in my body, I tell her, "What advancement? What kind of advancement is it, if it requires that people sacrifice their literal beating hearts? In what sense is it better than the world engineered by the Yibonn?"

"Sacrifice?" she says, looking at me dumbstruck. "I'm not asking people to sacrifice; I'm giving them purpose. One just has to breathe in order to make a living—even the most useless, small-minded citizen."

"You're insane," I hiss feebly.

She considers me a moment. Then a look of resignation comes over her face and she sighs a long sigh.

"It's so unfortunate," she says, at last. "I really wanted to make you a hero of the people, Miss Chobahm."

She reaches for the table and turns an invisible dial on the tabletop. The sound of a radio commercial promoting some kind of waterproof rain gear flows out of the speakers. In the center of the table, the glass teakettle filled with water begins to roar softly as tiny bubbles clinging to its surface start swimming up to the top.

"You must be pretty darn tired at this point, but I'd think

you still have enough energy left to boil some water for us," she says. "Oh, and your wheelchair's gravity amplifier operates on your energy, too, if you didn't know. Incredible, isn't it?"

Humming a tune, she pours a fistful of coffee beans into a grinder and begins cranking its handle.

"Thanks to the president being so thoroughly corrupt, I don't have to worry about cleanup. I can just tell the world that Miss Chobahm, too, perished from the same condition that killed all the underground residents upon surfacing. How simple and elegant is that?"

She tips the kettle and pours a slow, continuous stream of hot water over the fine coffee grounds, filling the air with a rich, nutty aroma. I gasp, my heart straining with the effort of creating so much energy.

"And don't waste your strength hoping that someone will swoop in here and save you. It's impossible for anyone to get here without my allowing them up."

She brings her coffee cup to her lips and takes a delicate sip. Lowering her cup, she gazes at me a long moment, the look on her face bittersweet. I can barely focus through the haze of pain.

"I'm going to be so sad when I eventually sit down and delete all your data from the system," she says, her tone soft now, nearly wistful. "So sad," she repeats after a moment. "You're my first and only friend to have visited my office."

Just then, the radio broadcasts the hour—noon—and the midday news begins with the host announcing the top headlines.

*"The sudden drop in temperature that descended upon Snowglobe around eight this morning continues. Current temperature is negative*

*one degree, the lowest summer temperature in Snowglobe history, folks.*
*While anxiety is high across the community, the Yibonn Media Group*
*has announced that President Yi will hold a special press conference at*
*one o'clock this afternoon . . ."*

"Oh my goodness, how perfect," Chairman Shin says, re-animating. "I can get her live, right in front of all those cameras then!"

She sets the coffee cup down on the table and clasps her hands like an excited child.

"I'll leave the radio on for you—hope you're still alive when the good news breaks that she's been captured," she says. Then she abruptly erases her smile and makes a sudden sad face. "Well . . . It's been lovely, Miss Chobahm . . . brief but lovely. I sincerely hope that your end will be quick and relatively pain fre—"

A loud pop cuts her off as her head jerks back violently. The smell of gunpowder fills the air. The next thing I know, she's pitched backward in her wheelchair, her wide-open eyes staring blankly at me, her mouth bright with blood. Everything is quiet and still but for the ringing in my ears and the news continuing to flow out of the radio. Then Somyung comes into view, perched in the doorway like a sniper, the barrel of her rifle still smoking.

"It was self-defense," she says automatically. "Your life was at risk."

As I blink at the surrealness of it all, Shinae pops out from behind Somyung and rushes over, crying, "Are you okay, Chobahm?!"

It takes me a moment to accept their presence through the agony of the cardioverter. This is real. I'm not dead yet.

"Turn off . . . turn this thing off for me . . . ," I rasp finally, but Shinae doesn't understand.

"What? Turn what off?" she cries, frightened and frustrated. Luckily, Somyung's already tapping her knuckles on the plastic heart on my chest, once, twice, three times, disabling the cardioverter. The radio news instantly cuts off, and I slump over in the wheelchair, my heart rate decelerating.

After a few minutes, I'm finally strong enough to ask them how they managed to break into Chairman Shin's lair—and how they even knew to come looking for me. By way of an answer, Somyung props her eye open with a thumb and forefinger and takes a careful fingertip to her eyeball, lifting out the contact lens covering her iris. Then Shinae lifts up her open hands. When she wiggles her fingers, their tips catch the light and shimmer, as if covered in shiny fish scales.

"Who would have thought that we'd live to see the day when Bae Serin offered invaluable assistance?" Shinae says. "Apparently, when Serin stabbed you in the neck and became Goh Haeri, Dr. Cha Sohm gave her extra fingertip covers and lenses that were designed to mimic your biometrics. You know, so she could access the studio and draw those weather balls that only activated with your fingerprints?"

"But Serin burned off her fingerprints," I say, still confused.

"Yes, she did," Shinae says, wiggling her glittery fingertips for me once more. "Unfortunately, she acted a bit too hastily. If she'd waited, Dr. Cha would have fixed the problem for her . . . but oh, well. Anyway, she still had some old ones left in her possession, so we got to put them to good use."

With the worst of the tension leaving my body, my head clears.

"Where's Sky?!" I cry.

"Who?"

"The little girl from the underground plant!" I reply, terror creeping into my voice again. "How about Ongi? Everyone else at the plant? How about Hyang? Did her memory return?!"

"Let's go," Somyung says. "I'll explain on the way."

"On the way to where?"

"To see the president. The others have already left."

"Others?"

I don't fully understand, but I trust my friends. Snatching up the steak knife on the table, I wedge the tip of its blade under the cardioverter and pry the thing off my chest, at last. A bit of skin comes off with it, causing a red spot to bloom on my white undershirt, but I don't care. Shinae's helping me up from the wheelchair when the sound of scrambling feet approaches, and Bae Serin slides in through the hallway.

"Guys . . . ?" she says, her voice high with panic. "I think we're trapped. The mirror portal has turned hard. I can't get through it!"

# THE FOUR SNOWMEN OF THE POSTAPOCALYPSE

I try all ten of my fingers, but none is able to penetrate the mirror's reflective surface. I turn to Serin.

"Are you sure that you didn't accidentally push a button or something?"

"What the heck?" she snaps angrily. "Is that how you talk to someone who's just saved your sorry life?"

She has a point, but it's not easy to be grateful when that someone is her. And especially not when my stress level is through the roof.

"You should have let me die, if you were going to be so bitter about it," I say reflexively.

"Oh . . . I would have, were it not for one thing," Serin says. "Credit me for everything, my ass . . ." A loud snort of contempt. "The others filled me in on what happened at the power plant—how they rushed in to save you, and all of the workers heard your real name. Your name, Jeon Chobahm, not mine. You said if your plan succeeded, I'd get the credit, but how do you propose that you make me the hero in anyone's eye now? Fool me twice, shame on me. I decided to take the matter into my own hands."

"You know what? At least you're consistent—I'll give you that . . . ," I volley, glancing over to Somyung and Shinae for support, but they won't give it.

"Would you two stop and think about how we're going to get out of here?" Shinae chides, her voice tight with frustration. "You two deserve each other."

Somyung doesn't even legitimize our pathetic little feud by responding to it. Her attention on the mirror, she mutters to herself, "For god's sake . . . It was working just a little while ago."

Then a dreadful possibility finally dawns on me.

"It may be because Chairman Shin is dead," I say. "She's the key to the entire system—she has to be alive for it to work. Not to mention, this mirror is for her personal use only. Not even the Yibonn knows of it."

"Then what do we do now?!" Serin screeches, glaring at me as if it's all my fault. "We can't bring the dead back to life!"

I fight off the impulse to fire something right back at her, and point to the coat rack where a handful of white coats hangs, all of them made with the same faux fur as the one I tried on during my first trip up here.

"We'll put on those and go from there," I say, already crossing the floor.

We all don the white coats—me over my blue inmate uniform, and the rest over the thick winter coats that Snowglobe's record low summer temperature has forced them to wear.

Hurrying back to the coffee table, I begin slowly running

my palm over the smooth tabletop, trying to find the right spot where the touch sensor, or whatever activates the table, is located.

"I'm pretty sure it's around here . . . ," I murmur, focusing as hard as I can.

I must brush over something, because all of a sudden, the whole tabletop lights up, shooting its beams up onto the glass ceiling and turning it into a mirror. A pang of relief going through me, I swipe my palm against the side of the table, just like I saw Chairman Shin do. In the next moment, the floor beneath us separates itself from the rest in a diamond shape, levitating us toward the mirror ceiling. Shinae briefly loses her balance and flails, but Somyung catches her. I'm holding on to the handlebars of Chairman Shin's empty wheelchair.

A few seconds later, we're through the mirror, on top of Snowglobe's dome, where the winnowing chill greets us. Negative twenty degrees, according to the tabletop's digital display. We seem to have emerged into a lively blizzard, on top of everything else.

"Which way is east?!" I shout to be heard over the wind.

Somyung points to her left, shielding her face from the wind and shouting, "There—that's the lake on the right of the SnowTower! So that's gotta be east!"

Serin shrills, "And just how are we going to get back inside the globe?!"

"The border office!"

"What?!"

"We have to get to the border office in the east!"

"How?!"

In lieu of an answer, I swing the wheelchair around and

shove it into the back of her knees. Serin helplessly folds onto the seat; before she can react, I plunk down on her lap. Next, Shinae stand on the back rest, and finally, Somyung, holding the handles behind Shinae, gives the chair a big push forward along the dome-top before straddling it with her legs.

I prepare for us to go hurtling down the dome's side. Under the heavy load of our cumulative weight, however, the wheelchair only jerks forward a few feet before coming to a complete stop.

Then I remember. I sweep the length of the armrest with my palm, like I saw Chairman Shin do. The wheelchair begins gliding forward on its own, picking up speed quickly on the snow-slick surface.

"Are you all crazy?!" Serin screeches mightily, but my own terrified scream drowns her out.

"Aaaaaaahh!"

The automatic wheelchair cruises forward at top speed, like a luxury sports car. Snow and ice pellets blast our exposed skin, my face turning numb as the jagged mountains of the open world come into view in the distance and the dome's curvature changes under us. Fresh panic surging inside me, I frantically sweep the length of the armrest with my hand, but this time, from front to back, screaming, "The brakes! Somyung! Squeeze the brakes!"

The wheelchair fishtails wildly on the icy surface, and after half a dozen harrowing spinouts, it skids to a stop to let us hang over the crest of the dome for a terrifying moment. Then gravity takes over, and we're plunging along the curvature as if on a descending roller-coaster track, our insides floating. The world zooms up to greet me; for a moment, I have the most thrilling and unobstructed view of our surroundings, sitting in the very front seat of this runaway ride.

"Mooooooomm!" Shinae screams over and over until—

Our chair drops off the dome and flings us into the snowy embrace of the open world.

**When I dig her out of the snowbanks, Serin lunges for me, in-**coherent with rage.

"You . . . you lunatics almost killed me!"

We tumble right back into the snow, where we wrestle until Somyung and Shinae trudge over and pull us apart.

Some minutes later, we are plowing through the deep, deep snow, like moles burrowing in the underground, while Serin lets the rest of us know how stupid and reckless she thinks we are.

"Remind me why we let her tag along again?" Shinae mutters under her breath.

"I know," Somyung grunts. "So damn noisy . . ."

Serin finally subsides into icy silence.

I take this opportunity to catch up on the details I missed while Chairman Shin was holding me captive.

"A few more people died while you were locked up in Chairman Shin's office," Somyung tells me. She explains how upon arrival at the blind spot via the mirror, Bonwhe found Sky alive and whimpering on the floor by Heart's desiccated body. Just as he discovered her, the people who he'd evacuated from the cave began flopping over like wilting plants, with sweat, tears, and all kinds of liquid pouring freely out of them. It was clear that something was terribly wrong with them, though what, he didn't know. He immediately paused the evacuation.

Luckily, once Sky recovered, she remembered where the stash of gel pills was hidden in Captain's room. She'd somehow gathered that they were some kind of cure to the condition affecting all those around them. Bonwhe's intuition told him to trust Sky, and so he went back, found the stash, and distributed the pills to as many prisoners as possible. Those who took them, Sky included, survived.

Meanwhile, Somyung was anxious to find me. Something about Chairman Shin didn't sit well with her, she said. Why did the chairman decide to swoop in at this stage of the mission, when she'd eagerly sent me down into the treacherous plant by myself? The only thing left was to defeat the villain, and Somyung assumed Chairman Shin wanted to claim a piece of the victory. There was also the odd fact that the mirror outside the blind spot wouldn't respond to Bonwhe's fingerprints even though he was a Yibonn, and that once they finally escaped back into Snowglobe proper and got Ongi into surgery, there was no news about my having snuck into the Yibonn mansion, or my having apprehended President Yi. If Chainman Shin had taken me to confront the president like she'd promised, why hadn't anyone heard about it? What was taking so long?

"So I called home to see if you were there, and Serin picked up the phone. The rest that followed—you already know."

I hang my head in grief. If only I hadn't been so quick to trust the chairman, Heart and the other workers wouldn't have died. My friends may have saved me, but we've still lost so many.

Somyung seems to sense this. "Come on," she says softly, putting a hand on my shoulder. "There's no use crying about our circumstances now. We have a mission to complete."

**The Snowglobe border office is set into the edge of the dome,** the bridge between the outside world and the one within. I breathe a sigh of relief when we see the landing strip outside the office, trudging through the snow and shoving open its doors along with the others.

"How may I help you—"

The attendant standing inside breaks off and gapes at us as we enter the building, our coats heavy with inches of snow and ice. Somyung lumbers stiffly over to the counter and asks to use the phone. But the officers behind the counter just glance at each other in bewilderment, rendered speechless by the sight of the four snowmen who've stumbled into their building.

"Don't you worry, folks. We're not hopping the border or anything this time—we live here," Shinae quips. All five officers were stunned, recognizing us. She glances through the windows at the back of the office, which face the inside of Snowglobe, past the dome. Through the glass, I can see a taxi lingering on the street.

"Oh, there's our car waiting for us already," she chirps.

A voice protests from somewhere to our left, shouting that the taxi's waiting for him, but we don't have time to argue. Moving in unison, we push our way through the security check, brushing aside the officers who try to hold us back. When it spits us out on the other side, we peel off our outer layers and throw them in the garbage can.

Then we're hurrying out of the building and piling into the taxi, with me riding shotgun and the rest in the backseat. When I give the driver—a woman—our destination, the Yibonn mansion, she turns to me with a frown on her face.

"The Yibonn mansion?" she says. "There's been a road closure—"

Her eyes lighting up, she gasps.

"Miss Haeri! Oh, I mean . . ."

It takes me a moment, but I, too, recognize her.

"Oh my goodness, it's you! You drove me to Haeri's house last Christmas!"

She was the first taxi driver I ever had, when I was pretending to be Haeri. The operator's license affixed above the glove compartment identifies her as Kwon Haejung.

"You remember me, Miss Chobahm!" Haejung says, clapping her hands with delight. Then her eyes flick to the rearview mirror, and she snaps her head around.

"For real?!" she squeals. "All four of you are in here?"

The three in the back respond with exhausted but polite smiles.

Haejung's face suddenly darkens, and she asks, "Are you storming the mansion? To get President Yi?"

We just blink at her, unsure if we heard her right.

"With everyone rushing over there right now, the roads are an absolute gridlock," she explains.

"Storm the mansion?" I murmur at last, my confusion only deepening.

She gazes from me to the three in the back, now looking as puzzled as we are.

"Don't you know?" she says. "There's a nasty rumor going

around. The power is down. At first, we didn't know what was going on, but now people are saying that the Yibonn have been lying to us all this time."

The girls and I share a look, our eyes wide with astonishment—except Shinae, who just grins and nods knowingly.

"Did you start the rumor? How?" Serin asks Shinae, incredulous.

Shinae just holds her grin, looking pleased with herself.

"It was a piece of cake," she finally admits. "I just picked up one of the business cards that journalists leave on our front steps every day and called them up."

At once, we're all congratulating Shinae on how amazing she is, when it dawns on me that we haven't heard anything about the rumor on the radio news. When I express this, Somyung answers immediately, "Obviously, the Yibonn have silenced the media. Remember—despite everything, the corporation is still in control for now."

"So the rumor's true? The Yibonn have been lying to us all this time?" Haejung reinserts herself, looking at us in disbelief.

We all nod gravely. Her jaw drops, and no one says anything for a few moments.

"Well . . . Do you think the president's still at the mansion, then?" Haejung says at last, sounding skeptical. "The press conference she announced might just be a smoke screen."

This fresh new insight gives me pause. I turn to the girls for their opinions, but they just stare back at me.

"I think she is," I say after a moment. "If she's looking for somewhere to hole up, there wouldn't be anyplace safer. From the angry people and from the cold."

If Chairman Shin was right, and what the Yibonn fears is a united people, then their worst nightmare is coming true. The people of Snowglobe are coming together around their suspicion of the Yibonn. Furthermore, the restricted woods might be too cold now for someone who's so fragile in the face of cold.

"Let's roll, then," Haejung says, cranking up the car heater to the max. "Do you know who has the most street cred among all the taxi drivers in Snowglobe? It's me, Kwon Haejung."

It's true. Though she's never had a major role in any show, Haejung is an essential bit-part actor—Licorice—who has survived Snowglobe for eight years and counting by giving rides to other, more famous actors.

The next thing we know, we're racing across the city in her taxi, winding in and out of side roads, back alleys, and unpaved paths, as occasional smatterings of frozen bubbles dump from the sky to shatter fantastically upon hitting our windshield. I watch the buildings roll by, their TVs flickering from within. Since Snowglobe officially imports most of its electricity from the outside world, facilities should still be running as normal. The cameras, of course, also keep rolling due to power from the sole nuclear power plant inside Snowglobe. But the warmth the city is known for—the warmth that makes it a paradise . . . with the underground plant shut down, that heat is dying fast.

I steal a glance at the tiny thermometer on the rearview mirror: nineteen. Even without its normal supply of heat,

Snowglobe's protective dome should keep it a bit warmer than the outer world, just like the retirees' village where I first met Hyang. Still . . . I shiver in my seat.

Then, with a final, dramatic throw of her manual shifter, Haejung's parking her car and turning off the engine. I don't think I recognize this alley.

"You're not going to have any luck getting into the mansion through the front," she says as I look around, uncertain. "Do you see that bush over there? There's a hidden entrance there that gets you on a path leading to the back of the estate."

"Amazing," Shinae says, counting our fare. "How do you know these things?"

"A trick of the trade. I've brought top-notch reporters and paparazzi here," Haejung offers proudly. "And security guards and butlers. They do play occasional hooky, sneaking in and out of the mansion on the clock. They're regular customers of mine, if you know what I mean."

Shinae hands Haejung our fare plus a tip, but Haejung gently pushes the money back toward us.

"Don't worry about it," she insists, smiling. "This ride is on me."

She gives a wink and a thumbs-up, and as she watches out for us in her car, we disappear into the bush.

**In the vast back corner of the Yibonn estate, security is shockingly** loose. When we emerge on the other side of the passageway, I brace for an onslaught of guards, but no one comes rushing at us. The few security team members I do see appear too busy infighting to even notice us.

It's total chaos. Some guards are actively aiding the demonstrators who are scaling and climbing over the high stone walls into the grounds, while others are trying to stop the intruders as well as the other guards who are helping them. Protected by the unexpected mayhem, we cross the yard and slip into the mansion.

Inside, the megamansion seems all but deserted. Once again encountering zero resistance, we search the basement bunker and the other secret hideouts Bonwhe told us about prior to our leaving, but President Yi is nowhere to be found.

"Did she flee already—" Shinae begins, when Somyung lifts a sudden hand to signal silence.

"Shhh," she hisses. "Listen."

I hold my breath and listen. A faint, high-pitched whistle separates itself from the low thrums of the basement. It seems to be peaking at a regular interval, like a distress signal.

With Somyung leading the way, we tiptoe upstairs toward the sound, arriving at a door across from Bonwhe's room. With a few determined glances and nods, we open the door and storm inside.

Nothing. The room appears unoccupied. Still, the feeble insistence of the whistle doesn't relent, and we follow it to the wardrobe standing against the far wall.

In a few moments, Shinae and I are positioning ourselves on the sides of the wardrobe, clutching at the doorknobs, while Serin stands crouched in the front, holding up the bedsheet she's stripped off like a net trap. Her rifle pointed at the wardrobe, Somyung mouths the countdown. "Three, two, one." Shinae and I throw open the doors.

"He-help . . ." a voice pleads weakly from inside the gaping wardrobe, where the fifth Haeri sits trembling, head down between her knees and clutching a small radio.

"Goh Haeri?" someone murmurs.

Slowly lifting her head, the girl looks up at us, her eyes going in and out of focus.

"I'm seeing things . . . ," she murmurs to herself, and raises a hand to rub her eyes.

That's when the headphone cable tangled around her wrist tugs loose from the radio jack, and a familiar voice jumps out of the radio's speakers.

*"We all know that cracks began to appear in Snowglobe since those wicked girls started poking at our system."*

It's President Yi, all composure and elegance.

Shinae turns on the TV on the shelf. On the screen, the president sits erect and regal in a pristine white suit before a microphone, her snow-white hair yanked back without a loose strand in sight.

The bold red caption on the bottom of the screen reads *Breaking News.*

*"But for you, beloved citizens of Snowglobe, I will not step down from my position—because I know for a fact that you will soon come back around with abiding trust in the Yibonns, in our missions and truths that have elevated us all this time."*

Wait. I recognize the backdrop. She's in her office after all!

We rush there. The door is locked, but it's nothing against Somyung's rifle power. When we kick down the door, Jin Jinsuh gapes at us, frozen in place behind the live camera she's operating.

President Yi, on the other hand, only directs a cool glance at us before turning her gaze back to the camera.

"Until that day, I will gladly bear the burden of defamation and libel hurled my way . . . ," she resumes, undaunted.

We share a final glance between us, steeling ourselves. Then, united, the four of us charge.

The next morning, the newspaper's opinion piece reads as follows:

*On live TV, the villain—President Yi—appeared resolute and noble, whereas our four brave girls appeared wicked and ghastly. We must remember, then, that truth is in the eyes of the beholders, even in the face of pure facts.*

# JEON CHOBAHM

Serin is the first to note the muffled TV sound leaking out of the room.

"The girl's up," she says.

In the kitchen, Somyung pauses mid-action, holding an egg above the hot frying pan. I rush to the bathroom and alert Shinae, who hurries out with suds on her face.

Together, we tiptoe to Miryu's old room, and holding our breaths, we click open the door. The Haeri once known as Wisher sits rigid on the edge of the bed, her already ghostly face turning a shade whiter as she takes us in.

"So . . . ," she tries after a long moment, her voice tight in her throat. "Which one of you filled in for me?"

She must have finally watched the tape. The exposé.

I bite my lip at the thought of her pain, the sheer disorientation and disbelief she must be experiencing.

"None of us," I tell her. "Her name was Jo Yeosu. She ended her own life."

Haeri lets out a low moan, curling farther back into herself.

"Come on out. We'll explain over some eggs," Somyung suggests after a moment, which prompts Serin to protest.

"Are you kidding? You're going to force actual, solid food on a girl who has been on an IV for a whole week?"

Somyung considers this a moment, or pretends to.

"Okay, fine, you have a point," she concedes. "But how about you pitch in for a change? Make some porridge for her?"

Serin rolls her eyes and sucks in a dramatic breath in preparation for her comeback.

"I was unconscious for a week?" Haeri murmurs then, stopping her short.

"Yes—at the hospital, mostly," I tell her. "It took the doctors three days to clear your system of Jin Jinsuh's hypnotic brew. Whenever a doctor tried speaking to you, you'd have a full breakdown and pass out again. Eventually, we figured out it was because Jinsuh appeared to you as a doctor herself whenever she first hypnotized you. So we moved you out of there yesterday."

She is silent a while, trying to process this information that just dropped out of the void.

"How about Assistant Yu?" she says finally.

While being transported from the Yibonn mansion to the hospital that day, Haeri, even in her barely conscious state, kept asking for Assistant Yu. Apparently, following the successful murder of Goh Maeryung, Assistant Yu had been tasked with the mission of eliminating Haeri, whose utility in the eyes of the president was exhausted. But even the loyal assistant couldn't find it in herself to fulfill that particular duty. Letting Haeri go free, however, was not even an option. So she took the girl to her room and hid her in the closet. As the chief of security, her room was largely off-limits, which made it an ideal hiding place for Haeri until a more permanent solution could be found. But then President Yi planted the false story of Bonwhe's airplane accident, and Assistant Yu had no choice but to take a real flight to make the lie believable, unaware that it would lead to her own death and leave Haeri alone.

"When we discovered you in the closet," I tell her, "you'd been without food for close to a week."

Haeri is silent again, reflecting on this. When she lifts her eyes back to me, a wave of terror peaks in them.

"How about the people at the plant?" she demands, her voice breaking with urgency. "Healer? Sky? Heart . . . ?"

"Healer will come see you today," I tell her, forcing a weak smile. "And Sky is scheduled to be discharged from the hospital sometime next week."

Haeri seems to find some relief in this. The stark dread in her face washes out a little, and she rubs her temples, as if finally catching up to her headache.

"All my memories since leaving the underground plant are patchy," she says.

"You don't have to try to make sense of them all at once," I tell her.

The Goh Haeri project. Heart's death. What became of Assistant Yu . . . It's already too much to take in. That she was used as a weapon in the murder of Goh Maeryung—under hypnosis, we've now learned—can wait until some other time.

Upon interrogation of Jin Jinsuh, the authorities decided

not to prosecute Haeri in Goh Maeryung's murder case. In fact, the focus of the investigation has shifted to President Yi and the Yibonns' breathtaking deception of the public and human rights violations all these years.

Some interesting facts were revealed during the investigation. President Yi had known of the Goh Haeri project long before any of us dreamed of the exposé. She even planned on destroying Cha Guibahng and Cha Seol, should they get anywhere with their ambition to put her family in front of the Snowglobe cameras. And the ace she held up her sleeve to bring them down, if need be—the proof of their criminality? Haeri, of course.

At the kitchen table, cradling a bowl of porridge made by Shinae, Haeri tells us of the day she ran off into the woods.

She emerged into a small clearing, where she couldn't believe her eyes. President Yi and Jin Jinsuh were engaged in a game of Baduk. *What amazing luck,* she thought. Surely President Yi would help her once she heard about Cha Seol's atrocious scheme, right?

"I had no doubt that I'd just run into my savior. Stupid me," she says sadly.

"We all thought the same," I tell her.

It's true. Serin thought of Cha Seol as her hero when the director first showed up at her doorstep in the open world. And I thought Shin Ichae was finally going to save us all, not just Snowglobe but the whole world. But we were mere tools to them. And that's not our fault.

Rising, I get ready to leave. The girls wish me luck, except Haeri, who doesn't know what I'm up to.

"I'm visiting our creator," I tell her, tongue-in-cheek. Then for no reason, I hear myself add, "The person responsible for who I am today."

And it's only then that I realize I'm telling the truth.

**In the visitation room, Hyang contemplates the figure behind the** glass partition, frustration creasing the space between her brows.

"I don't know . . . ," she sighs. "It's there one moment, and the next, it's gone."

Hyang hasn't recovered her memory. Everyone else afflicted by Jin Jinsuh's hypnotism has been making progress through various detoxes and therapies, but none has had any effect on Hyang.

From the other side of the partition, Cha Seol, clad in her prison-issued drab brown uniform, gazes at her little sister, a faintly wistful smile pressed on her lips. All around the room, where there used to be Snowglobe cameras, are small stickers instead. THE SHOW IS OVER, they read.

"How wonderful," Cha Seol says, trying for a smile. "It's only day one of my sentence, and my little sister's already visiting me."

Following the arrest of President Yi, Cha Seol requested a meeting with her lawyer whereupon she pleaded guilty to all charges. Her sentence might as well be life in prison. The court confirmed the prosecution's sentencing for the charges with astonishing speed and announced that it would deliver a swift and fair judgment regarding the Yibonn Media Group as well.

"I didn't think that you'd admit to everything you did," I say to Cha Seol.

She just smiles and says, "The world has changed. And so should I."

I don't know why, but I can't quite hold her gaze. I glance away, trying to maintain an exterior of cool disdain as I tell her, "Next time we meet, I suspect that we'll both have aged quite a bit."

"You plan to see me again?" She gazes at me, and I force myself to meet her eyes.

"I thought you might want someone to greet you at the gate on your day of release," I finally say. "By then, there will likely be no travel restrictions to and from Snowglobe and . . . I don't know, I'll probably have cultivated greater capacity for forgiveness . . . grace, or something like that."

She gives a puff of laughter, sweeping her brown hair back with a handcuffed hand.

"Thanks, but that won't be necessary," she says. "You go live your life. I plan to live mine."

Then I hear myself say, "I'll write whenever I think of it."

Her head snapping back to me, she seems to reflect on this a moment.

"Please don't," she says. "I can't stand the pressure of writing back."

Hyang, looking lost, finally inserts herself here. "What is your relationship again . . . ?"

"Archenemies," I reply.

"Two people who won't ever have to cross paths again," Cha Seol puts in.

Her words are harsh, but Cha Seol's tone is genuinely light, and I'm not sure how to feel about that. What's obvious, at least, is that not even this visit to her sister is doing anything for Hyang's lost memory.

"Let's go, Ajumma," I say, turning to Hyang. "We're done here, if seeing her face doesn't stir up anything for you."

Hyang's eyes bulge with outrage again.

"Ajumma this, Ajumma that . . . I doubt that I'd have kept company with someone so clueless. Are you sure we're friends?"

"I'm sure," I tell her. "One of the very few you have."

And on we go again, doing our little routine as Cha Seol, a nostalgic smile on her lips, quietly takes us in, filing the scene in her memory to feast on in the long and solitary years to come.


**Our next stop is the hospital where Ongi is still staying. On our** way, we drop by Miryu's grave for the first time.

Flowers, wrapped gifts, and letters are piled high around her headstone.

"The collection just keeps growing—it's even bigger than what we saw on TV," I say to Hyang. She straightens up a bouquet that's sliding sideways. Engraved on the back of the stone are Miryu's date of birth and the date on which Snow-globe's secret power plant came to a screeching halt, exposing for good the Yibonns' geothermal lie. The front of the stone only bears her name, but there are dozens of notes left by visitors.

*Thank you. You will forever be remembered.*

*We love you. You were a good person.*

*Rest in peace. Until we meet again.*

There's also a box of cookies. A note attached to it says, *From Thursday, who gets to live another beautiful day—thanks to you.*

Of course, this grave doesn't actually contain Miryu's body. With the underground power plant caving in completely, searching for bodies was impossible in the wreckage. Most of the people, including the vice-president, got out—but not Miryu.

"I bet Miryu is flying around in heaven, totally free to visit all the places she never got to in life, whenever she wants," I say.

Who knows. Her spirit might just be standing next to us, taking in the outpouring of love that she could never have imagined when she was alive. That would be nice.

Hyang gazes blankly at Miryu's name on the headstone.

"Jo Miryu, Jo Miryu . . . ," she repeats. "It's kind of a funny name—like yours."

I rub my eyes to drive back the tears welling up.

"You never ask about her. Why? Aren't you curious at all?" I say, sounding more accusatory than I want.

I expect Hyang to respond with a sharp and immediate pushback, but she doesn't, and silence falls.

"I don't know . . . ," she says at last. "Maybe it's this feeling that . . . the more I remember about her, the more it'll hurt."

The lump in my throat swells up again, and I really don't know if I can hold back the tears anymore. As if sensing this, Hyang whips her face to me and says, "Hey, Bambi," grinning comically. In times like this, it really feels like she's back.

"What, Ajumma?"

"What are you going to do with your life now?"

Every director in Snowglobe was sent an official letter of termination yesterday—every director in Snowglobe but Hyang, that is, because there's one more story left to tell. But it's not ours this time.

"I don't know," I tell her truthfully. "I'm going to think about it while Ongi recovers."

Ongi has told me that his near-death experience has given him a clearer sense of purpose in life.

"I'm going to take baking lessons. No matter how much the rest of the world changes, people always want cake for their birthdays," he said, adding that he's baking the cake for our special day this year.

Meanwhile, Somyung is back to training for the biathlon competition, and Shinae has expressed her ambition to plunge into the fashion industry, using Chairman Shin's cutting-edge heat-retaining fabric. As for Bae Serin, she has claimed co-ownership of the business, while also writing a memoir on the side.

"Is it true, Bambi, that you've always dreamed of becoming a director?" Hyang says out of the blue. "Ongi told me . . . So if you don't have a specific plan, you can help me."

"I may not have a plan yet. But that doesn't mean I don't have stuff to do," I respond, counting off the various obligations on my fingers for her. "One—Somyung needs a manager in the biathlon. Two—Shinae and Serin will need someone to keep them from fighting. Three, I'll probably have to help out with Ongi's bakery—"

"So you'll forgo the opportunity to take part in creating the last Snowglobe show ever?" Hyang cuts me off. "You know that I'll give you special recognition in the closing credits. Why don't you think it over?"

"Nah, I'm good."

Hyang looks at me slightly annoyed, as if I'm just being stubborn or something.

"You don't remember what my name means, do you, Ajumma?" I ask her after a moment.

"Chobahm," Hyang replies. "Isn't it just Bambi misspelled?"

I give her the side-eye, and she lets out a hearty laugh— which reminds me of Miryu all over again for some reason.

"Tell me about it again," Hyang says. "I want to know."

So I oblige. "The name means 'early summer night,' and it contains my parents' happiest memory, the dream of Snowglobe I nurtured every day inside my hamster wheel. Memories of watching TV with my family as we laughed and cried together to our favorite shows, and my epic adventure with my newfound sisters."

With a proud tilt of the chin, I conclude, "In short, the three simple syllables, Jeon-Cho-bam, contain a massive amount of meaning."

The look Hyang gives me then is, if not understanding, at least sympathetic, so I elaborate.

"My point is—I don't need to see my name in the closing credits, nor do I need my name to be known by everyone in the world. I like my name. It is already plenty special to me."

Hyang nods slowly, a smile dawning on her face. And somehow, my own speech has lifted my spirits, too. I breathe out a great big breath of satisfaction, which billows up in the air. Beyond the dead dome of Snowglobe, dark clouds float languidly across the sky.

# ACTOR-DIRECTORS OF OUR OWN LIVES

"**S**hinae! Chobahm!" Serin calls to us in the distance, waving her hand covered in a black leather glove. Even in a crowd, spotting someone with your own face is easy.

We make our way over to her, and Shinae gives Serin a friendly punch in her winter-coat-padded shoulder, saying, "Hey, Bae Serin! Did you stay out of trouble while I was busy making deals for us in the open world?"

Serin laughs off the comment. Then, narrowing her eyes, she gives each of us a long, appraising look.

"Eww . . . what are you wearing?" she says, making a face. "You two need to catch up to the trends now that you're back in Snowglobe."

Shinae and I glance at each other's plain hooded puffers. Without the secret power plant providing warmth for Snowglobe, the temperatures here have dropped to just above those in the outer world. Chairman Shin's cardioverter has been banned, along with all related research and products; but her innovative, heat-retaining fabric was salvaged by Shinae and

Serin, who legally acquired the rights to the technology. It is now used to produce everything from shoes to hats.

"How about you?" Shinae retorts. "What are you doing wearing that coat, instead of promoting our own products?"

"I had a meeting with the publisher I told you about today," Serin responds, ignoring the question entirely. "They loved my memoir proposal, which I already knew they would."

She gives us an elaborate smug smile, and Shinae huffs, "And you showed up wearing someone else's product? Girl, you need to develop some business sense."

In the next instant, we're all laughing together, finally dropping our act. Then we're heading into the stadium. I look up to the sky beyond the glass dome, from which snow falls softly.

The packed stadium buzzes with anticipation of the day's event. By the swamped concession stand, Hyang and Ongi call to us, lifting aloft a cardboard tray of hot drinks.

"Hey, guys! Here!"

Then we're all joining Mom and Grandma in the stand. I pass Grandma her tea, and she pauses to gaze into my eyes with such tenderness that I feel hope rising inside me again. Since our reunion, she still doesn't recognize me as me—her granddaughter. With an overly formal thank-you, she takes the drink from me, and I'm crushed. I search her face for some indication she's seen me—the real me—feeling bereft all over again.

"I can't believe I've lived long enough to see a championship in person," she tells me, smiling at me like I'm Ongi's girlfriend, which she still thinks I am.

Even so, she never confuses me for one of the other girls, a fact that floods me with liquid warmth whenever I think of it.

A few rows down, Haeri, who has legally changed her name to Wisher, claps her hands and bursts out laughing while chatting with Healer. I wish Heart could be here . . . Wisher and Healer are looking up at the sky, perhaps feeling what I'm feeling. Meanwhile, Sky is home, too young to join the rest of us in the stadium. I feel bad for her, I really do . . . but the thought of her cute little face screwed up in annoyance at being left out makes me let loose a small laugh. Plus, I'm sure the special Christmas dinner Aunt Knife is putting out for everyone at home can't be a bad deal as far as trade-offs go.

As for news of the world, the minimum work hours have been halved since the abolition of subscription laws that mandated payments in the form of electricity from the daily use of Actors. Instead, the average household income has increased since communities began selling electricity to Snowglobe—which still needs it to run the city, since there's no human power plant inside the dome. The consequence of these changes is time and money for people who used to have so little of either—and this translates into all kinds of freedom. Perhaps foremost among them is the freedom to travel to and from Snowglobe as we wish, so this year's championship spectators are a diverse mix of Snowglobe residents and tourists from the open world.

Perhaps the most important freedom of all, though, is that we in Snowglobe have become the directors of our own lives. We go to sleep each night with our hearts swelling with the stories we wish to write tomorrow. It's going to take some getting used to, and perhaps practice, but we're doing it—each and every one of us.

"Ladies and gentlemen, please take your seats as we're about to begin . . ."

The announcer's voice echoes across the stadium. A few moments later, Jumbotrons come alive with commercials, the first of which concerns some designer satchels made out of horse leather, a specialty of the Ba-E-5 settlement. The new world has ushered in an array of new occupations and careers available across communities in the open world, and people are furthering their education and learning new skills for better opportunities outside the power plants—like my own twin brother Ongi, who's taking classes with a master baker with the dream of opening his own bakery in our hometown someday.

Currently fading out on the Jumbotrons is a trailer for some new nature documentary about reindeers. Then the preview of *The Glass House,* the first and only reality TV show to air over the last six months, begins.

"It's the last hurrah! It's our swan song! We're returning to present to you the last show of its kind, one that will cap off the Age of Snowglobe," the voice-over rumbles as the faces of the former president Yi, the former VP, and Bonwhe flash on the giant screens. A deafening roar/boo erupts from the crowd and shakes the entire stadium.

Then the previews are over. The announcer steps up to the microphone and settles the crowd as the band begins to play. Music soars and falls. In a few minutes, athletes begin lining up at the starting line, and the crowd is once again stirred into all kinds of frenzy. We are no exceptions.

"Let's goooooooooooo, Myung Somyuuuuuuuuung!" I shout at the top of my lungs. "Come ooooooooooon!"

Somyung, bib number seven, steps to the starting line, her face somber with extreme focus. We up our cheer for her—scream for her—like the rabid fans we are, and when she turns her head in our direction and spots our faces in the crowd, her stony face briefly dissolves into a bright smile.

**"Ladies and gentlemen, here comes Chun Sahyun, arriving first** in the arena for the final leg of the race!"

The sportscaster cries as Chun Sahyun settles in her lane corresponding to her bib, number one, and the human target is thrown into the arena. The crowd is beyond berserk at this point, off their seats and drumming their feet.

The human target wears a red name badge above the chest pocket of her inmate uniform, which reads Yi Bonyung. She stands shaking like a person in an ice bath, on the far side of the snow-covered arena next to a few trees. The look on her face is one of absolute fright, disorientation, and vulnerability, which is in stark contrast to the face she wore for the press conference held in the office of her mansion the last time we all saw her. The Jumbotrons zoom in on her eyes, black and unblinking with terror.

How does it feel to be standing there? Can you still insist that the end justifies the means? Using people as entertainment to maintain what you call peace?

Then Chun Sahyun lifts her tranquilizer gun to her shoulder and, with cold composure, trains the barrel on the target. After this year, there will no longer be human targets, and the rules of the championship will be updated accordingly.

Meanwhile, Somyung arrives fourth in the arena and finds her lane, beating her time in the preliminaries. She, too, hoists her tranquilizer gun without a hitch or hesitation. In this year's final, the players carry tranquilizer guns instead of rifles, each loaded with dehydration pills that look like transparent bullets, but with dart needles at the front. These special pills are identical to the drug that the former president injected into the people trapped in the secret power plant—the very drug that took Heart's life through severe dehydration.

It is at this moment that something seems to finally jolt the human target from her terror-induced stupor, and she scrambles to the nearest tree in wild panic. Across the stadium, a chill descends and the crowd grows quiet. This vulnerable old woman was once a larger-than-life figure, our leader to whom we all looked up for so long. She is a sorry mortal, after all, the same as the rest of us.

Suddenly, the target runs out from behind the tree, crying, screaming, and pleading inarticulately—until the sound of firing tranquilizer guns puts a swift end to it all. Once exposed to extreme cold, anyone injected with that drug will have all the moisture drained from their body, leading to death. The moment she is thrown outside this heated stadium, outside this dome, the cold will take her life. In the chilling silence descending over the stadium, the ghastly execution of the former president airs all around the world.


**On our way out, the girls and I disperse in the hopes of keeping** a low profile. As luck would have it, though, Hwang Sannah, who's recently decided to explore a profession as a reporter, spots me by the bus stop. I'd ignore her if she were anyone else, but she is Sannah, who helped me back when I needed it most, and I owe her a great deal. She stands next to the cameraman and extends her microphone to me.

After a short interview, Sannah suggests that we catch up over lunch—her, me, and Hyang together. I don't know how to break the news that Hyang doesn't remember her, so I mumble some excuse and flee to the next bus.

Getting off at the right stop is always a trial when riding in a packed bus, but the championship on Christmas Day makes it absolutely impossible, and I count myself lucky when I manage to shove my way out of the stuffed vehicle only two stops past my destination.

**Dusk is settling over the city, reducing visibility, but I could find** my way through this neighborhood blindfolded. I let my mind drift as I walk, soon finding myself arriving across the street from Haeri's house. The two-story red brick house has been replaced by a three-story glass structure that allows a full view of the inside. It's the glass prison where Yi Bonshim, the former VP; Yi Bonwhe, her son; and several other core members of the Yibonn family/corporation are incarcerated.

Currently, a young man is seen exiting what used to be Haeri's room, a small wastebasket in one hand. Making his way downstairs and out the front door, he crosses the fenced yard to a dumpster parked in the corner. It's Bonwhe. Emptying the basket and turning back toward the building, he throws a lazy glance in my direction. Our eyes meet, causing him to pause in his tracks. I raise my hand in an awkward greeting. The streetlights come on then, illuminating the faint smile on his lips.

He doesn't greet me back, though. And I don't cross the street to him. Cameras for the show *The Glass House* are everywhere in and around this prison compound.

A car blasting loud music brakes to a sudden stop outside the fence where Bonwhe is standing. The music cuts off and the passenger window rolls down. I slip into the shadow of a nearby tree. A friendly young couple lean their heads out the window and introduce themselves to Bonwhe. They moved into the neighborhood a few days ago, they say, and would love to get together with him some time. Then they go on about how brave and heroic it was of him to expose his family's dirty secret and save those trapped in the underground power plant, and how unfair our judicial system can be, to be indiscriminately punishing him for the mere fact of having been the heir to the Yibonn. Maybe they can even appear in the glass prison as Bonwhe's neighbor, one of them jokes . . . The three of them laugh and trade niceties for another minute or so before the couple drive off.

Back inside his room in the see-through prison, Bonwhe lingers at the exterior wall, looking outside for me. I turn away and start back down the street. Passing a house with a big picture window, I see my face animated in their living room TV. It's my interview outside the stadium with Sannah. I can't hear a sound, but I don't have to. Watching my lips move, I remember what I said:

*We're all victims of the same con. It's just that I got to witness the inner workings up close, which was pretty darn horrible. And I know that the same abuse of power could be repeated at any time, if we're not careful, if we unwittingly hand over our freedom and rights to privacy—our lives—again to someone or something that claims to have our best interest at heart. We could run straight into the hands of the next Yibonn family, if we fall back asleep.*

Despite the heaviness of my speech, my tone and face are bright—likely with the excitement of seeing Sannah again. I hurry my steps to the bus station, where I plan to catch a bus headed back the other way toward the stop I missed, if only to walk off the embarrassment settling in. Does anyone ever get used to seeing themself on TV? That's when I feel someone's hand on my shoulder.

"Chobahm." Bonwhe's voice sounds behind me. I spin around in amazement, and there he is, face flushed, catching his breath. My heart picks up.

"How did you get away? Without the camera crew?" I say, astonishment fading into worry. "You'll get in trouble."

Bonwhe doesn't respond to this but holds a tightly folded square of pastel green paper out to me.

"I found it when they demolished Goh Maeryung's home. I thought you'd want to read it," he says. I take the folded square and murmur a thanks, studying its creases and worn corners. It looks like an old, unsent note.

"Happy birthday," he says, and he seems to brighten around the eyes. "May your special day be filled with warmth of all kinds."

A private smile plays upon his lips, one that I'd like to think he uses only for me. "I've gotta go. See you soon."

Then he's off—back in the direction of his see-through prison.

"See you . . . soon," I murmur, watching him trot down the sidewalk, swinging his arms like an athlete warming up. Finally, he slides out of view. I don't know how long I stand there, my eyes gone remote on the spot where he disappeared. A few seconds? Minutes? I don't know. Eventually, I turn around and resume my walk to the bus station, picturing my friends and family gathered at Serin's, their faces set aglow by the light of the candles on the cake Ongi baked for us.

# Epilogue

*If you're reading this, you most likely replaced me. I picture you with my face, of course, but under the familiar exterior . . .* Who might you be? *I wonder.*

*Every camera break, I search this room—our bedroom—in the hopes of possibly finding a note or message left for me by its former occupant, the Haeri who preceded me. Apparently, she died of a terminal illness, but her last wish was for this show to go on even after she was gone—or that's the story I was told.*

*But then doubts settled in, and once the first ones had sprouted, more began growing like mushrooms after a rain. Did she really wish for this life to continue on after her? To what end?*

*What unfinished dreams could she have had for a show that, behind its soaring ratings, hid the fact that its child star was being ruthlessly used and abused by parasitic adults?*

*Hence my desperate search for clues. Even a note as simple as* Thank you for stepping in for me, *or something like that, would have given me strength to believe that Haeri truly did want this. It would have bolstered me, even as my will to continue upholding her wish dwindled away inside me.*

*Eventually, though, I happened upon the truth. That it was not Haeri but the adults who wished for the show to go on for themselves. Not that anyone would ever admit to it . . . but I know. The show must end.*

*I doubt that I am her only doppelganger left on Earth. Still, my hope is that this letter will never be found by another one of us. That you, of my face and fate, will not be here in this room to witness this letter into existence. That you said no to being my successor.*

*I can't help but be curious, though. What might your name be? Whatever it is, don't ever give it up. Don't do what I did and give up who you are for a song. Not for this song.*

*I pray that if this letter is ever found and read, it will be in a new world where shows like ours are no longer needed. Otherwise, I pray that it will remain unread for eternity.*

*Wishing to be the last Haeri in the world,*
*Jo Yeosu*

## ABOUT THE AUTHOR

**Soyoung Park** majored in communication and media at university. She is a winner of the Original Story Award and the Changbi X Kakaopage Young Adult Novel Award. She is the author of the Snowglobe duology.

## ABOUT THE TRANSLATOR

**Joungmin Lee Comfort** is a Korean-English translator. Her translations have appeared in *Clarkesworld* magazine and *Best of World SF*. Her co-translation of Kim Bo-young's *On the Origin of Species and Other Stories* was longlisted for the National Book Award for Translated Literature.